Gray Widow's Walk

Dan Jolley

Cover art: John Nadeau

Editor: Linda Sullivan

Published by Seventh Star Press, LLC.

ISBN: 978-1-941706-39-8

Seventh Star Press

www.seventhstarpress.com

info@seventhstarpress.com

Publisher's Note:

Gray Widow's Walk is a work of fiction. All names, characters, and places are the product of the author's imagination, used in fictitious manner. Any resemblances to actual persons, places, locales, events, etc. are purely coincidental.

Printed in the United States of America

First Edition

Gray Widow's Walk

ACKNOWLEDGMENTS

This book would not have been possible without the help and encouragement of my family and friends. It's gone through many different forms, spent far too many years sitting on a shelf, and wouldn't have existed at all without...

Josh Krach, an invaluable first editor

Belinda Glenn, who spent long, laborious hours scanning every single page of the physical manuscript into an optical character recognition program

Joan & O.C. Jolley and Clint McInnes, who have always been stalwart, supportive fans no matter what

Linda Sullivan, who went through the manuscript with a fine-tooth comb and saved me from a number of embarrassing mistakes

And Stephen Zimmer, who decided to take a chance on a book that other people had described with words such as "too far out there," "too cross-genre," and "what the hell were you thinking."

My gratefulness to you all knows no bounds.

Dedication

For Tracy
My Reason. My Queen.

CHAPTER ONE

Preoccupied with thoughts of body armor and blunt instruments, Janey Sinclair locked her apartment door and walked down the ninth-floor hallway of the LaCroix Building to the elevator. It opened with a thunk and an off-key chime after a brief wait, and Janey stepped inside.

Tonight's the night. Tonight's the debut.

She knew she was ready for it. Still...her stomach had been uneasy all day, and she had a few hours to go yet before sundown.

A pair of college students already stood in the car, a boy and a girl sharing each other's personal space, and Janey nodded to them neutrally. They didn't respond except to stare at her, so Janey watched the red electric numbers until the doors opened again on the ground floor. She suspected the students had stared at her the whole way down; they moved past her toward the entrance, and she deliberately turned her head to avoid any further eye contact. The girl started giggling as the couple left the building.

Janey stopped outside the office door and pulled her rent check from her shirt pocket. She was dressed as she usually did: loose, faded jeans, running shoes, and a hugely baggy button shirt. Her only jewelry, aside from a wristwatch, was a simple silver cross on a steel chain around her neck.

Janey touched her recently and drastically shortened chestnut locks. For as long as she could remember, she had worn her hair in a glorious, curly mane that floated around her head and cascaded down her back. Now the mane was gone, and what hair she had left clung to the top of her head in a thatch of tight, springy coils. She couldn't deny the functionality—the mask fit much better this way—but she still felt self-conscious about it.

Not that she needed anything new to help her feel self-conscious.

At her first showing she had overheard a buyer talking about her, so she ducked behind a faux Greek column and listened. The buyer, a woman in her fifties with skin baked into leather by years of tanning beds, said, "Not exactly what you'd call a beautiful woman, but she's got a lot of character, doesn't she? And so tall!"

Janey put her hand on the office doorknob and began to turn it when a voice from inside stopped her. A man's voice. Through the door she heard him say, "It doesn't *matter* what's on your work order. I've got two tenants ready to move in *tomorrow.*"

Janey stayed outside and listened, thinking lightly of her behind-the-column eavesdropping at the show. A long pause stretched out, presumably as the owner of the voice paid attention to the speaker on the other end of the line.

"Look. Mr. Hayes. Our check has already cleared. Do you understand me? We have already bought those refrigerators. They are on your truck right now, and I want you to bring them here. To me. Today. All right?"

Another long pause, then a few terse monosyllables, then the sound of a handset slammed back into its cradle.

Janey cautiously pushed the door open.

Behind the desk, which was normally occupied by an affable middle-aged Indian gent named Raj Kapoor, a young man with a mop of black, wavy hair sat with his elbows on the desk and his face buried in his hands. Reams of paperwork almost hid the desktop from sight, and his lean, dark-bronze arms disappeared behind the stacks.

Janey said, "Um..."

The young man looked up at her, and she forgot why she was there.

He was beautiful. Like something out of a myth. His straight jawline and long, thin nose led up to a pair of eyes like the blackest ink. Janey stared at him, and couldn't stop even as she realized she was staring, and that he saw her staring, and still she stared.

Irritably, the man said, "Yes? Can I help you?"

Janey said, "Uh..."

He cocked an eyebrow. Somehow it made him even more appealing.

"Um, I..."

The young man stood up from the desk. He wore dark jeans and a tucked-in polo shirt that highlighted his narrow waist and flat stomach. Janey tried one more time to speak, and managed to say, "The, uh...I..."

"I guess that's your rent?" The man moved around the desk toward Janey, who still stood in the doorway, and held out a hand to take the check.

"Yes...uh. Yeah. Yes it is. Who, uh...where's Mr. Kapoor?"

"Oh." The man rotated his outstretched hand, a shift from taking her check to offering a greeting. Janey shook his hand dazedly. "I'm his son. My name's Tim. Dad had to leave for a while, so I'm filling in for him." He gave her a lopsided grin. "Sorry, I don't mean to be grumpy. I'm just really new at this, and it's been a long day." He paused, and carefully took the envelope out of her hand.

"Oh, sorry." Janey felt her cheeks burning.

Tim went back to the desk. "Do you want a receipt?"

"Uh...sure, yeah." She shifted her weight from one foot to the other and tried to find a place to put her hands.

Tim took her check out of its envelope, and when he read her name his whole face changed. He dropped the check on the desk and said, "You're Janey Sinclair!"

Janey's forehead wrinkled up. She said, "Uh..."

He bounded around the desk and again stuck out his hand, and when Janey took it, Tim clasped it with both of his as if it were something precious. "I've been dying to meet you! I saw your name on the tenant list when I got here a couple days ago, and I couldn't believe it! Janey Sinclair, living right here in our building!"

"Wuh...um. Yeah?"

He let her hand go and stepped back, as if to get a better look at her. "I saw your paintings! At the Slade Gallery, last week! You're *amazing*. That one, that one you did with the little mice? You know which one I mean?"

"Um...yeah—'Mind of a Field Mouse.'"

"Yes! That was so incredible! I took some art appreciation courses in college, so, y'know, I sort of know a tiny little bit about it, probably just enough to make some horrible mistake and sound like a moron, but your painting reminded me of El Greco. Y'know, 'View of Toledo?' With those deep blues and greens?"

Janey started sweating.

Tim said, "I'm sorry. You must have people bugging you about your work all the time. I didn't mean to attack you like that."

Blood rushed through her ears. "No...no...actually you're the first. Outside the gallery, I mean."

"You're kidding! Wow."

Janey started edging toward the door. Her face felt hot. Blazing.

He followed her.

"Listen, I don't mean to be a nuisance or anything, but I'd love to chat with you more about your work. Would you like to maybe go get a cup of coffee, or a drink, or maybe a milkshake or something after the office closes? And talk?"

Janey's hand trembled as it closed around the doorknob.

"Um, you're not being a nuisance, don't worry, but, I really can't, I'm sorry, I really need to go now." She opened the door, quivering like a rabbit.

Tim's eyes widened. "Oh—no, no, no, I'm the one who should be apologizing, I didn't mean to—"

Janey darted out into the hallway, and couldn't look back at him, wouldn't, would not. As she walked swiftly away, trying not to break into a run, she said over her shoulder, "It was very nice meeting you."

Tim came out into the corridor after her, but she'd already

pushed open the glass door to the street. "Hey! Do you want your receipt?"

"Please leave it in my mailbox," she called back.

Janey walked very quickly down the street, almost running. Running from him? *Better believe it, running from him.* She clamped her teeth together and shook her head, appalled at herself. *What was that? Flirting?*

Shame built up on her shoulders.

Still...

How long had it been since she'd actually sat down and talked with someone? How long had it been since she'd had any significant human contact at all?

She knew how long. She could count it out in years, months, days, hours, minutes. And it could go on longer. Would *have* to. For Adam's sake. Still...

With hardly any effort she could see him. *Tim Kapoor.* His image flashed on the insides of her eyelids.

She'd have to drop her rent checks in the mail from now on. Avoid the office if she could.

Janey stared at her feet as she shuffled down the sidewalk. She didn't *need* this. She couldn't afford the distraction, so soon before her first...what? First foray? First time at bat? She tried to concentrate on her checklist for gear and weapons. It wasn't easy.

Her fists clenched and unclenched, and the long, steely muscles in her arms bunched and rolled under the skin.

CHAPTER TWO

Hours passed, and light fled from the city.

Muted sounds of late-night Atlanta traffic drifted over the Hargett Theatre's wrecked walls as two men stood silently, waiting: one very tall, chalk-pale, and pitifully skinny, the other shorter, black, and nearly twice as broad as his companion. Standing side by side, they looked a little like the number 10. A mingled stench of garbage and urine drifted around them.

The taller of the men held a battered briefcase, and they both sweated in the August night's brutal, steaming heat. They stood among piles of rubble, bits of the past cast off among broken beer bottles and discarded syringes. A light rain had fallen earlier in the night, and now the men stood, motionless and gray, as water collected sluggishly in foul puddles at their feet.

The tall man, a near-skeletonized junkie named Chooley, grunted and closed his eyes. "Steady," warned the shorter one, and for the fortieth time glanced around, examining the place where they stood.

The Hargett Theatre shut down in 1995, slated for demolition less than a month later. Halfway through the wrecking job, the same absence of money that closed the theatre also canceled the demolition team's contract. Through the next two decades the theatre lay, half-destroyed, its ragged brick teeth and rusted skeleton bared to the sky. Part of the stage still stood. A catwalk hung from a twisted girder thirty feet off the ground, chopped off like a mangled limb.

The two men waited in the center of the theatre's dead body while the minutes scraped past.

Another hot breath of wind moved over them, the latest of several, and Chooley the junkie tried to fan himself with one hand.

"Shit," he mumbled. "They ain't kiddin' about global warming."

The other man, Zach Feygen, didn't respond. Feygen was burly, quiet, in his mid-thirties, with a naturally bald head and russet skin. His voice, when he chose to talk, came out slowly, deep and rough and rich.

After the better part of a year and a series of low-level buys, starting with ten bucks and working up to fifteen hundred, Feygen had finally set up this deal. Chooley, a regular customer of tonight's target, played an integral part in the proceedings, which led to Feygen's putting him on the list of departmentally protected informants. As near as anyone could tell, Chooley felt suitably grateful. Though he was articulate enough, for the most part, Chooley frequently lapsed into a kind of detached mumbling.

Over the long months, Feygen heard each link of the necessary chain slowly clink together. For the days leading up to the final deal he hadn't slept more than three or four hours a night, but *damn,* he felt good. Along with all the condemning evidence he'd gathered from users and street pushers and wire taps, this buy would, at the very least, take Maurice Tell off the streets permanently. At most, it would get rid of half a dozen of Tell's major contacts as well.

Almost certainly it would make Feygen's career. He'd caught himself breaking out in a big stupid grin a couple of times just thinking about it.

Feygen heard the car first, at ten minutes after midnight. Its engine died outside the walls. Four doors opened and closed. Footsteps crunched through the brick and concrete debris, and five long shadows slid up onto a graffiti-covered wall.

Chooley said, "Here they come."

Maurice Tell led the group of men rounding the corner. Tell stood just a hair shy of six feet, seven inches, and had at one time called himself "Breaker." Now, at thirty-four, most of the people he dealt with called him "Mr. Tell." The other men with him clearly deferred to him, and hung back like geese in a V formation, half-concealed by dense shadows.

Tell jerked a thumb at Feygen, but spoke to Chooley. "This the nigger you told me about?"

A muscle in Feygen's jaw twitched. Chooley hesitated before nodding mutely.

"You're alone?"

This time Feygen nodded. The microphone taped to his chest itched like a poison oak rash.

"And you brought the stuff."

Chooley held up the briefcase. His hand stayed steady.

Feygen tried not to eye the case more than necessary. The money it contained was coated with a fluorescent powder, so that anyone who handled it, or even came close to it while it was being handled, would shine like a Christmas tree under UV light.

"It's here," Chooley said. "Want to count it?"

Tell smiled—

—like a carnivore—

—and as Feygen murmured, "Oh...shit," Tell made a decisive gesture with one hand.

Two of the men behind him lifted sawed-off shotguns.

Feygen's stomach collapsed into a stone-hard knot, and beside him Chooley started shaking so hard Feygen thought he might be having a seizure.

The shotguns leveled at them, and Feygen screamed, "Wait, wait, wait a minute!" but the gunmen already had their feet planted, and the adrenaline saturating Feygen's blood didn't seem to work on his abruptly jellied legs. Wide open, away from any decent cover, Feygen knew he and Chooley wouldn't make it, couldn't possibly get out of the line of fire, but he tried, turned and lunged to one side, and even as he moved he heard Tell say, "Now," and screams lashed out against the theatre's crumbling walls.

Feygen landed face down in scraping bits of broken concrete and pulled himself halfway behind a shattered brick column. He thought, *What happened to the shotguns?* and peered around the edge of the column at a scene of chaos. Men ran in every direction, fighting…what? One of the gunners, a pale guy with curly red hair, staggered backward and held up empty, bleeding hands.

Now one of the sawed-offs did boom out. Feygen saw the muzzle flash, a flower of fire in the darkness of an empty doorway, followed by another scream. The shotgun flipped out of the shadows and landed near Feygen, splintered and broken.

Curly-hair started screaming, and Feygen realized there was someone in the theatre besides himself, Chooley, and Tell's gang. Something touched the ground—something gray—in the middle of Tell and his men, and things happened quickly.

Tell's hand had only brushed the .357 in his shoulder holster when something heavy struck him squarely between the eyes like a narrow battering ram. His knees turned to water, but the gray thing swept past him before he could fall.

The second shotgunner, an overgrown boy named Bryan Krago, stared at his broken hands and hissed out a litany of obscenities. He tipped sideways into the rubble and drew his knees up to his chest.

The two untouched members of Tell's entourage had by now pulled their own guns, but they couldn't tell at what to fire; one of them blazed randomly into the shadows, and Feygen felt a *whap* near one of his ears as a bullet sped past him. He tried to focus on the whirling gray thing across the theatre's floor, but only got more confused.

Something like smoke moved among Tell's thugs. Feygen thought it was human-shaped, but as he watched it seemed to flicker and dance, first in front of someone, then behind. A stray beam of light glistened off some kind of weapon, something oblong and narrow, and a series of fast hard sounds echoed through the demolished theatre, a machine-gun spatter of metal crunching into bone.

"Clarke..." Feygen murmured, unsure of his voice. He touched the wire, fumbled for it, shouted, "Clarke, there's something here! Something's in here with us!"

As Tell's last two men fell bonelessly, one swiftly followed by the other, Bryan Krago rose to his knees, a .44 Magnum the size of his forearm clenched in one mangled hand. To his left, Curly-hair's screams grew even louder, filled the night air, made it into a thick, tangible thing, and Feygen choked on the stink of garbage and cordite.

"Fuck you!" Krago screamed, and leveled his gun, and the mass of gray smoke turned and looked down the barrel.

Feygen saw in an instant of clarity what had torn through Maurice Tell and his helpers: a long, lean figure dressed head to foot in gray, segmented, form-fitting body armor. A tight gray mask clung to the head, and what looked like black mesh covered the eyes. A telescoping police baton rested lightly in one hand, blood dripping from the aluminum shaft.

The gray figure had to be at least six feet tall, but the shoulders, the chest, the hips... Feygen squinted, quickly certain: whoever was in that armor was female.

Bryan Krago had the woman dead to rights, point-blank, and opened fire after only half a second's pause. The muzzle blasts lit the ruined theatre with a hellish strobe and the stink grew stronger, overpowering, the weapon's report harmonizing with Curly-hair's screams...

...and Feygen saw something happen.

Krago's .44 would have required solid control under the best of circumstances, but with his hands damaged he had no hope of shooting accurately. The woman in the mask twisted backward into the thickest of the shadows as the gunfire roared around her, and then—between one flash and the next—stood *behind* Krago.

Feygen blinked and whispered, "Holy God." His mind latched onto the image: Krago, on his knees, the woman behind him with the baton raised high like a dishonored samurai's second, set to deliver the final blow of hara-kiri.

A sudden hot wind on Feygen's face made his skin tighten.

The baton came down on Krago's right elbow like a

hammer, and for an instant the sickening crack of breaking bones overwhelmed Curly-hair's screams. The gun flew from Krago's hand and clattered to rest on the far side of a pile of weed grown bricks.

The woman hoisted Krago to his feet, paused half a second to glance at Feygen, and hauled Krago out of sight into the shadows.

The force of the woman's stare, brief as it was, settled onto Feygen's skin. For just that half a second he felt like a bug under a microscope.

Curly-hair finally ran short of breath and dissolved into sobs.

Feygen stumbled forward, ears ringing, and stared into the darkness where Krago and the woman had disappeared. He saw nothing—and then the entirety of the theatre flooded with light as Clarke and everyone else arrived. Powerful flashlight beams washed the alcove where Krago and the woman in gray had vanished, but they illuminated nothing but spider webs, dust, and tiny puddles of water sending wisps of steam into the summer night air.

Feygen knelt, and touched one of those puddles, and jerked his finger back with a pained hiss. The steam wasn't rising because of the evening's humidity. The water was on the verge of boiling.

Feygen snapped his head up at the sound of Chooley's cries. He rushed over and found Chooley flat on his back, bleeding from a graze in his forehead. Feygen screamed for an ambulance.

* * *

Bryan Krago came to himself in a dark place, sweating and hurting and trembling violently. He gritted his teeth and strained to stop the shaking.

Krago half-lay, half-sat, propped against a brick wall, with cool smooth concrete underneath him. Groping around him, he touched something flat and rough propped against the wall next to him, and senselessly jerked his hand back. The sudden movement woke the pain in his right elbow, and he thought he could feel the ruined bones slide and click across each other. His vision tinged a crackling red, but he didn't quite pass out, though his heart pumped sick sweat onto his pallid skin.

Krago blinked and attempted to focus into the black, but his eyes had no adjusting to do; they stared into total darkness. He moved to sit up, and another flash of pain ripped up and down his arm, jangled into his neck and down to his feet—and from out of the black, rough hands grabbed the front of his shirt, yanked him to a standing position and pinned him to the wall.

A match hissed into life near his eyes, making him flinch and squint. The masked face floated inches from his own, alien and nearly featureless, and alongside the pain and the cold Krago still found room for fear.

Trying not to vomit from the agony in his arm, Krago thought he could make out eyes through the black mesh in the mask. He tried to talk, but the only thing that came out was a whimper, so he clamped down again and tried to salvage a few scraps of self-control.

Christ, his elbow, he didn't know there could be pain like that.

The gray figure held him pressed against the wall for several more seconds and let the match burn down. When the small gold flame drew near the gloved fingers, the figure spoke in a voice like skittering autumn leaves.

"Next time I catch you, I break a lot more bones."

Holy fuck, holy fuck it's a woman, a woman did this to me—

The woman waved the match out and, as the darkness returned, pushed Krago backward. Instead of grinding into abrasive brick, Krago felt himself fall into a space like the inside of an oven, and for one horrible instant knew he was about to burst into flame.

Consciousness lost him.

* * *

Feygen and Chooley stood near what had once been the back

entrance of the Hargett Theatre, lit alternately in red and white as the EMTs hauled away Maurice Tell and the three hired guns they could find. Eleven other police officers were on the scene now, and one of them, a thickset man with a large, square head and dark eyes, talked to Feygen in quick, brittle tones. Chooley sat down heavily, a thick gauze pad pressed to his head. He'd be leaving in an ambulance soon.

"So you're saying Tell's guys had you cold?"

Chooley scratched his nose, darted his eyes around like a rabbit. Feygen couldn't tell if he felt the pain from the graze or not. Chooley said, "We could've made it. No problem. No problem. Plenty of cover round here. I mean, the deal went all to hell, yeah, but we could've made it."

Feygen snorted. "We were dog food."

The thickset man, Clarke, eyed Feygen sourly. Chooley kept talking.

"As soon as they pulled their guns, man, the chick was right there. *Right there.*" Chooley squinted into the shadows and trembled. "We might've walked away from here, and we might not, but that wasn't *even* an issue once this bitch showed up. She just waltzed through those stiffs like...I dunno...like they were just standing there."

Clarke swept his eyes around the theatre's decayed interior. "And what did you say happened to the fifth guy?"

Chooley turned to Feygen and said, "You tell him. You *tell* him. What happened, you tell him."

Feygen shook his head. "I don't know. This woman, this woman dressed up like a fucking ninja, she carried the last guy off. I don't know where they went." He knew what he'd seen, but he still couldn't believe it. Chooley's corroboration wasn't very comforting.

Clarke turned and started to say something when a heavy thud sounded behind them. Spinning around, they saw Bryan Krago lying sprawled across the hood of one of the ambulances.

Krago slid slowly off and crumpled to the ground, where the

EMTs swarmed over him.

"Where the fuck did he come from?" Clarke shouted. "Get me lights! *Lights,* you shitheads, get me lights over here!"

The area around the ambulance, which had parked near enough to a wall for the shadows to be particularly deep along its side, immediately lit up with high-intensity beams. Feygen wasn't very surprised when the only thing they illuminated was a patch of paint on the hood that had bubbled up. He watched as one of the bubbles popped.

A scorching-hot breeze touched his cheek, and he flinched.

* * *

A short while later, in a place with no windows and no doors, Janey Sinclair concentrated.

Not bad for the first night. Not bad at all.

A pair of gymnastic rings hung from one of the steel girders crisscrossed over her head, and she gripped them, her body suspended between them, arms straight out from her shoulders in a position called the "Iron Cross."

Janey replayed the scene in her mind for the fortieth time. Gauged her reactions. Analyzed her judgments. She'd saved two lives: an undercover cop and, near as she could tell, a cooperating junkie. Not bad.

A leather gauntlet encircled her left forearm, seven slim throwing spikes nestled beneath thin straps. A leather sheathe held a telescoping police baton to her right thigh. She breathed slowly. Camouflaged beneath the Vylar suit, Janey's muscles stood out in forced tension, perfectly steady, each one burning and hard as steel. Janey brought her eyes into focus and willed the night vision on.

She looked across a large chamber, a cavernous space composed of smooth concrete floors, unadorned cinder block walls, and pure, smooth darkness. No light burned—no lamps, no flashlights, no silver streaks of moonlight allowed entry by high-placed windows or ill-fitting doors. Janey's space—she thought of it as her basement—was dark and seamless, with no entrance or exit save for a few narrow ventilation shafts.

Janey questioned her decision to bring one of the thugs here. She was confident the basement was inviolate, and she'd terrified the poor bastard even more thoroughly than she'd hoped to, but it bothered her. An unnecessary risk.

Thirty feet away stood a stack of hay bales supporting a shooting range target: a man's head and torso in black. Concentric outlines radiated from the heart.

Through the darkness, Janey's eyes ignored their need for light and saw the target with perfect clarity. She hung, arms parallel to the floor, teeth gritted, and began reciting the alphabet backward. *Z, Y, X, W...*

If she had turned her head, she would have found herself looking at one of a series of oil paintings that lined the basement, propped against the cinder blocks. All unframed, they were simple canvases expertly stretched over hand-built wooden frames.

Every one was a masterpiece.

No one would ever see them.

When she sent her bio and sample PDFs to Ben Gault at the Slade Gallery, against her better judgment she included one of what she thought of as her "angry" paintings, more to see what would happen than in hopes of displaying or selling it. It was a piece called "Consumption." She thought the effect might be lessened, since it was just an image file rather than the real thing.

Ben Gault called Janey the next day and asked if he could come and see Janey's work in person. Janey readily agreed, but Gault sounded strange, and Janey asked him if anything was wrong.

"No...no, not exactly," Gault said. "I think, though, I can safely ask you to leave 'Consumption' out of the works I see today."

"Okay. Why, if I may ask?"

Janey knew why, but this was the first time anyone had seen any of the paintings "Consumption" belonged with, and she wanted to hear the official response.

"Well...my wife and I both had nightmares last night after we saw the PDF. I don't think that particular piece fits in too well with the Slade Gallery's image. That's, of course, not to say I don't want to see the other ones."

Gault sounded stuck somewhere between fear and admiration, with a healthy dose of capitalism thrown in. The paintings could make the gallery a tidy sum, and both he and Janey fully realized it. Janey gave Gault a time to come over.

Counting the one finished that morning, Janey had completed one hundred seventy-three paintings that she felt accurately represented her mood at the time of their execution. Ninety-four of those, like "Consumption," had turned out unsuitable for public viewing. So they wound up here. In her basement.

S, R, Q, P...

Of the paintings which actually had been displayed, much was said. Critics drew comparisons with Friedrich, with Goya; her work, according to the *Journal-Constitution's* reviewer, "made occasional use of Dali's talent for the photo realistically surreal." Janey had no comment, and attended the initial showing only reluctantly. Her first sale, a four-by-six oil titled "Original Virtue," moved at the show for sixty-five hundred, an unprecedented price for a new artist. Janey graciously thanked the buyer, declined invitations to several parties, excused herself from the advances of a slender blonde in a push-up bra, and went home as soon as she could.

That was months ago, and since then her paintings had sold with astonishing regularity. Ben Gault had politely suggested on a couple of occasions that Janey sign on with the Slade Gallery exclusively, but Janey hadn't given him an answer yet. She'd probably say yes.

K, J, I, H...

Sometimes she wondered what Adam would have thought if he could have seen her like this. He used to comment on her body, an even mix of teasing and seductive appreciation. If he could see her now...

She grimaced. If Adam could see her now, she wouldn't be trying so hard not to think about Tim Kapoor.

If Adam could see her now, well, that would change a great number of things, wouldn't it?

D, C, B, A.

Still hanging, still in the perfect Iron Cross position, Janey took one breath slightly deeper than normal. With a grunt, she flipped around and launched herself off the rings, circling high and forward into the air. Spikes whistled out in a pointed whirring rain and made small tapping sounds as they punched through the paper of the target and into the densely packed hay behind it. Janey landed, rolled, and came up to a crouch, the baton extended and ready in her hand.

She held that position for a moment. Slowly Janey stood, collapsed the baton, and approached the target. One spike protruded from the center of the target's chest. Another had planted itself squarely in the target's right eye. Janey stretched, unzipped and pulled off the Vylar mask, holstered the baton and plucked out the spikes.

The paintings lined up around the walls of the enormous room broke their chain at one point to make space for a nineteen-foot-long segment of pegboard festooned with hooks and metal clips. Each of them held a melee weapon. Three different styles of police batons, bo staffs, brass knuckles, tonfas, hanbos. At the top of the board, separate from the rest of the weapons, hung an authentic Japanese katana. That was the only one Janey never considered using. It had belonged to her father.

Janey walked slowly over to the board, replacing the spikes in the gauntlet as she went, and unbuckled both the gauntlet and the baton sheath. Each item went on a separate hook. The baton she took to a small work table, in front of which sat a three-legged stool. She opened a gray metal tool box on the table, took out the various necessary items and began to clean the baton.

All of this she did in perfect darkness.

On the wall above the work table Janey had tacked a poster. Old and slightly wrinkled, it was a promotional bill for a Las Vegas-style lounge-act magician called The Astounding Alexander. Alexander appeared in the poster as a tall, thin, graying Caucasian man in his forties, clad in a red tuxedo with a black cape. An assortment of objects seemed to float in the air around his head and his grandly gesturing hand. Janey ignored the poster as she worked.

Throughout the vast chamber, the only sounds were those made by Janey's tools. Aerosol spray and cloth buffing lightly against metal.

When she finished, she stood and began pulling off the Vylar suit, but paused for a moment to run her fingers over its unique texture. Janey never quite tired of the sensation. Vylar, she remembered, was "composed of millions of tiny octagons, woven into a cloth with monofilament wire threaded through holes drilled by a precision machine press." The suit gave her peace of mind to a degree, though it had a tendency to chafe under the chest and back pads. She occasionally wondered if the military ever noticed it missing from its vault—or what they'd do to her if they ever caught her with it.

Not that they ever would.

"Got to buy some longjohns," she said aloud. The nights' temperatures would drop soon enough, and the last thing she needed was a cold. Particularly after tonight. After success.

Janey sat on the floor to unbuckle the steel-toed, leather-and-Vylar boots, and with a sort of rush realized how good it had felt, how good it still felt, saving those men's lives. Feygen and his informant, "Chooley," whose names she had overheard while listening from the shadows, could go home to their lives now. To their families, their children if they had them. And they could do it because of her. Janey wrapped her arms around her knees and rocked back and forth for a moment.

She stood, now wearing only athletic socks, boy shorts, and

a Porky Pig T-shirt. She folded the suit, tucked it under one arm, and picked up the boots. Concentrating briefly, she flickered once and vanished.

The basement stood empty, dark and silent, warmer with her passing.

CHAPTER THREE

The next day, far from the Hargett Theatre, Anna Grove twisted a crocheted pillow cover in her hands. Her voice shook a little. She'd been talking for some time.

"I don't know what to do anymore. I don't know where he goes at night."

The man she spoke to took a long puff on his pipe. "I wish I knew what to tell you. He's been out of my league for a while now."

A moth tap-tapped against a windowpane. Two clocks ticked in unison. Anna Grove, ex-actress and stunning at forty-five, sat in the den of her fourteen-room, white-columned house in a small town near New Orleans and tried not to shiver.

The man who'd spent the last hour and ten minutes hunched in a tall wing-backed chair, watching her closely, was Jim Fautsch, her family's doctor and a close friend. Fautsch looked a little like Wilford Brimley. He was one of the few people in whom Anna confided.

She moved closer to the edge of the couch and pulled harder on the pillow cover. Her voice stayed low, and every few moments she glanced over her shoulder, as though in an exaggerated tic.

"If Simon actually did the...what Sheriff Bowman said..."

She stopped and stared down at a framed five-by-seven on the antique cedar chest that served as the den's coffee table. She'd taken the picture down from its place, high on a shelf in her closet. "I'd like to think he didn't, *couldn't*. But after what happened next door, and then those others, I just, I..." Anna's face mingled sadness and regret. "I shouldn't have been so...controlling, all these years. Shouldn't have kept him so sheltered." Her words grew even softer. "I thought I was doing the best thing."

Fautsch took a while to respond. Unlike the general public,

he'd seen pictures of what had taken place in the neighbors' house. He couldn't think about it too much.

"It sure as hell wouldn't be like the boy I remember."

"No...no." Her voice faltered. "He's always been so *timid,* so..."

Anna had known from the beginning that Simon was different. Keeping him away from the other children, keeping him safe in the house, had only seemed natural. She thought initially that letting him attend a public school would solve any socialization problems he might have had, but... that wasn't the case.

Fautsch blew out a long stream of smoke. Anna continued, "Some of my son's friends... My son has told me how they treat him. When they see Simon in the halls. They call him names, push him down. You know how many fights he's been in. He's always run away."

She shook her head and, resisting it, started crying. Fautsch stood nervously, sat down next to her, and put an arm around her.

"He's always been like that," she said unsteadily. "He's always been so fearful. Never... He never could talk to anybody. Oh Jim, I made him that way, didn't I? Didn't I?"

Outside, late afternoon deepened into twilight. The sky descended into the dark, rich blue of late summer nights, and katydids filled the trees with their droning, two-note song. As a girl Anna had imagined they were calling her name, every evening, *Ann-a, Ann-a,* rising and falling, *Ann-a.* Sometimes it gave her bad dreams. She conquered that fear, or thought she did, when she became a teenager. But right now, tonight, combined with everything else, the sound made her want to scream.

A gust of wind moved over the vast expanse of professionally maintained lawn outside the house, touched a loose section of gutter, made it creak and groan against the eave, and behind the ocean of scorching air the first cool currents of fall winnowed their way through.

Autumn seemed to be arriving well ahead of schedule, pushing and shoving with no consideration for summer's desire to stay.

The Grove house, built on the eastern edge of her home town, had once been a place of joy for Anna. As she told *Life* magazine, it represented her triumph over the world...but in the course of the last two decades, the joy had slowly drained away, leached out, until the house stood gray and cold like a headstone.

Anna stared at the five-by-seven. It was a high school Valentine's Day dance picture: beneath an arch of red and pink marble-patterned balloons, a dark-haired young man in an immaculate tuxedo stood arm in arm with a wholesome-looking blonde in a snug green dress. The girl smiled tightly at the camera. Anna knew why. Every time she thought about it her heart broke. She knew her son would be furious if he discovered she hadn't thrown the photograph away, as he'd asked her to do.

The boy looked just as uncomfortable, but in a different way. He seemed ready to flinch, ready to throw his hands up to defend himself. Even with the girl on his arm his whole attitude radiated fear.

Anna reached to touch the photo, but her hand trembled. "It's just Jessica and me here now, you know that. I sent everyone else away. Jim, what am I doing? Am I losing my mind?"

Fautsch narrowed his eyes and stared at the toes of his shoes.

"I wish I could say I thought you were. I don't know what to do about this. It's too strange."

That tight smile in the picture. Michelle Mangrum, the girl's name was.

Loser of a bet. Simon hadn't found out till the prom ended, when Michelle turned on her heel and walked away from him, to a group of her friends. "Finally, it's *over,*" Simon had heard her say.

And faintly, from another friend as they filed out the door, leaving him standing there, "How could you *stand* that guy all night?"

Anna had tried to show him as much sympathy as she could, but he'd pushed her away. Once again, out of habit, Anna looked over her shoulder, and said, *"Oh!"*

Fautsch followed her line of sight and almost gasped himself. Simon Grove stood in the hall doorway, cloaked in shadows, watching them. His eyes glittered.

A few seconds passed before Anna could speak. "Simon! Wh-when did you get home, son?"

Simon moved into the room slowly. "Just now." He nodded at Fautsch. "Evening, Doc."

Fautsch nodded back, his eyes a little wider than normal. "Hello, Simon. How are you?"

Simon shrugged. He wore jeans and sneakers and a polo shirt, and in most ways looked like a normal young man. But something about the way he stared at them, swung his head back and forth between them, made Jim Fautsch's insides knot.

"I'm a little tired, actually," Simon answered. "I think I'll go up and lie down for a bit."

Anna said, "All right," but Simon had already moved past them, heading for the back stairs. They both watched him disappear up the steps, and waited until they heard the ceiling squeak above them. Fautsch exhaled slowly.

Anna covered her face with her hands, rubbed her eyes. "I think *I* know what to do. God." She snuffled and reached for a Kleenex. Neither of them said anything for close to fifteen minutes, and aside from the small sounds of Anna's tears the room grew claustrophobically silent.

Finally Anna said, "Jim—hand me the phone?"

* * *

Simon Grove lay down on his bed and stared at the ceiling. The familiar surroundings of his room gave him no comfort as he tried to recall the dream he'd had the night before. There'd been something, something in it he couldn't remember but knew he needed to.

Faces seen through wet red glass, Paul, Paul's mother and father. The girl with the broken-down car. The old man under the bridge.

Those, no, those were just memories, played out again and again for him.

No insights revealed. Just recollections.

Skin and muscle and bone, shifting, moving. The world in green and yellow.

More of the same. But there was something else, something new.

What, what was it?

Then ...

Simon sat up straight. *There.* He knew he could get it if he thought about it long enough. A new part of the dream, a new feeling, a new urge. It was ...

Traveling. Moving, moving toward the sunrise. Moving east, headed for ... a cylindrical tower, a dome shining gold.

There! That was it! And with the recognition his mind flooded with the need to make it real. Where was it? What city had he seen?

He swung his legs over the edge of the bed and stared around him.

Simon felt as if he sat in the room of a stranger. Nothing here was necessary, nothing here applied to him any longer.

It wasn't just the words he'd overheard between his mother and Doc Fautsch downstairs; it wasn't just the things people in town said about him. It wasn't just that he'd been getting careless—that he had left the last one to be found too soon. Now something else tugged at him, something new, and he felt no need to resist it.

Simon pulled a gym bag out of his closet and threw a few items of clothing into it, grabbed his toothbrush from his bathroom, and crept silently down the front stairs.

* * *

In the kitchen of the Grove house, Jessica Siede finished putting away the last of the dishes and turned to straighten the hand towels on their rack. She felt just as nervous as her employer, Ms. Grove, and performed her duties methodically. Like a neurotic's ritual. If the things she did remained relentlessly normal, maybe the world around her would as well.

She stopped, glanced at the door leading from the kitchen to the garage.

Quietly: "Simon? Is that you?"

Jessica was tall and slender, with clear green eyes and thick yellow hair pulled back into a tail. Only a few strands of gray hid among the blonde. *Not bad for a woman of forty-three,* she often told herself. She'd been thrilled when she first landed the job at Anna Grove's house. Even if Ms. Grove wasn't exactly A-list anymore, she was still a movie star, and Jessica enjoyed dusting the Academy Award Ms. Grove kept on the marble mantle of the drawing room fireplace.

Now, in the kitchen, Jessica's heart thrummed against her ribs and she struggled to keep her breathing even. Her hand fluttered near the oak knife rack.

"Simon?"

Another sound, soft and scraping. Jessica took a hesitant step toward the door, then another. She knew Ms. Grove and her friend the doctor were just two rooms, two doors away. She took a third step toward the door—and stopped as the knob turned. The latch clicked, and the door swung a few inches open.

"Jess..."

It *was* Simon, but his voice sounded strange. He stayed out of sight behind the door.

"Are you...Simon, are you okay? Are you hurt?"

Just two doors away, she could be through there in ten seconds, she was fast enough, he wouldn't catch her.

Jessica knew what the people in town said about Simon Grove. About what had happened next door, about all the others they'd found. They didn't have any proof, she didn't think, or they would have been out here to get him already. No proof...but they hadn't seen the way he'd been acting. Or the way he'd looked at her lately.

When she first started this job she'd have guiltily welcomed Simon's attention, maybe would've told her sister about it during their weekly phone conversation. Chuckled about robbing the cradle. Her sister used to make jokes about finding a boy, seventeen or eighteen, and "training" him; she'd suggested the possibility to Jessica more than once after Jessica showed her Simon's picture.

But a year was a long time, and Jessica carefully pulled out the sharpest of the carving knives.

"I'm fine, I'm fine," Simon said. He paused. "Could you..." The words came out strained, as if he had his teeth gritted. "Could you come out here? ...Just for a minute? I, uh, I...need..." He cut off in a strangle, as if his vocal cords had clogged.

"Simon..." Jessica knew she had to say the words, say them right now, or she never would—her knuckles, white around the handle of the knife, would cut them off. "Your mother, I, I think she's going to call the sheriff, and tell him something, and they'll come for you."

Oh Jesus. Oh Jesus, don't let this be a mistake, please don't. She *had* to tell him. She *had* to let him know. Sweat beaded on her face. It was the right thing to do. It was *Simon,* she *had* to tell him.

A movement caught her eye. Cast by the light from the garage on the floor of the kitchen, Jessica saw Simon's shadow.

There was something wrong with it.

She backed up a couple of steps. Slowly, the door started to swing open the rest of the way.

Jessica stared long enough to see the edge of something, some sort of mass, white and smooth and writhing.

She turned and bolted out of the kitchen, half-blind with sudden tears.

* * *

Simon watched her go. He sighed and closed his eyes, momentarily ashamed of himself, and pulled the door shut. He'd only wanted to say goodbye, really; he hadn't meant it to be anything else. Even though it almost had been. He whispered, "Bye, Jess," to the darkness.

Soon a gloss black Ford Mustang accelerated out of the Grove garage and squealed long burn marks into the road as it left the driveway.

A sheriff's cruiser arrived not thirty seconds later.

* * *

Morning dawned on a day of hazy sunlight.

On a badly-maintained two-lane road off I-75, slightly north of Atlanta, Garrison Vessler rode in the back seat of a Lincoln Town Car, simultaneously reading a news feed on a tablet and talking on a cell phone through a small earpiece. Two men in dark suits and dark glasses occupied the front seats.

A front page story dealt with the "gray-clad female vigilante" who had allegedly prevented a couple of members of the law enforcement community from being killed in a fouled sting operation. Vessler set the tablet down on his lap, distracted by the conversation.

"We settled this discussion at the meeting yesterday," he said. His voice didn't allow any argument. "I don't understand the point of your call." He listened for a few more seconds. "No. I'm through with this."

Vessler jabbed the END button, slipped the phone back in his coat pocket, and stared out the passenger window. They drove through rolling pastureland, with stands of pine alternating on both left and right. The morning sunlight glinted off patches of dew.

Gary Stillwater, the driver, spoke without taking his eyes off the road. "More grief from Stamford?"

"Just more horn-locking," Vessler answered, after a moment's pause. "Stamford's ideas didn't do anyone any good when Stalin and Hitler had them. They won't do anyone any good now."

The man in the front passenger seat, Benson Wong, said, "You realize, he's paranoid enough, he might have this car bugged." He raised his voice a hair. "We're all just kidding, Mr. Stamford, if you're listening."

Stillwater chuckled. "Jesus, Ben, that's the most I've heard you say in two days."

Wong shrugged. "Jorden's got me excited."

While Stillwater laughed, Vessler thought about Brenda Jorden, the woman assigned as Scott Charles' long-term caregiver. She didn't seem to have too much imagination, which Vessler thought a shame. It kept her from achieving perfection, but only just. Something of a karmic weakness, he supposed.

Brenda Jorden stood around five-six, maybe five-seven, and usually wore utilitarian suits in an unsuccessful effort to disguise the lush curves of her body. Long, wavy dark brown hair framed startling green eyes, set above a perfect nose and generous lips the color of red wine. At first he'd balked at the idea of someone so... *tempting* seeing after Scott. But Scott could barely relate to people on a human level in the first place, and Jorden seemed to be the most qualified choice, among the limited selection, as far as skills and training.

So a woman who personified many men's ideal of femininity supervised Scott—the boy who came as close as anyone ever would to being Garrison Vessler's son. And she waited for them at the house.

If she were an augment, now, *that* would be a different story. Then she'd have some chance of advancement within Redfell. But she wasn't. She'd volunteered to care for Scott just after he came out of his catatonic state, and had since done so without a hitch.

Vessler's thoughts shifted to Scott. Forty-nine years had honed and burnished Garrison Vessler to a needle point, and in his presence people stepped out of his way and called him "sir" as they did it. Black hair, swept straight back from a widow's peak, accented a long, weathered face punctuated by eyes like blue knife blades. Since he had accepted Derek Stamford's offer and taken him on as an equal partner in Redfell Security, Vessler had acknowledged only two chinks in his armor.

One was Derek Stamford himself, may he burn in hell, for undermining Vessler's position in his own company.

The other was Scott.

When Garrison Vessler discovered Scott Charles, Scott was a catatonic skeleton, starved to near-death by parents who'd convinced themselves their son's convulsions and strange cries evidenced possession by demons. When Vessler arrived at their house, which crouched far back in a New Jersey pine barren, he found the parents busy making preparations to boil their son in a huge iron kettle.

Vessler shot them both, one bullet to each head, snap snap. He took Scott, who'd been trussed like a hog on the living room floor, and put him in the back of his car, where Scott moaned and thrashed his emaciated limbs and bled from his nose and his eyes. Vessler dumped the parents' bodies in the kitchen, set fire to the house and drove away.

Stillwater swung the car onto a narrow, unlined blacktop road. Within seconds Vessler saw the house. He hadn't been to visit Scott in two months and felt enormously guilty about it, but still he hated the sight of that house.

Ten miles from anything, the two-story wooden structure looked to be a study in mediocrity. Off-white paint with charcoal-gray shutters, a half-dead ash tree in the front yard, acres of unused, grown-over pasture in back; the house was exactly the kind of place a motorist drove past without ever seeing, the essence of nondescript, decayed middle-class America. It reminded Vessler eerily of the house he himself had grown up in, outside of Houston, Texas, and for that reason he loathed it.

Stillwater brought the car to a stop beside the house. Vessler took a deep, silent breath and opened his door.

This arrangement was, without a doubt, the weirdest and most frustrating he'd ever dealt with. All the security measures, all the backups and teams he would normally have assigned to someone as valuable as Scott Charles had to go out the window. He knew that was necessary, but still didn't like it. If Vessler had had his way, Scott would still have been sequestered, but in the middle of a company-owned property, with a decent perimeter guard and at least fifty employees on constant call.

After a knock on the solid oak front door and a brief wait, unnaturally heavy footsteps approached from inside, and Ned Fields opened the door and greeted them. A small, mousy-looking man, Fields gave Vessler no real clue whether he felt bored, relieved, or happy to see them. Fields said, "Come in."

Vessler kept his face neutral as he nodded at Fields and moved past him.

Behind Vessler, Wong and Stillwater gave the smaller man a subtle but respectful berth. They'd heard more than enough about Ned Fields, and Vessler figured they'd keep their contact with him as polite as possible.

Fields moved away from the door, and the floor joists squealed beneath him. He went back and sat down in a specially reinforced chair near the front window. Vessler glanced around briefly; the interior was just as drab and unremarkable as the exterior, furnished as any other such home might be. Sofa, chairs, fireplace, television. Bookshelves.

Brenda Jorden walked out of the kitchen and greeted him. She wore a subdued dove-gray suit and looked twice as beautiful as the last time he'd seen her. She didn't smile. That helped; twenty-seven years of uncompromising, professional self-control let Garrison Vessler deny himself virtually anything, but he still found Jorden a temptation.

"Good morning, sir."

"Morning. How is he?"

"Just fine." The trace of a frown passed over her face. "He picked something up last night, as I reported, held it for about an hour. But of course you know that, that's why you're here." She paused. "It strained him. He complained of muscle cramps when he woke up, and I found a few spots of blood on his pillow."

"You've attended to that?"

"Yes, sir."

As he talked, Vessler started down the hallway, leaving Stillwater and Wong in the living room with Ned Fields.

Jorden fell in behind Vessler. He stopped outside the last door on the right, took a deep breath, knocked, and opened the door a second later.

Scott's room had once been two rooms, but Redfell had had one of the walls knocked out. Now Scott lived in a long, rectangular space, one end devoted to his own comfort, the other dedicated to company business.

In the company's half sat three desks, two computer workstations, and a portable fMRI machine equipped with a skullcap-style sensor cluster. The other end of the room, Scott's end, had a bed, a TV, a dresser, and another computer. His own personal one. Scott sat in front of it, playing a video game, but stopped and swiveled around to greet Vessler.

"Good morning, sir," Scott said. "How long are you staying?"

Vessler didn't reply, but came into the room and sat down on a straight-backed wooden chair near the door. "A day or two...maybe longer. We'll see."

Scott's eyes brightened, and Vessler felt about an inch tall, that even a bone that meager thrown to the boy could mean so much.

Redfell had classified Scott Charles as a "remote viewer." A few different government agencies in a few different countries had tried to cultivate remote viewing specialists for decades, with a tiny bit of unpredictable success here and there. Scott was, as Derek Stamford had called him, "the real deal."

The ability came with a heavy price. Scott's fragile mental well-being depended on a tightly controlled environment. Thanks to careful training, Scott could pick out other augments, but he couldn't abide the presence of large numbers of people, augmented or not. And so Redfell had placed him here, in the middle of nowhere, with at most a half dozen people around him at any given time. It was inconvenient beyond measure, but Vessler felt the benefits outweighed the costs.

Scott turned away from his computer, leaned back in his chair and stared at Vessler with huge, hollow magenta eyes. *So thin,* Vessler thought, a pang in his heart. He didn't let it show on his face.

"How are you?" he finally asked.

The question made the boy laugh: a weak sound. "I'm all right, I guess."

On some days Scott could display an acidic wit, but it didn't look as if this were one of those days. Still, Vessler felt immense pride in Scott's speech. The boy had only learned to talk about four years ago.

From the doorway Jorden said, "I'll be in the living room." Vessler paid her no attention, focused on Scott.

Scott Charles suffered from a severe pigment deficiency that left him extremely sensitive to sunlight—which didn't matter, since he never left the house. Scott had a tendency to go into seizures if exposed to the mental presence of more than six other people at once; in addition to that, he carried inside him a tightly packed bundle of phobias—a Freudian psychoanalyst's dream case—intense agoraphobia foremost among them. All windows in the house bore heavy, opaque draperies.

Scott's fears were numerous and varied: spiders, cats, knives, needles, darkness, automobiles, as well as several other, more esoteric terrors, such as white-haired men and sheets of heavy black plastic.

Scott was actually something of a success story among the behavioral therapists and research technicians on Redfell's payroll. When Vessler first brought him in, the white-coat types agreed unanimously: not viable. Don't expect him to last, they said. A month, maybe six weeks at the most. Too many problems, too many complications. Too many recessive traits, expressed all at once. But Vessler believed in him, took some leave time to stay with him, and together they changed the prognosis.

Scott wasn't normal, no, not by any standards, but after eighteen months of intense therapy, the child began to make real progress.

Away from the general population, Scott remained calm and focused. Now, sitting on the uncomfortable chair in Scott's room, Vessler could hardly believe he was looking at the same boy he'd pulled out of the rotting house in New Jersey.

"Did you bring me anything?" A pause, then, hopefully: "... Doughnuts?"

"Sorry," Vessler said. He reached into his inside coat pocket, brought out a video game and flipped it to Scott. The boy's face lit up.

"*Shadow Viscount 3!* Cool! Have you played it?"

Vessler shook his head wearily. "My brain's not geared right for those things."

Vessler recalled the end of his last visit here, when Scott had accompanied him to the living room, creeping along the wall of the hallway like a ghost. He remembered the sudden change in the boy as the door swung open and shafts of sunlight speared into the house's gloom.

Scott tried to stay, tried valiantly enough to make Vessler sick at heart, but his feet backed him away from the door. When the driver pulled Vessler's car up in front of the house, Scott disappeared with a yelp down the hall, into his room. Vessler couldn't get him to open the door, and had had to leave without saying goodbye.

The company fed Scott's fears. Vessler knew it, participated in it. Hated himself for it.

He knew that, with proper therapy, Scott could probably overcome those fears, learn to live a totally normal life, walk outside in the sunshine and drive cars and visit zoos and doctors. But no one knew how precarious Scott's abilities were, and since they functioned *now,* the company at large wanted him here, in its house, doing its work—*especially* now, since it looked as though he might become truly productive. Vessler wanted nothing more than to tell Scott, tell him everything about what they were doing.

Tell him why he had no reason to love or trust anyone like Vessler.

But he didn't.

Not for the first time, Vessler wondered when he had so profoundly lost control of his own company.

Scott popped open the game and tugged out the booklet.

As he read it, Vessler said, "Still in the book-of-the-month club?"

Scott didn't look up. "I'm in *three* book-of-the-month clubs. They can't keep up with me."

Vessler sat and watched Scott read for a few moments before reluctantly shifting to business matters.

"So. I hear you found something for us?"

Scott nodded. "I wanted to ask you something, first, though, if that's okay. Uh...sort of a private thing."

Vessler shifted on the chair. He thought he recognized the tone in Scott's voice, and didn't know whether to feel happy or scared. He settled on apprehensive.

Scott got up, went to the door and looked down the hall. Apparently satisfied, he closed the door carefully and sat down on the edge of the bed. It took him a while to get the words out.

"Do you...do you ever...um. Look at. Uh...gir, ah, girls? 'Cause, um, the bathroom door doesn't always close, I mean, it closes but it doesn't always latch, y'know, and I was going to the kitchen a couple of days ago while Miss Jorden was in there, in the bathroom I mean, and the door had come open just a little, and she'd been, um, in the shower, and..."

Scott trailed off.

Vessler took a deep breath. *Oh God. I am so unprepared for this.*

"And you saw her?"

The boy nodded, eyes on the floor. "I thought about asking Agent Fields about it, but, well, I...I wanted to talk to you. First, I mean."

Vessler ran one hand over his face and squeezed his eyes shut for a few seconds. "Tell you what. The company needs results from this trip, *fast* results, and I've got to get some answers right away. But as soon as we get this business taken care of, you and I will sit down and have a long talk, all right? Get all your questions answered?"

Scott's eyes were like finely worked crystal as he looked up. In a tiny voice full of confusion and shame and curiosity and fear and everything else Vessler remembered from his own distant adolescence, Scott said, "Okay."

"Okay. Well then." Crisis averted. No...crisis postponed. *Shit.* "On to business, yes?"

"...Sure."

Vessler's muscles relaxed a notch or two, and while he tried to think of someone to call concerning advice to give to a socially non-functional teenager, he made a small mental note: *Get the lock on the bathroom door fixed. Immediately.*

Business. All Scott had done up to this point had been tests. Accurate tests, tests on which he'd performed unbelievably well, but tests nonetheless. This was real, and Vessler knew Scott felt eager to prove himself. Scott said, "Let me show you," and opened the door to call to Agent Jorden.

Scott was so thin, thin and colorless.

This is wrong. This is so, so wrong.

Jorden came in and joined them in the end of Scott's room devoted to company work.

She sat at one of the desks, flipped through screens on a tablet, and tapped a button on the keyboard in front of her. Looking at the monitor, she said, "Another body fitting the description turned up three days ago in a little jerkwater town in western Alabama. We made calls, put a lid on the local establishment before anything got out. As usual." She paused, leaned back in the chair. "We've got detailed reports and files from each of the police agencies involved. It has all the signs of an augment, a powerful one, but we weren't entirely sure until day before yesterday when Scott saw something." She glanced at another sheet of paper. "If our hit is the same guy leaving these bodies around, we're pretty certain his name is Simon Grove. If not, we'll take the leash off. Let the Alabama state troopers have him."

She handed Vessler a photograph taken from a Facebook page. Simon Grove, pale and dark-haired, didn't look very happy.

Vessler's normally grim expression didn't change. "The mobile units are ready."

Jorden said, "That's another thing. The mobile units may not have to be so mobile. It looks like he's headed here. To Atlanta."

Vessler's eyebrows went up. "Really. Here. Well. Scott?"

Scott sat down, cleared his throat, and rolled his chair over to the larger of the computer setups. He picked up the fMRI skullcap and slid it on with a familiarity that made Vessler's stomach clench.

After a few seconds, Scott's eyes lost focus—became what Ned Fields had referred to as the "thousand-mile stare." The monitor in front of him flickered, turned gray and grainy, and slowly resolved into a series of shapes approximating Scott's vision. Vessler stared at them until he realized he was looking at a gas station. A door on the rear of the building opened, and an orange-red vertical waveform moved out of it.

Scott's talent registered inanimate objects more or less as they were, but that wasn't the case for people. Instead of their bodies, Scott saw humans' "signatures"—the distinctive patterns of energy that made each person unique. Ordinary people showed up on the fMRI monitor as thin, wavering lines, like an EKG readout turned on its side.

Augments, on the other hand, were impossible to mistake, their signatures much brighter, the waveforms heavier and more intense. And an augment had just walked out of that gas station restroom.

Vessler and Jorden pressed around him and watched the screen intently.

* * *

Forty-five minutes later Brenda Jorden left the house and drove into Marietta, ostensibly to buy groceries. She still saw the monitor whenever she blinked, filled with the grainy, static-distorted energy signature that represented their target. The new target resembled a blood-red bolt of lightning, dancing and flickering, and grew in intensity with every mile closer to them. Jorden drummed her fingers on the steering wheel as she thought about it.

The one remaining pay phone in the area was at a Hardee's. She stopped there and dropped several quarters into it.

The line only rang once before it picked up. Jorden didn't wait for a greeting.

"When does he go back to Chicago?"

"Soon." A man's voice. "Maybe tomorrow. It depends on the results he gets from the kid."

She paused. "I've got an idea. Can you hold off till I say?"

The voice tightened. "What idea? No one gave you clearance to modify anything."

Clearance. She smiled. "Just follow me on this. I'll give you details in a day or two." She closed her eyes and imagined the energy signature, growing stronger. "If this pans out it'll do your job *and* mine, with a lot less cleanup. If not, everything else is still in place."

Hesitantly, Derek Stamford said, "All right. But I want a full briefing by Friday."

"Not a problem."

She hung up, got back in her car, and headed for a nearby Kroger.

CHAPTER FOUR

Zach Feygen took yet another swallow of coffee and ran his fingers across his smooth, deep-brown scalp. He hadn't slept in thirty-nine hours, and his eyes felt as if they'd been sandpapered. He sat in front of a desk in an office on Spring Street, across from a small, slender white man with gray hair. Feygen felt exquisitely uncomfortable.

The gray-haired man was Lieutenant Burton Jenks, and despite his diminutive stature he could intimidate the hell out of anyone he chose to. Feygen was no exception.

"She disappeared," Jenks repeated flatly, staring.

Feygen squirmed.

Cops started calling Jenks "The Monster" after his third week on the job, and at first Feygen laughed about it. Until Jenks called him into his office one morning, after Feygen had rendered a piece of evidence inadmissible by overlooking a typo on a form. The evidence, a big syringe with the word "pecker" written on it in permanent marker, wasn't absolutely essential to the prosecution, but it would have saved them a chunk of time. When Feygen came back out of Jenks's office, both his ego and dignity were three sizes smaller. Jenks, with his deadpan stare and frosty voice, garnered enmity from a lot of cops, but got respect from all of them.

"I'm not saying she vanished into thin air," Feygen said plaintively. He swirled his coffee around. "What I'm saying, my point is, she grabbed this guy, Krago, and dragged him back where I couldn't see either one of them. And then everybody came in, and they weren't there."

Jenks breathed out slowly. "I don't think you've *made* a point yet." He flicked his eyes around the room. "Let's review, so I don't sound like a cretin when I try to explain this to my boss. Maurice

Tell made you. So instead of selling you drugs, he decided to kill you. A couple of his boys pulled out shotguns, and you and your pal with the odd-numbered chromosomes stood there sucking your thumbs until somebody, you don't know who, attacked Tell's men. Am I right so far?"

Feygen didn't respond. He thought about the bursts of heat he'd felt, and could predict what Jenks would say if he mentioned them. Jenks went on.

"Okay, now this woman, this ninja warrior, grabs one Bryan Krago and makes off with him. In a mostly enclosed space, surrounded by cops. Except a few minutes later, the woman comes back, tosses Krago onto the hood of an ambulance and disappears again. And not one man out of twenty sees her."

"That's correct, sir."

Jenks sighed and started drumming his fingers on the table. "I don't know whether to fire you or put your ninja on the payroll. This has got to be the most blatant display of incompetence I've seen so far this decade." Jenks's voice remained at conversational level, but the room seemed to grow cooler as he spoke. Feygen sagged. "This female, this masked woman, takes somebody right out from under you, puts him back, and you don't know how she did it, where she came from, or where she went. That is simply amazing."

Jenks stood abruptly. His voice still didn't get any louder, but Feygen nearly cringed from it. "Get back out to that theatre. Figure out where the woman went. She was *on foot,* for Christ's sake." Jenks went to the door and opened it. "I don't want some maniac thinks she's Batgirl loose in midtown."

Feygen got to his feet, stepped into the hallway, turned around to say something else to Jenks, and Jenks shut the door hard in his face.

Feygen let the crash of the door fade away, finished his coffee, and threw the Styrofoam cup in a nearby trash can. "Back to the theatre," he said to no one, and wandered down the corridor.

* * *

At roughly the same time Zach Feygen's boss slammed the door in his face, Janey Sinclair bounded down the front steps of the LaCroix and headed up Juniper Street, a spring in her step and a smile in her eyes. She still rode the high from the previous night's success, and the funk she'd been in the day before seemed very far away. Thoughts of Tim Kapoor were a lot easier to manage today, as well; the office door had been closed and locked when she passed it, so she hadn't had to contend with him on her way out.

Her destination was a little corner grocery several blocks up, where she planned to purchase the ingredients to her favorite lemon-herb chicken dish. She rarely ate meat, but she thought she owed herself something special by way of celebration. She already "had her mouth set" for it, as her father used to say, and could taste the herbed bread-crumb crust.

She laughed a little. *This is how exciting I am. Celebrating with chicken.*

Janey's thoughts abruptly derailed as her eyes fell on a copy of the *Chronicle* lying discarded on a bench. Not the main header, but still above the fold, were the words:

Masked Woman Saves Cops' Lives

The brief article had no art, but claimed that an "informed source within the police department" told the reporter that a masked female vigilante had stepped in last night and taken charge of things when a police operation went bad and endangered two officers' lives.

She picked up the paper and walked slowly, still reading. The police and everyone else knew she was out here now, which was inevitable, of course, but she hadn't expected it so soon. She'd hoped to operate for a few weeks, a couple of months even, before anything got out about her.

Guess that was unrealistic.

Janey rarely had anything to do with social media. She had never been able to shake the thought that participating in it was tantamount to rabid narcissism, and an outgrowth of that—along with strong, self-acknowledged Luddite tendencies—had kept her from buying a smartphone. But she also knew that social media's role in society had expanded far beyond simple social interaction, and that entities such as Twitter had evolved into legitimate sources of news. She wondered if she'd made it into the Twitterverse yet.

Maybe it's finally time to buy a new laptop. Her old one had broken down a couple of years ago, and she'd never bothered replacing it.

Janey shuffled on her way and tried to decide how she felt about the sudden publicity.

* * *

At 10:36 that night, Kaveyah Wilson pulled her books tighter to her chest and stared out across a vast expanse of pavement. She could just see her car from where she stood at the corner of the parking deck. It sat at the far end of the remote, dimly-lit, panhandle extension of the college's central dorm parking area, quietly nicknamed "The Rape Lot." Nobody liked to talk about it much.

Kaveyah straightened her slender frame and headed for her car. She tried not to be too conspicuous as she rearranged her keys in her right hand, so that they pointed out from between her fingers as she made a fist. Just like they taught in self-defense class.

Kaveyah Wilson was a sophomore dance major. Her instructors were unsure about her future as a dancer; they thought she'd be more suited to modeling. But Kaveyah wanted to be a dancer, and knew she had the talent, and daily thought of new places where her instructors could stick their opinions.

This is the last time I do this. It was after ten, and while the rest of the campus headed out for a typical night of fifty-cent beer and pick-up lines, Kaveyah had agreed to help her boyfriend Keith, a Journalism major who wrote for the school paper, study for an Accounting test. "Study," she said aloud, and snorted, wincing as the sound echoed around her.

He could barely be called her boyfriend. They'd only been on two dates.

That was apparently time enough for things to get horizontal, at least in Keith's opinion, and now she had to go all the way back to her car, out to the only parking place she could find on the overcrowded campus, alone and after dark to boot. Her eyes narrowed to slits. Under her breath she said, "Keith Gaffney, if I get attacked out here, so help me, I'll kick your ass up around your ears."

The car seemed only slightly closer.

The lot extended to the edge of a large square of bare earth, several months earlier cleared of trees for construction. Only a single line of mercury vapor lights lit the Rape Lot. The administration thought that was enough. They had agreed, grudgingly, to assign a twice-hourly security patrol to the area after reports of four rapes and two assaults were filed. Apparently it hadn't occurred to them to close that section of the lot.

Modeling. She turned the word over in her mind. Keith insisted she was a dead ringer for Chrissy Teigen, and was missing out on a fantastic opportunity by not auditioning for modeling jobs. *Yeah right. Chrissy got my chest and hers both.*

Four cars away from her own, she heard a sound. She stopped dead still, listening.

Kaveyah drove a gray Honda, a gladly accepted cast-off from her MBA older brother. Parked between her and the Honda were two sedans and two huge SUVs. The sound seemed to have come from between the SUVs. She strained her ears to hear it again.

Nothing. Silence.

Kaveyah looked back toward the dorms, hoping to see the flashing yellow light of the security patrol truck, but there was nothing. Not even other people coming from or going to their cars. She turned back toward the Honda and moved into the center of the aisle, as far away from the deep shadows between the vehicles as she could get.

It might have been a cat. There were plenty of cats around.

But it hadn't sounded like a cat. It sounded like something big. And it had come from between the two SUVs, where their high, square frames cast deep shadows.

She had parked next to the farther away of the two SUVs, and to get to her car she'd have to enter one of those deep shadows. Kaveyah took a nervous step sideways. Tried to decide what to do. She wouldn't have thought a parking lot could seem this threatening, and surely during the day it wouldn't. But the sun had set long since, and her heart pumped frantically, and she realized she was terrified.

Turn around. Turn around and walk to the dorm, simple as that. Call somebody. Anybody.

No no no. Dammit, stop being silly! You're no little girl. You handled Keith tonight. There's no reason you can't walk to your car, for pity's sake. So move. Go on. Go.

The seconds stretched out, and she didn't hear the sound again. Keys bristling from her clenched fist, she started for her car and waded into the shadow.

Nothing jumped out at her as she fitted the key to the lock.

Nothing jumped out at her as she opened the door and tossed her books in the back seat.

Smiling to herself, she took one foot off the ground to put it on the floorboard of the Honda, and a hand flicked out from under her car and clamped around her other ankle.

The hand felt like stone, and jerked her shin into the doorframe. She lost her balance and bounced off the side of the SUV, and the pavement slammed into her and drove all the air out of her lungs, and she gasped as a man pushed and pulled his way from beneath the Honda like a giant slug and fell on top of her.

He was big, *huge,* a massive wall of soft rounded flesh supporting muscle and bones like steel beams, and she couldn't believe he'd squeezed himself under her car. Kaveyah drew in a shocked breath and wished she hadn't, he smelled so bad, dirt and sweat and urine ground into his clothes and his skin. She got one flashing look at his eyes: palest blue, almost gray, and very wide, whites visible all the way around. With a lurch she recognized him as one of the college's landscapers. She'd seen him working around the dorms, and once or twice around Five Points, drinking and laughing with three or four other college employees.

He wore a work shirt with the name *Glenn* stitched above the pocket.

"Black bitch." Guttural. Forced. "Black bitch, black bitch." He curled one huge arm around her neck and hauled her to her feet. She clawed at the arm, gasping, unable to take another good breath, and he dragged her backward toward the edge of the lot. He told her in broken, muddled sentences some of what he intended to do to her. She still couldn't scream.

She kicked as well as she could, but it was like kicking a mattress. She tried to slam a foot down onto one of his insteps, but he held her almost completely off the ground, and her feet couldn't reach their target. Glenn twisted sideways, pulled her between the cars, still toward the trees. He began pawing at her with his free hand, shoved it inside her blouse, mashed her breasts. She made tiny hissing noises as the cartilage in her neck began to give way.

Kaveyah heard the sound of breaking glass, and the mercury-vapor light directly above them went out, enveloping them in darkness. Glenn stopped his chanting and let go of her breast as he turned his head to look up toward the dead light. His grip on her throat relaxed the tiniest bit, but he still held Kaveyah pinned. He made a strange, confused trilling sound in the back of his throat—and his arm sprang open convulsively. Glenn staggered away from her, out into the aisle between the cars.

Kaveyah had no idea what was happening around her, but

she did know she was free, and realized she still gripped her keys in her fist, forgotten till now. She stumbled to the Honda and climbed in, jammed the keys into the ignition, slammed her door and locked it, turned on the headlights, and the twin beams lit the scene before her perfectly.

Glenn and someone else stood not five feet from the front of her car.

Glenn kept his feet, but just barely. A long, freely-bleeding cut curved down across his forehead and onto one cheek. The other person wrenched Glenn's left arm into a punishing joint lock, and Kaveyah gasped.

A woman dressed head-to-foot in segmented gray body armor, a gray full-head mask covering her face, stood behind Glenn, forcing him onto the ground.

Relays clicked over in Kaveyah's mind, and she realized this must be the woman from the paper. The vigilante. The woman who, until now, Kaveyah hadn't really believed was real.

The vigilante turned her head and looked at Kaveyah through the windshield with eyes covered by black mesh, and Kaveyah didn't know who to be more terrified of, the masked woman or the man who'd attacked her.

Glenn let out a scream like a rockslide and broke away. The vigilante fell back, half-crouched; she moved fluidly, gracefully. Like a dancer.

Lord, she's better than I am!

Frozen, Kaveyah watched as Glenn knotted up a fist like a wrecking ball and slammed a punch at the vigilante's head.

The vigilante twisted aside. She caught Glenn's wrist as it passed her, pivoted, brought the arm up over one shoulder and snapped it cleanly at the elbow. Before Glenn could scream again, the vigilante shoved him a pace backward and delivered the most devastating kick to the groin Kaveyah had ever seen, in movies or real life. Glenn doubled over, his mouth huge and his great round gut heaving.

The vigilante pushed Glenn out of the way of Kaveyah's car. The huge man fell to the pavement with a thick, meaty sound.

The woman in gray came to her door—Kaveyah realized the window was rolled down a crack, and scrambled to put it back up, but couldn't find the button—but the vigilante only spoke to her.

"You're safe," she said, her voice cool and smooth and low. Kaveyah stopped fumbling for the window control and looked up at her. "But you'd better go now. Report this."

Bizarrely, for a bare instant, Kaveyah thought she smelled lemon chicken. The vigilante backed away from her, into the shadows, and faded from sight.

For about a second Kaveyah tried to see where the woman had gone, but couldn't.

She jammed the car in gear and got the hell out of there.

* * *

A little more than sixteen hours after Kaveyah Wilson called the police, a 2002 red-and-primer Camaro squealed its way down a narrow road in central Alabama, chrome flashing in the afternoon sun.

"You son of a *bitch!* Did you think I wouldn't find out? Did you think nobody'd tell me?"

Julie Worley felt her face turning red, the tears starting in her eyes, and hated herself for showing so much emotion. Brett said nothing. He just kept staring out the windshield. Julie could only tell he was upset by how fast he took the turns.

"Did you? Did you think I'd never know?"

Brett still didn't reply.

Julie Worley, a senior in high school, went out with Brett Griggs for the first time on her sixteenth birthday, almost two years ago. He was her first real date, her first real kiss. On her seventeenth birthday, their one year anniversary, he became her first lover.

She wished him dead.

Slumped back in her seat, eyes on the passing trees, she said, "I can't believe this. How long've you been screwing her? A month? Six months, a year, what?"

Brett tightened his grip on the steering wheel. "First time was at my dad's lake house, about two weeks after I popped your cherry." His knuckles whitened. "Happy now? That what you wanted to hear?"

Julie stared at him open-mouthed, and as the tears spilled out she screamed and attacked him, punched and clawed, and tried her best to rip off as much skin as she could. Brett shouted and fought her away. The car swerved all over the road, and the passenger-side mirror clipped itself off against a DEER CROSSING sign. Brett stomped on the brake pedal and, when Julie didn't let up, slammed his elbow into the side of her face. Her head bounced off the window and her fists fell into her lap.

Stunned, she sat for a few brief seconds of silence, and began to cry again. Brett curled his lip and pulled the car over to the side of the road, almost into the trees. He shoved it into PARK, reached across Julie, pushed her arm out of the way, and popped the door open.

"Out."

Julie looked him in the eyes and tried to say, "What?" but Brett cut her off and said, "Out! Get out, get outta my car!" He unbuckled her seat belt.

"Out here? You're just gonna leave me here?" Brett winced, and she immediately regretted sounding whiny.

"Just get the hell out!" he shouted, and Julie jerked back away from him. When she showed no sign of doing it herself, he put both hands and one foot on her and shoved her out the door. She caught herself on the doorframe and, when she got both feet on the ground, made as though to get back in. Brett hurriedly shoved the car into DRIVE and gunned the engine.

The Camaro sprayed Julie with gravel as it jumped away from her. Her books, which she'd forgotten on the floorboard, came flying out of the sunroof.

She stood and watched him go. Her cheek began to throb where Brett had elbowed her, and she felt the tears start again when she touched her face. Julie sank to her knees in the grass and for a few moments tried to think. When that didn't work, she settled for trying not to panic.

She stayed there, on her knees, for a quarter of an hour. No cars came down the road. She wasn't surprised, since not many people lived out toward her house, and those who did wouldn't be getting off their jobs for another hour and a half. She checked her watch: three thirty-six.

A breeze blew, lifted her hair. A mockingbird started singing. She waited. More minutes ticked past, and she had to try even harder not to lose control of herself.

Brett really wasn't coming back.

Julie straightened her shoulders, wiped her face as best she could on the tail of her shirt, stood and went about gathering up her schoolwork and textbooks. The idea of being stranded here didn't bother her all *that* much, really. Maybe in a big city, maybe in Birmingham, yeah, that'd be bad. But here, not too far from her home and in the middle of the day, no problem. Besides... concentrating on getting home ought to keep her mind off Brett. At least for a while. Ought to.

It didn't work out as she'd hoped. She hadn't been walking long when the reality of her situation hit her: she and Brett were over. Finished. She wondered how many people had known about it all along, how many people had laughed at her behind her back.

She and Brett had dated for *so long*. She realized with a sudden ache that she didn't know how to behave anymore, what to do or where to go. No more movies together, with his arm around her in the theater. No more dances. No more of his mother's cooking. No more trading music. No more kisses. No more nights together.

Julie gritted her teeth. She'd have to figure out how to spend Friday and Saturday nights again, and she'd have to face everybody in home room the next morning—*and* she'd have to explain it to her father, who'd convinced himself that Brett was a great guy, and told her on a regular basis how lucky she was to have caught him.

Well... She ground her teeth together as she walked. Screw 'em all. Screw 'em *all*.

Maybe she'd cry in the next few days, but damn it, it'd be for some other reason, because she wouldn't cry for Brett. Not anymore.

Bastard.

Son-of-a-bitch.

In the middle of a thought Julie heard something and stopped to look behind her. It grew swiftly louder, and closer, and became a song, one she recognized, one Brett's older brother Chad liked to listen to. Maybe...maybe Brett, coming back for her...?

But the vehicle that rounded the bend and bore swiftly down on her was not Brett's battered Camaro. It was a gloss-black Ford, and the sun's rays bursting off its windshield made it look less like an automobile than like something from outer space. She stood still and watched it come and let the music pulse over her.

The Ford blew past her without even slowing down and disappeared around another curve.

Julie let out a breath she hadn't realized she'd been holding and giggled. What was she thinking? Some handsome stranger would come along, pick her up, rescue her from her heartache?

She laughed a little more and started walking again—but heard the music, faintly, coming back. The song grew louder, and the Ford reappeared from around a curve.

It passed her again, did a lazy U-turn and pulled abreast of her. The music clicked off. Julie stood there, paralyzed.

Every lesson she'd been taught, every Alabama School Board educational video she'd ever seen, all of them pounded into her head the dangers of talking to strange men. But as she neared the unfamiliar car, the memory of Brett's cologne seemed to choke her, and her face throbbed, and all the anger inside her distilled.

Julie Worley decided to choose her own path for once, and to *hell* with what everybody else said.

Her determination doubled when she got a good look at the driver.

He was young, maybe a year or two older than she was, extremely pale and dressed completely in black. High-top sneakers, jeans, belt, T-shirt, and three-hundred-dollar sunglasses, all as black as his car, as his thick combed-back hair. He faced her, smoothly took off the shades—and she found herself staring openly. As he turned his head, she noticed a small earring dangling from his left ear: a skeleton key. He smiled at her, a little shyly.

"Hi," he said, his voice like ocean air. "You all right? Need a lift?"

It took a fraction of a second. Maybe less than that. "Sure." Julie smiled her best bedroom smile, felt a little slutty and a little dangerous and reveled in it. He reached over, opened the door for her. She said, "My name's Julie. What's yours?"

His smile got even better. "Simon." He slipped the shades back on and put the car in gear as she buckled in. "Where can I take you?"

* * *

Earlier that afternoon and several hundred miles away, the bell signaling the approach of the next period rang, and Nathan Pittman walked into his American History class and set his books down on his desk. Paige had already sat down in the desk in front of his, her back to him, talking to Drew Watkins. He was pretty sure she'd seen him come in, but she didn't turn around.

Nathan smoothed his dyed-red hair so that it all hung down on the left side, leaving the shaved part of his scalp uncovered, and out of reflex tried to adjust his nose ring. Of course it wasn't there. Piercings were against school rules. He sat down and tried to regulate his breathing. Paige continued chatting with Drew, and gave no hint of turning around to talk to him.

Even when he couldn't see her face, Nathan found Paige tremendously appealing. She was short, maybe five-two, with curly brown hair, enormous green eyes, a curvaceous figure, and a smile that made his insides spin.

From the first day of class eight days before, Paige had spoken to him every day, freely, and shown none of the reluctance that everyone else at the school seemed to. On the fourth day of class Nathan finally overcame the worst of his suspicions and started talking openly to her.

Nathan Pittman was seventeen, rake-thin, and utterly out of place.

At his old school he was one of the crowd; he hung out with his own group of friends and no one gave him a second glance. Then his mother's boss handed her the choice of taking a raise and moving to a new city or losing her job, and Nathan had two weeks to say his goodbyes to his friends and his hometown.

"You'll thank me later," his mother had said. "I'm making enough money now, we can get you into a *good* school. A *private* school."

Attending classes his first day at Grover Cleveland Academy seemed very much like stepping into an alternate dimension. He'd jotted down a few possible names toward the end of the day: The Uptight Zone. Top Forty World. Planet Button-down. Every single person he passed in the halls, teachers and custodians included, stared at him as though he were actually a member of some alien species on an inter-dimensional exchange program. He wondered how much worse it would've been if they'd seen him with all his piercings and in his normal wardrobe, instead of the bland-as-white-bread clothes he had to wear to follow the dress code.

But Paige was different. As soon as he sat down in History, she greeted him with, "Hi! I'm Paige. What's your name?" And it went from there.

Each day became tolerable because he could look forward to

talking to Paige. When no one sat with him at lunch, and no one spoke to him in the halls, and he got picked dead last every day for the football games in P.E. like some nine-year-old fat kid, he could think about talking to Paige before and after History class. When the starting quarterback and three of his buddies trashed Nathan's car, he thought about Paige. When Charlie Greene, a trust fund baby encased in a solid block of entitlement, walked past him in the hall and casually slammed his head into a locker, he thought about Paige. When Jimmy Tullo wrapped his fist around a roll of pennies and rammed it into Nathan's shoulder so hard it knocked him off his feet, turned to his friends and said, "Hey, that does work," Nathan thought about Paige, even as three teachers pulled him off of Jimmy Tullo. And with the thought of her he'd made it through each day of the preceding week of hell.

So yesterday, after the end-of-class bell sounded, Nathan leaned slightly forward over his desk and said, "Um, hey Paige, I was wondering if you'd maybe like to go out, maybe this weekend? I'm sort of broke, but I was thinking we could watch a movie, maybe, or something?"

His words stopped her dead, and she regarded him with wide eyes for a long moment before answering. He knew what the look meant, or at least he was pretty sure he did, but he hoped he'd misread her.

Paige said, "Well. Why don't you let me think about it?"

Of course he said sure, sure, no problem, sure.

And today she would give him her decision, yes or no. When Nathan felt reasonably confident that his voice wouldn't shake, he said to Paige's back, "Hey, Paige."

She turned around, and her decision was as obvious as if she'd been wearing a mask with the word NO printed across the forehead. He sucked in his breath and waited anyway.

"Yes?"

And that was it. That was her response. All of it.

Nathan let out the breath and took in another, stunned. Not,

Hi, Nathan, listen, I've thought about it, and I'm flattered, but I don't think so. Certainly not, Nathan, I'd love to go out with you! Instead...nothing. As if he hadn't said anything.

"Uh, I was wondering if you'd maybe reached a decision, about what I asked you about yesterday. About maybe going out with me. This weekend." He wanted to crawl under his desk.

Paige smiled, but it was the kind of smile you'd give a moron.

"I don't think it'd be a good idea," she said, and turned back around to talk to Drew again.

"But...uh...Paige. Paige? ...Hey, Paige?"

She ignored him.

Nathan lowered his head and stared at the top of his desk for the rest of the period.

CHAPTER FIVE

"Creep. Bastard. *Bastard.*"

Simon watched as Julie hugged herself and stared out at the parking lot. Her cheek had begun to darken where Brett struck her, and she had a small knot on her head where it smacked against the car window. She ignored the menu on the table in front of her.

Simon Grove cleared his throat nervously and said again, "Would you prefer, um, Supreme or Super Supreme?" He took a sip of his iced tea and tried to make eye contact with her. She may have felt him looking; she finally turned her head and smiled softly.

"Oh, Simon, I'm sorry. I ought to be paying a lot more attention to you. Instead of thinking about him."

Simon shook his head. "It's okay! It's okay, really. I mean, you just had sort of a personal trauma, right? It's only natural for you to be upset."

Julie put her elbows on the table and leaned forward, watched him intently. Her eyes narrowed slightly. "Y'know...I just met you. Not two hours ago. How come I feel like I can tell you anything?" Her smile still hovered about her lips, which were thin but well-shaped. Simon cleared his throat and squirmed in his seat.

"I...feel sort of...connected to you, too," he said quietly. "'Cause you don't know me. You don't have any preconceived ideas of me. It's nice." He touched his clothes, his earring. "All this stuff is sort of new, actually. I'm kind of going through a change of image."

"I like it." She stretched, and her shirt pulled tight across her ample chest. Simon tried his best not to stare, or at least not to look as if he were staring. Several seconds later it occurred to him that she might have *wanted* him to stare, and he couldn't decide whether that pleased him or scared him.

"Y'know, if anyone had asked me this morning if I'd accept a ride from a total stranger and let him buy me dinner, I wouldn't even have bothered to answer. But here we are."

"I don't know that I'd call this dinner. It's just pizza."

"Hey, around here this is as good as it gets for a date."

They both fell silent, and the word "date" bounced around in Simon's mind among all the uncertainty. He only had to think back a few days to remind himself why he was on the road. But Julie was ... different? Was that the word? Or maybe it wasn't Julie that was different. Maybe it was the new surroundings. Maybe it was *him*.

"So you're headed east? Got a destination, or're you just driving?"

"I'm not sure," he said, truthfully. "I knew I needed some time away, but I didn't know where I wanted to go. But something clicked in my head, sort of, and now I think I'm going to Atlanta."

She smiled a little. "Mmmm...never been there. I'd like to go sometime." Julie tilted her head slightly to one side. "So Simon... what's your secret?"

He flinched, and saw her eyes widen, and forced his smile back into place.

"Are you okay?" Julie asked, all concerned and caring, all sweet and sugary like frosting.

Abruptly another name came to him, another face. Another girl who'd also acted concerned and caring. Julie Worley began to seem ever so slightly...

...fake.

"I didn't mean to pry. I mean, you just said you could be yourself 'cause you were here with me...on neutral ground, right? Like starting over? I'd just like to know more about you. Like, y'know, your last name and stuff. If that's okay with you."

He shut his eyes, thought of his mother. People said she stayed so beautiful because of exercise, and diet, and genetics. Simon knew better. He knew full well the connection between himself and his mother. Not that she'd ever admit it. Not after what had happened. What he'd done.

"My last name is Brown," he said.

"Simon Brown. Well. I'd really love to know how you got to be in Crawford Shoals. But, y'know, only if you want to tell me." She smiled again, and he returned it, at least on the surface.

Fake. She was fake. So obvious. He resisted the urge to look around the restaurant, try to spot her friends, no doubt watching him from a far table. Had someone known he was coming? Known what road he was on, and put this girl there for him to find?

But Simon surprised himself with how well he hid his suspicions. The two of them talked freely and easily; their food arrived, but didn't hinder the conversation, and they stayed long after they'd both finished.

Simon spun the Alabama schoolgirl a tale of a rich grandfather and an inheritance which, coupled with a long-standing desire to see the world, had led to his purchase of the Ford. "I wanted a Porsche," he said, gnawing on the end of his straw. "But, y'know, just 'cause I have some money, doesn't mean I need to spend it all on a car with only two seats."

Julie listened more than she talked, but she seemed comfortable enough to relate the high points of growing up in a tiny, far-removed Alabama town, dealing with a distant, loveless mother and a well-meaning but spineless father.

Simon thought perhaps that sounded a bit too pat, a bit too Lifetime Channel, but he decided to let it pass. For now.

Equally difficult, she said, were the boys she had to choose from. "Pickings are slim. Most of the guys around here are just dumb rednecks, and the few that aren't..." Her eyes unfocused, slightly, and she slumped a little. "Really, I guess, *all* the guys around here are sort of like that." She straightened her shoulders again, gave him a small, coy smile. "I guess I'll have to look for a guy from somewhere else."

Simon finished his tea, set down the glass. Watched her. Her with her blonde hair and pretty eyes and big tits. Miss Popularity, no doubt. Trapped in a small town. What a tragedy. He said, "How would you like to take a spin? Just drive around for a while?"

* * *

"You're sure, now? This is the place?" Simon steadied himself in the dark, one hand on her upper arm.

"I'm the one who grew up here, right? I know where I'm going."

Full dark had come, and Julie led the way down a narrow path choked with Bermuda grass and wild blackberry bushes, their only illumination a penlight she carried in her pocketbook.

Not that Simon really needed the light.

More than once he pricked himself on one of the long, sharp blackberry thorns, and the first time he nearly screamed. He stopped short in the darkness and held up his hand, and Julie rushed back to him, sugary sweet, and he examined it in the penlight's weak beam. A small, ragged hole had punched into the fleshy part of his left palm and torn slightly, so that a tiny red ribbon of blood seeped out of a teardrop-shaped wound.

As he stared, the bleeding slowed and stopped, and the blood reversed course, retreated into the wound. He turned his hand away so she couldn't see the skin start to close.

"Did it get you real bad?" There was that concern again, so thick and treacly. If she hadn't had the light near his face he would have sneered.

"No, no, I'm okay."

Julie pulled him further into the darkness. "Come on. It'll be worth it, I swear."

After several more minutes of tripping over roots they came out of the trees and onto the shore of a lake. Simon leaned against the trunk of a pine and stared.

"Wow," he breathed out, solemnly.

"Glad I brought you here now?"

Simon wavered. It was so *beautiful.* Michelle...Michelle wouldn't *ever* have brought him to a place like this. Maybe Julie wasn't trying to trick him after all. Maybe she really did want to be here, just with him, just for him.

He felt so confused now, he didn't *know*...

He reached out, took Julie's arm and pulled her gently to him. She nestled against him, her back to his chest, and the two of them gazed out over the water. She made a small, pleased sound, and he twined his arms around her waist.

The half-moon rested on its side in the sky like a shining cradle. The water's surface rippled with tiny, breeze-driven wavelets, and the moon's radiance infused them, so that the water itself seemed liquid silver. After a few moments Julie moved away from Simon, but took his hand again and led him to the water's edge, farther away from the trees.

"You can see the stars better from here," she said, and when she tilted her head up to look, Simon kissed her. Her hand glided up his arm to rest on the nape of his neck, while the other pressed into the small of his back.

Could he have been so wrong about her? Could this be something real? The grass was soft on the dark earth of the lakeside, and he laid her gently down on it, and stretched out beside her. She kissed his lips, his cheeks, his eyelids, his neck. She nipped the skin just to the side of his Adam's apple—

—and he felt it begin.

No. No! Not here, not now!

Just a touch, just a tingle. But a part of his mind already knew: though Julie's lips and body felt so sweet, so perfect, though he was already hard and straining for her, nothing she could possibly give him compared with what he could take.

He discovered her unbuttoning his shirt, and her light kisses covered each exposed portion of skin. Simon stared at the top of her head in the moonlight and ran his fingers delicately through her hair.

He felt it coming. And on a level just above his subconscious, he wanted it to.

But, damn it, he could talk to this girl! How many other girls had he ever been able to talk to? How many other girls had ever gotten past what their parents had told them about him? Maybe… maybe he could stop it, keep it down, control it, take Julie in his arms and make love to her. He could take her away, away from here, from her dried-up little town. Keep her with him. Protect her.

She looked up, and the moonlight reflected in her eyes, made them sparkle and shine like the eyes of some mythical woodland creature, a dryad come to life just for him. At that moment she was the most beautiful girl he had ever seen. Her hand trailed down, lower, and she touched him lightly, just with her fingertips.

But that pushed it over the edge, and with a self-hatred blacker than coal Simon welcomed it.

Julie's eyes reflected the change even as it happened, and she would have screamed, but twisting white coils entwined her head and filled her open mouth.

* * *

As the next day dawned on Crawford Shoals, Robert Worley fumbled with his necktie and hurried toward the door. He had a habit of showing up for work five minutes late, almost every day, even when he didn't have a good reason for it. This morning he promised his reflection in the hallway mirror that he'd make it to work on time, no matter what. He miss-tied his tie for the third time, and pulled it off in disgust.

Julie hadn't come home the night before. That worried him a little, but it was nothing she hadn't done in the past. Standing at the bar in the kitchen, Julie's mother Irene muttered to herself and methodically ate a bowl of high-fiber cereal.

Robert finally got the knot in his tie right and, feeling positive about the day ahead, opened the front door.

Gray Widow's Walk

Annoyed, Irene Worley strode into the living room when she heard her husband violently retching.

"Robert? Robert. What's wrong with you? What's the matter?"

She saw the thing on the porch, and her voice left her. She continued walking. Slowly. Drawn to it, couldn't keep her eyes away from it. On the floor, Robert retched again, spewed his breakfast across the hardwood, and started to sob.

Something that had once been her daughter sat propped against the porch railing, its hands folded in its lap, still dressed in the outfit Julie had left the house in the day before. Irene recognized her only by the clothes.

Pinned to Julie's brown-stained, crusted shirt was a note written on yellow legal paper, printed in clean block letters.

I'M SO SORRY.

* * *

That night, Jake Friskel's breath hung unexpectedly in the air before him as he kept a lookout. It flickered and danced beneath a blinking, dying streetlight. Just in the last few minutes, just after 11:00, the temperature had plummeted. Jake didn't think much about it. He did think for a second he felt someone watching him, but he was sure the place was clean, so he didn't say anything to Marko or De'shan.

De'shan had picked up enough knowledge of wires and circuits over the years from his older brother, the electrician, to take care of the simple alarm system rigged to the chain-link fence. Now the three of them, pressed into the shadows in the loading zone of Grant's Discount Electronics, moved silently up the concrete steps to the heavy back door.

De'shan and Marko looked as if they'd been stamped by the same cookie cutter: both well over six feet tall, both skinny as scarecrows. They dressed alike most days, and they both drove customized Honda Civics with enormous sub-woofers taking up the trunks. De'shan's head was smooth and bullet-shaped, though, while Marko wore his hair in rows. Tonight they both carried 9mm revolvers, but Jake didn't like the idea of anything that couldn't take down more than one target at a time. He held a sawed-off, 12-gauge, pistol-grip pump shotgun pressed against his left thigh, one finger on the trigger.

De'shan and Marko worked on the door, and gave Jake time to think.

Every so often it occurred to him how needless their crimes were. Not one of them came from a family that took in less than sixty-five grand a year, and Marko's dad was president of a bank. They only did it for the thrill. Still, Jake loved it. Loved the rush. They all did.

Jake massed nearly as much as De'shan and Marko put together. At six feet one inch, Jake weighed in at two hundred sixty-seven pounds, very little of it fat. De'shan and Marko referred to him as "Cinder," short for "cinderblock." Jake was two years younger than his friends, and that was the only reason he wasn't in charge.

Long seconds passed, and the feeling of being watched grew stronger, though the night remained perfectly still and Jake couldn't see anything moving. The clicks from the lock sounded unnecessarily loud.

Jake whispered, "What's takin' so long?"

"Shut the fuck up, nigga," De'shan hissed, in his best "hard" voice. "It's comin'."

They heard a thump from inside the store, and Jake watched as the lock flipped over of its own volition under De'shan's fingers. As De'shan and Marko traded panicked glances, the door popped open, and the Grant's night manager backed his way out onto the dock, humming a tune, his arms filled with empty boxes.

He was a short, overweight Hispanic man with receding hair and a moustache, dressed in cheap slacks and a short-sleeve button shirt with a loosened necktie through the collar. The door thumped into De'shan's leg. The manager pushed harder, didn't look around, thinking it was just some innocuous obstruction that kept the door from opening. He still hummed.

The three boys froze for several seconds. Jake saw De'shan's face clearly, and his expression said *Shit! What now?*

Marko spoke in controlled, icy tones meant to sound grown-up and dangerous: "Get out here, bitch!"

He grabbed the manager by his shirt, from which hung a name tag that read "Hi, my name is RICO," and yanked him out onto the loading dock. The door immediately swung shut. Rico swiveled his spherical head around, realized what was happening, and said, "Don't hurt me! Don't hurt me, I just work here! Don't hurt me!"

"Shut the fuck up!" Marko barked out, and shoved the barrel of his revolver into the manager's cheek. By this time, Jake had moved up the stairs, and said, "What the hell, man? You said everybody'd be gone by now!"

De'shan had his mouth open to answer, but before he could say anything the latch clicked again and the door punched open.

Marko said, "Shit, another one?" and De'shan cocked his gun and had just started to turn when a narrow gray boot pistoned out of the darkness inside the doorway and crushed his nose. His head snapped back and he pitched nervelessly off the loading platform.

Jake scrambled down the stairs, the shotgun forgotten in his hand, and watched De'shan fall the six feet to the concrete lot. De'shan landed solidly on his back, and his head struck the pavement and bounced. He didn't get back up. Jake glanced at the open doorway and felt his bowels loosen.

A tall woman dressed in gray body armor stepped out onto the loading platform.

Jake tried to make out her face, and realized a mask covered the woman's entire head. Solid black eyes floated in the mass of smoky darkness. The woman remained silent, but moved quickly forward, toward Marko and the night manager.

Jake had momentarily forgotten about Marko, but he stepped back and away, and waited. Marko would deal with this. Jake was big, sure, and strong as a bull, but Marko had a black belt. He was *fast.*

Marko stood halfway up the stairs, Rico pressed to his side, and even as the woman approached him he took the revolver from Rico's face and raised it toward her.

As soon as the barrel of the gun moved away from his head, Rico screamed, *"Hijo de puta!"* and rammed his elbow into Marko's ribs.

Marko gasped, surprised, and his gun hand faltered. Rico jumped off the steps, but landed badly and crumpled. He rolled over onto his back and clutched one ankle.

Alone and confused on the stairs, Marko tried to speak, but before he could get anything out, a police baton seemed to leap into the woman's hand. It flashed, lightning fast, and Marko's gun clanged out of his grip.

Marko howled and jumped off the stairs, landing beside the writhing night manager. He looked around for his gun but couldn't see it.

The masked woman slammed into him.

Marko had studied tae kwon do and jujitsu since he was thirteen, had trophies to prove it, but the woman in gray never gave him a chance. The baton flew out and down and connected with Marko's ankle bone. Marko landed hard on the pavement. He absorbed the impact with one arm, as he'd been taught, but it still shook him.

Instead of wading in after him, the woman collapsed the baton, slipped it into a sheathe on her right thigh, and stepped back, and motioned for Marko to get up.

The young man surged off the ground, teeth gritted. He launched a brutal kick at her head—and shouted as she blocked it with an arm that looked solid as a tree limb. Marko spun off-balance and the woman in gray moved into him.

The woman's armored back was to Jake and partially blocked his view, so he couldn't see exactly what happened next, but it didn't sound like punches landing on Marko's ribs and chest and face. It sounded more like his friend was getting pummeled with a baseball bat. The sound of impacts rattled together like a great ratcheting, and when the woman stepped calmly aside, Marko slumped forward onto his face on the concrete.

Rico lurched up to one knee, pale and sweating. The woman turned toward him and began to extend a hand when Rico saw Jake, back in the shadows at the base of the concrete steps. Rico's eyes grew huge and round. The woman, who had not yet spoken a word, spun around and threw herself between Jake and Rico.

Jake didn't realize he'd raised the shotgun until he felt it buck in his hands. He hadn't fired it more than three times in the past, and he didn't have a tight enough grip on it: even as the roaring battered his ears, he felt the weapon jump backwards, and the hammer embedded itself in his hand between his thumb and index finger, slid and grated against bone.

But pain or no pain, an image struck him, stamping itself on his eyes: the woman in gray, her feet planted, taking the shotgun blast straight to the chest. The spread was too big, though, the woman hadn't positioned herself quite right, and several pellets ripped into Rico's face and neck even as the impact of the shot slammed the woman backward. Blood sprayed from Rico's skin as the woman in gray landed heavily beside him.

A land mine seemed to go off inside Jake's hand, and he started screaming. Tears filled his eyes.

Under its own weight the shotgun dropped. The hammer slid out of his hand with a wet sucking sound. Jake collapsed against the wall, his hand gushing blood, and squeezed his eyes shut as he screamed.

Because of the pain, it didn't fully register on him that the woman in gray, who'd just taken most of a shotgun discharge at five yards, immediately stirred and rose shakily to her feet. All Jake could think about was his torn and broken hand, even as the woman spoke briefly to Rico and helped the shorter man to his feet.

Jake's attention narrowed down to a needle point, however, as the woman in the mask threw a long, slim, metal dart and blew out the guttering streetlight.

The loading area plunged into absolute darkness, and a breath of scorching-hot air raked across Jake's tear-stained cheeks. He could see nothing but a huge greenish-purple after-image amid the black, but he knew the woman wasn't there anymore.

De'shan groaned.

Marko made no sound other than ragged breathing.

In the distance Jake heard sirens.

* * *

Unable to sleep, Zach Feygen staged a rule-bending after-hours visit to Chooley, who had benefited greatly from getting shot. After admission to the hospital, the nurse who examined Chooley found five separate ailments he needed immediate treatment for, not the least of which was acute malnutrition.

"I'm amazed this guy could walk around," the nurse had said. "I've seen healthier corpses."

Ill or not, Feygen had never seen the man quite so ...*intact.* "It's the hospital food, buddy," Chooley said. "It's like a laxative for the brain. Purges you."

Odd declarations aside, Chooley seemed clearer of mind than Feygen had ever known him to be in the past, and had engaged the detective in an unexpectedly cogent discussion of the second season of *Supernatural,* which he'd apparently been watching for the last several weeks in one of the common areas of the Georgia Tech student center. Feygen surprised himself by not really wanting to leave when his cell phone rang.

Feygen left Chooley and made his way down to the E.R. According to the dispatcher, an ambulance was making its way to the hospital, carrying three young men who may or may not have been assaulted by the same woman who'd both humiliated Feygen and saved his life at the Hargett Theatre. One of them was still conscious.

Lounging against a wall and wishing he could smoke in the ER hallway, he'd already checked his watch three times. He couldn't believe it was taking the EMTs so long to get there.

* * *

Chief Resident Carla Gates leaned wearily against the admissions desk in the emergency room of Gavring Medical Center.

Her shift was almost over, no car wrecks or third-degree burns were on their way in, her husband's return flight from Tokyo would arrive at Hartsfield International in another two hours, and she looked forward to doing absolutely nothing but spending the entire night in bed with him. Awake or asleep, it didn't matter; she was exhausted and knew he'd be jet-lagged as well. But for the first eight or nine hours, she only wanted to lie next to him, breathe in the smell of his skin, and let the rest of the world drain away from her mind and body.

An odd sound shook her from her half-dream. She looked around and tried to pinpoint its source, and heard it again. Harry, one of the admissions clerks, came to the counter and said, "What was that?"

"You heard that too?" Gates frowned and moved toward what she thought was the noise's source. It came a third time, a muffled rattling, from a supply closet tucked away in a small alcove.

As she reached for the handle, the door swung partway open, and two people stumbled out. One was a portly, gray-faced Latino, clutching a square of cloth ripped from his own shirt to his bleeding face and neck. The other, supporting the first, wore some kind of gray body armor—and a full-head mask, featureless except for two patches of black mesh over the eyes. Gates backpedaled and said,

"Oh my God." The Latino's shirtfront was soaked with blood, and he grunted and sank to one knee. As the person in the mask turned to face her, Gates felt a chill skitter over her skin.

That's a woman. Gates backed up fast.

That's a fucking terrifying *woman.*

"He's been shot," the masked woman barked. "Twelve-gauge shotgun pellets. I don't think they pierced anything essential, but he's losing blood."

A team of nurses rushed forward while Gates gave orders, focusing on what she knew best. The wounded man held onto enough consciousness to cooperate in getting himself onto a gurney, but she thought he was going into shock. Gates glanced once over her shoulder at the woman in gray, but focused her attention on the wounded man completely as she followed the gurney through the swinging door.

* * *

The masked, armored woman turned and stepped back toward the closet. When she saw Feygen standing in the middle of the corridor staring at her, she froze for a couple of seconds before she ducked into the tiny supply room and snicked the door shut behind her.

Feygen turned his head aside for a second at the blast of heat as he yanked open the closet door. He flipped the light switch. Fluorescent bulbs hummed and lit up, revealing mops, buckets, cleaning supplies, and a haze of steam around the back wall.

Feygen's stomach shrank, his balls drew up tight against his abdomen, and his brain did a hitching little dance.

He tore into the closet, pulled bottles and boxes and sacks off the shelves as he searched the back wall for concealed doorways or traps. After five minutes he growled in frustration and backed out of the tiny room.

This couldn't be what it looked like.

But he'd seen it. First at the theatre. Then here. Tonight. Just now.

After a few moments he wiped a sheen of sweat from his face and muttered, "I'll be damned."

Feygen shut the door, turned around and stuck his hands in his pockets.

He lumbered down the hallway with unfocused eyes, shaking his head.

CHAPTER SIX

Despite the weather services' forecasts of scattered showers, the next morning dawned with an intensely blue sky, marred only by a few thick clouds on the eastern horizon. Traffic was noisy as usual, but the air tasted clean, and Darius Clay enjoyed it as he walked to work.

A neatly-kept man in his late thirties with coffee-colored skin and a few threads of gray in his tightly cropped hair, Darius adjusted the lapels of his double-breasted suit as he made his way down the sidewalk.

Monolithic buildings rose all around him, and every now and again he amused himself by imagining they were all made of stone, each one a single colossal shard meticulously carved out by a giant sculptor.

He related them in his mind to the Chinese ivory eggs he'd seen in a museum: each piece of ivory, about the size of a large man's fist, intricately fashioned into an egg and covered with tiny figures of people on bridges and balconies, in windows and doorways. And yet, inside that egg was another egg, completely separate from the outer one, that had been carved *inside* the larger carving. No seams, no hinges. The sculptor had to send tiny picks and probes through the openings of the outer sculpture to fashion a totally separate egg.

Staring at one such egg, mightily impressed by the feat, Darius thought about describing it to his friends—and realized there was a third egg inside the second, and a *fourth* inside the third, each of them unconnected to the outer ones and all of them just as exquisitely carved.

The patience and mastery of skill required to accomplish such a thing, the *lifetime* it would have taken, boggled his mind.

Thinking of it still filled him with a delicious sense of awe.

And so he tried to imagine, every so often, that all of the city's buildings were like the Chinese eggs, all of them the products of a master craftsman's life work. Every hallway, every elevator, every light fixture carved from living rock. In this way he could sometimes appreciate them as something besides the festering ant hills they so often turned out to be.

Darius moved up Peachtree Street and prepared to turn onto Ellis. The newsstand he passed every day would be there, he knew, and he switched from his contemplation of the city's architectural structures to the somewhat less lofty debate he'd held internally, for about twenty seconds each morning, over the last seven weeks. Rounding the corner, he stopped at the stand, picked up copies of the *Chronicle* and the *AJC*, and stared at the latest issue of *Mandate,* the gay skin magazine his new lover, Frederick, enjoyed so much.

They'd laughed about it when Frederick first mentioned it, Darius wondering aloud why Frederick didn't just get his porn free online like everyone else in the developed world. "I guess I'm old-school when it comes to my prurient interests," he'd said.

Darius had been trying to decide whether or not to buy one of the magazines for Frederick, bring it home and surprise him with it. He'd seen how much pleasure Frederick took from the glossy photos, and he agreed that the men in the pictures were indeed beautiful, but Darius had never bought a magazine of that kind in his *life.* He felt, and would admit it readily, unreasonably squeamish about it.

He took his hand out of his pants pocket, made as though to pick up a magazine. Hesitated. Glanced up at the proprietor, who favored him with a dull stare and said, "Decisions, decisions."

Darius had his mouth open for a retort when a tortured voice carried over the ambient sound of traffic.

"Justice has come to Atlanta!"

Darius swiveled around, searched for the source of the voice, and heard it again: *"The city hath responded to the wickedness that plagues our world today, and sent a predator!"*

Darius spotted it: an old homeless woman, clad in rags, stood on the opposite street corner and waved a scrap of newspaper. Darius thought he recognized the scrap, but couldn't tell for sure at that distance. He dropped his own newspapers back on the rack, waited for the light to turn green, and crossed the street.

Atlanta had more than its fair share of the homeless. Many of them were frighteningly aggressive in their requests for money, and many more left little doubt that they were mentally ill. But the woman across the street seemed different right away. Her voice, though badly strained, held a note of coherence and purpose that Darius suspected had come from formal training.

"Thieves, murderers, rapists! Thine evil ways do not escape the sight of justice! Thy days of chaos are numbered, know ye this!"

Darius drew close enough to see the newspaper clipping. It was one of the front-page *Chronicle* articles from a few days before, describing the "masked woman" who had allegedly appeared out of the night to save the lives of a couple of cops in a screwed-up drug sting. A couple of subsequent sightings had surfaced, carried by several of the smaller papers as well as the *Chronicle* and the *Journal-Constitution.* The tattered orator waved the clipping like a flag.

"No longer are you the apex predators! The city has risen up, and the old hunters soon will be prey! A gray widow walks among you! And she will feed!"

Darius stared at the woman as he passed her. *Gray Widow...* He rolled the name around in his head. The old lady had undeniable charisma, and Darius wondered what she might have been earlier in her life. A preacher? A motivational speaker, perhaps? Maybe a drill sergeant?

His conjecture cut off abruptly as he jolted hard into a stringy teenager who seemed to be equally mesmerized by the homeless woman.

The kid had shaved one side of his head bald and dyed the straight hair on the other side a brilliant red. It hung down past several facial piercings to the collar of a battered leather jacket. Until Darius bumped into him, the kid's eyes were big as the proverbial dinner plates, staring alternately at the old woman and at the clipping.

Startled, the kid and Darius made mumbled apologies, and Darius hurried along his way, faintly embarrassed by his clumsiness. The homeless woman's voice grew fainter behind him, and faded completely as Darius turned another corner.

The voice stuck in his head, though. Through the lobby, into the elevator, up to the sixth floor and the *Chronicle's* rabbit warren of desks and privacy dividers, the street orator wouldn't leave him alone. One name rang in his ears: *Gray Widow.*

Through a window, he noticed the sky beginning to turn overcast after all. Darius rapped on the glass wall of his editor's office and pushed on the door just below the name "Edgar Watts." Watts looked up as Darius entered. The antithesis of the harried, cutthroat newspaper editor, Watts dressed even more neatly than Darius, with razor-cut hair and a meticulously trimmed gray beard. He didn't wait for Darius to speak.

"This woman in gray thing is turning into something real." His voice flowed out clear and smooth. Darius loved to listen to him. "Fodder for your column, I'd say. There's a doctor over at Gavring who claims this masked female delivered a patient to her last night and then vanished into thin air. Doctor's name is Carla Gates." Watts paused to take a long swallow from a bottle of spring water, and Darius casually and with faint and lingering disappointment regarded the framed pictures of the man's wife and children on his desk.

"Well, then, the fates have smiled on us this morning," Darius said. "Forget calling her 'masked woman' or 'woman in gray.' Her name is the Gray Widow."

* * *

Outside, on the street, Nathan Pittman shuffled along the sidewalk toward the MARTA station, the homeless woman's speech echoing in the back of his mind. Nervously he adjusted his eyebrow ring. He couldn't stop thinking about school, though. Couldn't stop thinking about Paige.

At his old school he'd made the dean's list every quarter. He maintained at least a 3.87 GPA. He was staff photographer for the yearbook, and had five trophies in his room from kickboxing tournaments. It hadn't mattered what he looked like; he'd chosen his own appearance and been accepted that way, and whether or not he dyed his hair or put a ring through his eyebrow hadn't mattered one bit. Nobody said, *Hey, there's that freak with the crap in his face.* Or *Man, what a loser.* If anyone said anything at all, they said, *Hey, that's Nathan Pittman, he's up for Star Student.*

Well. Maybe not *total* acceptance. The old administration wasn't too crazy about his appearance, no. But the principal was pretty liberal, and the few times a teacher had called his parents...

Ha. Wrong place to look for concern.

The two ghouls he had to call "mother" and "father" didn't give a rat's ass about him, unless he somehow directly inconvenienced them. They hadn't even put him in a private school because it would be good for him; they did it because it would make *them* look better.

Here no one knew him. Though more than ready to prove himself, to show his new classmates who he was, no one gave him the chance. No one except Paige.

He closed his eyes briefly, and corrected that thought. No one at all.

When Nathan opened his eyes again, the day had darkened. He glanced up at heavy rolling clouds as rain began to fall.

* * *

At 12:22 that afternoon, Tim Kapoor stood in the hallway outside Janey Sinclair's apartment and stared at the door. He held a stack of honeycomb air filters in one hand and a sheaf of work orders attached to a clipboard in the other. Leon, the man his mother had hired to handle maintenance in the building, was at that moment across town on a loading dock, arguing about refrigerators. Tim's mother would have let the air filters go until Leon got back, but Tim saw no reason to wait. He shifted the clipboard to his other hand, where he could just barely hold onto it with his thumb, and rapped on Janey's door a second time.

"Ms. Sinclair?"

No one answered. Rain lashed the window at the end of the hallway, and the lights dimmed for a second as another huge wave of thunder crashed over the building. Electric blue-white flashed again, and Tim smiled.

He loved thunderstorms. As a child at home, back in Florida, when his mother sat agonizingly still in her armchair and tensed her muscles against the next boom of thunder, Tim always went to stand at the sliding patio doors, face pressed against the glass. He reveled in the storm. He loved the saturated feel of the air, the way the trees whipped in the driving wind. He loved the sound of the thunder itself, from the single basso booms to the high, brittle, crackling crashes that lasted several seconds at a time. The thunder always kept him company.

Now, in the hallway, despite the storm's companionship, he felt paranoid for a second or two. He imagined Janey Sinclair just inside the apartment, watching him through the fish-eye lens of the peephole. His cheeks heated up.

Rarely did he bungle anything as badly as he'd bungled meeting Janey Sinclair. He could only imagine what he must have looked like. An art groupie, at best—at worst, a puppy dog, yapping at her feet. No wonder she practically ran away. He might have too, in her place.

Tim set the stack of air filters down and dug the huge jumble of keys out of his jeans pocket.

The door opened smoothly when he worked the lock, and

he poked his head inside. "Ms. Sinclair? Are you here? I need to replace your air filter."

No one answered. He stepped through the doorway.

The LaCroix Apartment Building housed two kinds of apartments: small one-bedrooms and minuscule one-bedrooms. Janey Sinclair occupied one of the small one-bedrooms, but judging from the decor and amount of furniture she owned, Tim suspected she could have lived comfortably in a minuscule. No lights burned, but he saw well enough not to trip over anything, despite heavy, charcoal-and-black draperies that blocked out nearly all of the storm-filtered sunlight.

A striped cloth couch and matching chair, both tasteful but not very expensive, formed a sparse conversation corner against the far wall. A small TV sat on an old typing desk, positioned so that someone could watch it while lying comfortably on the couch. He didn't see anything like a game console or a stereo. Tim wondered if, like one of his former roommates, Janey Sinclair preferred to keep all her expensive electronics in her bedroom.

A glass-topped table stood near the kitchen alcove, but the four chairs surrounding it didn't look as though they'd been moved in months. The sink stood empty and scrubbed clean. Tim figured that for either a very good or a very bad sign, depending on whether the empty sink resulted from a healthy respect for neatness, or a streak of anal retention.

He stopped, surprised to find himself building a mental image of Janey Sinclair based on how she kept her apartment. He hadn't done that with any of the other tenants.

Of course, none of the other tenants were anything like Janey Sinclair, either. Tim closed his eyes and remembered her paintings. They were like...he searched for comparisons. *Beautiful music. A perfectly cooked meal.* They were like expressions of the best qualities humanity had to offer.

He tried to deny it, but he felt a serious, guilty thrill, being in her apartment alone.

Okay, Tim, that's some heavy-duty creepy you've got going on. You need to get out of here.

He set the stack of air filters against the wall beside the door, took one of them and went to the utility closet that housed the AC/heating unit. It was near the door to the bedroom, next to a slightly narrower door, which he knew opened onto a coat closet.

He had his hand on the utility closet doorknob when he glanced at the door to Janey Sinclair's bedroom. It was pulled to, but not shut completely. A sudden thought made him twitch.

What if she didn't use a studio? What if she painted here?

"Hello? Ms. Sinclair? Are you here?" He let his voice get louder and louder with each word. The silence that came back to him was broken only by the sound of an upstairs neighbor turning on a vacuum cleaner.

This is creepy. By being in here, and thinking about taking a look in her bedroom, I'm being a creep.

He shifted his weight from one foot to the other.

Just a quick peek!

Hating himself a little, Tim went to the bedroom door. He felt more and more like an intruder with each passing second, but...to get a glimpse of a Janey Sinclair painting in mid-process? He put his ear to the door, sure that Janey was gone but fearful enough to make doubly certain before he *truly* invaded her privacy. Finally he sucked in a deep breath and pushed open the door.

Tim stayed that way, rigid and staring, for a full minute.

A tremendous clap of thunder sounded, and his hand fell away from the knob. The air filter dropped to the floor and propped itself against the wall. The maintenance chores forgotten, Tim took a few small, hesitant steps into Janey's bedroom, his breath shallow and fast. The door, not hung quite properly, swung shut behind him and tapped against the door frame.

A huge painting rested on an easel beside the window. Illuminated only by the storm's thin, gray light, its details remained stunningly clear. It nearly touched the floor and stood almost as tall as he did, and he couldn't take his eyes off it.

The rest of the bedroom registered on his mind only peripherally: a narrow twin bed, a battered chest-of-drawers, a small night table that held up a reading lamp. A three-legged stool sat in front of the easel, and orderly stacks and rows of painting materials rested on a small work table a few feet away. Tube after tube of oil paint pointed to a coffee can frenzied with different styles of brushes. Beyond that sat a complete set of Design Markers, each one upright in the stand, bristling like grown-up Crayolas.

But the painting, not its surroundings, demanded his attention and took away the air from his lungs.

"Wow." He'd taken a class in college, "Criticism of the Arts," and for a semester had forced himself to come up with words that would "codify the physical expressions of the minds and hearts" of a selected group of artists. Sometimes he did it successfully, sometimes not, but he'd left the class believing he could verbalize *something* about any creative subject.

Nothing came to him now except awe and, he couldn't deny it, a growing spike of *fear.*

The painting depicted a small house, a cabin really, at the edge of a vast, snowy forest. Yellow-orange light like that of a fireplace shone from the windows, but reached no further. Icy blue dominated the work. It utterly defeated the light of the fire. Beat it back into the windows.

And Tim *saw something* in the painting.

He blinked, and searched the canvas for an actual image of what he *knew* was there. He backed away a step.

On the surface, the painting was simply a photorealistic depiction of a cabin near a forest, nothing more. But the longer he stared at it, the more convinced he became that something lived there, in the woods.

Ridiculous. What am I thinking?

Tim's heart banged against his ribs. Involuntary tears filled his eyes.

Something was *there*. Something lurked, waiting, waiting and watching. The firelight from the house wasn't enough to keep it back. The safety of the house was an illusion, a shell of false hope. Something lurked in the woods, something that *hated*...something that would act. Soon.

He felt the cold from the snow all the way into his bones.

He felt it *watching him*.

Thunder hammered at the building, and Tim jumped.

A sharp click sounded out behind him, from the apartment's living room. Panicked and light-headed, he looked wildly around, searching at the same time for a place to hide and something he could use as a weapon. A closet with two folding metal doors took up most of one wall, but he knew the doors would squeal if he tried to open them, which would alert anybody in the living room.

He heard footsteps draw closer. Feet brushed across carpet. Right outside the bedroom door.

Tim backed swiftly into the corner, squeezed behind the easel and crouched down, hidden behind the canvas. He didn't want to be anywhere near the painting, and shuddered as the edge of the canvas touched his skin, but he held tenuously to a sliver of rational thought, and even more than the painting itself he feared whatever it was that crept through the apartment.

For long seconds, as the footsteps drew nearer, he knew beyond doubt that the thing in the woods had come out after him, come right out of the painting and followed him, and was about to rip him into bloody chunks.

The footsteps stopped, and Tim realized with a thump in his stomach that whatever made them now stood before the air filter he'd dropped, staring down at it. He pictured the head swiveling around, searching for the intruder who obviously hadn't left the apartment.

Tim's heart began to ache, his limbs glistened with panicked sweat, and he feared he might vomit.

The bedroom door swung open and he saw, beneath the

easel, a pair of feminine feet enter the room. Silently, carefully, he exhaled. The feet, clad in athletic shoes and white socks, looked completely harmless. Not the clawed feet of a supernatural beast. Not cloven hooves. Just Reeboks. What sounded like keys clattered on the chest-of-drawers.

He almost laughed. Edging ever so slightly to one side, he peered out from behind the easel.

Janey Sinclair was home. Dressed in baggy sweats, she held a dark gray bundle of some kind under one arm and moved the other arm in circles, as though trying to work out a muscle kink. She seemed to have been sweating, though her shirt wasn't wet.

Tim pressed himself against the wall and closed his eyes for a moment, letting himself de-fuse. Of course it was Janey Sinclair. It was her apartment, wasn't it? In a rush he grew acutely conscious of how stupid he'd been, jumping and hiding because...why? Because he'd been frightened by a painting. A painting! Oil smeared on canvas! What an *idiot!*

All his terror switched to embarrassment and shame. He'd set his mind to figuring out how he could salvage even a single scrap of personal dignity from the situation when he heard another door open, and realized he might not have to try. Janey looked as though she were about to step into the bathroom.

Tim waited, hoping she'd be neurotic enough to pull the door closed, even though she believed herself to be alone in her own apartment. If she did, he thought he could creep out silently, and she'd never have to know he'd been there.

Yeah, except you should come clean and tell her, you creep, you freaking stalker.

The air filter wouldn't get installed, no, but if she called to ask about it he could tell her he'd been there earlier and gotten distracted, maybe gotten a call about some maintenance emergency. He had a way out, an easy and clear one, if she only closed the door. Excited, he silently planted one hand on the floor, ready to spring up and wriggle out from behind the painting as fast as possible. He risked another peek.

Tim tried to keep his breathing even and silent, and succeeded, barely. Setting the gray bundle aside, Janey Sinclair had taken off her sweatshirt, revealing a red sports bra, and was unlacing her sneakers. She straightened, stepped out of the sweatpants, and stood in front of her dresser, clad only in the bra and black boy shorts.

For three long seconds Tim stared, before tearing his eyes away. The shame threatened to choke him, and he squeezed his eyes shut, but her image remained, vivid in his mind's eye.

She was *magnificent.*

Tim held his breath and gambled on another peek, ready to bolt as soon as she entered the bathroom. Janey Sinclair turned slightly toward him. Above the tantalizing swell of her sports bra, two circular scars, each about the size of a dime, marred her upper left pectoral.

Gunshot wounds?

They looked old. Tim's eyes widened as he judged the distance from her heart to the nearer scar. Janey Sinclair was very lucky to be alive today.

Moving to the closet, Janey opened one of the metal doors—which squealed loudly—and dropped her sweats into a hamper. She returned to the chest-of-drawers, picked up the bundle she'd brought in with her, and entered the bathroom. The door clicked shut behind her, and a few seconds later water started running and music came on, small and tinny. The tone of the water changed as it switched from faucet to shower head, and Tim unfolded himself from behind the easel.

He crept out of the bedroom, didn't spare even a glance at the air filter—and stopped dead, looking at the stack of other filters still leaning against the wall beside the front door.

His story of getting distracted wouldn't hold up very well if Janey had seen the other filters when she came in, but found them missing when she got out of the shower.

But, if the emergency that called him away were pressing enough, he might have left all of them behind, and could maybe chalk it up to simple forgetfulness. Or, maybe, Janey hadn't noticed them when she came in. If that were the case, he could take them with him now and possibly get the rest of them installed before five o'clock when the office closed.

Trying to decide what to do, he turned the doorknob, and with a start realized it wasn't locked.

He let go of it.

Janey Sinclair had returned to her apartment while he was inside, so she would have found her door unlocked when she went to open it. Yet she'd shown no signs of alarm when she came in, and he hadn't heard her make any phone calls, to the police or otherwise. Had she not realized her door was unlocked? How was that possible?

Unless she came back, tried the door, found it unlocked...and came into the apartment anyway, fully conscious that someone was there, but acting as if nothing were amiss.

Why would she do that?

Had she figured out Tim was in the apartment, and decided to play a game with him? He glanced back over his shoulder at the bedroom, scowling. The shower still ran, the tinny music still played. He recognized "These Boots are Made for Walking" by Nancy Sinatra, a perennial favorite on a local AM station.

Surely to God Janey Sinclair wouldn't have undressed in front of him if she'd known he was there.

Or was she so forgetful that she might leave her apartment and simply forget to lock the door? Odder still to think about, was Janey *that* trusting, not to even bother locking her door in the first place?

Tim saw something, a tiny detail, but striking: the coat closet, the one he had noticed earlier, stood open about four inches. He was absolutely certain it had been closed, *latched*, when he came in. Against his better judgment, he quickly crossed to it and looked inside.

It was empty. Nothing on the floor, nothing on the single shelf. Even the light bulb was gone.

All right. So Janey came in, grabbed something out of her coat closet and took it into the bathroom? That bundle?

Tim couldn't think straight, and tried to keep from shuddering as he picked up the stack of air filters and hastily left Janey Sinclair's apartment. More out of reflex than anything else, he locked her door behind him.

As he hurried away down the hall, huge raindrops spattered like a shower of rocks against the window, and another detail struck him: Janey Sinclair's sweatsuit hadn't had a single spot of rain on it.

CHAPTER SEVEN

The bell sounded, signaling the end of another day in hell.

Nathan stood, gathered his books under one arm, and walked out of his classroom. He made his way calmly down the hall, ambled past a cluster of football players standing by the main entrance, and headed for his car in the parking lot. More than once he heard people snickering after he'd passed. He slammed his car door shut a lot harder than necessary and laid rubber on his way out of the lot.

Trying to find a good song on the radio, he came across yet another news report of the vigilante working in the city. They'd started calling her "the Gray Widow" now. Nathan decided he liked the sound of that. This time, according to the announcer, the masked woman was responsible for the near-maiming of two suspected crack dealers. Both men were taken to Gavring, one with both arms broken at the elbows. The Gray Widow had not as yet made any attempts to communicate with the police or the media. She simply showed up, beat the living shit out of one or more people, and vanished. Nathan smiled as he thought about it.

Now there's someone I can get behind. Someone who doesn't take any shit off anybody. Someone who sees something that needs to be done and does it.

Nathan had been following the exploits of the Gray Widow for the last few days, since the story first showed up in the *Chronicle.* He remembered seeing the homeless woman on the street, flapping around a torn-out article about the vigilante, right before he'd just about knocked that guy in the suit off his feet.

According to the media, the Gray Widow was now believed to have committed at least five brutal assaults on criminals, all within the city limits.

Even though Nathan enjoyed the idea of a real-life masked

vigilante fighting crime on the streets, it shot a pang of homesickness through him, because that was exactly the kind of thing he would have talked about with his friends. He and Peter and Whit would have sat around and shot the bull for hours, speculating on what the Gray Widow would be like in real life. Trying to profile her, like bargain-basement versions of John Douglas. They'd try to get in her head, figure out what motivated her, speculate on what must have happened to her in the past to make her put a mask on and wreak such killer havoc on unsuspecting dirtbags.

"I know what makes her tick," Nathan said aloud, over the song that came on after the announcer finished. "I know exactly why she does what she does. 'Cause she's pissed off, that's why."

He fell silent again, but something was there now, in his mind, that hadn't been before. He switched off the radio and squinted his eyes as he drove, the mental gears whirring and clicking.

Both his parents were gone, of course, when he got home. This was the time Nathan liked best, when he had the house to himself. When the two ghouls who'd brought him into the world weren't around to ignore him. He let himself in, went upstairs to his bedroom, and started rummaging around in the back of his closet. After twenty minutes of digging, tossing wrinkled comic books and old, battered action figures over his shoulder, he found what he was looking for: a souvenir from a past Halloween. He dusted it off and held it up to the light.

It was a black domino mask attached to a black nylon hood. Nathan slipped the mask over his head and adjusted it so the eye holes felt comfortable. He glanced in the mirror and smiled.

Nathan pulled the mask back off, stretched out on his bed and grinned like a fool. He began making plans.

* * *

Shortly after Tim fled from her apartment, Janey finished her shower, clicked off the radio that hung from the shower head, toweled dry while she stood in the tub, walked out into her bedroom and began going through her underwear drawer. The air filter bothered her. She didn't know exactly why; maintenance had never been great in any of her other apartments, she didn't see why it should be any different here. Nonetheless, something about it worked under her skin.

She took out a pair of white silk boy shorts and pulled them on. Lightning flashed outside, rendered the room in chiaroscuro for a split second, and caused Janey to glance over toward the window.

She froze, and by reflex clicked off the overhead light.

As thunder pealed, Janey pulled an aluminum baseball bat from under her bed.

With both hands on the bat, she crept from the bedroom into the living room. The small apartment afforded very few potential hiding places, but Janey checked them all quickly and efficiently. Satisfied, she returned to her bedroom and leaned on the doorframe.

Someone had moved her painting.

Not much; only a few millimeters. But she'd deliberately aligned the tallest of the trees with the center of the easel's upper tension knob that morning, before she'd finished up the painting and left to go to the basement. Now the tree rested to the left of the tension knob, and she hadn't touched the painting or the easel since she'd been back.

Maybe the thunder? The vibrations, jarring it? She went to the painting, braced the easel with one hand, and pushed on the side of the canvas with the other. It moved, but only with more effort than thunder would have provided. Janey narrowed her eyes, stepped away...and scrutinized the floor around the easel and the work table.

The carpet in Janey's apartment was standard institutional beige, but thicker shag than most economy apartments had. This came with pros and cons. While very kind to bare feet, it clearly showed the tracks left by a vacuum cleaner, and sometimes even preserved footprints.

Janey found a footprint in the carpet behind her easel, along with five evenly spaced scuffs. Just about right for fingertips, if they—like the footprint—belonged to someone with larger hands than hers. Thunder crashed outside, very close, and the floor vibrated.

Tim?

Janey straightened up, leaned the bat against the work table and tried to think.

Yes, he had access to the apartment. No, it wasn't unreasonable to think he might perform low-level service, such as replacing air filters. But why would he hide...?

The painting. He came in, saw she wasn't there, hoped to find a work in progress, maybe, and took a peek into her bedroom. Janey covered her mouth with one hand. *"Oh no."* As raw as the painting was, as much power as she'd poured into it, Tim could have easily had a seizure…or worse. Freaking out and hiding was probably the best outcome she could've hoped for. Guilt flooded through her. *This is the last time I work on one of these anywhere but the basement.*

Her heart jolted as she realized something else.

Tim saw the suit.

He'd hidden right there while she came in and got ready to shower, must have, that was the only time it could have happened, and she'd had the suit with her, right in plain sight. She tried to remember how she'd carried it. The boots, the boots were back in the basement, that was no problem, he wouldn't have seen those, but could he have recognized the suit for what it was? Maybe... *think, come on...*

No. She'd had it folded up when she took it into the bathroom to wash it by hand. Routine, as always. All he would have seen was a big gray wad of stiff material. Could have been anything. No reason to get upset.

She slumped down on her bed, scooted across it to put her back against the wall, and hugged her knees to her chest.

No reason to get upset, my ass. This is a perfect reason. What happens, when you finally meet someone who makes you feel something? One of your paintings tries to drive him insane.

All right. Best to concentrate on one thing at a time. Pick a job, do it.

She let out a long, slow breath. Two years. Surely two years of self-imposed exile was enough. Enough time to mourn. To heal.

Of course that was absurd. She hadn't healed. Healing involved dealing with grief in a healthy way: learning to accept loss and getting on with life as a productive, mentally balanced member of society. It most definitely did *not* involve jumping around in bad parts of the city every night, or stealing prototype suits of military body armor.

Janey groaned. "What the hell am I doing?" She thumped her head on her knee a few times, rolled over on the bed and picked up the phone on her nightstand.

* * *

Tim sat in the office and stared at the paperwork covering his desk. Badly rattled, he'd returned to familiar surroundings seeking a sense of security, but hadn't really found one. He couldn't stop thinking about it—Janey, her apartment, the painting, the closet.

Get a grip, Tim. You're freaking out. Why are you freaking out? Nothing happened! If you were going to freak out, it ought to be about how perverted you are, sneaking around in some strange woman's apartment!

The LaCroix had no gym, no laundry facilities. Janey would have had to come in from the outside. But no one not wearing a full rainsuit could have avoided getting at least partly wet, and he hadn't seen any rainsuits while he was in her apartment. Was that what the gray bundle was? But why would she have wadded it up and carried it into the bathroom with her?

The office phone rang, and Tim jumped again.

"LaCroix Apartments, how may I help you?"

"Um, hi, this is Janey Sinclair, in apartment 9C."

Tim took a deep breath. *Stay calm. Calm!* "Hi! What can I do for you?"

"Well, I came home a while ago and found a new air filter in here. Did you want me to replace the old one? I didn't know if someone was coming back, or what."

Her low, rich voice over the phone sounded open and polite. Tim couldn't hear any unpleasant undertones, no smugness, nothing accusatory. His mind whirled.

"Oh," he began, and tried his best to sound genuinely surprised. "I did forget to put that one in, didn't I? Sorry about that. Got distracted with a phone call. Let's see..." He shuffled papers around on the desk. "When would be a good time for you that I could come back and do that?"

"I could do it, if you'd rather not. It's no trouble. I mean, it's just an air filter."

"Oh, sorry, but I have to do it. Insurance reasons." That much was true. The tenants weren't supposed to do any of their own maintenance beyond changing light bulbs. But as he said the words, he realized he'd set it up so he would have to go back to her apartment.

What am I doing?

He thought Janey actually sounded pleased. "Well, right now would be fine, I guess. If it's okay with you."

"Oh, uh..." Tim faltered for a second. "Yes. Um. Well...I guess I'll be right up."

Numbly Tim turned on the answering machine, locked the office door behind him, and headed for the elevator.

* * *

A few minutes after she hung up the phone with Tim—who had sounded exactly like someone caught where he wasn't supposed to be—Janey dressed in dark brown leggings and a rust-red button shirt, slipped on a pair of worn but comfortable flats, and stood in front of a mirror.

She thought about putting on makeup. But she hadn't done that in so long, hadn't even touched any foundation or lipstick since…well. Since Adam. No, whatever twisted version of social interaction she was about to engage in, it wasn't worth makeup.

She studied her reflection, turning her face right and left.

Janey had always thought of herself as "funny-looking." Taken individually, she supposed, her features weren't objectionable. Her lips would never rival Angelina Jolie's, but they were full and dark. And she liked her tawny complexion, which her father had always said was the exact color of a lion's pelt. But she had the long, straight, somewhat pronounced nose of her German grandfather, which didn't quite work, she didn't think, with the slight epicanthic folds above her eyes, while her eyes themselves—a blue so light they bordered on gray—looked as if they belonged in the face of someone else entirely. And now, with what suddenly seemed a ridiculous new haircut, the whole effect from the neck up made her want to hide inside some huge, baggy hoodie. Or maybe a ski mask.

Janey took a deep breath. *This is no good.* She lifted her shirt and flexed her abs, turning left and right again as the light outlined the rigid, perfectly symmetrical muscles. Keeping the shirt up, she pivoted and glanced over her shoulder. The leggings clung to the curves of her ass, and try as she might, Janey couldn't find a damn thing wrong with the way that looked. Feeling a tad better, she grinned and let the shirt fall back into place as a knock sounded at her door.

Tim was taller than she remembered, and even thinner. *He's built like a swimmer.* He wore brown loafers, blue jeans, a vivid green polo shirt, and an expression that combined elements of frustration, apology, and...maybe a little fear.

She opened the door wider and stood aside. "C'mon in."

"Thanks." He nervously gave her just the barest glimpse of straight white teeth.

As Tim entered and headed for the air filter, which leaned against the wall where he'd left it, Janey said, "I really appreciate the prompt response. Some of the places I've lived, you were lucky to get any kind of maintenance work done the same month you reported the problem."

Tim didn't make eye contact. "It's not really that big a building." He opened the utilities closet and began removing the old filter. Janey crossed her arms and watched him. Twice, as he worked, Tim cut his eyes toward the door to her bedroom.

Mm-hmm.

As he finished, she said, "Hey, listen, I was wondering if I could get your opinion on something."

Tim shifted the old filter from one hand to the other, hesitant. "What?"

She uncrossed her arms and started walking toward the bedroom. His eyes got wider.

"Well, I just finished this new piece today, and I was wondering if you could tell me what you think of it." She reached out and put one hand against the door as if to push it open. Tim's reaction confirmed every suspicion.

"*No,* I mean, I'd like to, really, but I have a ton of paperwork to do back in the office, and I should really get back to it, and—"

Janey pushed the bedroom door open, and Tim couldn't help but look inside. His lips parted, slowly formed a small, perfectly round O, and Janey grinned. He stayed completely silent long enough for her to prod him.

"What do you think?"

Tim still didn't answer, but moved to stand in the doorway, his eyes locked to the painting on the easel. Janey looked over his shoulder.

Predominantly golden brown, with splashes of blue and ice-white, "Pure Thought" was one of Janey's favorites. The painting depicted a vast wheat field, out of the middle of which sprang an enormous tree composed of blue-white crystal. Cotton clouds decorated the azure sky, and both the clouds and the gold of the wheat reflected perfectly, thousands, maybe millions of times, from every crystalline branch, stem, and leaf.

She knew its effect, a total reversal from the unnamed piece Tim had seen earlier, and on a number of occasions she'd come close to selling it. She hadn't, partly because she loved it too much, and partly because she'd felt, since its completion, that the painting was meant to be a gift. She just hadn't ever been sure for whom.

His breathing grew shallow. "Ms. Sinclair, that is *beautiful.*"

She took a step inside the room. "You can call me Janey."

He didn't seem to hear her. She started to confront him about the hiding, but changed her mind; instead she left him there, with the painting, and walked slowly into the living room.

The apartment was small, yes, but a large picture window near the couch let in light from the storm. Janey pulled aside the heavy curtains, leaned against the frame and watched the clouds. Lightning flashed from one to another, electric veins of the sky. She let her eyes half close and took in the display.

Quiet thoughts nagged at her. *You're making a big mistake. You shouldn't be doing this. You're only going to screw things up.*

But it wasn't his fault. The painting would have spooked anyone. He's not saying anything about it because he's embarrassed.

Embarrassment doesn't mean you hide like a peeping Tom.

Am I this desperate for human contact?

Something touched her arm, and she found Tim standing beside her. "What are you doing?"

Janey looked back out at the sky and the clouds and the rain. "Just watching the storm."

An enormous bolt of lightning touched down halfway to the horizon, and moments later brittle thunder crashed. Janey smiled, and glanced at Tim. They looked each other straight in the eye, exactly the same height, and just stood there like that for a long moment. A moment no one could have engineered, a gift from nature.

At this distance, Tim smelled *fantastic*. She didn't recognize the scent, some sort of after-shave, and she could only detect it from this close up, which meant he knew how to apply it properly. Lightning flashed, reflecting a heartbeat's worth of sapphire blue highlights in his coal-black hair.

Janey wanted to slide her arms around him.

What am I doing?

Another blast of thunder exploded against the building, and all the lights went out. Tim jumped. "Damn! Sorry, I've got to get back to the office. Everybody'll be screaming about the power."

He turned to go, but hesitated, about to speak. Janey's night vision revealed his eyes, huge and dark, on the line between deepest brown and true black. They left her without a coherent thought in her head. Tim opened his mouth, and Janey waited… but he seemed to think better of it.

He backed away, turned, and moved swiftly to the door.

Janey caught up to him as his hand turned the knob.

"Tim. If you're interested...that is, if you'd still like to go somewhere—" Her throat threatened to close up. "—and chat, for a while, I'd like that."

Tim didn't respond immediately. His eyes drifted toward her bedroom/studio, but he seemed to realize that and hurriedly brought them back to her. "I'd like that very much. Can I—I'll, uh. I'll call you tomorrow? We can work out logistics?"

Janey smiled in what she hoped was a non-threatening fashion. "That sounds great."

"Great, then."

And he was out the door.

* * *

Later that night, Tim sat on the edge of his bed while his cat, a giant, fat gray tabby named Elmer, rubbed around his ankles and purred. He watched the animal, but thought of Janey Sinclair.

"All right, Tim," he said quietly. "Try to be objective about this." He attempted a mental list: Janey was 1) gorgeous, 2) talented, 3) intelligent, 4) mysterious. Her paintings in the gallery had touched him...intimately? Was that the appropriate word?

But she was also a little creepy.

Jeez, look at me, calling her names, after I'm the one crawling around her place.

He shook his head. No, not creepy, that word made him think of greasy-haired pedophiles. Janey was kind of...*sinister?* He remembered her face in the storm's lightning.

And the painting, the horrible one she'd replaced with the crystal tree—a tiny sliver of his mind insisted that he'd only imagined that painting, since simple paint on canvas couldn't do what that painting had done to him.

He remembered an H.P. Lovecraft story he'd read in college, "Pickman's Model." The artist, Pickman, had painted pictures of horrible, twisted creatures, pictures that drove anyone who saw them to the edge of insanity. But there weren't any horrible creatures in Janey's painting. Not any he could see, anyway. The horror was...inherent? Maybe that wasn't the right word. Maybe *saturated* would be better.

Tim shuddered. He felt as if he'd been touched by some kind of spectre, as if the painting had been a sort of doorway into a dark, cruel place. As if it had swung wider and wider as he stood there. Could he spend time with a woman who'd created such a thing? Could he be exposed to more of it?

And for that matter, painting aside, how had Janey not known someone was in the apartment? He'd gone over it and over it, and unless she was the archetypal scatterbrain, she should have realized something wasn't right when she found the door unlocked. She *had* to have come in from the outside; she'd dropped her keys there in the bedroom.

Tim didn't believe Janey Sinclair was scatterbrained for a second.

He suspected he was missing something obvious, some perfectly sensible explanation for all the weirdness, but he couldn't think of what it might be.

He picked up the cat and regarded him seriously. "What do you think?" The cat meowed in a way that Tim knew meant, "Please put me down or I'll scratch you."

He dropped Elmer back down on the floor. Tim shook his head and ran a hand through his curly hair. "The hell am I getting myself into?"

* * *

After spending four days with Garrison Vessler, Brenda Jorden was thoroughly sick of him. She'd discovered that, after so long with just Scott and Ned Fields there in the house with her, she'd grown accustomed to the relative isolation. Apart from her professional loathing of Vessler, now he was getting in her way and on her nerves.

Maybe if Scott had gotten more solid results from his nightly scans, Vessler would already be gone by now. But Scott hadn't, and Vessler—"The Icicle," they used to call him—decided to stick around and offer his own brand of misguided fatherly encouragement.

It made her want to retch.

On returning from a trip into town, she opened the front door and found Vessler standing in the kitchen, slicing thin disks off a pepperoni. Over his shoulder he said, "What do you like on your pizza?"

She hesitated, closed her gaping mouth, and said, "Doesn't matter. Where'd your boys go?"

"I sent them to their hotel. I'll stay here."

She closed and locked the door, bit back words. Garrison Vessler, standing in a kitchen in stocking feet, making a *pizza,* for God's sake. Ever since he found Scott Charles he'd been on his way down. Down and out. She repressed a shudder at the thought of what might happen if Vessler were allowed to remain in charge of Redfell.

Jorden slipped off her own shoes and padded down the hallway to Scott's room, where she opened the door without knocking. He lay on his bed, reading a magazine, and when he saw her his face went a little slack.

The magazine dropped out of his fingers as she sat down on the edge of the bed, and she plucked it off his chest and let it fall to the floor. For a few seconds the air around them filled with a scent, a heavy, musky aroma with an acrid undercurrent. Jorden touched Scott's neck and the scent quickly faded. His eyes glazed over completely.

Jorden glanced out the door at the hallway, listened for approaching footsteps, and heard Vessler clanking around in the kitchen. She wrinkled her nose and turned back to Scott.

"You're doing very well," she said. He nodded, trancelike. "Do you remember the rules?" He nodded again. "Say them."

He barely whispered. "Do what you say to do. Don't do what you say not to do."

"Correct. And what else?"

"Keep it our secret."

"Right. And?"

"Act natural."

"Very good. Very good. Now, it's time to forget about this again and just be Scott. Ready?"

Nod.

Scott's eyes closed. Jorden got up from the bed and went to the door.

He'd wake up in a few seconds, forget about today's dose just as he had every other day's dose, and be his usual neurotic, psychologically crippled self.

She closed Scott's door, secure that her own energy signature would never show up on his screen. A few people knew—Stamford,

Fields, a handful of others. Those who had to. Aside from them, her own augmentation, as well as the plans she had for its use, were none of the company's business.

Brenda Jorden was born in Shinehull, Georgia, a barely incorporated little collection of truck stops, diners, brothels, and a few other meager businesses just north of the Florida border. Her mother, a prostitute, was knifed to death in the sleeper compartment of a tractor-trailer when Brenda was two, and Brenda went to live with her grandparents, who also lived in Shinehull.

Her grandmother, Leigh, was a petite brunette with pale skin and green eyes who waited tables in one of the diners. Leigh's husband, Arthur, was a gigantic man with dark copper skin and arms as big around as most men's thighs. Arthur worked as a mechanic.

On summer nights Arthur read Brenda stories before she went to bed, with a voice so deep it nearly shook the bed frame, and on each of those nights he promised her that he'd always protect her. She believed him.

Three weeks before Brenda entered junior high school, Arthur died of a heart attack. That night, Leigh got very drunk, took Arthur's .38, and put a bullet through the roof of her own mouth and into her brain.

Due to a clerical mix-up, the county Department of Family and Children's Services at first placed Brenda in a home for troubled youths, where a developmentally disabled girl named Ricki savagely beat her behind the school's equipment shed.

Brenda spent sixteen days in a hospital bed before she was released into the custody of the first in a string of foster families. At the fourth foster home, a bowling pal of the father's got high one night, came to the house when the parents were gone to a movie, and tried to rape her. When she fought him off, he apologized but, fearful that she would tell her foster parents, he stabbed her with a hunting knife and threw her in the deepest part of a nearby stream. A deputy sheriff named Jay Clives pulled her out of the stream thirty-two hours later and took her to another hospital, where she stayed longer this time.

That fall Brenda entered high school. Her class was predominantly white, and when a couple of the students learned her grandfather was black, they began a campaign of harassment that would last two straight years. Brenda found the words "nigger" and "coon" and "spade" spray-painted on her locker, on the ragged-out Lincoln Continental Arthur had left her, and eventually on the walls of her current foster home. Her tires were slashed. Students tripped her and shoved her in the halls. She tried to approach the tiny group of black students at the school, but they took in her green eyes and milk-pale skin and refused to speak to her.

Brenda dropped out after her sophomore year and took a job at a day-care center near the diner where Leigh had worked. She seemed to have a knack for connecting with children, and for a while thought she'd found her place.

A few weeks after her first night on the job, a man named Rafael approached her as she was walking to her car and offered her a chance to make several hundred dollars a night, without ever having to leave her room. When she refused the offer, he became violent, pulled a switchblade, and was about to use it when Jay Clives, the deputy who'd found Brenda in the stream, shot Rafael in the hand at point blank range. He'd been driving past and seen what was happening. Deputy Clives gave Brenda a ride home that night, since she was too shaky to drive.

Eight weeks later Brenda became Mrs. Jay Clives, and moved in with him to his double-wide trailer.

For a little over a year Brenda was genuinely happy, the first time since the day her grandparents both left her. With her income from the day-care center plus Jay's salary at the police department, they were able to start a decent savings account, and talked about the possibility of having children. Brenda bought a book on crocheting, and tried to make a baby blanket.

But on a damp night in July, Jay Clives came home drunk,

after losing his job as sheriff's deputy, and demanded that Brenda have sex with him. He was loud and frightening, and when she pulled away from him he clubbed her on the side of the head, bent her over the back of a kitchen chair and took her forcibly.

They were just far enough away from the neighbors so that none of them heard Brenda's screams.

Jay Clives adopted a different attitude toward his young wife after that night. He spent his days on the couch in their trailer, rarely without a bottle in his hand, and demanded sex both before Brenda left for work and when she got home. If she did anything to displease him, he shouted and called her "little nigger bitch." At one point, angered because his eggs had gotten cold, he hit her with an electric skillet and broke her arm.

The Clives family stayed that way, with Brenda at the day-care center and Jay mostly on the couch, for two years and seven months.

Until one night the sky opened up and touched her.

It happened just past eleven, as the news was coming on, after Brenda had finished satisfying Jay for the fourth time that day. Raw and sore, as she seemed to be all the time, she put on a bathrobe and went outside to sit on the trailer's back steps. She liked to sit out there if the weather was nice, look up at the stars and pretend she could still hear Arthur's voice. Crickets chirped in the long grass around her, and a cool, gentle wind blew in from the west.

One star seemed to be particularly bright, and as she watched, it quivered and flashed like a small sun.

Something like a grenade went off in her head.

When she came to herself she was lying in the grass next to the steps, and her nostrils were filled with a pungent aroma, something she couldn't place but which seemed terribly familiar. As she attempted to get back to her feet, the scent still filling the air around her, the back door slammed open and Jay planted one thick foot on the top step.

"'M hungry," he slurred, nearly blind drunk. "Gitcher ass in here 'n cook me sumpthin'."

Brenda locked her eyes on Jay's. She slowly stood and climbed the steps toward him. She figured he'd grab her ass or one of her breasts as she passed and hoot or make a vulgar comment. The scent filled her head, saturated her brain, and she felt as though her feet barely made contact with the rough wood as she climbed.

Brenda reached out, and smiled, and touched him.

The scent drained away out of the air, into him, and Jay's eyes filmed over.

His jaw went slack, and he dropped the bottle of Milwaukee's Best he'd been holding. It hit the floor without breaking, splashed beer on the cracked linoleum, and rolled out the door and into the grass.

Brenda said, "Get out of my way, asshole."

Jay did as he was told. He backed up, turned, and cleared the doorway for her. Brenda couldn't believe it—but neither did she question it. She couldn't smell the strong scent anymore, but she still felt it in her brain, deep inside her, and it felt right. *Everything* felt right. She took her time going through the knife drawer and finally came out with one she'd won as a door prize at a county fair. It had a thick black plastic handle and a long, serrated blade. She thumbed the edge, flipped it over and handed it, handle-first, to Jay.

"Here. Take this."

He did. Holding the knife, his hand fell back to his side, limp. Buzzing. Buzzing in her brain, like a million wasps, whisper compounding whisper till it became a roar. Somewhere in her mind she thought, what's happening, why is this happening, what am I *doing?* But that wasn't the part of her mind in control just then. Calmly, evenly, she said, "Jay, I think you should take off the fingers on your left hand now."

Jay tottered, uncertain. Brenda said, "You can use the kitchen table, that's all right."

Jay loved that table. It was nothing more than particle board with an "oak veneer," but it had been a gift from his mother, and Jay said it fit him perfectly. Brenda hated it.

Slowly but deliberately, Jay moved over to the table. He set his left hand on its surface and used the knife to chop off his fingers, one by one. Brenda smiled. "Good job, honey. That was real good."

Jay held up the bloody stump of his hand, and tears began to roll down his cheeks. He made a small, high sound in the back of his throat.

Brenda said, "Now. Honey. You'll do whatever I tell you, won't you?"

Jay nodded.

"And you like using that knife, don't you?"

Jay's neck muscles strained. His keening grew louder. He nodded again. "Good. Real good. Now, Jay, drop your pants for me, will you?"

Seven hours later Brenda walked away from the raging torch that used to be her home, the shadows of her and her suitcase thrown long and wavery on the driveway.

Things happened quickly after that. She didn't go to jail. Instead, a man in a dark suit spoke to the sheriff and the Georgia Bureau of Investigations officer assigned to the case. Brenda was promptly released into the man's custody, and asked to accompany him to Savannah where, he said, a few new options might be opened to her.

The man walked with a silver-headed cane, and said his name was Stamford.

CHAPTER EIGHT

Friday night came, and Janey Sinclair tried very hard not to fidget.

Tim had a first-floor apartment, two doors past the elevator. Janey knocked five times, quietly, and stood waiting with her hands folded in front of her. Then she decided she didn't like the way that posture looked, and held her hands behind her back, but she was afraid that made it look as if she were drawing attention to her breasts, plus her messenger bag purse got in the way. When Tim opened the door, Janey's arms hung loosely by her sides, and she wore what she hoped was a steady smile.

"Hi!" Tim said brightly. "Wow...you look great." He was dressed casually, in new running shoes, faded jeans, and a brilliant white Oxford shirt with the sleeves rolled up to his elbows. "C'mon in, I'm on the phone, sorry, it's work, it won't take a second."

Janey stepped inside and looked around. Tim's apartment was a mirror image of hers, and it struck her how different the reversal made it look. The kitchen to her left, on the right in her apartment, seemed bigger here, and the hallway didn't look the same length. Several cardboard boxes were stacked in one corner. He hadn't quite finished unpacking yet.

Janey caught sight of her own reflection in a mirror, and it almost startled her. She'd forgotten how much a bit of mascara and eye-liner could make her blue-gray eyes flash. Maybe the makeup *was* worth it...now and then.

Tim's taste in furnishings was definitely classier than hers. It looked as though he actually spent time and effort in picking out items to coordinate with each other, as opposed to Janey's technique, which was more like a blind stab at furniture store clearance sales. Tasteful prints decorated the walls. The coffee table was oak, she thought.

As Tim stood in the kitchen, talking to someone about installing carpet, a big fuzzy gray cat wandered out of the bedroom. The cat stared at Janey with enormous yellow eyes, and as she watched, the animal's tail puffed up.

"That's Elmer," Tim said, his hand over the phone. "Don't worry, he's harmless."

Janey didn't move. She knew where this would go, and lost her smile.

His stare never wavering, Elmer began growling. Low in his throat at first, the growl rose in volume as Elmer's ears flattened back against his skull, and as Janey winced, Elmer hissed and darted back into the bedroom.

Janey glanced over at Tim. He had finished his phone call, and was staring after Elmer.

"Sorry! I don't know what that was," he said. "I've never seen him act like that before. He even loves the vet."

Janey shook her head sadly. "Animals don't like me much." He seemed to be waiting for her to go on, but she didn't have anything else to tell him. "Maybe I smell funny."

Tim hesitated, but then laughed. "Crazy cat. Who knows what got into him. Well. Ready to go?"

A lot of people trusted their animals' judgments. Was that why he hesitated? Was Tim deciding maybe this wasn't such a good idea, but going through with it anyway?

A familiar train of thought ran through her mind. *What the hell am I doing? I should be training. Or patrolling. Or painting. I shouldn't be here. This is selfish.*

Instead of any of that, Janey said, "Sure."

Tim opened the door and smiled. "After you."

She tried to match the length of her strides to his as they went to the car. She'd often been told she walked too fast. *Is that too…what? Accommodating? Subservient? Let him catch up with me if he's walking too slow!* In the middle of a rising storm of conflicting thoughts and emotions, Janey realized she had forgotten entirely how to go on a date.

"So, uh...how was your day?" She ground her teeth and wondered if she could sound any more inane.

"Not bad. A lot like yesterday. This full-time job arrangement...y'know, it takes up a lot of time."

"I've heard that. Guess that's why it's called 'full time.'"

"Yeah." Tim chuckled.

He laughed! He laughed at the lamest comment I could possibly have made, but he laughed! The tiny step forward boosted her flagging confidence.

They took her car. Janey explained that she never got into a guy's car on a first date, and Tim agreed her policy was sound. So his old Monte Carlo sat in its reserved spot, and Janey drove her Civic.

"I'm...a little nervous," she said as she turned the ignition. "I figured I'd go ahead and tell you, in case it wasn't obvious."

"Okay. Why is that?"

"Why am I nervous? Well...I haven't done...anything like this, ah...any kind of social engagement in a couple of years. I'm not sure I'll remember how to act."

"Oh yeah? Why such a long time?"

She shook her head. "Long story. Long *boring* story. I'll tell you some time when you've got insomnia."

"I don't know. I doubt any story you told could be too boring."

Janey didn't respond to that. Instead she said, "So. What's the place we're going? What's it called? It's a vegetarian place, right?"

"Right. You do like vegetarian food? I hope?"

"Yeah, yes I do. I guess we should've ascertained that before now, huh?"

He cocked an eyebrow at her, and one corner of his mouth quirked up.

"What?"

"'Ascertained.' You just used that word in a regular sentence."

Janey cringed.

"Oh, hey, no, I liked it! Spend too much time on Twitter—which I will admit I do—and you forget that people have actual vocabularies."

A pause, as Janey thought about that.

"I, uh…never really got much in the way of education."

Tim shrugged. "Could've fooled me. Besides, it's not like I'm using my degree. I mean, except for paying for it. Which I'll be doing until I'm dead." He smiled to lighten the words. "So, no college for you?"

She shook her head. "Wasn't in the cards."

"Nobody can teach the kind of talent you've got anyway."

"Thank you." She felt her cheeks get a little warm.

They didn't say anything else until they got to the restaurant. It was a small, narrow brick building on North Highland, not far from Taco Mac, with a couple of wrought iron tables and chairs outside. The whole front wall was glass, and Janey saw about a dozen people inside, seated and eating. She followed Tim in.

A waitress greeted them. "Sit wherever you want to, I'll be right there."

Tim gave her a questioning look, and Janey shrugged. "Maybe that table in the corner?"

Tim nodded and led the way. Janey took a chair backed up to the wall, and Tim said, "Do you want your back against the wall so nobody can sneak up on you?"

Janey glanced behind her. "Hey, now that you mention it, that is kind of nice." Tim chuckled again. *That's twice. Am I doing something right?* "It's actually a sort of neurotic derivative of my movie-watching habits."

"Which are?"

"Well, I guess it's only one habit. I like to sit in the very back row."

"Why? So you can neck with your date?"

"No...so nobody can throw popcorn at me."

Tim laughed at that, a full-blown *real laugh,* and Janey felt the knot of her insides begin to untangle. Tim opened his mouth to say something, but the waitress showed up again. She gave them each a glass of ice water, silverware wrapped in a paper napkin, and a menu.

"Are you both ready to order now, or do you need a few minutes?"

Tim opened his menu, but didn't really look at it. "I know what *I* want, but I think you'd better give us some time."

Janey opened her own menu and was bombarded by dishes she'd never heard of before. "Yeah, I think I'll need a couple of minutes at least."

The waitress, who wore a hand-made name tag that read "Lynn," smiled and nodded and left them alone.

Janey felt Tim watching her as she looked over the selections. A silence stretched out, and Janey broke it with, "Uh, can you recommend anything?"

He seemed happy to make suggestions. "Well, everything they serve is good. Except the cornbread—they cook it with bits of purple cabbage in it, which is pretty weird, *I* think. But aside from that, everything is good. I can vouch for the lentil burger and the barbecued tofu especially, but I'm going to get the vegetable samosas and dal soup."

Janey's eyes wandered across the paper until she found what he meant.

"Ah. In the Indian section." She peered over the top at him. "I guess that makes sense."

He dropped his eyes, and Janey set the menu down on the table. "Did I just put my foot in my mouth?"

"No, no..." He paused briefly. "See, the first time I had any Indian food was in a restaurant."

"No kidding?"

"No kidding. My dad was never all that interested in preserving my, ah, my cultural heritage. He used to go back to Mumbai, when

I was little, to visit my grandma, but then he finally talked her into moving over here, and that was pretty much it. He kind of cut ties."

"Your mom was okay with that?"

"My mother…my biological mother…died when I was four. Dad re-married about a year later. Met a perky redhead with freckles, and that was all she wrote, as they say."

Janey cocked her head. "Did they have any more children?"

Tim nodded. "I've got a brother, and Mom—my step-mom—already had a daughter. Depending on what part of the country we're in, we get a lot of confused looks when we're all out together."

Janey tried a smile. It felt good. "I can imagine."

"So, in answer to your question, no, you didn't put your foot in your mouth."

"Thank goodness." She chuckled—her own laughter foreign and new—and said, "That would have been number 146 on my List of Things To Do Around New People: 'make offhanded racial slur.'"

Tim laughed again, and Janey went on: "That's right after 'complain of incontinence,' and right before 'comment on new person's weight problem.'"

He laughed harder, and before Janey could think of anything else to say, Tim reached across the table and gently took her hand in his.

Janey drew in a deep breath. This didn't seem real. *Tim* didn't seem real.

His skin was warm and smooth and, as his laughter subsided, with the index finger of his other hand he slowly traced a line across the back of her knuckles. He slowly turned her hand over and glided his fingertips across her palm. "If I'd paid more attention to my grandmother, I might know how to read these lines."

She flexed her fingers a tiny bit. "Best not to know the future."

He grinned. "That fits in with something Grandma used to tell me. She always said, 'Tim, there is only one thing in this world you can truly control. And that's yourself.'"

Janey considered that. "She sounds like a smart woman."

He nodded. "She was. She died last year."

"Oh, I'm sorry, I didn't—"

"It's okay. It's okay. It was the kind of thing that, by the time it happened, it was a blessing."

Janey carefully pulled her hand back, hoping she hadn't finally managed to ruin the whole evening.

"So what about *your* background?" Tim asked. "Where's your family tree planted?"

Janey made a sort of shrugging gesture with her eyebrows. "It's more like a family hedge. I come from everywhere."

"Yeah? How so?"

"Well, let's see..." Janey started counting off on her fingers. "On one side Dad's family was Scottish, Irish, and German. On the other side they were Cherokee and Jewish."

Tim grinned. "Traditional! Okay. How 'bout your mom?"

"Mom's folks were from Florida, with some Seminole influence—so they were a mix of Caucasian and Native American and African-American. Mom's father went overseas and brought back a young lady from the Philippines, and Mom showed up not long after that. Then Mom and Dad got together and had me: an official mutt."

"Wow. That is..."

Janey waited. "Yes?"

His grin widened. "That is the most *American* family I have ever heard of."

"Isn't it, though?"

"I can sort of relate. Growing up with my super-Irish-American step-mother and step-sister, and an Indian-born father who wears cowboy hats and drives a Dodge Ram."

Janey's eyebrows shot up. In what she hoped was a playful tone, she said, "Your dad...sounds a little bit like a certain Louisiana governor...?"

Tim groaned, but grinned while he did it, and threw his hands up. "I know! I know! I think Bobby Jindal is his hero. Don't worry, though. I love my father to death, but we haven't seen eye to eye on politics since I was about ten." He took her hand again, and squeezed it. "But where I was going was, I recognize what you are. My friends and I used to talk about this in college—you're a *future of humanity* person."

Janey's heart thudded. "I'm a what, now?"

"You're what every human being is headed toward! As technology advances, and travel gets faster and cheaper and easier, human populations are blending. Y'know, instead of different, genetically identifiable groups—Africans and Chinese and Indians—we're starting to meld together. Another hundred fifty, two hundred years, there'll be a lot more humans who look like you than look like, say, Idris Elba."

"I *like* Idris Elba."

"Of course you like Idris Elba! What's not to like? But that's hardly the point."

Janey nodded. "I get what you're saying. I guess."

Still holding Janey's hand, Tim held his water glass up for a toast. "To the culturally ambiguous."

Janey lifted her own glass. "To weird loners."

"To Americans!"

"I'll drink to that."

They clinked their glasses and drank, and when Janey set her glass down, Lynn the waitress appeared next to their table. Tim grinned, just a tiny bit, and slowly pulled his hand away.

"Ready?" Lynn asked, tentatively, as if sensing the interruption. She had a small pad and pen.

"I think so," Tim said, and turned toward the waitress. Janey couldn't think over the whirring of blood in her ears. "I'll have the samosas and dal soup. And iced tea."

The waitress dutifully scratched the order down and turned to Janey. She said, "Same for me."

Janey watched the waitress go, and after a pause that might or might not have been awkward, she couldn't tell, mumbled, "So, uh...what were you saying?"

Tim leaned back in his chair, smiling. Something had changed, but Janey didn't have the presence of mind at the moment to try to figure out exactly what. She decided to concentrate on listening, and on observing basic table manners, such as not stabbing herself with a fork.

"Y'know, I can't read you," Tim said.

Janey swallowed hard before she tried to talk. "I'm not..." But her throat clamped shut, made her words come out quavery. *I'm not hard to read. Say it!* Instead she mumbled, "Whoo... Sorry." She covered her face with one hand, and looked at Tim through her fingers. "I don't get out much. In case that wasn't really, really obvious." She touched her cheeks. "Am I blushing? I feel like I'm blushing."

Tim chuckled. "Maybe just a little."

Janey grinned self-consciously. "It's like I'm in seventh grade again. Okay." She took two deep breaths, and put on a mock-serious face. "All right. I'm okay now. In control."

Tim's dark eyes glinted with humor. "As long as you're sure."

* * *

The dinner went smoothly from there. Janey didn't have any more visible emotional spasms, and Tim graciously pretended she hadn't had any in the first place.

She listened as Tim told her about his childhood, and the wretched time he spent in high school, and his four years in college. He asked her about her own past twice, but both times she sidestepped the question and asked him another one about himself. She could tell Tim was aware of the evasions, but he didn't press her.

The food was good. The dark green dal soup was spicy

enough to warrant long sips of iced tea, but not hot enough to burn the tongue, and the samosas' crusts were wonderfully flaky and light. Janey had never tried either of the dishes, and was pleasantly surprised.

"So," she began at one point as he set down his glass of tea, "does your family actually have these? At meals? Ever?"

Tim swallowed a bite of samosa and smiled, shaking his head. "No. That's what I meant before. I first had this stuff at an Indian restaurant when I was seven. I'm not sure how authentic it was. For that matter I'm not sure how authentic *this* is. But that's what I meant. I can't tell, 'cause I don't have any first-hand experience. They wouldn't teach me to speak Hindi, either."

He paused, drew in a breath as if to speak, paused again. Janey said, "What?"

He smiled a little sheepishly. "Along the same lines... authenticity and such...my, ah, name isn't really Tim."

Janey didn't know what to say. She finally managed, "Oh yeah?"

"Yeah. It's Tarik. It means 'Morning Star,' among other things. Mom—my step-mom—her boss, when I was a boy, was named Tim, and I wanted to be just like him. So I told all my friends to call me Tim, and, well, it just sort of stuck. Even Mom calls me Tim now. Most of the time."

Janey shrugged slightly. "I think Tarik is a beautiful name."

He smiled lopsidedly. "Yeah...I'm okay with it too, now that I'm grown. But I'm too used to Tim to switch back."

Janey hesitated. Glanced around at the restaurant and back to him. "I like this place. Authentic or not, I like it. I'm glad you wanted to come here."

"Good."

At her suggestion they split the bill. In the parking lot, as Tim waited for her to unlock the passenger-side door, he said, "Do you really want to go to the movie?"

Janey took a half step backward. "Don't you?"

"Well...no, not really. Look, when you go to movies you sit for an hour and a half and don't say anything. And I was thinking, to begin with, that that would be okay, 'cause I wasn't sure how this was going to go. But as it turns out, I really enjoy talking to you. So no, I don't really want to go to the movie."

Janey shrugged. "Okay. But I've got to tell you, as a by-product of not going on any dates for two years, I'm clueless as to what there is to do around here. I mean, as far as social activity goes. What do you have in mind?"

Tim grinned again, his flawless white teeth flashing. "I love the way you talk." While Janey tried to think of a response to that, Tim said, "C'mon, I've got an idea."

* * *

Tim said, "Oh, good, there's a parking place."

Janey swerved the Civic into an empty slot in a six-space parking lot that faced a circular area of well-kept, very green grass. Nestled between a post office and a long, gently sloping embankment covered in kudzu, the clearing managed to preserve a certain pastoral serenity, if one could overlook the discarded beer cans and fast food wrappers littering the parking area. A white wooden post rose from the ground at the far edge of the pavement, and looked as though it might have once supported a sign, but it ended in worn splinters after four feet.

"Welcome to Anonymous Park," Tim said as Janey got out of the car.

"I never knew this was here," she said, gazing at the statue that rose from the grass in the middle of the clearing.

"Not many people notice it. That's what makes it so cool. C'mon."

He took her arm, a very cordial gesture, and guided her out onto the grass, which felt springy and soft under her feet.

In the clearing's center stood a fifteen-foot-high bronze man dressed in Revolution-era clothes, holding a massive book under his left arm and gesturing passionately with his right hand. Thoroughly imposing, he stood on a bronze rock partially overgrown with vines. Janey noticed a square indentation in the rock directly below the tips of his shoes; a plaque had once rested there, Janey guessed, but now the space was empty. Three low concrete benches surrounded the statue, and Tim dropped onto one of them and patted the space beside him. She sat down slowly.

"Isn't he great?" Tim asked, waving at the statue.

"Yeah." Janey didn't quite know what to think about it. "Who is he?"

"I have no idea! That's why I call this place 'Anonymous Park.' I found it a couple of years ago, and neither the sign nor the plaque was here then either." He craned his head to look up at the massive bronze face. "I heard somewhere he might be Francis Bacon. Who knows? He's pretty awesome, though."

Janey tried to think of some kind of comment concerning the statue that wouldn't sound like total garbage, and realized Tim had moved slightly closer to her. She looked over at him and, before she could change her own mind, put one hand to his face, quickly caressed his cheek, and kissed him.

It was brief, but there was heat in it, and as soon as their lips parted Janey wanted to disappear. Jump up and run away. She felt split down the middle, as one side of her desperately wanted to touch him again, while the other side jammed a pitchfork of guilt into her stomach.

Tim gave her that smile that continued to kick her in the ribs. She didn't scoot away from him, but instead swiveled on the bench and pulled her knees up to her chest. It was an elegant way to stay close to him while establishing a sort of barrier.

Tim said, "I...wasn't expecting that."

Janey rested her forehead on her knees for a second. "I don't think I was either."

She tried to calm her breathing and her heartbeat, and hoped none of her sudden panic came through on her face when she raised it again. "It's hard work. This being-an-average-human thing."

Tim grinned again, and as he did Janey caught another trace of his after-shave. He said, "I don't think there's a single average thing about you."

Janey blushed deeply.

The two of them sat on the concrete bench and talked, under the watchful eye of the bronze statesman, until night fell and the cicadas began their determined droning. They talked about movies, and religion, and touched briefly on national politics. They discussed the space program, and whether they liked green or blue glass bottles better, and what their favorite rides at Disney World were, and the pets they'd had as children.

Somewhere along the way Janey realized she was falling in love with him, and it felt like dying, and she couldn't stop it.

* * *

Tim felt adrift, somewhere far away and warm and comforting.

Objective, objective, stay objective.

Tracing squiggly patterns on Janey's shoulder with one finger, he drew in a deep breath and said, "Okay...here's a hot-button topic. What do you think about gun control? For or against?"

Janey grimaced, and didn't answer immediately. "I'm hesitant to say. How do *you* feel about it?"

"No, no, I asked you first."

"Well, I'm fine with guns, honestly. It's those hard little pieces of metal they fire that I have a problem with."

"Come on, I'm serious."

Janey tried for a smile. "So am I, actually. …You realize you're handing me a soapbox?"

"I like tall women. Climb on up."

She sighed, and ducked her head. "I just…it's…"

Janey fell silent. Her jaw clenched tight. The air around them turned hot—stifling—and a sudden fear Tim couldn't explain crushed his lungs. *What the hell?*

She turned away, breathing heavily.

"Janey…I…"

Janey slumped forward and put her face in her hands, and a cool breeze swept away the strange, oppressing heat as quickly as it had appeared. It took with it the baffling fear, leaving Tim trembling from what now seemed to be pointless adrenaline.

What the hell just happened? He tried his best to think straight.

Janey exhaled, long and slow.

"Tim…could we just not talk about it?"

Normal! Act normal! No nervous breakdowns!

"Of course." Tim took a few deep breaths and, once the trembling stopped, he put a hand on her back. "I shouldn't have pushed." When she didn't pull away, he lightly scratched the area between her shoulder blades, and when she still didn't pull away, he added, "Think there's any way we could get back to a, uh, a more light-hearted tone?"

Janey straightened up and met his gaze, and before he could stop himself he said, "My *God* your eyes are gorgeous."

She closed her eyes, and her cheeks turned a vivid pink. Finally, a slow grin crept onto her lips. "I could go for some dessert. You know any good dessert places around here?"

* * *

Janey hadn't thought she could feel like this again.

Driving back to the LaCroix, they stopped at a small ice cream shop—she got two scoops of strawberry in a waffle cone, he got a cup of orange sherbet—and both of them had just finished when Janey parked the Civic in apartment 9C's reserved spot.

She turned to Tim. He set his cup on the dashboard, and leaned over and kissed her. His lips and tongue were cool, and tasted like oranges, and she made a small sound in her throat as they kissed, not quite a moan. She could tell he liked that, and she felt the pitchfork twist.

After their lips parted, Janey sighed and unhooked her seat belt.

"I guess we should go in," she said softly.

On the way into the building Tim quietly took her hand, and Janey didn't know if her feet would stay on the ground or not.

Inside, Janey followed Tim past the elevators to the door of his apartment. He pulled his keys from a pocket and unlocked the door, and turned to her before he opened it.

"Janey... I've had a great time tonight. Would you...like to come in? For a while?"

He touched her side. Very lightly.

Oh God. Oh *God.* There'd been nothing...no one since Adam, and she couldn't...she just *couldn't...*

The pitchfork tore into her and the wound filled with salt.

"I, uh, I can't, really, I..."

Tim's forehead wrinkled. She was blowing this, and knew it, and she backpedaled a few steps anyway. "I'd like to, really, but I can't, um, I have to go. I, uh, I had a really good time tonight too, though." Stupid, *stupid,* that sounded patronizing, dammit!

His eyebrows drew together. "Oh...okay. So, do you want to text me? ...Just wait till we run into each other in the hall again?"

Janey forced herself forward, took his hands in hers. "Tim, you're great, you really are, and—I'm sorry, I know I must seem like a lunatic, I just...I do want to see you again. Maybe...maybe tomorrow? I'll come by the office?"

"Sure. If you want." Pain filled her eyes, her face, and Tim's expression softened. "Janey, are you okay? Do you want to talk about this? Whatever it is that's bothering you?"

She made a tortured sound. "Yes. Yes I do. But...not...not right now. Not yet. I'm sorry."

She released his hands and turned and moved down the hallway, through the glass doors, into the darkness outside.

* * *

Just inside his apartment, Tim leaned against the door and ran his tongue over his lips. He could still taste her. *Strawberries.* Aloud he said, "Well. That was surreal."

No it wasn't.

If this bat-shit insane idea turns out to be right…

It would all line up perfectly.

A new feeling, an icy thrill rippled through him. Objectively, intellectually, he called himself a reckless dumbass, and knew he ought to promise himself he'd stay as far away from Janey Sinclair as possible.

But he knew he wouldn't.

What else did Grandma say? "Try your best to minimize the crazy in your life?"

Tim took a deep breath.

So this is what the inside of the rabbit hole looks like.

The taste of her danced across his tongue. He savored it.

CHAPTER NINE

Nathan Pittman made the turn out of his subdivision and drove away from his home, slowly and more or less aimlessly. He liked to drive at night, by himself. It helped him clear his thoughts.

Nathan owned a 2000 Grand Am, originally black, now black with a red driver's side door and a white left front quarter panel. Nathan referred to the car as "Frankie."

He pulled into a Jiffy Mart two miles from his house and parked next to the self-service pumps, but kept the car running for a couple of minutes and remained in the seat, eyes closed. The last few seconds of an ancient grunge metal song ground its way out of the custom-installed speakers. When the song ended, Nathan shut off the car and got out.

The night had turned foggy and cool, almost cold; the Georgia fall was coming in early this year. Nathan unscrewed the gas cap, but dropped it, and went down to one knee to grab the cap where it had rolled under the car.

As he straightened back up—at the moment his eyes rose above Frankie's rear window frame—something inside the store caught his attention. He froze in place and stared through the glass.

Nathan had good eyes. Years before, as a Boy Scout, he'd gone for a physical before a trip to summer camp. The technician administering the vision test actually got excited by Nathan's results and made him repeat the procedure.

"You've got good eyes, man," the tech finally said, respectfully. "Take care of them."

Now those eyes picked out a movement inside the store, something that shouldn't be there, and Nathan's heart began whirring in his chest.

A tall, gaunt man in a camouflage hunting jacket and a red

toboggan cap stood at the counter opposite the clerk, a twenty-year-old girl named Cindy. Nathan was almost positive he had seen a knife in the man's hand.

When he realized he was doing nothing but crouching and staring, Nathan tried to look busy. He bent down behind the car and pretended to do something with the rear tire, but he kept his head craned back and watched the store through the car windows.

Nathan knew the clerk's name was Cindy only because he'd read her name tag one of the other times he'd stopped there for gas. She was a slender, pretty blonde girl, a bit too heavy on the make-up, maybe, but still sort of attractive. Not that she'd shown any interest in him at all. He watched intensely, and didn't blink even when his eyes began to burn. He saw Cindy's shoulders move as she handed something to the man at the counter. Cigarettes? A magazine? A box of condoms? Nathan kept watching, and saw her give him something else. Again. And then again.

The man glanced out the window, at the Grand Am. It occurred to Nathan that his car was the only one there, so the man must have been looking at him. As he watched, the man gestured, and light flashed off the blade of a knife. Clear as day.

This is it! Much sooner than he'd expected, but here it was. He focused on slowing his breathing as he opened the driver's-side door and pulled out his book bag. He slung it over one shoulder and walked in what he hoped was a convincingly casual manner around the side of the store, to the restrooms. He didn't turn his head to look in the window on his way past, but he could see the man there out of the corner of his eye.

When he got around to the side of the building, Nathan pressed his back to the white-painted cinderblock wall and unzipped his bookbag with shaky hands.

Nathan went over the moves in his head as he pulled the mask out. The man inside was most likely not a trained knife fighter, and would come at him slashing. He envisioned the man, arm raised high, bringing the knife down toward his face.

Gray Widow's Walk

Nathan rolled the nylon hood up, tugged the mask down as far as his eyebrows, remembered his rings and stopped to take them out.

He knew the moves. He'd rehearsed them time and again at the dojo, with a partner and a practice knife. The mask was smooth and cool on his skin as he made some final adjustments, and it didn't impair his vision at all. Looking down, he took in his combat boots, black jeans, black T-shirt and blue-and-red plaid overshirt, and decided he looked like a high school student with a funny mask on. Pulling off the overshirt helped; he was all in black now. Not gray—not like the Widow. But it would do. Goosebumps rose on Nathan's arms in a sudden chill, and he heard the door of the store open, and his heartbeat kicked all the cold out of him.

Nathan came around the corner and dropped into stance, his eyes fixed on the tall man, who still stood half in and half out of the store, holding a large brown paper bag. A glance confirmed Nathan's suspicions; a couple of twenties stuck out of the bag, one from the top and one through a two-inch tear in its side.

The man met Nathan's eyes—

—and Nathan couldn't decide what to do.

For an awful moment he expected the man to laugh at him, immediately recognize him as a skinny teenager in a weird mask. The tall man's mouth did open, but Nathan didn't want to hear anything he might have to say, and he screamed, *"That's it, dirtbag, I'm taking you down!"* and charged.

In the next two seconds, as he ran, a moment of stunning clarity came over him. He wasn't a masked crime fighter. He was just a high school student, nothing more. He had no business wearing a stupid Halloween mask, shouting bad comic book dialogue. He had no business pretending to be someone he wasn't.

The realization came too late. The tall man pulled a revolver out of his jacket and shot Nathan three times in the chest.

* * *

Tim held open the door of the club for Janey. She flashed him an appreciative smile as she dug in her purse for her wallet. Their second date. She hadn't scared him away with that ridiculous display outside his apartment after all.

They both showed their IDs at the door, paid the cover charge and walked in. The darkened interior had already half-filled with smoke. It consisted of one large, square room, with a raised stage against the wall opposite the door, and full bars on both the left and right walls. Tables were scattered across the floor, leaving a space open in front of the stage for dancing, and plush chairs and couches tucked themselves into the corners. There were only a half-dozen other people there. The show wouldn't start for another twenty minutes, and even then the crowd would most likely be small for the opening act. Canned music blared over the PA system, and Janey had to raise her voice.

"Do you want to sit down? Or get something to drink?"

Tim motioned with his head toward the bar, and Janey followed him.

The bartender was a whip-thin blonde in her mid-twenties whose eyes slid past Janey to examine Tim boldly. Tim didn't wait to be asked what he wanted.

"Jim Beam and Coke." The bartender nodded and looked back to Janey, expectantly.

"I don't guess you have Grape Crush?" Janey asked. The blonde gave her a blank stare. "Didn't think so. That's cool. I'll take a diet Mountain Dew."

Drinks in hand, they turned from the bar, and Tim took her arm and led her toward one of the couches.

"You don't drink, I take it?" he asked.

"Not too often."

"Do you mind if I do?"

"No, no, of course not. All things in moderation, as the

saying goes." They reached the couch. It was set back into a small alcove, still affording a clear view of the stage but slightly isolated from the rest of the crowd. Janey hesitated. "Would you rather sit at one of the tables?"

"Nah." He plopped down on the couch and motioned for her to join him. She did, sinking back into the spongy cushions. "You can hear yourself think a little better back here," he said, and laughed at the sight of his own knees, which were almost on a level with his eyes. "If you can put up with the less-than-firm padding."

Janey folded her long legs under her as she sat, and poked at the couch. "Sort of has that Salvation Army thrift store charm, doesn't it?" Tim laughed, and Janey turned her head away and scanned the club as she took a small sip of the soda. Neither of them spoke.

Tim broke the silence. "I still can't get over that painting of yours. I've never known a painting to have that much of an effect on me. I mean, the ones I saw in the gallery were fantastic, but nothing like that one. Are you going to show it?"

"No...I've got something special in mind for it."

"Oh really? What?"

She took another sip of Mountain Dew, straining to remain casual, and changed the subject. "So, ah, you said your brother would be here tonight?"

He paused, switching gears. "Well, he's supposed to be, anyway. His girlfriend's in the opening act. He said he'd find us and say hello. He sort of plays guitar himself..."

"Sort of?"

"Well, he's pretty good, really, if he's just, y'know, dicking around at the house. Get him on stage and he gets all nervous." He sipped at his own drink, and set it on the floor. "So how much do you get from selling one of your paintings? I mean, if you don't mind me asking."

Janey let one corner of her mouth quirk upward. "It varies. Depends on what I think they're worth, what kind of price I put on them. Did you really like 'Pure Thought'? The crystal tree one?"

He nodded vigorously. "Yeah! I mean, like I said, I've never seen a painting before that made me *feel* so much. And that one really did."

Well. He'd just given her the perfect opening. Acting on a decision she'd made earlier in the day, she took a deep breath and said, "So you liked it better than the other one?"

Tim's smile froze. Janey experienced a touch of sadistic pleasure at catching him so flat-footed, and immediately felt ashamed of herself.

"The ones at the gallery? Which one do you mean?"

She calmly drank from her cup. "The other one I had in my bedroom. You know, the one you saw before I came home the other day. When you were in my apartment." He looked like a deer caught in headlights. "If I'd realized you were there I wouldn't have walked around almost naked, y'know."

Tim half rose from the couch, shifting between guilt and anger. "Look, I don't know what you're—I mean, I'm sorry that... " When her face didn't change, he sank back down onto the cushions. "How'd you know I was there?"

"You left a couple of signs." She shifted around to face him directly. "I'm not upset. Not really."

He looked suspicious. "Then why did you pretend you didn't know? All this time? Through that whole date?"

She stared down at her soft drink. "I'm not sure why I didn't go ahead and ask you if you'd been there. In my bedroom, I mean. I guess I was waiting to see if you brought it up first. I was going to talk to you about it before, out at the statue, but I couldn't ever seem to find the right time. And...I really didn't want to ruin things."

Janey looked up, into his narrowed eyes, and shrugged. She felt the heat rising into her face, and wondered if he could see it in the dim light. "I know, it's not exactly standard for the beginning of a rel—" She stopped, unwilling to say the word. "Um. Well."

Neither of them spoke for several seconds, and Janey finally said, "Awkward, huh?"

Tim slumped backward and nestled into the corner of the couch. "Sort of, yeah." Janey started to say something else when she saw his face darken, as though remembering something unpleasant. He sat back up. "Well, okay, but...how come you weren't soaked? When you came in? It was pouring rain outside."

"I'd gone downstairs to take out my trash." The dumpster for the LaCroix was in back, outside an access door. "I just stuck my head out and pitched the bags around the door, y'know, to try to keep from getting wet." She paused. "I took the stairs...you must've just missed me."

Tim's eyes got wider, and he smacked himself on the forehead. "Of course. Of course I did." He laughed self-consciously. "Okay, okay, I'm a total moron. I mean, I guess you know why I was spooked when you came in. That first painting would give the undead nightmares." Janey smiled. "But how come you didn't notice the door was unlocked? When you came back? You had your keys with you."

That stopped Janey cold. She slowly opened her mouth, wondering what was going to come out of it, when an unfamiliar voice sounded from over her shoulder.

"Tim! Hey! Thanks for coming, bro!"

Tim looked up and grinned and rose off the couch, heading for a rail-thin, long-haired young man in ratty jeans and a blue T-shirt with the Superman emblem on the front. He and Tim embraced briefly, then he turned to Janey, flashed what looked like every one of his teeth, and stuck out one long, bony hand.

He looks like somebody grabbed Tim by the head and feet and stretched him.

There were a few more differences. The young man's skin was a shade or two lighter, and he'd inherited his mother's freckles. But, putting him side by side with Tim, it was obvious at even the barest glance that they were brothers.

"Hey! I'm Cary."

Janey stood and returned the handshake. "Janey Sinclair."

"Great to meet you!" Cary gave Tim a mischievous smirk. "For that matter, great that Tim finally managed to talk to a girl." Over Tim's loud protest, Cary went on: "And listen, I'd love to stay and talk, but you won't believe this. Kate's guitarist has the flu, and I talked them into letting me play tonight!"

Janey watched Tim's face. He was clearly surprised, and not pleasantly. Before he could say anything, though, Cary shook Janey's hand again. "I've got to get backstage now. Nice meeting you! Wish me luck, guys!" He sprinted away.

Tim watched him go, and shook his head. "This is going to be a disaster." He sat back down. Janey followed. "Kate takes this band pretty seriously, and if Cary makes them look bad she'll kill him."

Janey pretended to watch the stage, but kept glancing at Tim out of the corner of her eye. Maybe he'd forget what they had been talking about...?

"So," he said. "What about that door?"

Shit.

"Well, I'll tell you, but it's sort of embarrassing."

"Yeah?"

"Sometimes I just forget to lock it. I mean, y'know, the building's got security, cameras and what-not, so it's not like my door just opens onto the street or anything. Plus, where I grew up I never had to lock my door at all. So sometimes I just forget. When I came back yesterday I figured I'd left it unlocked again, and nothing was missing, so I didn't think about it."

Tim fell silent. She didn't think he believed her and, considering it, she wouldn't have believed such a lame explanation either, but before he could respond, a voice crashed out over the PA. Easily five times louder than the canned music, it made Janey wince and wish for ear plugs.

"All right!" the voice said. Janey turned toward the stage and saw that a tall, bony girl with lustrous purple hair stood at the center mic, a big guitar slung across her chest. The other members of the band were all guys—kids, really. A swarthy, shirtless young man with long, unkempt hair and a fretless bass took up his position near the west corner of the stage. The drummer came out and sat down, also shirtless, with shaggy blonde surfer hair and enormous biceps. He grinned at the girl and twirled his sticks in his fingers. Then, finally, Cary appeared, clutching a blinding white Les Paul six-string. He already looked nervous, and the harsh lights made the sweat on his forehead sparkle.

"We're Flay," the girl, Kate, barked into the mic. She turned and nodded to the drummer, who cracked his sticks together, *one, two, one two three four,* and the band launched into their first song.

The drummer and the bassist seemed at least adequate. Their pounding rhythms nicely complemented Kate's vocals, which she belted out in an oddly melodic growl. The song progressed smoothly through the intro, which did not involve guitar at all—and then Cary started playing.

Tim shook his head and mouthed the words, "Oh, no." Janey couldn't hear him at all over the din, and her ears started to hurt. She squinted, tried to decide whether or not to stick her fingers in her ears, and watched Cary play.

He made mistakes almost from the first note. To begin with he couldn't find the rhythm of the song, and when he did find it he couldn't get the right chord. What probably would have been a good song instead became unlistenable. Kate turned from the mic halfway through and gave Cary a look that, to Janey's surprise, didn't kill him where he stood. Cary saw it, though, and flinched.

Tim pulled Janey up from the couch.

"Come on," he shouted into her ear through cupped hands. "I can't take this anymore."

Janey let herself be led outside, and felt sorry for the kid.

* * *

The cool night air smelled faintly of pine needles as they walked back to Janey's car and drove to Hammerfield Park. Intended to be a safe, family-friendly alternative to Piedmont Park, the carefully landscaped Hammerfield spent its days filled with college students, small children accompanied by watchful parents, and dogs, along with a lot of Frisbees. Squirrels more or less infested the well-maintained trees, and ducks quacked in the man-made pond.

By night the park wore a slightly more forbidding face but, according to the Atlanta safety commission, stayed well enough lit and was patrolled by police frequently enough to afford safe passage to joggers and others out for evening strolls.

So Janey and Tim strolled, following a pine needle-covered walking trail.

After a few moments he tentatively reached out his hand, and Janey took it.

"Tell me about Cary. Were you two close, growing up?"

Tim's grin flashed. "Well, we spent a lot of time torturing each other. So, yeah."

She concentrated on his voice, and as he talked about the times he used to have with Cary and their sister Lauren, she thought of Adam. Now and then, over the weeks and months, she'd found herself staring at the ring finger of her left hand. When she let it, the bareness of it struck at her like a phantom pain. Blonde hair floating around his head in natural ringlets, ocean green eyes...

Tim squeezed her hand, and she jerked back to the present. As they walked, he turned her hand over in his own, running long, slender fingers down each fold and line.

"Forgive me for saying so, but this doesn't actually feel too much like the hand of an artist."

Janey was glad of the subject change, since she hadn't heard a word he'd said in the last few minutes.

"Well, uh...I work out a little."

"A little. Really."

She smiled, but took her hand back and shoved it in her pocket. A not very comfortable silence followed, until Janey said,

"Hey, how's your dad? I know he's on a trip somewhere, but I never heard any details."

Tim's face fell. "He and Mom are taking care of my aunt and uncle, up in Cincinnati. They were in a car wreck."

"Oh, I'm sorry! I didn't know it was anything like that."

Tim stared off at the night sky. They came to a bench, and he moved to sit down. Janey joined him, but after a second's consideration left a good foot and a half between them.

"They're all right, or at least they're going to be. Aunt Tasneem in particular needs a lot of time to recuperate, and Uncle Sanjay's pretty old, he can't get around too well, even when he's okay. So Mom and Dad went up there to help. And I'm here, until they get better." He laughed. Short, derisively. "Or maybe longer than that."

"What do you mean?"

"It's…I didn't really plan to be anywhere. Not in any practical way, at least. Growing up, Dad always told me how important it is to get a good, steady, paying job. He said if you had that, you had no limits. As long as you had a solid base under you, you could *reach for the stars*. Well, I didn't buy that. I wanted to be a writer, make my living selling stories. So...after I graduated with my nice little BA in English, I worked for a while in a bookstore while I submitted stuff. I figured, hey, every writer goes through this, getting back rejection slips, it's just part of the game, paying my dues, I'll get published soon enough. But...I didn't."

He paused. Janey waited for him.

"Every once in a while an editor wrote me a personal letter and encouraged me to keep writing, but by and large I got form letters. My favorite one had, 'Dear... ' and then a blank line, and some intern misspelled my name on it. How the hell do you misspell 'Tim?' Anyway, Dad kept telling me I needed to get a nine-to-five job, he said I could make money during the day and write at night. But I was bull-headed about it, and I kept on trying to live the dream, y'know? But I just…rode that plane right into the ground. I had about a week and a half's worth left in my bank account…

and then Aunt Tasneem lost control of her car. I think, probably, what happened was there was a spider in the car. She's always been terrified of spiders. She won't admit it, about the spider, but she was a very good driver, very safe, and in the middle of a dry, sunny afternoon she just ran off the road and into somebody's front yard and hit a tree."

Tim rocked back and forth on the bench. "Now she needs a lot of help for a while, and Mom volunteered herself and Dad. So I packed up my cat and my laptop, and that's why I'm here, because Dad can't be, and he needed someone to run the building. So I'm in the family business. And Dad was right all along." He sighed. "Not a very interesting story. I'm just sort of a slacker who finally saw the light and realized he couldn't buy food with rejection letters."

Janey said, "Interesting stories are overrated."

Before Tim could reply, a shrill, rasping scream punched out of the darkness from somewhere to their right.

CHAPTER TEN

Janey jumped up from the bench. "Come on!" Before Tim could protest, she took his hand, and the two of them darted off the walking trail and into the trees, running toward the scream.

Along the way, Tim said, "What are you *doing?* Let me call 911! Janey!" but she didn't stop. The pines only stood in a narrow line, and seconds later she and Tim crashed into a small clearing with a fountain in the center. A brick pathway encircled the fountain and led out through a metal archway covered with ivy. A tremendous oak, hundreds of years old, stood off to one side in the clearing, and dark shapes writhed and struggled in the shadows on its far side. Behind her, Janey heard Tim say, "Yes! I want to report an attack!"

The scream came again, a little weaker this time, and Janey rushed toward the tree. She couldn't tell exactly what was happening, but it was obviously an assault, and she shouted, "Hey! *Hey!*"

Janey reached the tree and rounded the far side, entered the shadow, and willed her night vision on. A college-age girl lay on her back on the ground, her head and shoulders emerging into the dim light. She wore a jogging suit, and an iPod lay on the ground nearby, smashed apart. Her attacker had torn open her shirt and ripped off her sports bra. He knelt on top of her with his back to Janey, a wiry man in black clothes, both of his hands out of sight as he clutched the girl. The girl saw Janey over the man's shoulder and screamed again, and the man twisted around and looked Janey in the eyes.

There was something very very wrong with the mugger's jaw, and the length of his arms and hands, and his eyes. A stray beam of light glinted off slick, glistening spines like the teeth of deep-ocean predators.

Janey skidded to a stop with her mouth hanging open and

stifled a scream of her own.

* * *

"Miss Jorden!" Scott Charles shouted.

Garrison Vessler stepped out of the hall bathroom as Brenda Jorden and Ned Fields, who'd been watching a movie in the living room for the last hour, sprinted down the hall toward Scott's room. The walls shook with Fields' pounding footfalls. Jorden helped Scott across the room and into the chair in front of the mobile fMRI unit. She slid the cap of sensors onto his head. Scott's eyes stayed wide, unblinking, as he stared into another place.

Seconds later a grainy image coalesced on the screen, with a familiar energy wave shimmering in the middle of it.

"That's Hammerfield Park," Fields said.

Vessler hit a button on his phone. "Mobile units 3 and 10. Target is located."

The energy wave flickered and shook on the screen. "Jesus." Scott sounded less like a young boy than an old man. "Look at that signature."

A voice came over the phone. "Mobile unit 3, ETA ninety seconds."

Vessler stood near Scott, barking orders into the phone, when he heard the boy gasp. He turned, glanced at the screen and almost dropped his handset.

Another signature shone on the display. It moved after the primary's, throwing off energy like a magnesium flare, the waveform half an inch wide and dancing like a bolt of lightning. The lines and contours of its surroundings began to distort around it.

Jorden paled when she saw the new signature. Her eyes flicked over to Fields.

"What the hell is *that?*" Vessler hissed, but Scott couldn't answer. His body shook with a sudden convulsion, and small, tendrils of smoke rose from the cage of sensors around his head.

On the screen, the immense energy signature approached the smaller one, rolled over it, consumed it like an amoeba enveloping its food. The fMRI itself began to smoke.

Vessler jerked the sensor cage off the boy's head, pulled Scott away from the console, and screamed into the phone: "Mobile units! Pull back! Pull back! I say again, mobile units, pull back!"

Brenda Jorden disappeared from the room, reappeared almost immediately with a cool, damp wash cloth. She laid Scott down on the bed and sponged away the thick, greasy sweat that had popped out all over his face. To Vessler she said, "What was that? On the screen, what *was* that?"

Vessler had to leave, and knew it, and hated himself for abandoning the boy. He spoke without looking at her or Fields, who'd stepped back out of the way.

"I don't know. The second signature must have been another augment, but good lord, it was *huge*. Damn it, I have to get back to the temporary HQ. Take care of him."

"Of course, sir."

Jorden sat down on the edge of Scott's bed. The boy shook with small tremors, and Jorden dabbed at his temples with the cloth.

Teeth gritted, Vessler ran for his car, cursing as he went. He knew he wouldn't see Scott again for days, probably weeks. Damn it all to hell.

* * *

The mugger flung himself at Janey, gave her no time to think. Out of reflex Janey clamped one hand on the mugger's right upper arm, jammed the other one under the man's left armpit, and dropped to one knee as she twisted. The mugger's feet shot over his head as his body flipped, and the force of his own momentum slammed him into a young pine. Needles showered down. He immediately rolled to his feet, still cloaked in shadow, as Janey sprang up.

They faced each other, frozen. Janey blinked. She stood

opposite a perfectly normal young man. What the hell had she seen a few seconds ago? The jogger on the ground moaned, and Janey yelled, "Tim! This girl's hurt!"

The mugger stood there, frozen, for just over three seconds, before he sprinted away like a cat through the trees. Tim rushed past Janey to the girl's side. He started to say something, but Janey cut him off with "Stay with her!" and bolted after the retreating figure.

A dozen yards into the woods, safely out of Tim's sight, Janey stopped briefly, cursing the time it took but too scared not to do it. She found a cleft in a lightning-struck tree and plunged her purse into the darkness inside it. Immediately the air temperature around her soared, and a number of nearby leaves cracked and fell to the ground, dry and brittle. Janey drew her hand back out of the cleft holding the Vylar suit.

Ten seconds later—the result of long hours drilling this very task—Janey dashed after the mugger, her body protected by gray segmented armor, the mask covering her face.

* * *

In Scott's room, Ned Fields came and stood over Brenda Jorden until she looked up at him. On the bed Scott wheezed and didn't open his eyes. Fields motioned with his head, and followed Brenda out into the hallway.

"Well," she sighed. "Our job just got twice as complicated."

Fields sighed. "I suppose we'll have to find that one too. Ourselves, I mean."

"If we do this with the first one, we'll have to do it with the second. It's our asses now." She looked thoughtful for a moment. "...Unless we can make the primary go after that new one."

"Christ. We could've stuck with the original plan. For that matter, Vessler's *right here*. Why couldn't you just zap him, like you do the kid?"

She shook her head. "I tried to sell that to Stamford to begin with. He doesn't think the other lieutenants would buy it. Too much faith in Vessler. It's got to look like plain incompetence. Plus, Stamford already approved the new idea, so we're stuck with it."

"Grand." Disgusted and abruptly thirsty, Fields turned and headed for the kitchen, floorboards squealing beneath his weight. He'd spent a good deal of time thinking about what the company would be like, once Vessler was out of the way. Once Jorden took his place.

Fields got the feeling that, no matter who she worked with, Brenda Jorden would be the one in charge, sooner or later. Not for the first time he wondered what the chances might be of getting a letter of resignation accepted.

Behind him, Jorden went back in to tend to Scott.

* * *

Janey caught up with the mugger underneath a small stone bridge leading out of the park. Harsh streetlights illuminated the bridge, but cast thick black shadows beneath it. Janey saw brilliant white pinpoints set in onyx, and thought, *Those are eyes?* The rest of the man became visible slowly in the darkness.

He was young, early twenties maybe, and strikingly handsome. Janey blinked, even more unsure of what she thought she'd seen under the tree. The guy was crouched down just beneath the road, wedged into the corner formed by the bridge and the embankment.

He made no threatening moves, just crouched, one hand raised, touching a massive archway stone. Janey approached slowly, hands open, unthreatening, but young man cringed away from her.

Guess I can't blame him, given how I look.

Janey called out, "What's your name?"

"Simon." The mugger winced. "Please...I'm sorry, I didn't..." He trailed off, uncertain and—what? Scared?

Janey stood like a statue. Somewhere a clock struck, the first of eleven chimes, and in her mind she replayed the horror show in the darkness under the tree. It *couldn't* have been real.

Just then they both heard the rumble of an approaching truck on the road over the bridge, headed out of the park. Simon tensed, telegraphing, and Janey took a quick step forward. "Wait a minute!"

As the truck passed overhead Simon moved, fluid as an animal, swung himself up and onto the bridge. By the time Janey scrambled up the embankment and vaulted over the guardrails into the flat white light of the street lamps, the truck, and Simon along with it, were rapidly becoming a distant pair of taillights, about to blend smoothly into the midtown traffic.

Janey ducked back off the road, into the shadows, as another vehicle swept past, but she never took her eyes from the truck's taillights. She saw them come to a stop in a line of cars at an intersection a few hundred yards away, where the park surrendered to the city's concrete.

Paralleling the road, Janey sprinted toward the truck.

If it hadn't stopped at the red light she would have lost it, and wouldn't have tried what she attempted now. As it was, some of the city's traffic signals took a long time to change, and this looked like one of them. The light probably wouldn't hold the truck long enough to reach it on foot. But Janey had other options.

She tried to think clearly as she ran. She'd had only the chase through the park for a warm-up, but her breathing came deep and unlabored as her arms and legs pumped.

The truck still sat at the light, waiting for her.

She squinted, trying to make out the details of the vehicle. Bright yellow, formerly a Penske, with the black letters overpainted by a slightly different shade of yellow. A private citizen, most likely, hauling who knew what. Janey watched for silhouettes poking up from the truck's roof, afraid the mugger would be on the lookout for her. There wasn't much she could do about it, running out into the open, and the farther into town the truck moved, the fewer chances she'd have to flicker out and get anywhere useful.

The light changed, and the truck rolled slowly forward, Janey still a hundred yards away. The grassy shoulder of the road abruptly changed to concrete sidewalk, and the thick soles of the leather-and-Vylar boots slapped against the hard surface.

There: a wide ledge ran around the third story of a squat, cube-shaped building on the corner where the truck had turned, and street lights below it cast deep shadows between the ledge and the side of the building. The nearest pedestrian was easily sixty feet away, and Janey veered from the road and plunged into the darkness beneath a magnolia tree.

The tips of several branches withered and died as she disappeared beneath them.

Emerging onto the ledge, Janey saw the truck stopped at another red light. From her new vantage point she had a clear view down onto the street.

Simon still perched spread-eagled on top of the former Penske—and Janey gasped. Simon's fingers had *elongated,* become more like tentacles than actual digits, and clamped onto the forward corners of the truck's cargo compartment.

I wasn't imagining things!

The light flicked to green, but pedestrians still moved in the cross-walk in front of the truck, and the driver leaned on his horn. Janey saw one of the pedestrians flip off the driver before skittering out of the way. The truck accelerated. She found another jumping point on the roof of a six-story building three blocks away, and flickered away from the ledge, leaving steam and blistering-hot concrete behind her.

The truck moved deeper into the city, and Janey followed, flickering from one pool of shadow to another, always in sight of it. Simon stayed on its roof until it slowed and came to a creaking halt outside a lower-class apartment building. Janey watched as Simon flung himself from the roof of the vehicle to the side of the building and bounded onto the rooftop of a nearby shop. She couldn't believe it; the two leaps together totaled about fifty feet.

But the leaps, those patently impossible leaps, proved the point Janey hadn't quite allowed herself to accept yet. The fingers *could* have been a trick, some sort of weird gloves, and the teeth might just have been a mask or an oral prosthesis. But no kind of cosmetics allowed their wearer to deny freaking gravity. Simon, the young man who'd attacked the girl in the park, wasn't human—at least, not any more human than Janey herself. A kinship was there, a connection of some kind. Janey felt the certainty of it in her bone marrow. She had to catch up with Simon, contain him if necessary, but above all she had to talk to him. *Had* to.

The truck's doors opened, and two college kids got out and went around to the back, unaware of the ride they'd provided. Janey could see the roof Simon had jumped onto, several sections of it covered with inky shadows, thrown by both the low wall that ran around its edge and by two huge air conditioning units that stood twenty feet apart, like sentries. With a sigh and a burst of heat, Janey was there.

She kept perfectly still for long moments, listening. She edged around an air conditioner housing and found herself facing an open door, a wrecked lock hanging from its hasp, stairs beyond it leading down into the building. Simon was inside, Janey could feel it, and she knew she'd lose him if she didn't follow immediately. Janey eyed the ruined lock. Had Simon found a crowbar somewhere? ...Or had he destroyed the lock with natural strength? With a sinking feeling Janey hoped it wasn't the latter.

The rooftop lay in icy silence. Janey went to the stairs and flickered down, into the darkness.

She stood at one end of a short hallway, polished hardwood floors partially covered with plush green carpet. Five heavy wooden doors opened off the hall. The two on her right stood open, and Janey peered into square rooms filled with expensive office furniture. Set into the north walls of both rooms were ornate, non-functional fireplaces, smooth concrete filling in where flames had once provided heat, and Janey realized the building had once been a hotel.

A glass door closed off the far end of the hallway. Through the door was a landing, with stairs going down to the right. She could see another glass door on the far side of the landing, and beyond that another hallway, a mirror-image of the one where she now stood.

The doors around her, according to the plaques on the walls next to them, led to the offices of a realtor. She squinted, and saw a similar plaque affixed to the door on the far side of the landing. A brokerage firm.

The building felt lifeless. No air currents moved. The offices had no doubt closed down and emptied at five o'clock. She could see deadbolt locks on the nearer glass door, engaged at both the floor and the ceiling.

So. Two doors open, three more shut, maybe locked. Simon had come through the door from the roof with no problem, but he'd left the lock mangled when he did. Nothing here appeared to be disturbed. Janey made adjustments to the Vylar gloves, swinging hinged metal braces from the backs of the hands around to the palms. They interlocked with a steel ridge running across the knuckles, and when they clicked into place, functioned as built-in steel knuckles.

Janey hadn't spent much time actively looking, but in the past seven years she'd met no one else like herself, no one else who could do things no human should be able to do—until tonight, when the skinny, pale young man who called himself Simon did things that made Janey's mind ache. She focused on regulating her breathing.

One of two possibilities: Simon came down the stairs, went into one of the two rooms with the open doors, and immediately left through a window. If the windows opened. It wouldn't surprise her to find them painted shut. Or, Simon came down the stairs, got into one of the other rooms, closed the door behind him, and decided to wait.

Which didn't make any sense. Simon wouldn't have known Janey had followed him at all, much less that she had trailed him here, to this specific building. Simon had no reason to wait. He'd be long gone by now.

Unless he'd seen Janey following him.

Or unless he could feel Janey's presence somehow?

The windows in the open rooms, as Janey had suspected, were painted shut. The building was old enough not to have any closets, and the desks she'd seen faced the walls, their knee-holes exposed and hiding nothing. If Simon were here, he'd have to be in one of the three other rooms.

Janey approached the first door.

She closed her hand around the knob, still breathing slowly and deeply, turned it, stepped to one side of the doorway, and pushed the door open.

Nothing flew out at her.

For an instant Janey flashed on the girl in the park, lying behind the tree. Her skin had glistened, wet with black blood. Janey hadn't seen any knife. But those fingers...

Swiftly now, Janey pushed the door the rest of the way open and stepped through it, one steel-jacketed fist drawn back and ready.

Ready to punch an empty bathroom.

Her shoulders slumped, and she smiled under the mask.

The next door she tried was about ten feet down the hall, and also opened when she turned the knob. She didn't know if the realtor simply wasn't concerned with people breaking in, trusting in the locks at the ends of the hallway, or if Simon had somehow managed to open this lock without destroying it.

Janey opened the door the same way she'd opened the one to the bathroom, and paused in the doorway, scanning the room's contents. Two desks and a copier didn't present much of a threat. She couldn't decide whether to be annoyed or relieved.

The third door was also unlocked, but opened onto a room

smaller than the others she'd seen. Set into the far end of the wall to Janey's left was another door, more than likely to an inner office. Several shafts of yellow-orange light from the downtown street lamps sliced through the darkness of the room, casting distorted window-shaped patches across the carpet and furniture. *This is the last place he could be. If he's not behind that door I've been wasting my time.*

She didn't want to take the chance of having the floor squeal under her feet as she approached the last door, and the shafts of light from outside illuminated only a small portion of the room. Janey crossed the room with a small flicker. She emerged right beside the door, and the hot air from her jump steamed up the window just as she heard the gasp from behind her.

Whirling, Janey saw Simon tucked into the corner above the door to the hallway like a fat, grotesque spider. Simon's arms reached back behind him and his toes touched the lintel of the doorframe. He let go of whatever he'd been holding on to and dropped to the floor.

"Oh my God," Simon choked out. "Oh my God, oh my God, oh my God."

Janey realized two things at once: first, Simon had seen her teleport. Second, the kid was terrified of her.

Simon scrambled backward, out the door, without taking his eyes off Janey.

As she watched, Simon's eyes shifted and changed, warping back and forth between normal blue and the solid-black-with-white-pinpoints Janey had first seen in the park. Simon's jaw opened, and Janey sucked in a sharp breath. The jaw was distending again, with a greasy popping sound.

"Oh my God, get away from me, get away from me!" Simon screeched, and bolted away toward the door to the roof. Janey instantly flickered into the hallway. Behind her the antique window pane cracked with the sudden heat.

Simon only had a few feet to go before he reached the door, but another flicker brought Janey to the foot of the stairs, blocking

Simon's path. Janey said, "Wait," and was going to follow it with, "I just want to talk to you," but Simon screeched again, wheeled and barreled headlong toward the glass door at the other end.

Flicker. Janey was there, in front of him again. She held up her gloved hands. "Stop, please, I'm not going to hurt you!" Simon's eyes looked like saucers by now, and Janey realized he wasn't *going* to stop just before Simon rammed into her, sending them both through the glass door and onto the carpet at the head of the staircase.

The Vylar suit protected her from any jagged edges, and she tried her best to make sure none of them cut Simon. They landed in a tangled heap, and Simon exploded off the floor, shoved Janey away from him and scrambled toward the stairs. Janey slid a couple of feet across the floor, and her head cracked hard against the stock broker's doorframe. She blinked away stars and tears.

Janey shouted, "Stop, would you?" and, lunging across the carpet, reached out and grabbed Simon's right ankle. Simon fell forward, his hands flailing out into the empty space at the top of the stairs, and he slammed into the topmost step. His breath whooshed out of him and he curled on his side, jerked his foot out of Janey's grip and started wheezing. Janey sat up just as Simon swiveled his head around and glared at her, his eyes solid black and filled with hate even as he struggled to breathe.

Janey said, "For crying out *loud,* man, I don't want to hurt you, would you just stop for a second and *listen* to me?"

"You're her. That Gray Widow bitch. You're *her.*"

Janey didn't realize what was happening until the last instant. From somewhere Simon produced a knife, or something like a knife, and lurched at her with it clutched in both hands. Janey yelped and rolled out of the way as the blade punched through the carpet and wooden flooring where she'd been half-lying.

Simon screeched again, ripped the knife out of the floor, and threw himself at her. Knife? The thing looked more like some kind of *sword.* Janey made it to her feet and sidestepped Simon's rush, planted a foot on Simon's butt, and shoved. That sent him through the second glass door. Simon's head connected with a huge oak desk right outside the stock broker's office with a sickening crack that coincided with a deafening alarm. The broker's office *did* have a security system.

That would mean police response in a matter of minutes. Simon jumped up out of the shower of broken glass and raised the knife over his head. For a second, less than a second, Janey got an eyeful of Simon's weapon: it looked for all the world like a unicorn horn, and spiraled down from a broad base to a needle-sharp tip.

In the next instant Janey realized she couldn't tell where the horn-thing ended and Simon's hands began.

Still making an ear-splitting racket, Simon turned and charged the length of the broker's-office hallway, headed straight for a huge picture window at the far end. He dove head-first through it and plunged out of sight in a shower of glass shards.

Just before he jumped, Janey saw him pull his arms apart, and the horn weapon *unraveled,* separated into long, tendril-like fingers.

Janey ran to the window. Several pedestrians stopped on the sidewalk below to peer up at the noise, but Simon was nowhere to be seen. Glittering electric blue lights and sirens swerved around a corner, approaching swiftly, and Janey retreated into the shadows.

* * *

Red and white emergency lights strobed through the trees and sirens split the night air as Janey walked back out of the woods and into the clearing, once again wearing her street clothes, the Vylar suit stashed safely in the basement. An ambulance approached, driving carefully on the brick walkways. Tim sat next to the jogger. He'd draped the girl's torn sweatshirt over her, and kept a knot of curious passers-by from crowding in too close. He looked up as Janey shouldered her way through.

"Janey? Are you okay? Why the hell did you run after him like that?"

Janey squatted on her haunches. "I'm fine. I was just trying to get a good look at the guy, but he was too fast. Is she hurt?"

Tim's eyes looked hollow. "I don't know. She's breathing all right, and her pulse is steady, but I think she's in shock. And she's lost some blood." He gestured with one finger, traced a curving path up the girl's arm. "From here. These marks." Janey looked where he was pointing, and her stomach clenched tight.

Simon had covered the girl's right forearm with deep purple bruises that shone slickly with blood in the diffuse light from the walkway lamps. The bruises encircled her arm, wrapping around it again and again, starting at her wrist and winding up past the elbow. Janey hissed involuntarily as she saw the same marks around the girl's neck, like a high collar.

"She was strangled?"

The ambulance was almost there, its sirens deafening, so Janey had to shout. Tim shook his head.

"I don't think so! I can't tell what the hell happened here! There's bleeding, but I don't think she has any cuts or wounds!"

The sirens shut off, and Janey got out of the way as two paramedics rushed toward the girl. The onlookers scattered. Tim answered several terse questions, and moved aside as the paramedics loaded the girl into the ambulance. Janey stayed apart from them since she knew she'd only get in the way. Se felt too distracted to be of much use in any case.

Weird fingers aside...the thought of someone losing blood without being cut made her flesh crawl.

Tim's touch on her arm startled her.

"Listen, Janey, I'm going to ride along with them in the ambulance. Come with me?"

"Ah, no, no, uh, listen, I'm—uh, I'm going to go back and get the car. To, uh, so, y'know..." She was babbling, and knew it, and wondered how much of it was an act. As Tim watched her, his eyebrows bunched together.

"Are you okay? Did that guy hurt you?"

"No, no, I'm fine, really! I'll just, um, call you later, or you can call me. Can you get home from the hospital okay?"

"Yeah, no problem, I can get home." She could see the thought in his eyes: *she's lost her mind.*

"Okay, well, I'll talk to you tomorrow, then?" She backed away, headed toward the trees.

* * *

Tim watched her go for a moment before he yelled after her. "Hey, wait a minute! You're going to have to talk to the police!" But Janey was already gone.

He climbed aboard the ambulance after the EMTs loaded the college girl, and before the doors swung shut, the paramedic riding in back asked, "Where's your girlfriend headed?"

Tim chewed his lower lip for a second. "I think she's going to go change clothes."

CHAPTER ELEVEN

Janey's thoughts spun as she drove back to the LaCroix. She'd originally intended to go to the basement before she did anything else, but she realized that, if her story were to hold any water at all, she'd at least have to put the car back where Tim would expect to find it. She wasn't sure how much sense her actions made to an observer—first rushing off to face the attacker, then freaking out and leaving—but she felt sure she could think up some explanation to cover the weirdness.

Hard empty eyes, fingers white and jointless and twisting.

Janey screeched to a halt in the LaCroix's private parking lot. She jumped out, slammed the door, looked around briefly, and sprinted for the unbroken shadow behind the building's dumpster. She fell into it and flickered away.

Janey rolled to her feet in the basement. The Vylar suit hung there on its rack, just as she'd left it. Another ten seconds and she was wearing the suit, more comfortably now since she didn't have to drag it on over her street clothes.

Her heart hadn't stopped pounding since she'd first heard the girl's scream in the park. She took a deep breath and calmed herself. Focused and centered.

Janey vanished in a breath of blistering air.

* * *

Thousands, millions of lights everywhere sparkled and glittered, but reached only so far; darkness surrounded each one, and she flickered there, a hot, heavy presence wherever the light fell short.

Only a few people felt her passing, and then only as a sudden sweltering wind. A uniformed policeman, sitting in his patrol car in an alley between a convenience store and a CVS, froze with his lukewarm coffee halfway to his lips, abruptly certain that someone was watching him. He turned, scanned the alleyway and saw nothing, but gooseflesh crawled over him—and his windshield abruptly fogged. When he lifted a slightly shaky hand to take a sip of the coffee he discovered it was steaming.

A prostitute lounging against a burned-out street lamp gasped as a breath of tropical air brushed her. The metal of the lamp almost burned her partially bare back, and she jerked away from it with a startled yelp. She tried to rub the spot, but her tight dress restricted her movement. As she cast about for someone she could ask to look at her back, she saw something move around the corner of a nearby building and vanish into an alley. She thought it might have been a woman...but for a second, just a second, she thought she saw *through* it.

The heat from her back twined itself with fear, flashed into her stomach and out along her bones, and she turned and ran.

* * *

Janey had never covered as much ground as she covered tonight. From shadow to shadow, darkness to darkness, she flickered in, took in her surroundings, flickered away again. Twice she broke up muggings and left the assailants stretched out on the concrete. The first of the would-be victims began to offer shaky thanks before Janey left. The other bolted away without a word.

"I'm sorry..." It was like a plea. The young man had sounded so pitiful.

And frightened.

"I'm sorry..."

Janey had just stepped out of the shadows beside a dilapidated frame house in one of the metropolitan area's worse residential districts when she heard the distinct sound of flesh striking flesh, followed by a howl of pain. She reached into the dark, back to the basement, and brought a second police baton to her. Janey snapped both of them open and moved closer to the nearest window.

The house was a two-story, built onto the side of a hill and separated from the next one by a fifteen-foot-wide alley that sloped sharply down toward the backs of the structures. Lights visible through thin curtains burned in all the windows of both houses, but if she stayed quiet, there was no reason anyone should see her. Not until she wanted them to.

Janey crept forward and raised her head to the window. Dingy, faded beige curtains had spots of mildew on them. Hung incorrectly, they left a half-inch gap below the right panel, which let her see into the house's front room.

Her hands tightened around the batons.

A huge white teenager with long, greasy blond hair stood unsteadily in the middle of the room. He couldn't have been more than eighteen. He wore blue jeans and a white T-shirt emblazoned with the Confederate flag, and he clutched a young, shapely Hispanic girl by one wrist, and even as he weaved on his feet he drew back a block-like fist and smashed it across her face.

The teenager's words through the glass were badly slurred, and the only one Janey could pick out was "whore." The girl screamed. Her face ran purple and red in a mass of bruises and contusions, and one split lip bled openly. Janey thought he heard her call the young man "Jeff."

Janey's teeth ground together as she left the window.

Jeff dropped the girl and spun around as the front door exploded off its hinges. It slammed to the floor and kicked up a huge cloud of dust as the glass in its one small window shattered. Janey came through the doorway, batons held ready, and Jeff grunted and pulled a knife.

The girl backed into a corner, forgotten, her one good eye widening. She whispered *"Gray Widow,"* and jumped up and fled into a back room.

Janey watched Jeff carefully. The kid was flying high, that

much was clear, but she couldn't tell from what. She held the batons ready and waited for him to make the first move.

Obligingly, Jeff raised the weapon, a bone-handled sheath knife with a five-inch blade, and swung at Janey. Janey stepped aside, brought a baton down on Jeff's elbow and kicked his feet out from under him. Jeff landed face-down, but held on to the knife, so Janey knelt beside him and cranked his elbow up, pinning the back of his hand flat to the floor. Jeff's tendons obligingly spasmed open, and Janey took the knife out of his unresisting fingers.

Pinned to the dirty floorboards and helpless, Jeff began screaming at her. "Fuckin' bitch! *You cain't come in here like 'is!*" Jeff tried to spit at her, but his face was pressed too tightly to the floor. "Fuckin' cunt, I'ma bend you in half an' pound yore pussy till it bleeds, y'hear me? *Y'hear me?*"

The hatred in Jeff's voice took Janey off-guard. Not enough to make her loosen her hold on him, but enough to realize the sheer depth of it. She lowered her voice to a smoky growl. "You're not going to do a damn thing."

"Fuck you! I'll rape you till yer dead, bitch! Gitcher cunt hands off'a me, *git 'em off'a me you fuckin' cunt bitch!*"

A feminine voice somewhere else in the house shouted, "Gray Widow! Gray Widow!" and multiple footsteps pounded up what sounded like a wooden staircase. Janey had just enough time to realize she might have made a serious mistake when a door burst open and five more redneck teenagers boiled out of it, a collection of neck beards and "Don't Tread On Me" T-shirts, and every one of them was armed.

Janey rolled out of the way as the first spray of bullets kicked at the floor and wall. She thought a couple of the rounds might have hit Jeff, who didn't try to rise from where Janey had pinned him. Janey dropped the police batons, and throwing spikes whickered and flashed in the air and sank deep into the gun hands of two of the youths.

The other three fired madly, randomly, screaming at her and

each other. The room filled with the roar of gunfire, and Janey heard bullets buzzing past her like super-sonic hornets. Dust and bits of plaster clouded around her as the gunshots tore huge chunks out of the floor, walls, and ceiling, and for an instant Janey grew disoriented.

A large-caliber round took her in the side, kicked her off her feet and forced the air from her lungs in a whoosh. Gasping, she rolled again, throwing more spikes. Two of them sank into the right legs of two more of the teenagers, but the rest went wide. The pain of the impact began to reach her, and she doubled over, clutched her ribs, but didn't lose her balance. She knew the Vylar padding had dispersed a lot of the force of impact, and probably kept her ribs from shattering.

Janey straightened, willing her eyes to focus, just as the one unhurt youth fired an Uzi. Seven bullets stitched their way across Janey's chest and knocked her backward through the front window. A shower of broken glass followed her down into the shadows.

* * *

Simon dropped away from another truck onto an ill-lit section of street.

He straightened his clothes, set off at what he hoped looked like an easy stroll down the sidewalk, and tried not to let his outward appearance reflect his emotions, which yawed wildly between rage and shame.

Absently he pulled an inch-long shard of glass out of his lower chest. He didn't notice as the wound sucked the blood back in and sealed itself shut.

The sudden interruption of the proceedings had done nothing to stop his urge. He needed it. And hated himself for needing it. His mother and the house in Louisiana called to him, and he wanted to go home, but that line of thought slammed into the urge, which strummed along his nerves harder every second.

He'd have to do it. Again.

Briefly he thought about the tall woman from the park, the woman who'd put on the gray suit and chased after him. The woman who...stepped into the darkness and...moved *through* it... Simon shut his eyes and waved his hands in the air. Couldn't think about *that.* That wasn't real. He said it over and over again, first silently, then out loud.

Simon stopped abruptly and stared down at his hands. For the first time it hit him: the monster under the bed. The monster in the dark. Maybe it was the bitch in the mask...but it was also *him.* Simon Grove, himself. The face in the mirror. The thing in the dark was *him.*

He felt more afraid than ever, and wanted to cry. *Concentrate. Come on, think about something else!*

Simon glanced around him as he walked, taking in his surroundings.

He hadn't been in Atlanta for long, and was still unfamiliar with it. He didn't recognize the place where the truck had unknowingly delivered him. The dull, steady vibrations of I-285 hummed from a nearby overpass. The street he now walked down appeared to lead into a low-income housing district after it passed under the freeway.

Up a steep hill on his right, however, a brightly lit apartment complex looked out over the city. The units, stacked three high, presented perfectly square faces, white stucco faded to gray, decorated with wrought iron railings on patios and balconies. *Straight out of the sixties,* Simon thought. He looked over his shoulder and saw an entrance to the complex, a steep blacktop drive winding up the hill. He reversed his course and walked quickly toward the sign.

Bright lights artfully concealed in low shrubbery illuminated the words.

"Crestwood View," Simon read aloud. He started up the smooth, recently re-paved drive, and whistled a tune.

The drive was lit better than the street it branched off of.

Every sixty feet or so a street lamp overhung the way, giving Simon enough light to notice a macadam jogging trail that wound its way down the hillside, crossed the drive, and angled back up toward the apartments. He eyed the path and thought for a moment about late-night joggers, until a car's headlights washed over him.

He stopped walking and raised a hand to shield his eyes.

A late-model Chrysler made its way up the drive, and thanks to the street lamps' illumination Simon could see the driver. He locked eyes with her for a long, heart-stopping moment before she rolled past him.

Simon remained perfectly still, stared after her, and savored her image like an aftertaste.

He sprinted after the car.

Its taillights had already disappeared around a bend in the drive, so he didn't worry about her seeing his pursuit, though he did have to hold himself back to keep from catching up with her. He'd discovered he could move at a good thirty or forty miles an hour when he tried.

Long, golden hair. Bronze skin.

The driver. Simon knew he had to have her. At the top of the hill he stopped, ducked down behind a hedge, and scanned the parking lot. No cars moved, no doors thumped shut, so he dashed to the edge of the first building, where the lot turned to the left. *There.* He saw the Chrysler pull into a space in front of a building with a three-foot-high letter G on it, and the girl got out. He couldn't see her face clearly at this distance, but her athletic body was visible enough, and he felt the twinge, the need to change, and fought it back.

Light eyes, blue, maybe green. Wide mouth.

She went to the trunk, opened it, got out two small bags of groceries, and disappeared into the front central door of the building. Access was only possible through one of the two central doors; all the doors to the apartments opened onto a long hall down the building's middle. Simon almost panicked. He couldn't see her anymore, had no way of knowing where she was, and his throat began to close up with anxiety.

He ran across the parking lot, almost on all fours in his haste, and came up hard against the back of her car, his breathing ragged and his eyes glued to her building.

Simon gasped with relief when a light came on in one of the second-floor apartments. A silhouette moved over the blinds, and he crawled around to the side of her car, trying to calm down a little. He drew his knees up to his chest and sat there, fingers clenched into white-knuckled fists.

Simon could feel the bones of his jaw loosen, and he ground his teeth together. He saw his mother's face, so sad and disapproving whenever she caught him doing something wrong. He couldn't imagine what she'd say if she caught him like this. *I'm sorry, Mama. I've tried to stop, I have, I promise.* He tried to think of something, anything but the woman, but he knew it wouldn't make any difference.

"Ace of spades," he mumbled into his knees. "King of spades. Queen of spades. Jack of spades." Simon worked his way down to the deuce, then started with diamonds. At the ten of diamonds he felt in control of himself enough to stand up, so he made his way as quickly as he could around the building to the back side, and clung to the wall once he got there. Maybe...maybe if he just *saw* her. Maybe that would be enough.

The view was impressive. The hill hadn't looked all that high from the street below, but the Crestwood View apartments weren't kidding about the View part. A strip of grass about ten yards wide separated the complex from an almost sheer drop of roughly fifty feet, tumbling down to end at the street where Simon had begun his climb. A chest-high chain link fence ran along the edge of the drop-off, protection for careless toddlers and drunken college students. Simon crept out to the fence, trying to keep in the deepest of the shadows, and looked back up at the apartments.

The railings of the second-floor balconies leered down at

him like multiple sets of teeth, and he felt afraid. His jaw was back to normal, and his hands unclenched after some effort. He rubbed the joints of his left hand, lingered over them, paused to work his ring finger back and forth. He pulled, and the knuckle popped.

Simon sank down against the rust-spotted fence and began to cry.

The urge wasn't nearly as strong as it had been, not now. He could walk away. Walk away, find a quiet place, call his house, call his mother. She'd know what to do, know where he could go. Maybe...maybe she could tell him how to keep from...from doing it anymore. It wasn't right, wasn't right at all, and he knew it. How many nights had he screamed himself awake from the nightmares? How many nights since it first happened? He remembered the look on her face, in her eyes, *remembered,* ha, he couldn't make himself forget, when she heard about what had happened at the neighbors' house. He knew all the stories in the paper by heart. Every word.

He knew another word.

Addict.

Simon got to his feet, forced himself to breathe slowly and deeply. He touched his jaw, his eyes, and held his hands up in front of his face. They were thin and pale and normal.

"Can I do this? Can I just, can I just stop? Can I quit?" The sound of his own voice seemed very small and weak.

The light in the girl's apartment came on at that moment, and Simon shoved his hands behind his back with a small whimper. A sliding glass door opened, and she came out onto the balcony, her golden hair turned dark in the moonlight. He stood, rooted, waiting for her to scream and disappear into the apartment—but she stayed there for long minutes, staring out at the city, before she turned and went back inside.

She hadn't seen him.

Too bad for her.

His eyes hard white pinpoints, Simon crept across the strip of lawn, his torso long and pale and brushing the grass.

His movements were quick and fluid and sure, and as his joints reconfigured themselves, things like heavy white worms writhed below his wrists.

* * *

Darlie Gilbert closed the glass door to her balcony but didn't lock it. She planned on going back out as soon as her hot chocolate was ready, to relax in her white plastic lawn chair and prop her feet up on the railing. Darlie emptied the essentials from her purse, as she always did, placing wallet and keys and loose change on the kitchen counter next to the microwave, ready to transfer to another handbag. She had seven different ones and liked to rotate them.

Attached to the keys was a canister of pepper spray, an item her father had practically demanded she carry.

"If you insist on living alone," he'd said, about four thousand times, "the least you can do is keep some protection with you."

Protection from the big bad men out there. Darlie smiled to herself. She might not have been very tall, though she had always felt that five feet three inches was certainly tall enough, but Darlie was very nearly solid muscle, and wasn't afraid of much. Still, no harm in granting her dad's request.

She contemplated the young man she'd seen on the way in, the dark-and-handsome type who'd stared at her as she drove past. She hadn't seen him around the complex before, but that didn't mean anything. She wasn't even sure who lived two doors down from her. Maybe she'd look for him around the laundry room.

While she waited for the water to boil she went through her voice mail. The first one was her boss at the art gallery, where she worked as Assistant Manager, a job which ranged from giving tours to arranging exhibits to helping with the framing. He wanted her to work an extra shift next week because of the new paintings from Janey Sinclair, which were scheduled to show up on Tuesday. She smiled at that, and felt a tiny thrill; she hoped Sinclair's new pieces would be as electrifying as her previous ones.

The other message was from her father, who called her every few days, "to make sure you're all right." She listened to and deleted both messages. The kettle began its steam-driven harmonica chime.

As she poured the water into a Kermit the Frog coffee mug she heard a thump on her balcony. Frowning, she put the kettle back on the eye and moved to look around the corner, expecting to see one of the several stray cats that made their rounds of the neighborhood. Before she could tell what had caused the sound, she heard the latch click open, which only caused her a bit of puzzlement in the half-second she had to think about it. Then she rounded the corner from the kitchen to the living room.

The Kermit mug crashed to the floor as her arm spasmed. Her lungs wouldn't work, and she stood in the kitchen doorway in silence and watched.

Something that might have been a man stepped from Darlie's balcony into her apartment and grinned at her. Eyes like two tiny search beams speared out from its face, set deep above an impossibly distended jaw that bristled with glistening spines. Its chest and legs were normal, but the arms were half again as long as a regular human's, and the hands... Dead-white tentacles squirmed and writhed where the fingers should have been, ten undulating tendrils at least two feet long, each one terminating in a sharp, bony point. The creature spread its arms wide, and the finger-tendrils fanned out and lengthened until they tapped and scraped the walls and ceiling. Grotesquely, it wore normal clothing, a black T-shirt and charcoal gray jeans.

Darlie's breathing stopped as she made a connection. *The guy on the road.*

"Yoo aghe ee doo ghis," the creature said, and repeated the words, and she realized what it was saying: *You made me do this.*

It crouched, pulled the fingers back in and coiled to leap at her.

Darlie pulled the can of pepper spray off the counter and

fired a stream directly into the creature's eyes.

Two seconds later both her ears began to bleed as every piece of glass in the apartment shattered.

The creature sucked in air for another scream and flailed toward her, but she backed up against the wall and fired again, and this time hit not only the creature's eyes but also its open mouth. It screamed again, louder than a jet engine, than ten jet engines, and Darlie thought her skull would come apart.

As she watched, the jaw wriggled and retracted, became human again, and the creature shouted, "Ow! *Ow!* Shit shit shit *shit!*"

The writhing tentacles gouged runnels out of the walls and ceiling and tore gashes in the carpet as the creature jerked and twisted like a tornado. It ran and smashed its way back out through the sliding doors as if they'd been made of construction paper.

Just before it jumped over the railing of her balcony, the creature screamed, *"Bitch!"*

She stood with her knees locked and stared after it, and realized numbly that she still had the plunger pressed on the can of pepper spray. She took her thumb off it. She further realized she wasn't completely deaf when she heard the neighbors banging on her door.

* * *

Simon hit the ground badly and felt the bones of his shoulder break. He heaved up off the ground and got away from the apartment as fast as he could, propelling himself forward as much with his extended fingers as with his feet. His eyes felt as if they'd been scooped out of his head and replaced with burning embers, and each breath he took drew acidic fumes into his lungs. He didn't see the fence until he'd crashed into it, and didn't remember its significance until he'd levered himself over it.

The slick grass of the hillside offered no traction at all as he fell. The rock outcropping he met halfway down could have provided a handhold if he hadn't been agonized and blinded. As it was, his bad shoulder slammed directly into it. Another jet-engine scream tore out of him, abruptly cutting off when he bounced off the trunk of a tree. He felt his ribs splinter.

Simon rolled to a stop in the ditch along the street where he'd originally jumped off the eighteen-wheeler. All his insides seemed to have changed into tiny, sharp-edged rocks that ground together when he breathed. His vision began to clear, just the tiniest bit, but his eyes and mouth and lungs still burned unbearably.

He closed his eyes and tried to shy away when a car pulled to a stop on the street and headlights fell on him.

Two sets of footsteps approached. Even through the pain, the urge was still there, lingering at the back of everything with a needling, despicable insistence. His fingers were still extended, and with a feeble grasping twitch he tried to send them toward whoever made the footsteps.

A man's voice said, "Oh...sweet *God.*"

A woman spoke, sharply. "We can't let anybody see him. Come on, give me a hand here."

Simon felt a sharp sting on his neck, separate from all the other pain, and his limbs went completely numb. Two people grabbed him roughly under the arms and legs and lifted, and he realized he'd been dropped in the trunk of a car just before the lid slammed closed and he blacked out.

CHAPTER TWELVE

Images slammed through Janey's mind in pain-rimmed jump cuts. *Flash.*

Sixteen years old, calling for her father. An unfamiliar car sits in the driveway. She hears the sound of chains through the open kitchen door, a shadow moves, and something like a tree falls on her head.

Flash.

She sits in a chair next to her father. Chains bind them both. They're in the chairs Janey's mother picked out when they bought this house. Janey misses her mother, and wants to call to her when she sees her father crying. Shadows move toward them.

Flash.

The men are huge, distorted, like ogres. When one of them pulls a gun it gleams small and slick in the light from the fixture overhead. Her father tries to talk, tries to beg, but the hammer cocks back and the barrel swings around, centered on Janey's chest. Her father screams, and the air goes cold.

Flash.

The ogre with the gun clamps a hand to his own face and curses, and there's something on the floor next to his foot, it's small and wet, and he staggers and steps on it. The other men draw back from him, and he digs the gun into the skin between Janey's father's eyes and pulls the trigger. Janey's throat hurts from screaming and crying and begging, and she can't see because there's something hot and wet in her eyes, and the gun turns on her and fires again, and a third time.

Flash.

Janey opened her eyes on darkness and aching pain, and started to panic when she couldn't see. Her breath caught in her throat as she strained. She tried to focus herself by reciting the alphabet backward, but only got to W when the first wave of real pain crashed across her chest. The memory of the kid with the Uzi came back to her just as her night vision did. Her mind hitched, and for less than a second she was there again, back in the kitchen, lying on the floor next to her dead father. A flash, quickly faded. She groaned and tried to sit up, but collapsed onto her back.

She didn't think any ribs were broken. The Vylar was intact, and the armor padding seemed whole. She took a deep breath, which rewarded her with stabbing pains, deeply felt but not—quite—debilitating.

Janey pushed with her elbows and managed to rise into a sitting position, and only then realized she had no idea where she was.

Oh my God. I traveled blind.

Stunned, she sat frozen for several moments. Shudders skittered through her body. Nauseated and weak, she did her best to put out of her head thoughts of what might have happened. Anyone who'd ever read any science fiction knew what was *supposed* to happen if someone teleported into a solid object. Janey didn't know how accurate the stories were, had no plans to find out, and was horrified that she almost had.

She quickly patted herself down, took a fast inventory, and eventually decided all of her was still there, though she'd lost both the police batons. She unzipped the Vylar mask and rolled it up, exposing her mouth and nose, and took deep breaths regardless of the pain—but just as quickly pulled the mask back down. The smell of rich damp earth and the heavy, musty stench of mildew filled the air, but rolling over those two scents was the stink of human urine and feces. Janey wrinkled her nose and tried to take in her surroundings.

She sat on a packed, damp dirt floor, in a space maybe five feet high. Pipes emerged from very old brick walls to disappear both through gaps in the mortar and into the ceiling. The ceiling itself was composed of massive crossbeams and tongue-and-groove two-by-sixes, covered with mold and cobwebs. Against the far wall, maybe fifteen feet away, a squat water heater sat, housing a steady blue flame.

I'm in a cellar. She winced at the pain in her chest, knowing she would be a mass of bruises soon if she wasn't already...and something touched her shoulder. She almost left the ground.

Janey whirled, a fist drawn back, and saw the edge of a ragged shape scuttle behind a brick support column ten feet away, the motion punctuated by a metallic clinking. *A chain.*

The sound knocked her back into the memory, blood in her eyes and two bleeding holes in her chest. Her stomach lurched, but she steadied herself, and soon the sensation faded.

Once behind the column, whatever had touched her remained still.

Janey crept forward slowly, eyes narrowed. The clinking sounded again, and she saw it now: a heavy iron chain connected to a bracket driven into the brick wall at the other end of the cellar. The chain dropped into the dirt, ran across the floor...and ended at the shape behind the column. Whatever it was didn't move, and she heard its breathing, fast and shallow.

The cellar where Janey crouched was rectangular, about thirty feet long and half that much in width. Four brick columns rose out of the dirt to connect with the flooring above. A few cardboard boxes sat here and there on the floor, all of them placed near the water heater, far from the chain and the thing attached to it.

The chain clinked again, and the tattered, dark shape behind the column moved, just enough for one eye to emerge.

Janey's spine froze over. Her pain entirely forgotten, she scrambled forward, bent almost double for the low ceiling.

A little girl hid from her behind the column. Dressed in decaying gray rags, she looked to be about ten years old. The chain in the dirt was welded to a thick iron ring around her left ankle. The girl stared at Janey with enormous eyes as she knelt before her, and

Janey realized she could see her. Janey unzipped and pulled off her mask, ignoring the stench, let her night vision relax, and saw that a few thin threads of light made their way into the cellar through a square patch on one wall.

She brought the night vision up again, and saw the patch was actually a window. A window that had been bricked over. A few cracks had developed in the cheap mortar, and let in the weak, purplish luminescence of a mercury vapor street lamp.

Returning her attention to the girl, Janey kept her voice low.

"I'm a friend," she said, and the girl grunted and moved away from her.

The girl never took her huge eyes off of Janey, but she jerked away even more quickly when Janey reached out a hand to her. The girl clutched something to her chest like a prized possession—held it the way other children hold blankets or teddy bears—and it took Janey several moments to figure out what it was.

Scratched and scarred, every line filled with dirt from the cellar floor, the girl's prize was the black plastic bottom from an old two-liter soft drink bottle.

The full extent of what she was witnessing began to dawn on Janey, and she sat down heavily.

When she didn't move for a bit, the girl came closer, still staring at her.

With a sense of dread, Janey tried again. "My name is Janey. What's yours?" She smiled, her best, warmest smile, but the girl didn't answer. She only stared, and jerked away whenever Janey moved her hands. "Can you say anything?"

No answer.

"Can you talk to me?"

No answer.

"Can you talk at all?"

She only stared.

Slowly, trying not to spook the girl again, Janey moved to the bracket where her chain attached to the wall. Above it she noticed a short ladder, folded and nestled between two of the crossbeams, covering what looked to be a trapdoor. A trapdoor leading up to the house above.

She heard the chain clink, and the girl joined her, staring up at the trapdoor. The girl made a sound...a low moan—a sound that shouldn't ever have been made by someone so young, saturated with pain and hurt and longing. Janey's eyes filled with tears, and her jaw muscles clenched tight. She turned to the girl.

"I don't know if you can understand me or not. But I want you to know that I'll be back for you. You're not going to stay here. I don't know how you got here, or who put you here, but you're not going to stay here. I promise you that."

The girl's stare didn't change, but Janey thought she clutched the bottle bottom a little tighter.

Janey went to the window and began pulling the bricks away from it. The girl followed her, but the chain stopped her short. The mortar was old and poorly applied, and Janey soon had the window completely exposed. A square, solid beam of light made its way into the cellar now. The girl stayed out of it, squinting her eyes, but she never stopped watching Janey. Janey looked outside for a moment, moved away from the window into the darkness, pulled her mask back on and flickered out.

The world transformed outside the cellar. This far into the wee hours, the night had grown cooler, but the neighborhood Janey saw seemed to exude warmth no matter what the temperature. Tall, beautiful pin oak and pine trees lined well-lit streets. Immaculate sidewalks framed manicured lawns, and most of the mailboxes were brick, many with ivy or flowers growing on or around them. The houses themselves, while not huge, were decidedly upper-class, each of them with enough yard space for children and dogs to play in, yet not so much that a neighbor would seem far away. Janey turned slowly, taking it all in, and finally stopped when she faced the house from which she had just emerged. It was beautiful, and at a glance seemed to be the oldest in the immediate area. Lights burned inside, several on the ground floor and one on the second. An expensive mountain bike rested against the front porch railing. A mini-van sat in front of the garage.

Janey's chest throbbed again, joined by a white-hot spear behind her eyes as her teeth ground together. The grass underneath her burned and died, and two more batons nestled into her hands. She snapped them open, walked steadily to the side of the house, flickered into a shadow, and emerged in the dining room.

The interior of the house seemed to be just as well-appointed as the exterior. Heavy, dignified oak filled the dining room, a table seating at least eight surrounded by chairs upholstered in a stately sea green. Light glimmered from an open doorway to Janey's left, and she approached it, moving silently.

The living room.

A teenage boy, maybe seventeen, sat slumped on the plush couch, watching a huge TV with the sound piped to a set of headphones. A premium channel was showing the original *RoboCop*, and the boy sat mesmerized. His mouth hung slightly open, his eyes glazed. A bag of Bugles rested next to him on the couch, and he held a two-liter bottle of soda laxly in one hand.

Janey backed away and moved to the other side of the dining room, where a stairway led to the second floor. Shadows draped the house, and a flicker took her to the top of the stairs.

Light shone from a door to her right. It stood slightly ajar, and she peered inside. Another teenager, this one a girl slightly older than the couch slug downstairs, lay in bed reading a magazine. A box of tissues lay beside her on the bed, and every few seconds she sniffled. Janey stepped away, still totally silent. The door she was looking for stood at the end of the hall, also slightly ajar. Not that a lock would have made a difference.

The man and woman asleep in the king-sized bed looked blissfully happy.

He was big, barrel-chested and thick-armed, with a full head of silver hair. One of those arms rested under the head of his wife, a handsome dark-haired woman in a silk nightgown. Janey stood beside their bed, stared down at them as they slept, and couldn't decide which she felt more, fury or disbelief.

Two worlds sat atop one another: one filled with PTA meetings and apple butter and house payments, the other narrow and crusted with dirt and mold and stench. These people lived their lives, walked among everyone else, while they kept a ten-year-old girl chained in their crawlspace.

With sick fury gnawing at her heart, Janey knew that if she had had a gun at that moment, she would have blown the man's head off, and the woman's right after.

She stood there, trembling, for so long that her muscles began to cramp. Her chest ached unmercifully, as did her side, where the first bullet had struck her. Her breathing grew erratic.

The big silver-haired man rolled over, opened his eyes, and looked directly at her, and Janey didn't think she'd ever seen a human being look more surprised in her life. The silver-haired man tensed and opened his mouth, probably to scream, but before he had the chance Janey stepped backward, into the thickest of the room's shadows, and flickered away.

* * *

The silver-haired man lay very still as the gray wraith vanished in the darkness, and didn't move as the temperature in the bedroom skyrocketed. He got up, staring into the shadows all around him, and turned down the room thermostat as sweat popped out across his brow. Scared witless, he got back into bed, pulled the covers over his head, and spent the next forty-five minutes telling himself that what he had seen was just a nightmare.

Long accustomed to convincing himself of his own version of reality, he finally drifted back to sleep.

* * *

For close to an hour Janey crouched on the roof of a Wal-Mart, grinding her teeth and hurting and hating.

What if it was some kind of special circumstance? She had no proof the child's captivity was long-term, she'd only seen her this once.

Except that the girl was encrusted with dirt, and unable to speak.

But maybe...maybe she needed to be kept down there. Maybe she was a psychotic killer.

Sure. That explained her timidity.

But what if the people in the house didn't know about it? What if a neighbor, or someone else, kept her there, chained up like that?

With only one access, through the house. Right.

Janey opened and closed one of the police batons. Snap. Click-click-click. Snap. Click-click-click.

Eventually she remembered a name, and made a decision, and vanished into a patch of darkness.

* * *

7:09 a.m.

Zach Feygen's apartment was a modest townhouse on Briarcliff Road, narrow and squeezed into a line of six identical units. Janey stepped out of the shadows into Feygen's living room.

A light burned in the kitchen, and Janey pressed her back to a wall and sidled closer to it. Upstairs a radio played. A pass-through bar linked the kitchen and the living room, and Janey stooped to look through it. A bowl sat on a counter next to a box of Grape-Nuts and a drinking glass.

A board creaked over her head, and Janey's pulse sped up. Either Feygen came downstairs, started to prepare breakfast, then went back upstairs for something, or there was someone else in the apartment. Feeling stupid that she hadn't considered that, Janey leaned against the wall and tried to decide what to do.

Just then a door off the kitchen popped open, and a slender young woman wearing only a pair of white lace panties stepped out into the room, carrying a shirt and a pair of slacks that looked as though they'd come straight from a drier. Her skin was as dark as Feygen's, but her eyes and cheekbones indicated Asian blood, probably in the immediate family. She missed Janey entirely, hung the clothes over the back of a chair, and poured the cereal bowl full of Grape-Nuts.

Caught flat-footed and embarrassed beyond belief, Janey was set to flicker right back out of the townhouse when she heard a handgun cock about three feet behind her head. Simultaneously the living room's overhead light flipped on. Janey carefully stepped away from the wall and slowly raised her hands, fingers splayed.

"Heather, put my shirt on." It was Feygen's voice, and from the sound of it Janey thought Feygen might shoot her in the back of the head without further preamble. She didn't try to turn around.

Heather came out of the kitchen, still mostly nude and holding her bowl of Grape-Nuts. "Why, what's—" When she saw Janey, she set the bowl down on a counter, wordlessly snatched up the shirt and covered herself with it. She stepped back into the kitchen to put it on.

Janey remained motionless, hands in the air, and fervently wished she could go back out and try this again.

"All right," Feygen said. "When I tell you, you're going to take two steps forward, real slow. Then you're going to use two fingers to take out those batons, and you're going to toss them on the couch. Nod if you understand."

Off the top of her head, as she nodded, Janey thought of eleven different ways to disarm Feygen. Still, she took the steps forward and dropped the batons onto Feygen's couch, exactly as ordered. "This isn't necessary. I'm here to talk to you."

Heather came back out of the kitchen, practically swimming

in Feygen's shirt, and edged past Janey with wide eyes. She stood behind and to one side of Feygen. Janey said, "May I turn around?"

"No, you may not. I'm trying hard right now to think of a reason not to put five or six big holes in your ass. The hell do you think you're doing, coming into my home?"

Janey closed her eyes and let her shoulders slump. "I can only ask you to believe me on this. I'm here to talk to you. I didn't realize you weren't alone. I didn't mean to scare anyone."

"Heather, baby, call 911, all right? Get your phone and dial the number, then hand it to me, all right?"

Janey said, "Wait, wait a minute, please. I'm here asking for your help. There's a little girl who desperately *needs* help, and much as I'd like to be the one to give it, the kind of help I can give isn't the kind she needs. Please listen to me."

Janey waited, still with her back turned to them, and when she didn't hear the beeps of a phone being dialed, she took a deep breath and very slowly turned around.

Heather stood with a phone in her hand, uncertain, and kept shooting glances back and forth between Janey and Feygen. Heather had long black hair in loose ringlets, and Janey figured her for early twenties, maybe twenty-two. Feygen stood like a mahogany carving, thick arms locked forward and feet set apart at shoulder-width. He wore a pair of pajama bottoms with little sailboats all over them, and no shirt. Janey would've smiled about the sailboats if Feygen hadn't looked so competent with the gun.

"Please. I'm not kidding about this. There's a little girl, and she needs help, and I'm only asking you to listen to me for two minutes. I'm serious. She could die."

The detective held a Beretta nine-millimeter. The Vylar would stop the rounds effectively enough, but Janey really didn't feel like getting shot again. She kept her hands up and waited.

Finally Feygen said, "Put the phone down, baby. Let's hear what the woman has to say before we haul her ass in." His eyes were solid black and cold and sharp, and Janey hadn't seen him blink yet.

"So go ahead. Talk."

Now that she had the chance, Janey couldn't think of where to start. She tried twice before she got it right. "I want to see some justice done. And I want it to be final. By the book."

Feygen didn't lower the gun, and Janey started to get annoyed. "Look, could you just put the gun down? I'm sorry I scared your girlfriend, I didn't mean to, it was an accident, but in case you haven't made the connection, I'm the one who saved your thick neck at the Hargett Theatre. The same one you saw bring that clerk to the hospital. You could at least give me the benefit of the doubt here."

Feygen studied her with slitted eyes. Finally he uncocked the gun and lowered it. Janey crossed her arms over her chest and leaned back against the edge of the pass-through bar. Heather said, "This is her? This is the woman from the theatre?"

Feygen's eyes never left Janey. "...Could be." To Janey: "The chick who showed up at the theatre that night kept me and a friend of mine from getting cut to pieces. If that was you...all right. I'll listen. Talk."

Janey told them about the little girl. She fudged on a few of the particulars, but didn't hold back on the details of the girl's living conditions.

Feygen shook his head when Janey finished.

"Well, that's the most full-of-holes story I've ever heard. Granted, if you are who you say you are, I'm in your debt. But that's a big if."

Janey sighed, exasperated. "That's why I came to you in the first place. I figured, since I'd already saved your life once, maybe you'd be a little more inclined to believe what I say. Listen, I swear to you, I'm telling you the truth. I couldn't just take the girl away. There'd be no way to prove her family had done that to her. People would think *I'd* taken her and abused her myself. The only way to help her is through Family and Children's Services, or some other agency with the proper authority, somebody to go through the right channels."

Janey leaned forward, her voice rising. "I don't want that girl near those people anymore. Not ever again. I want them in jail, for the rest of their worthless lives if possible, but more than that I want that girl taken care of. Cared for. Educated. They've already taken away most of her childhood. I don't want to let them have any more of her life."

Silence fell on the three of them. Feygen stared at Janey, Janey stared back at him, and Heather's eyes flitted from one to the other.

"All right. There was some weird shit at that scene, stuff we kept out of the papers. You tell me what that was, and I'll see what I can do."

Janey laughed once, short and sharp. "You mean the disappearing act, or the heat?"

Feygen's dark skin went a little gray around his face. He said, "Give me an address."

* * *

At 9:30 that morning, a patrol car pulled up in front of the home of Reggie Troland. Troland sold wholesale air conditioner parts and had already left for work. So had his wife June, a health care specialist at a nearby nursing home. Their son Chet was already at school, and that left only the daughter, Yvonne, still in the house.

Zach Feygen, along with a well-dressed, dark-haired woman and a uniformed officer, got out of the car and walked up the front steps. Feygen knocked on the door.

A minute later the door swung open and Yvonne greeted them, pasty-faced and in her bathrobe. "What do you want?" she asked through a cough. "You got me out of bed. I'm sick."

Feygen showed her his badge. "I'm Detective Zach Feygen. This is Officer Cardi and Kate Rodek, from the Department of Family and Children's Services."

Yvonne Troland's eyes got huge, and her face drained of what little color it had to begin with.

Feygen continued, "We'd like to ask you a few questions. About a little girl." He handed her a search warrant and walked past her into the living room as he spoke, so he didn't see her face and the further effect his words had on her. Kate Rodek did, and knew in an instant that everything Feygen had told her was true.

Without any further prodding, Yvonne Troland slumped to the floor, pulled her knees to her chest and curled her arms around them. Hid her face. She started crying. Feygen glanced at Rodek and Cardi, motioning with his head for Cardi to look around. Feygen found the door to the cellar himself, in the floor of a utility room at the back of the house. Taking a deep breath, he opened it, pushed down the short wooden steps, and made his way down into the darkness.

Kate Rodek stayed with Yvonne in the living room, in front of the open door, as the girl cried. Yvonne tried to say something through the tears, but she couldn't stop sobbing long enough to speak clearly. Rodek looked up as Feygen came back into the room, his eyes ancient, and pulled out his cell phone.

* * *

An ambulance and two more squad cars arrived a short time later. The paramedics brought the little girl—Yvonne said the child's name was Laura Jean—up out of the cellar on a stretcher. Her arms and legs were restrained, but still she kicked and thrashed and howled, partly at the strangers, but mostly at the light. Her eyes stayed screwed tightly shut. Kate Rodek stood close to Feygen as they took the girl away.

"It was just like you said," Rodek murmured.

Feygen's low voice rumbled just loud enough for her to hear. "The Gray Widow...I can't believe I'm gonna say this. And I hate to say it, I really do. But the Gray Widow's a good woman, Kate. I can feel it."

Rodek was silent for a moment. "Good or not, she's still a vigilante. You can't just decide the law doesn't apply to you. She's still a criminal."

Feygen didn't answer her.

At ten minutes after ten o'clock, in response to a call from one of her neighbors, June Troland arrived at her home to be met by Zach Feygen and six other members of the law enforcement community. Slamming her car door, she stormed up the sidewalk and shouted, "What the *hell* is going on here? Who's in charge?" Officer Cardi met her and tried to read her her rights, but she cut him off with, "Get off my lawn, you assholes! You're screwing up my grass!"

Feygen approached her. "Mrs. Troland."

June Troland rounded on him. "Are you in charge here? What the hell are all these people doing at my home? Where's Yvonne?"

"We have your granddaughter, Mrs. Troland," Feygen said.

He found June Troland's reaction to that immensely satisfying. All the blood drained from her face, seeped away down into her neck and disappeared. Her mouth hung slackly open. Feygen stepped forward, took her hands, cuffed them together, and finished reading her rights. She didn't reply or make any sound as he put her in a patrol car.

As the car with Mrs. Troland in it pulled away, a Channel 5 news van turned the corner and bore down on them. Feygen scowled and made a small growling sound. Vicki Chamberlain would be in that van, and a bigger pain in the ass he'd never encountered. He turned and started toward the house, away from her and her microphone and her questions, when a thought popped into his head. He glanced around until he saw Cardi standing by the side of the house.

Cardi was twenty-three, baby-faced, a decent rookie so far, and a good target for somebody like Chamberlain. Feygen ambled over near the young officer, turned partly away from him, pulled out his phone and leaned against the house.

"No, listen, that's what I'm saying," he said softly into the dead phone. He figured Cardi could hear him if he strained at it. "I got it from higher up... No, seriously, we got this tip from the Gray Widow."

He heard a small intake of breath from over his shoulder, and smiled a little, out of Cardi's sight. "That's right. She called somebody, brass I guess, and gave 'em this location. Told 'em about the little girl. ...'Oh shit' is right, man. ...Okay, thanks."

Feygen pocketed the phone again, leaned his head back against the wall, and turned to look at Cardi as if just noticing the young officer's presence.

"Hey, Cardi," he said, and motioned him over. "Listen, we got these reporters out there. Head out to the front, keep 'em out of the house, all right?"

"Ah, yeah, yeah sure," Cardi said, the impact of Feygen's one-sided phone conversation practically stamped on his face.

"Good, thanks." Feygen put a hand between Cardi's shoulder blades, gave him a gentle shove to send him on his way, and ducked inside the house.

Through the window in the front door he saw Vicki Chamberlain and a cameraman coming up the sidewalk. Chamberlain called out to Officer Cardi, who turned around and froze like a deer on the road. Vicki Chamberlain powered up her stadium-lights smile—which Feygen knew camouflaged a personality like a shark with a chain saw—and started asking Cardi questions.

Feygen chuckled and moved farther into the house.

* * *

At 11:15 that morning, Janey Sinclair rolled leisurely down the Trolands' street in her modest little Honda Civic, the driver's side window down and Bruce Springsteen on the stereo. She saw the squad cars clustered around the Troland house, piercing blue lights aglitter. Neighbors congregated to crane their necks and ask questions of uniformed officers. A news van sat at the curb.

Allowing herself her first totally unreserved, unselfconscious smile in two years, Janey rolled up the window and sang along with the Boss.

CHAPTER THIRTEEN

Janey walked into the police precinct on Spring Street that afternoon, asked a few questions, and was directed to Detective Chester Kraitz. The policeman waved Janey to a battered gray metal desk and said, "Have a seat while I get the right papers." Janey took the nicked and scarred wooden chair in front of the desk and sat, glancing around. Her chest and side hurt unmercifully, and deep breaths hurt even worse. She let her eyes unfocus briefly.

Z, Y, X, W...

Soon her breathing eased.

Kraitz was a stocky, barrel-chested man in his thirties, slightly below average height, with very closely cropped red hair, a neatly trimmed mustache, and brown eyes that could punch holes through concrete. His demeanor was cordial enough, but he made Janey uneasy.

"So you're here to give your statement about that mugging in Hammerfield Park last night, right?"

Janey nodded. "Yeah."

"And it took you till now to come in? Talk to us?" Kraitz glanced at his watch. "Fifteen hours later?"

Janey sat with wide eyes for a few seconds, and decided to act really, *really* stupid.

"Well, uh...I had to, like, get my car, y'know?" She tried to let her eyes glaze over. That part wasn't hard. *God, I'm tired.* "I didn't wanna just, like, leave it out there, y'know?"

Kraitz stared at her. Janey said, "Hey, I'm sorry, I didn't realize it was so important, I woulda come in already. Anyway, it was, like, really freaky out there."

The detective's pen hovered over a statement form. "Freaky? How?"

"Well, I mean, that poor girl, y'know? With all the blood and stuff. And I was thinking, holy shit, that coulda been me, y'know? What if he'd cut me up like that?"

Janey knew the girl hadn't been "cut up."

Detective Kraitz sat unmoving for some time. Janey began to think the man would spring across the desk and cuff her.

"Okay," Kraitz finally said. "So did you get a good look at this guy? At his face? Your boyfriend didn't. He was asking about you, by the way."

An unexpected jolt throbbed through her side, and the effort required not to gasp made her eyes unfocus again.

"Yeah, I totally got a good look at him."

Janey had tried to decide, the whole way to the police station, whether or not to be truthful in describing the young man who'd called himself Simon. She'd finally settled on a partial truth, since she couldn't do much good herself if she were locked up in a padded room somewhere.

Not that a padded room could hold her.

"He's a young guy. Pale, dark hair, thin. Sort of pretty, y'know? He had on black clothes, I couldn't tell exactly what. Jeans, maybe."

Kraitz said, "That's a pretty detailed description of somebody running away from you in the dark."

Janey shrugged, and gave Kraitz her absolute best ditzy grin.

"I was trying to take a photo. Y'know, like, with my phone. Couldn't get a shot, though."

"Did he say anything?"

"Nope. Not a word."

Kraitz handed Janey a sheet of paper with departmental letterhead on it.

At the top were the words, "VICTIM/WITNESS STATEMENT."

"Just write everything down there," Kraitz said. "Exactly as you told me. And fill out the stuff at the top."

Surprised, Janey looked at the piece of paper uncertainly.

She'd expected to come in, say what she had to say, and leave. Now she had to spend more time there, and—her eyes widened—one of the blanks was, "Highest level of education completed."

Completely aside from her agitation at last night's events and anxiety about being in the police station, she felt a little pang of shame.

Janey was twenty-seven, and officially had nothing more than an eleventh-grade education. She wasn't destitute, she had no health problems. Thanks to the ACA, she even had insurance now that didn't cost the proverbial arm and leg. There was no real reason she couldn't have gone back and at least gotten her GED. She just hadn't. Normally she didn't think about it much, since her life was progressing, after a fashion. But now, with it staring her in the face, she couldn't help but feel like sort of a loser.

Her face held carefully neutral, she checked the box beside "High school," and felt a little slimy. She quickly wrote down her abbreviated version of what had happened in the park.

It took about fifteen minutes. As Janey stood to leave she felt Kraitz's eyes on her back, drilling two little brown holes, and kept feeling them until she got outside.

On the way to the car she thought, *Well, that could have been worse, I guess, all things considered.*

* * *

Janey hadn't noticed Zach Feygen, sitting mostly hidden behind a partition, watching her. A few moments after Janey left, Feygen stood and wandered over to Kraitz, who glanced up at him and leaned back in his chair.

"Zach," Kraitz said, friendly. "What's up? How's your woman? Still lookin' good?"

"Better than ever," Feygen replied. "Hey, who was that girl you were just talking to?"

* * *

Dark dreams played out on the screen behind Simon's closed eyelids, filled with heavy, crushing weight, and...something else. A scent...? What was that? Something heavy. Musky.

He tried to stay asleep, but Ruby wouldn't leave him alone. Her whining grated on him, filled his head. He tried to reach out a hand to her, to pet her, maybe scratch behind her ears or thump her on the ribs. But he couldn't reach her, and when he tried harder his fingers started to feel strange.

A beautiful Alaskan Husky, Ruby belonged to Paul Burney, Simon's next-door neighbor. He and Paul were...what? Sixteen? No. Paul was sixteen; Simon was older by a year. Both his and Paul's houses had huge, perfect lawns, and a thin line of trees separated them. Paul and Ruby ran around their yard almost every day, played catch with Frisbees or wrestled on the ground. So Simon walked over one day, asked if he could play, too.

He'd never had a dog.

Ruby was so good, so sweet. Such a smart dog. Simon saw the intelligence in her eyes. She really looked back at him when he looked at her.

Eventually Paul began to let Simon take Ruby on walks by himself, if Paul had other places to be. Simon was happy to do it.

She was fun just to pet, with her thick fur and fuzzy ears and beautiful blue eyes. Whenever Simon stroked her neck Ruby pointed her nose straight up in the air, offered her throat for scratching, where the fur was dense and deep.

Ruby was such a good dog. She never barked for no reason, was always warm and friendly. Simon missed her. He began to cry, softly, as he reached out for her, tried to stroke her head, scratch her ears. But his fingers weren't right, and Ruby's whining wouldn't stop...

...and he realized he was the one whining.

Simon tried to open his eyes, but could only pry the lids apart the tiniest bit. He lay on a bed, indoors somewhere, in a place with white walls. He thought he saw two people nearby. They were talking.

Two people, a man and a woman, he could tell by the sounds of their voices, but he couldn't make out what they said. Only one word really got through: it was "nicely," maybe with one or two words attached to it. *"Coming along* nicely"? He couldn't quite understand it. He tried to move, and that caused him to feel his shoulder, and the gouging pain blacked him out again.

* * *

Dusk, and Simon's eyes opened again, clear and calm.

The memories hung there, and he walked through them: the golden-haired girl—he winced—the fall down the hill, the headlights. Frowning, he very carefully tried to move his shoulder, just an inch, just lift it off the bed. It worked. A little stiff, but no real pain. His eyes and throat felt cleansed, and he drew in a few deep breaths. Pleased, he sat up.

He was in a small bedroom in a house, on a twin bed. Dark brown wood paneling covered the walls. A small night table stood beside the bed with a reading lamp on it. Huge, overlapping squares of heavy gray plastic covered what looked like a hardwood floor. The closet, a wide type with two folding doors, stood open and perfectly empty, except for a hanger on which his clothes were draped. They looked to have been recently washed.

Guest bedroom, he thought.

He lifted the sheets and saw that he was wearing a pair of boxer shorts he didn't recognize. That started to freak him out, but before he could make any clear decisions the bedroom door opened and a woman walked in. She flipped on the overhead light and Simon flinched away from it for a second.

Older than he was, late twenties or so, she wore a burgundy silk jacket with a matching skirt and a white ruffled blouse. He'd thought for a moment she'd be bringing him a tray of food. That's what he always saw in the movies, when the main character woke up in some strange place, the first person he saw was always some attractive female with a tray of food. This woman was attractive, all right—more so the longer he looked at her—but empty-handed. She stood in the doorway and watched him with a blatantly speculative expression.

Attractive, yes... Simon felt himself responding, and almost immediately the other urge flared up right behind it. He remembered vividly the girl in the apartment, how much he'd wanted her, how he'd been so rudely denied, and the full need of it settled onto him.

He felt his eyes change. The woman saw it, and her own eyes narrowed, but she didn't move from the door. She crossed her arms just below her ample bosom and leaned against the doorframe, only watching him. That made Simon angry. He wasn't sure why, but it did. He didn't even try to fight it this time. He threw the sheets off him with already lengthening fingers and rolled forward, up onto his knees. His jaw dropped, distended, and the teeth came in, and he brought one leg up, ready to lunge off the bed toward the woman, and she said, "I think you need to calm down and get back in bed."

Simon stopped in mid-motion. His fingers rapidly returned to normal.

Calm down and get back in bed. Okay. That sounded reasonable. He nodded, his jaw re-formed and clicked shut, and he gathered up the sheet.

The woman pushed off of the doorframe and came into the room as he settled down onto the mattress with the covers around his chin.

"Now you just stay right there, like that, and listen while I talk to you."

Simon nodded, and stared at her. She was maybe a little heavy, a little more rounded than he liked, but the closer she got to him the more he found himself straining at the boxer shorts. He was acutely embarrassed, and he wanted to lift one leg, at least, to camouflage himself. But she'd told him to *stay right there, like that,* and that sounded pretty good, so he figured he'd go along with that. Even when she sat down on the edge of the bed.

But...but the need was on him *bad.* His fingers began to throb as the bones softened, re-formed, softened again, echoing his pulse. He saw the white pinpoints of his eyes reflected clearly in hers, and his jawline rippled. But she'd told him to stay, to listen. So he did, and it made him want to howl.

The woman leaned back, away from him, her expression speculative. "My name is Brenda, and I have a lot that I need to tell you." She stood up from the bed, went back to the door and pushed it all the way open. In the hallway outside the bedroom stood a small, dull-looking man in dark slacks, a white shirt, and a tie. He held a slim teenage girl by the arm, in such a way that he seemed to be keeping her upright as much as she was herself. The girl looked frightened, but made no move to break the man's grip. Drugged, Simon thought. That girl is sedated. And *pretty...*

"But I know you must be absolutely starving," Brenda said. "I'll come back and speak with you when you're better able to concentrate." She nodded at the small man, who shoved the girl into Simon's room. Brenda walked out and pulled the door shut behind her. Simon heard several locks engage.

He and the girl stared at each other for about ten seconds before Simon felt a release, a catch thrown open inside his head, and thought his blood would boil out of his veins.

He bore the girl down to the floor in a tangle of white squirming coils. She never made a sound.

* * *

Later. How much later...? Simon didn't know. Couldn't tell. His toes still quivered.

For the first time, the sheets of gray plastic covering the

hardwood floor of the bedroom actually registered on him. That was good planning. Both he and the girl were soaked, dripped red everywhere they moved.

Well, everywhere *he* moved.

Simon lay on his back beside the bed. When he rolled up onto his side, the plastic stuck to his skin, and he had to peel it off. The girl's body lay a few feet away, curled and shrunken and looking a bit like a cast-off insect shell.

He closed his eyes. He knew from experience that as soon as the buzz wore off he'd feel it, all the remorse and guilt and pain. It was a unique time for him, this blood-fueled high, when he could survey his actions and their consequences intellectually, distanced from every emotion but pleasure. He tried to savor it.

The door opened. Brenda, just as striking as before, said, "Get up and take off your shorts."

Simon scrambled to his feet, happy to oblige. Off with the shorts, sure, no problem with that. He left them on the plastic, and she said, "Now follow me." Well, that wasn't a problem either.

She pointed him toward the bathroom and told him to wash off all the blood. Still no problem, quite a reasonable request, glad to do it. The shower felt pretty good, anyway, though he really hated to see the blood disappear down the drain. He liked it when it dried on him, and cracked a little when he moved. Anyway. He tried to think of a song to sing while he bathed, but nothing good came to mind, so he hummed "Row Row Row Your Boat."

When he finished and stepped out of the shower stall, he found clean, fluffy towels and a fresh change of clothes waiting for him. Just plain white socks and tighty-whiteys, and dark blue jeans and a solid green T-shirt, looked like they came from K-Mart. But it beat walking around naked, so he got dressed.

Brenda waited for him in the hall. He started to say something, but the air filled up with that scent, the scent he'd smelled before, and she stepped forward and put her arms around his neck and kissed him, and oh, oh *wow,* even though she didn't give him any tongue, *damn* but that was the best kiss he'd ever had, and everything got sort of white and weird and his head went strange.

Next thing he knew he stood in the bedroom again. All the plastic and the bloody underwear and the girl were gone. Brenda stood next to him and told him to sit down on the bed, so he did, and that felt better. She pulled a chair across from another room—Simon thought he saw a kid in that room for a second, but he wasn't sure, maybe the kid wasn't real, 'cause he was really pale and *maybe he was a ghost*—and she sat down in the chair and looked at him.

"All right," she said. "This is what we're going to do. I'm going to ask you some questions, and you're going to answer them truthfully. Okay?"

He shrugged. "Sure."

"Good. Now. Earlier tonight you were in a park in the city."

He nodded affably.

"What was the name of that park?"

"Uh...I think I saw a sign...Hammer Field?"

"Good enough. You met someone...unusual in that park tonight, correct? Do you remember that?"

Simon squinted and thought about it, and the rest of the night came back down on him like falling masonry. All of the good feelings, the thrill of the teenage girl, the incredible kiss from Brenda, everything went sour.

His eyes started watering and he scuttled back on the bed and jammed himself into the corner, and hugged his knees to his chest and darted his eyes around. His heartbeat went crazy.

"Please," he said, in a voice like a little boy's. "Please, she's not here, is she? The woman from the park isn't here, is she? I don't, I don't wanna see her, I don't, don't..." He trailed off, and Brenda scowled.

"What's wrong with you?"

Simon started crying. He grabbed handfuls of hair and hid his face.

"Hey. I asked what's wrong with you. Answer me."

Simon wailed, *"I'm scared!"* and really started sobbing, and couldn't talk.

* * *

Brenda counted to ten, very slowly. She'd seen this happen once or twice before, when she dosed someone. Sometimes it brought emotions closer to the surface. If she'd had to predict which of Simon Grove's emotions would float to the top, though, she wouldn't have picked *fear.* After a few moments, when she felt collected, she fixed her eyes on him again. "Simon. You do what I say. Look at me."

Reluctantly he raised his head. His whole body shook, and tears rivered down his face. She'd never tried what she was about to try, but what the hell, it was worth a shot.

"I can't believe this," she muttered. Louder: "Simon. Stop crying." It took a few seconds, but the tears dried up. He still shook, though, obviously still terrified. She said, "You're afraid of this woman? It was a woman, you said, right?"

He nodded pitifully.

"Okay, well, no more of that garbage. You're not afraid of her. Hell, you're not afraid of anything except me. Got that? Do you understand me? Except for me, you're fearless. All right?"

She sat back and waited to see what effect that would have. It took a few more seconds, and then—

The change scared her.

Simon stopped shaking, and grew unnaturally still. He partially uncurled from his fetal position and lifted his head, slowly took in the room around him as if seeing it for the first time. Quickly he focused on Brenda, and as he looked into her eyes she sat back a little farther in her seat and swallowed a sudden lump in her throat.

Something in there had shifted, melted, realigned itself, and Brenda understood that she had unintentionally, radically transformed this young man.

She thought for a moment that his features had changed, that he had softened and reshaped his face into someone else's. But the only difference lay in how he *wore* his expression. The effect rippled out from there, through everything about him. The way he held his hands, the set of his shoulders. The tilt of his head. As if some outside force had scooped out the old Simon Grove and poured a stranger into the empty shell.

He wiped the tears off his face with his shirt, straightened his back and folded his legs under him, and regarded her with total calm.

"Y'know, I'm not sure what just happened..." This he said in a different voice, even. Lower, better modulated. "But I think I owe you for it."

"Ah...well. Remember, you're doing what I tell you to do."

He arched his back and rested his forearms on his knees. And smiled.

"Oh, absolutely. I'm all yours."

Thoroughly unnerved and trying hard not to show it, Brenda said, "Okay, back to the park. You ran into somebody in the park tonight?"

"Did I ever! That bitch was something to see! Popping around, all over the place. Wore a mask, too."

"A mask?"

"Yep. Gray one, black over the eyes. Scary chick. Real badass."

Brenda flashed on several articles in the paper over the last several days. She groaned and put her face in her hands.

"What's wrong?" Simon asked helpfully. She ignored him.

Exactly what we need. An augment with an agenda. And right off the scale, to boot. She said, "We need to find that woman. Did you see her without the mask?" Simon nodded again. "Good. All right, come over here across the hall. There's someone I want you to meet."

"Sure," he said. "But first I've got a couple of questions for you."

Brenda frowned again. It looked as though she'd have to give him another dose as soon as possible. "Such as?"

"Like, okay...how'd we get this way? I mean, you and that mask woman are the first people I've met who could, y'know, do things. Like *I* can do things. So what caused it? This is the first chance I've had to ask someone who'd know. Well, I think my mom knows something about it, but she wouldn't ever tell me."

"This isn't the time for lengthy explanations. All right? When I have time I'll tell you everything I know."

"Okay," he said. "So give me the abridged version for now."

Brenda decided she didn't much care for the new Simon. "The abridged version? Fine. No one knows how it happened. It just did. About one out of every four or five million people got it. Usually people who already had a little bit of it...like your mother. Like you."

Simon nodded. "I knew Mom had to have *something*. She couldn't've looked that good for that long without some kind of help."

"So. Satisfied? Can we get on with things?"

He nodded.

"Good. Now come with me."

* * *

Janey came dragging back into the LaCroix Building with her eyelids at half-mast. Her side hurt, her chest hurt, she had a swiftly building headache from not having eaten anything in the previous seventeen hours, and the need for sleep weighed her down like an anvil on her shoulders. All the exhilaration from seeing cops crawling over the Troland house that morning had deserted her.

The office door stood propped open, and Tim rushed out as he passed. "Where have you been?" he asked. "Are you okay?" He walked at her side as she headed for the elevator.

Janey couldn't decide if Tim sounded angry or relieved.

He smelled amazing, as usual, and a part of herself she found immensely annoying at the moment couldn't help but notice how his black eyes sparkled.

"Yeah, I'm fine." She absently rubbed a spot high on her chest, and wrinkled up one side of her face as she did. "Sorry I freaked out. I just came from the police station, gave my statement."

They reached the elevator, and she punched the UP button.

"Listen...Tim, I know I owe you an explanation, and I'll give you one, I promise, I'll tell you everything about last night, but right now I can barely hold my eyes open. Can I call you? And tell you all about this? But, later, I mean?"

Tim cocked one eyebrow up and folded his arms. Janey tried to figure out what was going on in his head, and couldn't even come close. So she stood and waited and tried not to look too pained.

"Yeah, that's fine," he said, finally. "You can call me."

"Thanks."

Tim walked away from her, slowly.

The elevator doors opened, and Janey stumbled inside and pushed the button for her floor. On a whim, she stuck her head back out and looked down the hallway at the office. Tim stood in the doorway, and stared right back at her, and he looked...*smug*.

Janey didn't have the mental capacity to deal with that, and pulled her head back inside the car. The doors closed.

* * *

Janey woke briefly around midnight that night, ate some crackers and drank a glass of orange juice, and went back to bed. She hadn't been an early riser for some time now, but she *was* accustomed to getting at least some sleep during the night and early morning. When her head hit the pillow that afternoon she'd been awake for over twenty-four hours, and the slumber she fell into swallowed her without a ripple.

She woke again the next morning, a little past eight, feeling remarkably refreshed considering what she'd been through. She peeled off her T-shirt and bra, and examined her chest and side in the bathroom mirror, grimacing at what she saw.

A huge band of repulsive purple and yellow bruises crossed her chest, starting at her left collarbone and tracking down between her breasts—she lifted the right one to get a full view, grimacing as she did it—to the lower right part of her ribcage. Testimony to the firing pattern of the Uzi. Another livid contusion flowered on her side where she'd taken the pistol shot. All of them were too sore to touch in any way but very lightly, and they hurt even more when she bent over. She did a few stretches and discovered that the bruises hurt pretty much whichever way she moved, no helping it.

She could still function, though. Time to get back to the issue at hand.

Simon.

Janey fixed a picture of the young man in her mind and replayed the few words Simon had said to her.

...I'm sorry...

Janey had to find him. Her subconscious had gnawed at it the whole night, and now that she'd gotten some rest it seemed clear as glass: some way, somehow, she and Simon shared some sort of similarity, some kind of kinship. Janey had to know more.

And unless Simon had a good reason for doing what he did to the girl in the park, he not only had to be found, he had to be stopped. Janey decided to head down to the basement and get some preparations done.

She left her phone on the kitchen counter. There was no reception in the basement. Janey took a quick look around the apartment, walked out of her bedroom, opened the door to her empty coat closet, stepped inside and vanished.

As soon as she left, her phone started ringing.

CHAPTER FOURTEEN

The opening sequence cut to the *Good Morning Sheree* logo over the studio audience as the theme music finished playing. At Camera One's signal, Sheree Baker shined her best smile into the lens.

"Good morning, Atlanta, and good morning all our Internet viewers!"

"Good morning!" the audience roared back at her, and her smile broadened, accenting the dimples in her cheeks.

In the control booth Ted Swit, her producer, sighed and allowed himself a small grin. Sheree Baker was gold and everyone knew it.

Sheree stood six feet tall, with long, lustrous red hair, carefully-tanned skin and enormous blue eyes, and since Swit had successfully halted the posting of her spread on BigTaTas.com, had no significant obstacles in the way of her career in broadcasting. Swit leaned back in his chair, laced his fingers over his beer paunch and closed his eyes. Sheree's voice came to him over his headset like hot caramel.

"We're going for a change of pace today, people." The words sounded like an invitation to sex. Swit hummed softly.

Sheree Baker's show achieved success for one reason and one reason only: Sheree Baker. The writing was mediocre at best, and Swit had no illusions as to his own production skills. He'd hired the director away from a children's show about a petting zoo because the woman worked cheap, and every piece of their equipment was easily five years out of date, if not more. *Good Morning Sheree* debuted with a segment about professional square dance callers and had gotten only worse from there—or better, depending on your point of view. Sheree herself was the soul of the show. Quite simply, no one could take their eyes off her.

Swit vividly remembered seeing the first click-through numbers to come back. Their show started at seven thousand, moved to three hundred thousand the following week, then hit a million-five and stayed there. It didn't matter, apparently, that *GMS* never covered any topic weightier than what to do if you discover your fly unzipped in public. The show became, in the words of the *Chronicle* reviewer, an "inexplicable hit, in the tradition of *Jersey Shore* and every living Kardashian." Swit didn't care. The ad rates just kept going up.

He felt a little nervous about today's show, since it departed from their usual meringue-light format, but *Good Morning Sheree* was never a program to miss exploiting a trend. They had today's topic operating right here in the city, after all, practically on their doorstep, and with everybody between five and fifty-five fascinated with the Gray Widow, why not do a show about her?

Sheree spoke, and Swit wondered if it really mattered what came out of that mouth, as long as its lips moved just the way they did.

"Our country's criminal justice system has been criticized more than once, both by Americans and by citizens of other nations." A few notes lower than one would have expected from her, her perfect voice carried authority without intimidation. With just a touch more steam, it could have been a phone sex junkie's fantasy.

"Now, here in Atlanta, someone has decided to take the law into her own hands. Our show's topic today is the masked vigilante the news media has dubbed 'the Gray Widow.'"

Sheree let her voice drop slightly at the name, allowing it the proper gravity. "Here with us today to debate the Gray Widow's presence are columnists Greg Thatcher, on the anti-Widow side, and Chinira McCallum, representing the pro-Widow opinion."

Sheree turned from the camera and moved to the discussion set. Camera Two showed the home viewing audience three comfortably padded chairs in a small half-circle, the center one still empty. Sheree Baker settled into the empty chair and smiled at her guests. Neither of them returned it, but Chinira McCallum nodded courteously.

On her right sat a stocky, aggressively clean-cut white man in his mid-forties, wearing a stiff-looking charcoal gray suit: Greg Thatcher. Across from him sat Chinira McCallum, an African-American woman in her mid-thirties, in a tasteful, expensively-cut blue dress. Thatcher scowled. McCallum wore a pleasant, if somewhat bemused, expression.

"The Clash of the Columnists," said one of the technicians in the booth, leaning over toward Swit. "How did you get these two in the same room together?"

Swit shrugged. "Wasn't too hard. Thatcher's been drooling over Sheree from the start, so he'd take any excuse to get here. McCallum, I don't know; probably just wants to take a few shots at Thatcher."

The technician thought about that. "This is not what you'd call a typical episode here."

"You're telling me. But let's see what happens."

Somewhere between talking to the audience and sitting down, Sheree had disposed of the hand-held, and now used her lapel mic. Thatcher and McCallum were similarly wired. Her electric smile turned about half-way up, Sheree said, "How are the both of you today?"

McCallum said, "Just fine, thank you, Sheree," and Thatcher grunted. Sheree took a deep breath and asked her first question.

"Chinira, in several of your columns you have addressed the Gray Widow's activities, always in a positive light. Could you tell us exactly why you're in favor of someone who so blatantly operates outside the law?"

McCallum cleared her throat softly. "Well, Sheree, I think we have to look at the state of our city since the Gray Widow first appeared. In just a few days, the incidence of street crime has already seen a drop. People are starting to feel safer. Women have begun going out to stores and malls by themselves after dark again. The criminals are still out there, yes, but the Gray Widow is out there with them, and they're realizing that."

She would have said more, but Sheree turned to Thatcher.

"Greg, you've spoken out sharply against the Gray Widow. What do you think her activity here means?"

Thatcher shook his head, as if sad and disappointed. "Vigilantism has existed for as long as there have been laws. But the fact remains, she is breaking the law. It's a slippery slope, Sheree. If one person can disregard the law, what's to stop anyone else from doing the same thing?"

The audience murmured.

McCallum shifted in her seat. "You're ignoring half the picture, Greg. Yes, technically, what she's doing is against the law. But she's also setting an example. What about Kaveyah Wilson, the girl the Widow rescued from a rapist? According to police reports, the Gray Widow has *prevented* four rapes so far, and those are just the ones we know about. Who knows how many others we don't? She was there before they happened, and she kept them *from* happening. To me that's worth a hell of a lot more than prosecuting the offender after the fact. And what about Federico Ruiz? In Ruiz's sworn statement, he said the Widow saved his life, *stepped in front of a shotgun* for him, and then got him to the hospital so what little injury he did suffer could be treated."

Thatcher raised one eyebrow. "And who's to say that if the Widow hadn't been there at all, Ruiz might not have gotten hurt in the first place? That's what happens when someone goes on a vigilante kick like this. They step outside the law, and sooner or later, people get hurt. That's why we *have* laws in this country, Ms. McCallum, that's why the public voted those laws into place. We have to have a system. You can't go out and start making up the rules as you go along, because if you do, someone's going to get hurt, someone's going to get *killed*. What's going to happen when someone else starts to do the same thing, but *doesn't* have those golden ethics you seem to admire so much?"

McCallum tried to answer, but Thatcher talked over her. "I'll *tell* you what: we're going to have someone who hates blacks, or gays, or Jews, or single mothers, out on the streets and hurting people."

Calmly, McCallum spoke to Sheree: "May I speak now? Or does Mr. Thatcher want to spend more time answering his own questions?"

Thatcher sputtered, but Sheree said, "No, no, please, Chirina."

McCallum thanked her. "I have a question for *you*, Greg. What's the difference between the Gray Widow and George Zimmerman in your eyes?"

Thatcher recoiled. "What? What are you talking about?"

"I'm talking about what you just said. You're condemning anyone who hates blacks, or gays, or Jews, or single mothers, I believe those were your words, out on the streets, taking the law into their own hands. And yet, during the Zimmerman trial, you wrote no fewer than seven columns in defense of what George Zimmerman did."

Thatcher said, "See here, now, I won't have you put words in my mouth!"

McCallum grinned. "I didn't, Greg. I'm just telling all these good people what you already said. But I *will* put some words in your mouth, if you don't object." Thatcher very clearly did object, but before he could speak, McCallum steamrolled right over him. "I think what you're really objecting to is that it's a *woman* taking the law into her own hands. You were fine with it when it was a man. You stood up for George Zimmerman, even though actual law enforcement told him in no uncertain terms that it was not his place to follow Trayvon Martin. You stood up for him even though he pursued Trayvon Martin and provoked the incident that led to Trayvon's death. But now, *now*, when it's a female out there, stopping actual crimes *as they're being committed*, oh, no, that's unacceptable. Fascinating double standard, Greg. Maybe you can explain to everyone why you feel that way?"

Sheree clearly had no idea what to say or do. She sat, silent.

Thatcher huffed and straightened his suit jacket. "That's ridiculous."

He seemed to be struggling with how to follow that statement up, so McCallum stepped back into the opening. "Now, just to be clear, I am not saying the Gray Widow is anything like George Zimmerman. He acted as an opportunistic, violent bigot, whereas the Widow is more like…a symptom. A symptom of a larger, systemic problem. Is what she's doing illegal? Yes, of course. But so far, she hasn't killed anyone. She hasn't caused any life-threatening injuries. She's waited until there actually was a problem, and she's stepped in and *solved* that problem. If you ask me, the Gray Widow is a role model. Not just for females who could by God use some empowerment in this society, but also for law enforcement as a whole. You called her a vigilante, Greg, but that's not how I see her. I see her as an *enforcer*. One this country badly needs."

Greg Thatcher's face had been getting redder and redder, and as soon as Chirina McCallum stopped talking, he stood up and stalked out of the studio.

Sheree smiled desperately into the camera. "We'll be back after this short break!"

Ted Swit sat in the control booth with his mouth hanging open, trying to decide whether or not to laugh. The only way this could get any better was if they had the Gray Widow herself out there in a chair. He tried to say something, and finally managed to choke out, *"Damn."*

The technician said, "Well, I like this show better than the one we did on quilting."

In the booth, every light on the phone board that wasn't already glowing lit up.

* * *

While Greg Thatcher and Chirina McCallum traded verbal punches, Tim stood outside Janey's door in the hallway, his back pressed to the wall, a pass-key held tightly in one hand.

"This is insane," he said quietly. "By standing here, I am proving myself to be an insane person. Plus I might get arrested. Or killed." He shifted the key to the other hand and looked at the one he'd been holding it in. Its imprint was very clear in the pale skin of his palm, which trembled slightly. He dropped the hand to his side, went to the door and knocked loudly.

"Janey? Janey, are you in there?"

No answer. He wasn't surprised, but he still got a peculiar sinking feeling.

He'd watched the video from the security camera in the building's entry hall, fast-forwarding through the periods of inactivity. Both the elevator and the staircase let out onto the entry hall, and there'd been no sign of Janey.

And now she wasn't answering her phone.

Tim pressed his ear to the door, listened intently, and heard nothing.

He sighed, annoyed at himself.

Logically, Janey Sinclair was one of two things. One, she was indisposed, asleep or in the shower or something, maybe with the ringer off, so that she couldn't hear the phone. Two...she actually was hurt, and couldn't come to the door or answer the phone.

"This is stupid, Tim," he said in a quiet voice. "What are you doing? Why are you here?"

He knocked again, louder this time, and waited. Still no answer. "Janey? Hey Janey! Open the door!"

Nothing.

"Dammit, dammit, dammit." He jammed the key into the lock and turned it, popped the door open.

The apartment was mostly dark, lit only by the shaft of light coming in from over his shoulder and a weak yellow glow from a lamp on one end of the kitchen counter. Tim closed the door, and immediately missed the light from the outside hallway; the small lamp lit the apartment's interior well enough for him to get around, but seemed to create more shadows than it dispelled. It was the same apartment he'd seen the first time, but now it seemed unrelentingly weird.

He tried to think of the right word. The painting of the cabin by the woods came back to him, and he resisted the impulse to jump back out into the hallway and slam the door.

Sinister. That's the word. Just like that freaky painting. Only now it's the whole place. He flicked the nearest wall switch, and an overhead fixture came on. Three high-wattage bulbs scattered the darkness. "That's better."

Janey had become a puzzle he couldn't resist trying to assemble. He thought he'd already figured out one of the big pieces…but he got the feeling the other ones were even bigger.

"Hello? Are you here? Asleep? In the tub? Hello?"

The walls soaked his voice in and gave nothing back. He took a few hesitant steps to the middle of the living room, near the couch. The apartment had the stillness of the abandoned, and Tim forced himself to look through it, room to room.

In just under two minutes he determined that Janey Sinclair was indeed not in the apartment.

"Okay," he said, in a normal voice. "So you're not here, but you're still in the building. Fine. That's normal. You could be visiting friends on the next floor up. Kicking back, watching the game, drinking beer. That'd be perfectly normal. At eight-thirty in the morning."

He didn't believe *that* for a second, and wondered again exactly what he hoped to prove by doing this. He went to the kitchen, poured himself a glass of water, sat down on Janey's couch and turned on the TV. A rerun of *Grimm* had just come on, and he settled back into the cushions, content to wait.

Minutes stretched into hours.

Embarrassment and self-doubt had somehow transformed

into a belligerent need to figure this out. *I'll sit here. I'll sit here until she shows up, and if she doesn't kick my ass, maybe I can get her to come clean.*

The next time he glanced at a clock, it read 2:52. Tim still sat alone in Janey's apartment, reading Robert McCammon's *Gone South,* a novel he'd found in a small bookcase in the corner of the living room.

He knew he should be down in the office. It wasn't as though he didn't have enough paperwork to do. But his cell number was on the door, and any maintenance emergencies would get to him that way. So he sat and read.

He'd turned off the TV shortly after turning it on, since he didn't want Janey to hear it before she came in. Every so often, when he could force himself to pull his eyes away from the book, he glanced up at the apartment door. He tried not to think about what he'd say when Janey came home from wherever she was. Maybe, "Hi, I couldn't figure out where you went, so I thought I'd break in and wait here to ask you, because I've got a suspicion about you that might land one or both of us in the looney bin."

Something like that.

Sure.

He closed his eyes and went over the building's floor plans in his head, trying to remember...what? A blank space? Somewhere for a secret passageway to go? When the door opened and she stepped inside, probably holding a bag of groceries, he knew he'd look like an idiot. Almost certainly an unwelcome idiot. But he had to know. Had to stay and find out.

But—what if she'd left right after she got back yesterday? ...What if she was staying with someone else?

What if she was sleeping in someone else's bed?

That was a thought he refused to entertain. He went back to reading, and almost jumped out of the chair entirely when two loud thumps sounded from his left.

He tried to think of some reason why he shouldn't bolt out of the apartment, and couldn't come up with anything good, but he stood up anyway and moved hesitantly toward the source of the noise. There'd been two, each very distinct. *Thump,* and less than a second later, *thump,* just like the first one. He thought they'd come from the coat closet.

Tim had looked in that closet when he first got there, just as he'd looked around the rest of the place. It was empty, with the light bulb missing. Just a perfectly ordinary closet, vaguely coffin-like, with a single shelf at about head height, nothing on it. He took a couple of deep breaths and glanced around the apartment. With the overhead fixture still burning, it looked cheery enough, though it was painfully clear that the place belonged to a single person. He turned back to the closet door, put out a hand and touched the knob.

"What's behind door number one?" he said aloud. The sound of his own voice made it a little easier. "I'll turn the knob, open the door, and a corpse will fall out, right into my arms. Just like on TV."

No, no. That'd be too easy. Although...a few images came to him, probably spawned by reading too many Stephen King novels, of dead bodies and expanding intestinal gas and rupturing flesh, and what if those thumps were the corpse's arms falling off? Or a couple of internal organs squeezing out through a big hole in the stomach? He'd turn the knob, open the door, and something would be in there waiting for him, and reach out and pull him in. He thought of the painting again, of whatever it was he thought he'd seen in there.

"Jesus, I'm making it worse," he said quickly, and with a swift turn and yank he pulled the door wide open and stepped back so the light from the overhead lamp could reach inside.

Tim thought about laughing. On the floor of the closet lay a pair of gray combat boots.

Thump-thump. One-two. Hitting the floor. He tilted his head and looked up at the shelf, a couple of inches above eye level. There hadn't been any boots there before when he looked, he was sure of that. Even if he'd missed them, why would they have fallen *now?* He knelt and picked one up, turned around and sat down with his back to the wall beside the open closet.

He'd thought they were combat boots—they were the right height, they laced up—but that was only at first glance. He turned the boot over in his hands, examining it. It wasn't all leather, that was certain. He recognized the other material as some kind of synthetic, but not like anything he'd seen before. He brought it close to his nose, stared hard at the material, and thought it looked like...scales? Tiny scales? No...too regular. The sole was thick black rubber, like the sole of a hiking boot. He couldn't find a brand name anywhere on it, or even a size, for that matter.

He heard the sound in his mind again. *Thump-thump.* As though they had just been dropped. Just like someone sitting on the edge of a bed, ready to sack out: pull off the boots, maybe look at one of them to see if anything was stuck to the bottom, then toss them into the corner. *Thump-thump.*

Slowly Tim pulled the boot's tongue out, loosened the laces further, and touched the inside of the boot. It was warm against his fingers, and very slightly damp. He made a face and, hesitantly, brought the boot up to his nose and sniffed. There was the scent of sweat there, yes, but not offensively strong. He picked up the other boot and held them side by side. They were very high quality, clearly enough. Well-maintained. And recently worn.

Tim hopped up from the floor and went quickly through Janey's bedroom to the adjoining bath, which he knew shared a wall with the closet. The bathroom was empty, and the molded acrylic wall of the shower-and-bath unit covered the place on the bathroom wall where any kind of concealed door would have opened.

He went back into the short hallway where the closet stood and opened the door next to it. The heating and cooling unit and water heater sat there, undisturbed, exactly as he'd left them when he'd finished with the air filter. He knocked on the wall shared by the two closets and found it satisfyingly solid.

Thump-thump. It wouldn't get out of his head.

"Stuff doesn't just appear out of nowhere," he said. Hearing the words out loud didn't do much to make him feel better. He kept talking anyway. "And if something did, it wouldn't be a pair of *boots,* for God's sake. It'd be something else—a little toothy creature, or an old book. Or a wheelchair. Or something. Not a pair of sweaty boots."

Before he could say anything else he felt a change in the air. He couldn't put any kind of name to it, but he felt it, just as surely as he would have felt the airflow from an electric fan suddenly turned on him. Sweat popped out on his skin and seemed to evaporate as soon as it appeared.

Something was coming.

Maybe he wouldn't have felt it if he hadn't already been so tense, waiting for something to happen. But something was coming, he knew it, the same kind of feeling he'd gotten from the painting but ten times stronger, twenty times. Every hair on his body tried to stand on end. Tim put the McCammon novel back on the shelf, straightened the couch cushions, and ran to the wall switch and flipped it down, plunging the apartment back into the shadows. The closet itself received no light at all, and seemed endlessly deep, a cavern to enter and never exit.

Tim fumbled with his keys, tried to sort out which one was the right key—and heard a soft sound. Something brushing against the carpet. Something like skin. His hands began shaking too badly to hold the keys, and he dropped them on the floor.

He turned around, his back to the door, and was facing the closet just as Janey Sinclair stepped out of it, and for an instant, just a heartbeat, the light from the lamp shone straight *through* her, so that Tim saw the wall of the hallway and the door to her bedroom through her chest. She wore only socks, a sports bra, and white panties. Sweat beaded on her head and ran down her face, and she carried the same gray bundle under one arm that Tim had seen the first time.

Janey saw him immediately. Tim didn't think anyone could move as fast as she did then, and his shout cut off abruptly as her hand clamped over his mouth. Quickly and gracefully, she spun him around and held him tightly to her.

A hole in the world opened up and Tim fell through it.

CHAPTER FIFTEEN

At first Tim couldn't tell if his eyes were open or not. He blinked several times, touched his eyes with his fingers, and decided they were open. He stared wide-eyed into total darkness, and called out, "Where am I?"

The words echoed around him, in a manner that reminded him of the gymnasium at his grammar school. The gray concrete walls and the polished wooden floor had flung sound back to him much the same way his voice returned to him now.

He quickly patted himself. All his clothes were in place, and he couldn't find any injuries. The air was cool and slightly musty.

"You're safe," Janey's voice said from the dark.

A candle lit ten feet directly in front of him, and he jumped. Dressed in a strange, segmented gray suit, Janey Sinclair stood behind it, holding a match, which she slowly raised to her lips and blew out. She watched him intently, but he didn't think there was any malice in her expression. "Janey—"

She calmly pulled a gray mask over her head. Tim stared into the black mesh eyes.

Without surprise, Tim said, "You're the Gray Widow."

She faltered, and pulled the mask back off. "...You knew?"

Tim glanced around, trying to get a better feel for where they were. "Well, it's not like you're Barbara Gordon. Anybody could've figured it out."

Janey shuffled one foot self-consciously. "I haven't been at it that long."

"Where exactly are we? And how'd we get here?"

She came forward, holding the mask in both hands. "That'll take some explaining."

"I bet it will. Where'd you come from, out of the closet like that? What, you've got mirrors set up or something?" He reached out and took the mask from her. "And Jesus, Janey, was that theatrical enough back there? You scared me to death!"

"Sorry. Look, I only brought you here because I wanted to tell you about, uh, this." She gestured at the gray suit. "Would you mind going back to the apartment? To talk, I mean?"

"No, I'd—"

He stopped.

It clicked with him, then, that what had happened was no illusion with dry ice and mirrors. He remembered, the way he sometimes remembered fragments of a dream minutes after he'd awakened from it. The hole, the doorway opening up. The heat inside.

Janey took his arm, and he had time enough to say, "Oh shit" and grit his teeth before it happened again.

* * *

About an hour later Tim sat on Janey's couch, sipping a cup of hot tea.

Janey sat at the opposite end with an identical mug. She had showered quickly, and was now dressed in blue sweats.

Tim shook his head, blinking.

"And...you said the heat, that was..."

"It happens every time I do it. Near as I can tell, the farther I go, the hotter it is where I've just left. I think—I think some of the. . .energy, I guess, the energy I use gets lost. Like a light bulb. You want the light, but you get the heat as a by-product."

"All right...all right, so, what happens if you take a running start? You come out moving on the other side? So you could all of a sudden come shooting out of the shadows?"

Janey's eyebrows drew together. "Actually, ah, I never really tried that."

Tim scowled at her. She shrugged.

"Okay. Fine. But I want to see you do it. Not in any closets, or behind closed doors. I want to see you do it, right in front of me."

"What, taking you to the basement didn't convince you?"

"I don't know *what* that was, but I do know if I'm going to believe what you're saying, I want to see it myself. With these eyes. On my terms."

Janey set her mug down on the coffee table. "Well, that's just it, that's why I do it where nobody can see it. It has to be in the dark."

"Oh, convenient. Why? Why in the dark?"

"I don't know. I've never known. That's just the way it is."

Tim thought about it for a while. "All right. We can deal with that." He looked around, considering. "Here. I'll turn off the overhead lights, and—get up." They got off the couch, and he shoved the coffee table over so that it touched the seat cushions. "Now." He peered under it. "It's nice and dark under there. If you can really do this, this stuff you've been telling me, I want to see you crawl under that coffee table and come out somewhere else."

Janey wrinkled her forehead again. "...Okay. Where?"

"Anywhere, I don't know! Here, okay, how about this." He went to the kitchen, climbed up on the counter, and sat down with his legs folded. "All right, I can see you get under the table from here, and, uh, switch off that lamp there, would you?"

Janey obligingly turned off a floor lamp in one corner of the living room. "Good. Now there's lots of nice dark shadows right here behind the counter. So crawl under the table, and come out here, right below me. No sleight-of-hand. No secret doors." He set down the mug of tea and crossed his arms, his jaw set. "And you can let me know when you get tired of lying there on the floor."

Janey walked over, looked behind the counter, and went back to the couch and the coffee table. Tim watched her closely. She set her own mug of tea on the table and got down on the floor. "I feel really stupid." She pulled her knees up to her chest and scooted underneath.

Tim started to say, "How you doing down there?" when he

noticed the mug of tea on the coffee table begin to boil. A wave of hot air touched his cheek, and Janey rolled out of the shadows below him and stood up in the kitchen.

She said, "How was that?" and had to lunge to catch him as he pitched backward off the counter.

* * *

Tim sat and shivered. Janey stood a few feet away from him and tried to think of something to say, but eventually decided to wait for him. Outside, fat raindrops started pattering against the window.

After a few minutes he said, "Oh my God. Oh my God. Oh my God."

Carefully, Janey asked, "What?"

He looked up at her. "The—all the things—wait a second. Okay. All the stories I used to read, the movies I used to watch, when something really bizarre happened. I'd always wonder what I'd do, y'know, if I got faced with something like that. And now here it is. You just teleported across the room."

She shrugged. "Yeah."

"I just...I feel like somebody just proved the world is flat."

He shook his head and shivered some more. Janey walked over and sat beside him.

"You're the first person who's known. Well, almost the first. I didn't know how you'd take it."

"How I'd take it! Jesus God, it's...aaah! I don't know, I don't know! I mean, of course, you just did it, right there and I saw you do it, but... Oh, Jesus. How...how did...what...you were born able to do this? What caused it? What's..." He trailed off.

Janey touched his face, lightly, and turned it toward her. "I'll tell you. All of it. But I want to take you somewhere." Tim tensed, and she quickly said, "In a car, in a car, don't worry."

"Where? Where are we going?"

She went into her bedroom for a couple of minutes, and came

back out in street clothes, carrying an umbrella. "I want you to meet someone."

* * *

They headed out of the city. For the first five minutes or so the silence remained unbroken. Tim had stopped in at his place and grabbed a long gray raincoat, and he sat in the passenger seat, playing idly with the belt buckle.

"I keep waiting for a commercial."

"Sorry?"

"I said I keep waiting for a commercial. I feel like I'm watching a show on TV. None of this seems real." He stared out the window. "You said you'd tell me about it."

Janey hesitated.

"It…started about seven years ago. Well, no, actually before that, when I was sixteen. So. Eleven years. My dad—"

Janey stopped. Her throat seized unexpectedly, and she fought back sudden tears. She hadn't tried to recall that night in a long while. She blinked a few times and swallowed, breathed deeply.

"My dad was a stage magician." The words came out okay, as long as she kept her breathing right. "He made things disappear. He was good, *really* good, and nobody ever figured out his tricks. That's 'cause they *weren't* tricks. The stuff actually disappeared."

"What, like cars and statues...?"

"No, no. Small stuff. Apples, keys, rabbits. But oh, it looked great. The crowds loved him. So. These guys approached him and asked him to do some tricks for *them*. Basically, they wanted him to make some money disappear out of a safe and reappear in their pockets."

Janey took a ramp onto I-85 north. Tim said nothing.

"He refused. I think he refused more than once, and maybe said he'd go to the police. ...Not the wisest thing he could have done. So they showed up at our house one night, a couple of days after my sixteenth birthday.

"I'd just gotten my black belt in karate, and I was studying jujitsu and aikido at the same time, and I thought of myself as a real tough kid, y'know? The kind of kid who could handle anything? And it didn't make a damn bit of difference. A guy was waiting for me when I came through the door that night, and he hit me in the back of the head with a lead pipe. They chained us both up in the kitchen, and killed my dad, and shot me." Her fingertips brushed the scars high on her chest, through her shirt. "I guess they thought I was dead.

"Before they shot him, he... The guy, the one in charge, his name was Sammy Kyle. He kept pointing his gun at me, said he'd kill me if Dad didn't cooperate with him. I don't know what happened, if Dad tried to kill him first, or if he just lost control, or what. But when Dad did his trick, made something disappear, there was always this feeling in the air. I could tell when he was doing it. Well, the whole kitchen lit up with this feeling, and Sammy Kyle started screaming, and...um.

"Dad made Sammy Kyle's left eye disappear out of his head. One second Kyle was just standing there, and the next second his eye was hanging in the air beside his head. It fell on the floor, and Kyle staggered, and he stepped on it. It made this *pop*...

"Anyway. Kyle realized what my father had done, and he put his gun between Dad's eyes and pulled the trigger. Then he turned and shot me twice, and I went over backward in the chair—but the gun he was using, it was really small caliber, a .22. He used that, I think, because he thought it was the kind of gun a real Mafioso would use, like in a mob-style execution—but he wasn't seeing that well, y'know, so his aim wasn't great, and he didn't manage to puncture anything too vital. And I lived."

Janey kept her eyes straight ahead.

Tim said, "Dear Lord."

"I stayed in a hospital for a while, till my body healed. But my head was another story. I needed a lot of therapy. One day, one of the interns brought me some paint and paper. I started painting. I've kept that up."

She gave him a tiny smile.

"Anyway, I was lying in bed one night, about half asleep I guess, and there was this *thing*. This thing happened. I've...been trying to put words to it ever since then, and I can't really, it was just…something happened, and I really really wanted to be outside, away from there. And bang. I was out on the lawn, in my underwear."

"In the dark."

"Right, in the dark. And it felt just like what my Dad used to do, except so much stronger. *So* much stronger. And there was the heat."

"So you inherited it?"

"I think so. I must have gotten it from Dad, and then—whatever that thing was—whatever happened, it boosted the power. Dad never knew anybody else that could do anything like this, and I hadn't ever met anybody either until we saw that guy in the park."

"The mugger?" His victim, the girl, flashed in Tim's mind, curling bloody welts on her arms and face.

"Yeah. I think he's like me. I mean, not *just* like me, but I think something similar happened to him. I've been looking for him."

"What, and you've found him? Is that where we're going?"

"No! No. This is…something that'll explain a lot. I think."

They made the rest of the trip in silence. Soon Janey got off the freeway and took them down a two-lane road lined with oaks, pines, and hickories. Tim spent the time staring out the window, trying to decide whether or not he was going insane.

More and more made sense now. Of *course* she wasn't wet when he saw her during the storm. She hadn't been outside. She'd been wherever that place was. Her hidey-hole. Her basement.

And the painting...the painting must have soaked up some of her power. He wanted to ask her about it, but she didn't look as though she had anything else to say for a while. So he kept quiet.

Soon they reached their destination, and Tim got an inkling of why Janey had brought him.

They turned off the road onto a wide circular drive, which curved up through a very green, perfectly clipped lawn and stopped in front of a massive three-story white brick house. Huge columns on the front porch supported a small balcony on the third floor. On a small, tasteful sign near where they parked were the words, "Leslie O'Brien Care Facility," and below that, "est. 1946."

Janey left the car. She tried to open her umbrella, but it ripped as soon as it sprang open, so she threw it in the backseat and sprinted through the rain. Tim followed wordlessly, alternating between looking around him and watching her. Waiting for him out of the downpour, Janey's jaw was set hard, but her eyes glistened.

A young woman dressed in white met them in the lobby. She wore an identification badge clipped to her left shirt pocket, which gave her name as Loreen Fugett. Loreen lifted the corners of her mouth in a smile that Tim had seen before. In hospitals.

Janey asked, "How is he today?"

"He can see you," Loreen Fugett said. She looked frankly, but politely, at Tim. "And who might this be?"

"This is my friend, Tim Kapoor," she answered, her voice mild. "He's my captive for the day."

Tim and Loreen Fugett shook hands cordially. To Janey, Loreen said, "Call if you need me." Janey nodded and led Tim through a door and down a hallway.

The house had once been spectacular, and still preserved some of its former grandeur, but it couldn't hide its purpose. Whitewash covered everything, and the place smelled faintly of disinfectant. Janey stopped in front of the third door on the left, and seemed to collect herself before she opened it.

As the latch clicked and a gap appeared between door and frame, Tim noticed two things: a faint scent of blueberries, and a clear male voice halfway through the A-B-C song.

Tim followed Janey into what had once been a medium-sized bedroom, but which now carried the unmistakable air of professional care. The off-white walls matched the beige curtains on the window, as well as the light brown cover stretched across the neatly made hospital bed. A small table and three chairs, all built of blonde wood, sat in a corner, and a metal wardrobe stood against one wall with a door half-open. Tim saw several shirts and pairs of pants on hangers inside it.

In the middle of the floor sat another nurse and a handsome, pajama-clad young white man with a mop of curly yellow hair. A partially completed large-piece jigsaw puzzle lay on the floor between them. They both looked up as the door opened, and the nurse smiled and said, "Ms. Sinclair."

The young man surged up, arms wide, and shouted, "Janey!" He caught her in a fierce hug, and though he was a good three inches taller, Janey lifted him off the floor as easily as if he'd been a tiny child and spun him around in a circle. As they turned, Tim saw tears in Janey's eyes.

Janey set the young man back on the floor, brushed away her tears with a thumb, and said, "Here's someone I'd like you to meet."

"Okay!" the man said, and Tim noticed he slurred his speech slightly. A lock of his blond hair shifted, and Tim saw a large, irregular indentation marring the left side of his forehead. He smiled brightly at Tim and stuck out his hand just as a tiny line of saliva escaped from the corner of his mouth. Janey deftly dabbed that away.

"This is my friend Tim," Janey said, as the yellow-haired young man pumped Tim's hand. Janey pulled a small Matchbox car out of one pocket and held it out for him. "I brought this for you." He squealed and thanked her and ran to show the nurse.

Janey's eyes made Tim's whole body ache. "That's Adam," Janey said, barely above a whisper. "My husband."

* * *

Zach Feygen visited Nathan Pittman in the hospital in mid-afternoon.

He'd gotten a call twenty minutes earlier. Nathan had regained consciousness at just after two, and spoken lucidly, but passed out again. Feygen got there as soon as he could.

He'd talked with Nathan's doctors. The convenience store robber had used a .32 revolver, and all three of the bullets he put in Nathan had struck bone. If Nathan had been incredibly lucky, the gunshot wounds might not have been all that serious. As it was, fragments of bone had penetrated one lung and sliced a chunk out of his liver.

Feygen reached Nathan's room, pushed the door partway open, and knocked lightly. No one answered. He stepped inside and found Nathan's parents staring at him, one standing on either side of Nathan's bed. They had on expensive clothes but wore them badly.

The mother grunted, "Who're you?"

Looking at the two of them, Feygen couldn't help but think of the nursery rhyme, "Jack Spratt could eat no fat, his wife could eat no lean," except in reverse. Nathan Pittman's father didn't appear to have eaten anything lean in quite some time, although, judging by his wife's brittle frailty, he might have eaten all of her food along with his.

"I'm Detective Feygen, Atlanta PD," he said. He let the door close behind him. "I was hoping to ask your son a few questions. About the Gray Widow."

The mother said, "Nathan can't answer any questions." The father stayed quiet. Feygen stepped farther into the room, and for the first time got a good look at Nathan Pittman.

Tubes sprouted from the boy in far too many places, and an oxygen feed ran up his nose. Feygen had seen pictures, and knew Nathan was normally very thin. Now the kid looked worse off than Chooley. His cheeks and eyes were sunken, his skin the color of chalk. He looked like a corpse.

"He did regain consciousness a few minutes ago, didn't he?" Feygen asked politely.

"Yes," the mother said. Her expression—the kind of expression someone has right after they swallow half a glass of curdled milk—

hadn't wavered since Feygen entered the room. He began to suspect she looked like that all the time.

"For about a minute and a half, he woke up. He said something about that Gray Widow bitch. And he asked for water, and I couldn't give it to him. He's not up for any kind of third degree." She put her hands on her bony hips. "We've already talked to the police about five times, Detective. What's the point of this?"

It hadn't taken long for the investigation of Nathan's shooting to turn up the trove of Gray Widow-related items in the boy's room. He practically had a shrine to her Scotch-taped to his walls.

Feygen stuck his hands in his pockets. "I don't intend to give your son any sort of 'third degree,' Mrs. Pittman. I tried talking to his friends at school, but no one there seems to know him very well. I only wanted to ask him what kind of prior contact he had, if any, with the Gray Widow."

"None, that we know about," Mr. Pittman said, speaking for the first time. He settled heavily into a chair in the corner. His wife remained standing.

Mr. Pittman sounded as if he were gargling wet cement when he talked, and Feygen thought, *Christ, what a pair.* The father continued, "Far as we can tell, he went and did this all on his own, just readin' about shit in the papers and such." Mr. Pittman's hairline was severely receding, and he ran one hand across it, tugged on the hair. Several strands came away with his fingers. He shook his head. "Still can't believe he went and did this. Just can't believe it."

Mrs. Pittman said, "It's practically all I've heard about. Whole family calling about it, newspapers, TV, folks at church." She, too, shook her head slowly. It was like a twisted, mean-spirited parody of a Norman Rockwell painting, the two parents hovering over their hospitalized son, shaking their heads and looking...looking how?

Mrs. Pittman's face soured even further, and Feygen realized how they looked. His stomach rolled queasily.

Nathan's parents weren't grieving. They were *embarrassed.*

Feygen remembered the photographs he'd seen of the boy.

Head half shaved, multiple facial piercings—all of which had been removed, and he wondered if the hospital or Nathan's parents had done that—but good Lord, was it any wonder the kid felt alienated, raised by these two? Feygen started backing slowly toward the door. Nathan Pittman's parents both stayed silent, and both stared at him.

"Well," Feygen said carefully, "I know you've both given your statements, and I really wanted to talk to Nathan, so, ah, I'll come back once he's awake and clear-headed."

Neither of them moved or spoke. They both just stared at him.

He had his hand on the door when Nathan Pittman made a sound. Both his parents flinched away from him. He made the sound again, slightly louder this time.

Feygen went to his side immediately. Nathan's eyes opened, just a tiny bit, and focused on him. Feygen said, "Nathan? Can you hear me?"

In a weak whisper Nathan said, "I hear you...detective."

Feygen glanced up at the Pittmans, neither of whom made any move to come closer to Nathan's bed. He looked back down to Nathan. "I know this is a lousy time for it, but I need to ask you a question or two."

Nathan nodded faintly.

"I need to know what kind of contact you had with the vigilante known as the Gray Widow. Before you got shot."

Nathan stared at him, and rolled his eyes. "Never met her," he whispered, before grimacing in pain. "Only read about her, heard about her." He glanced down at himself as best he could without moving his head. "I really screwed up, didn't I?"

His eyes slid closed, and his breathing evened out. Feygen figured he'd passed out again, but the boy's eyelids cracked back open. *"Hey,"* he whispered, a little more energetically. *"Hey.* Did they catch her?"

"The Gray Widow? No. She's still out there."

Nathan smiled a little. "Good." He swallowed, stayed quiet for a few moments, then whispered, "C'mere a second."

Feygen bent close to him, turned his ear to the boy's lips. So softly Feygen was sure only he heard the words, Nathan breathed, "Get these two ghouls out of my room, will you?"

Nathan's eyes shut again, and he slept.

"What was that?" Mrs. Pittman barked. After the quiet of Nathan's exhausted voice, his mother sounded like an air-raid siren. "What did he say to you?"

Feygen glanced at Mr. Pittman, back to Nathan's mother, and said, "Don't know. Couldn't make it out." He nodded to both of them and excused himself, and he could feel them staring at him as he headed for the door.

Feygen had the door halfway open when someone else pushed on it from outside. He backpedaled as a very tall, very thin young man in a pinstripe suit entered the room. He carried a briefcase, and smiled quickly at Feygen, but focused his attention on the Pittmans.

"Mr. and Mrs. Pittman?" the man asked in a smooth, practiced voice. Nathan's parents switched their stares to the newcomer, to Feygen's relief. "My name is Krach, and I represent the law firm of Kurth & Serrano. Mr. Pittman, Mrs. Pittman, could I talk to you about the potential legal aspect of your son's condition?"

Feygen moved out into the corridor. The door closed slowly behind him and cut off the lawyer's words. On another day he might have gone back in and forcibly ejected young Mr. Krach, on grounds of terminally inappropriate behavior if nothing else. Today...he was too distracted, both by Nathan Pittman's sub-human parents and by Nathan himself. *Did they catch her?*

No. She's still out there.

Good.

Those words played on a loop in Feygen's mind as he left the hospital.

CHAPTER SIXTEEN

Janey and Tim stayed there in the room for about half an hour. They helped Adam put together several jigsaw puzzles and listened to him sing. Tim didn't say a word the entire time.

With a small sigh, Adam's energy drained away. He said, "Lie down," to the nurse. The nurse and Janey helped him to the bed and pulled a blanket over him, and he fell asleep immediately.

After a few moments, as Adam breathed deeply and slowly, Janey said, "No change." It wasn't a question, and she didn't look at the nurse as she said it.

"No," the nurse replied. "He'll probably sleep for several hours."

Janey nodded, spent a few more seconds watching Adam, and led Tim out of the room.

Before they left, Tim shrugged out of his raincoat and handed it to Janey. She started to protest, but he said, "I wore it in. No point in getting soaked twice." Janey nodded a silent thanks to him as she slipped the coat on, and Tim made a soft snorting sound. "It looks better on you than on me."

They made their way to the car.

Headed back to the city through the rain, after half a dozen false starts Janey said, "Adam and I are still legally married so he can stay on my insurance. He had no family of his own. Neither of us did." She paused. "We lacked a few weeks getting to our first anniversary."

"And...he doesn't..."

"He doesn't know me. According to the tests, his mental capacity is right on par with a three-year-old." She blinked a few times. "When he woke up, the nurses had to introduce me to him. He has no recall of his former life. He only knows me as a friend who comes to visit."

"Janey, I'm so sorry." He put a comforting hand on her leg.

She looked sharply at him, as though she might snap at him. Instead she glanced down at his hand, ran one finger lightly across the back of it, picked it up and placed it gently back in his lap.

"Thank you. Tim...I'd like to tell you. The rest of it. Everything. I think I need to."

"Of course. ...Anything."

The words came haltingly to begin with, but soon they poured out of her as if draining from a wound.

* * *

Janey first saw Adam Kendrick on a Wednesday afternoon, in the art supply store where he worked. Adam was trying to help three different customers at once, was clearly stressed, and Janey accidentally made that stress much worse when she reached for a Scharff brush display just as Adam walked by. Janey's hand knocked the half-gallon jug of yellow acrylic paint he was carrying out of his grip, and it landed in just the right way for the lid to crack and fly off, spraying yellow across the concrete floor.

"I'm so sorry!" Janey looked around for something that might help mop up that much paint. "That was totally my fault, I'm so sorry, let me help you!"

Adam declined her offer of help, and stiffly—yet still politely—suggested that Janey just let him clean it up on his own. Mortified and humiliated, Janey fled the store.

That night she went home and painted a picture of him.

It was the first of her paintings that took on the unearthly quality for which she would eventually become known. She used watercolor, on a nine-by-twelve sheet, and framed it herself. She was up the whole night doing it, and took it to the art supply store the next day.

Janey found Adam straightening some crow quill pens, took

a deep breath, and said, "Um, hi. I made a huge mess in here yesterday, and I'm really sorry, and I felt terrible, and this is a peace offering."

Frowning, Adam took the painting and stared at it silently.

"My name is Janey. Janey Sinclair."

After an excruciating fifteen seconds, Adam dragged his eyes up from the watercolor and really looked at Janey for the first time. "You painted this last night. From memory."

"Uh...well, yeah."

The painting captured Adam perfectly, just as she'd seen him the day before, in jeans and T-shirt and his employee's smock, but she had no idea if he'd like it or not. For that matter, she didn't know if he'd think she was crazy or not. Finally he lowered it and, to her relief, held out his hand. "I'm Adam."

She shook it. "It's nice to meet you, Adam."

"I, uh, I'm gonna be done here at 6:00. There's a coffee shop down on the next corner—would you like to meet me there?"

That evening's shared pot of coffee marked the first date of many. Ten days after Janey gave Adam the painting, he started saving money for a ring. Four months later he asked her to marry him.

At the age of twenty-four, Janey Sinclair carried more than her fair share of demons. Her father's death and her own injury, all the time spent in psychiatric care, and now the presence of—she could only think of it as a *power,* a power she knew she couldn't let anyone else know about—lent her a gravity, a deep-rooted sadness, and a great deal of forced maturity.

It also left her with an unshakable feeling of isolation.

Her life was well-organized, much more so than those of many other women her age. She had a steady job as an assistant instructor at a dojo, she painted in the evenings in her apartment, and—since she hardly ever went anywhere or did anything that cost much money—she was well on her way to saving up enough for a down payment on a house.

And she felt more alone than she would have thought possible, and didn't know what to do about it.

She had no shortage of dates. Tall, lean, graceful, with her startling blue-gray eyes and resplendent mass of hair, Janey could get attention if she wanted it. But the shallow young men she met, the handful of flings—she couldn't think of them as relationships—did nothing for her loneliness.

All of that changed with Adam.

A little taller than she was, and not quite bony, he had a natural athleticism Janey appreciated. His personality was a mass of contradictions and surprises: painfully shy in public, when they were alone together Adam revealed a razor-sharp sense of humor and a surprising capacity for silliness.

He followed a firmly defined moral code, and had a very strong sense of what he considered *proper.* He was by far the most dignified man she'd ever spent time with. Yet his sexuality could have been described with the kind of clichéd words found in bad romance novels: "unbridled," or perhaps "volcanic."

In Janey's mind, the day she first saw Adam marked a new beginning in her life. A fresh start, not bogged down by the weight of all the grief and horror that had for so long occupied such a large part of her. When she started seeing Adam, the nightmares which had come to her at least two nights out of every seven stopped cold.

After their wedding, they got a small but comfortable two-bedroom apartment together, and with their combined incomes Adam enrolled in night classes at Georgia Tech. He said he wanted to be an architect, and Janey supported his decision.

What began so beautifully ended in a rush of pain.

It was the night of the judo test at the dojo, and Janey had to work late, letting students flip her onto the mat over and over. Adam went without her to a Wednesday night church supper. At a little past seven o'clock one of the elderly women there complained of a headache, and Adam went out to his car to get some Advil from the glove box. He kept it there right next to his .38 caliber revolver, for which he had a concealed carry permit.

Whoever attacked him was never caught. The assailant, or assailants, took Adam's wallet, which police found later in a public trash can, and made off with the seventeen dollars he'd had in it. What the police were able to determine, following a ballistics test, was that the gunshot to Adam's head had come from his own gun.

Janey got the call just as she arrived home from work. She was at the hospital five minutes later...far too late for Adam, far too late to make any difference. Her husband was deep in a coma by the time he reached the ER.

A doctor met her in the hall outside the room where Adam lay. Her face drained of blood and her heart kicking, Janey almost shoved the man out of the way and burst into the room, but the doctor said, "Mrs. Kendrick, please wait, I need to talk to you," and something in the tone of the man's voice stopped her. When Janey realized what the doctor must have to say, her insides went numb.

"It's Sinclair," Janey mumbled.

"I'm sorry, what?"

"My…I kept my…my last name." Something was dying inside her, withering away the longer she stood there. She couldn't feel her lips. "It's Sinclair."

"Mrs. Sinclair, your husband suffered a gunshot wound to the head. He's receiving the best care we can give him, but he's lapsed into a coma. I'm...afraid there's been brain damage."

Janey's vision grew hazy and ragged around the edges.

"The damage is extensive. It is likely that your husband won't survive. I'm sorry."

Janey stayed there, at Adam's side, for four days straight. She didn't sleep, or eat. She hardly moved. Each day the doctors told her Adam's condition was growing worse. They showed her charts, gave her literature to read, explained it all in their technical ways—and they gave her husband another few weeks, at the very most. Finally they convinced her to go home and get some rest.

Janey spent the time after Adam's attack on something like autopilot, a cardboard-cutout woman. She went to work, taught her classes. Came home. Visited Adam. Went back home, stared at the canvas, painted nothing. Went to sleep. The cycle repeated, and Janey felt nothing. People from their church tried to see her, but she had nothing to say to them. She had nothing to say to anyone.

The one-month limit the doctors had given Adam came and went, and he lay in the hospital bed and kept breathing.

Another month passed. And another.

Janey took books to the hospital, and read to him for hours every evening.

She softly touched his face, and told him how much she loved him. He didn't open his eyes for her. Didn't talk. Didn't move.

Then one evening she received a call from the duty nurse. "Mrs. Sinclair? Janey Sinclair? I have...I have some news for you."

Janey bolted up from where she'd been lying on the couch. "What? What?"

"Mrs. Sinclair...your husband has emerged from his coma."

"*What?* He's conscious?" A hydrogen bomb detonated inside her.

"Yes, he is, but there are—"

"I'm on my way!" Janey shouted, and ended the call. In her near-delirium she completely missed the tone of the nurse's last sentence. Not for an instant did she consider that Adam's recovery might have been less than total. With a hope in her heart hotter than the sun, Janey stepped out her back door into darkness and flickered away to the hospital.

In a miracle recovery that defied all of known medical science, Adam Kendrick was awake and alert, and less than ten minutes after she got the call Janey burst into his room, crying like a little girl, and rushed to his side and put her arms around him.

Adam screamed and burst into tears and fought her and kicked her away.

* * *

"It was worse than if he'd just died."

A sudden burst of rain hammered down, shrouding them. For an instant they were trapped in the car, alone in a gray soulless void.

"That was two years ago. Tim... I can only imagine what you're thinking. But this is what happened, and it's what's caused me to do what I've been doing. I never told him, what I could do, I never shared that with him. But after Adam woke up, I..."

She trailed away.

Tim said, "You got pissed off."

Janey stared at him, amazed, and slowly nodded. "I got pissed off. I got pissed off at Sammy Kyle, and all his goons, and I got pissed off at the cowardly piece of shit who did that to my husband, and I got pissed off at everybody else in the world. Most of all… and the counselors have told me this is normal, but it doesn't make me feel any less terrible about…I got pissed off at Adam, because if he hadn't had that God-forsaken gun in his car, they wouldn't have taken it away from him, and he wouldn't have gotten shot."

Tim nodded solemnly.

"So I trained and trained and trained. I mean, I was already pretty damn good, and the…the teleporting…it made me a little stronger, too. Physically. I went *way* beyond what I thought I could, and I stole a suit of prototype body armor from a military research lab. And I decided to go out and find some of the same assholes that fucked up my life, and make it so they wouldn't, or *couldn't* screw up anybody else's."

"And the Gray Widow was born."

"Yeah. …But I didn't come up with that name. That was somebody else."

Tim watched the rain. "This is so much, Janey. I don't even know what I think about all this."

She flicked the windshield wipers a notch higher. "I don't

blame you."

"Wait, you got *stronger?* Are you saying you're like…Spider-Man strong?" When Janey gave him a truly frosty look, Tim held up his hands. "You're right, you're right, sorry, that's not important right now."

Janey sighed. "No, I'm not Spider-Man strong. But you probably don't want to arm-wrestle me."

They fell silent. After a few long minutes, Tim said, "Do you…has this helped you any? Talking, getting it all out like this? Has the anger gone down any?"

Janey wrinkled her forehead and drummed her fingers on the wheel. "Not really."

* * *

Simon Grove parked Brenda Jorden's brown Ford in the parking lot of the shiny new high-rise next to the LaCroix, and settled in to wait.

The rain on the car's roof lulled him. Made him sleepy. Drew him back...

After Prom night with Michelle,—after she and her friends had humiliated him so thoroughly he thought his heart might collapse in his chest—he'd been convinced that every last person he knew despised him. So when he got back to his house and changed out of those ridiculous formal clothes, Simon Grove left his Louisiana home and went for a walk.

Temperatures were down in the forties, and Simon decided to wear his favorite fleece-lined denim jacket. He knew his mother wouldn't have wanted him out this late alone, but he felt restless and went anyway. He couldn't really talk to her anymore. Not that they ever shared secrets with each other...but over the last few years he'd found that he could hardly talk to her about *anything*.

Since his teeth got straighter. He thought that was when she stopped wanting to talk to him. They'd been crooked, and she told him maybe they'd straighten out as he got older, but they didn't. The canines punched forward, and the upper incisors turned at odd angles. "We'll have to get you some braces," she said.

He didn't want braces. The other kids made fun of him enough already.

But his mother took him to the orthodontist, and they made plans to put the braces on, and that night he came home and stared into the mirror for a very long time. He wanted his teeth to straighten out, focused on it, concentrated as hard as he could.

And they did.

While he watched.

He was afraid to show his mother for days. He thought he knew what she'd say. It turned out he was right.

She hadn't really talked to him much since then.

He kept it up, though, and not just with his teeth. Sometimes he'd will his muscles to grow, and they would. He'd make his hair get longer, or change the color of his eyes, or turn his skin a darker shade. It felt nice.

Of course he didn't tell anybody else about it, not even Paul next door, since he knew nobody else would understand. And even if they did, they'd probably still stop talking to him, just like his mother. So except for his teeth, which he kept straight, he didn't let anyone else see his changes. That was private. That was his.

Simon pulled the jacket tighter around him and walked into the trees behind the house. His mother paid people to come in and keep the undergrowth cleared out, so it was easy walking. And so quiet, in the cold of the winter. No birds. Not even any katydids. Just him and the fallen, decaying leaves and the light from the moon.

Restless. Was that the right word? He'd surely been feeling something lately, more and more. A little more each time he changed, in fact. What was it? He felt as if he needed...something. What?

He heard a noise behind him and whirled around, frightened,

ready to run, but it was only Ruby. She came running toward him through the carpet of leaves, tongue wagging out, her breath hanging in the air around her. He knelt down to pet her and she whined as if in pain.

"Whatcha doin' out here, girl? Huh? Whatcha doin' out here?" Simon knew she was supposed to be leashed behind Paul's house. He noticed a few dark streaks on her fur.

Was that...blood?

She whined again.

He smoothed the fur away from a deep abrasion around her neck, where the collar had been. "Did you break your leash?" he asked. He kept his voice soft and comforting. "Did something make you run away?" He remembered hearing a dog barking earlier in the evening, but he hadn't connected it with Ruby. Again she whined. Simon parted more of her thick gray fur, tried to get a better look at her wound in the moonlight.

He felt strange. Simon looked up, through the trees, and saw a star right above him grow very bright, and a wave of something thick and dark crashed through his mind and along his limbs, and he fell backward into the leaves.

Ruby danced away a few steps, but came back, concerned. Simon's stomach knotted, and his jaw and hands both blazed with pain as if they'd been smashed with hammers.

"What...oh *God...*" Pain. More pain. The cool blacks and grays of the woods flip-flopped, and his eyes burned in green and yellow. "Ruby..." he whispered, gasping. "Get...somebody. Bring somebody." He rolled onto his side and gasped again as the agony ripped into his lungs, his heart. Ruby whined and chuffed, hovered over him. He reached out to her—

—and his fingers twisted, stretched and writhed. They circled Ruby's neck as he tried to haul himself up off the ground, and the tips found the leash abrasion and dipped into fresh-flowing blood.

Simon blacked out.

* * *

Later. Hours? Minutes?

White skin glistened red, and tendrils like steel cables flung away the dry, spent carcass. Jaws of ivory spines caught the moonlight, a cluster of narrow blades, and eyes filled with silver fire scraped across the yellowgreengold woods. Acid sweet as cider filled his veins, set him alight, more powerful than a hundred orgasms, and Simon Grove wanted more.

His joints clicked and ratcheted free of their restrictive sockets, and he skittered through the woods, moving like a bloody golem built of pipe cleaners and knives. Within seconds he reached Paul's house.

Something had happened here. He would've known that even without his new eyesight. Ruby's leash hung frayed and broken, and the back door stood ajar. On all fours Simon scuttled across the Burneys' side yard, out of the woods, with his fingers curled up onto the backs of his hands and his feet pointed the wrong way. His distended jaw brushed the grass, and when a fat cricket made sluggish by the cold lodged in the spines of his teeth, a long reddish-purple tongue flicked out of his mouth and dragged it inside.

He could hear someone moving around inside the house, but he didn't think it was Paul or either one of Paul's parents. He pushed the door wider and went inside.

He found Paul first.

His friend lay just outside the kitchen, in the living room, and his head was flat on one side. The floor all around him was slippery with blood. Simon stepped over him and continued into the house, and where his hands touched it, they soaked up Paul's blood. This act of absorption sent tremors out along every nerve, and thin streams of red ran down from Simon's eyes.

Paul's father lay sprawled on the stairs. A double-barreled shotgun rested in one out thrown hand, unfired. Only a few strands of skin and tendons held his head to his body. Simon heard a sound from the second floor, and started up the stairs.

Heavy rhythmic breathing came out of the parents' bedroom. Simon recognized it from the websites his mother didn't know he visited, the websites he'd masturbated to with his door closed and locked, but this didn't sound right. Uneven. One-sided. He peered around the door.

A huge naked fat man knelt on Paul's parents' bed. Paul's mother lay on her back in front of him, and he held her thighs across his, shoving himself into her, over and over, over and over. Her ribcage had been smashed in, and part of her face was gone. All the breathing came from the man.

Outlined in brilliant green, a heavy spade lay beside the bed. Its blade had been sharpened, and both it and the handle were covered with blood.

Simon rose to his feet. He let his fingers uncurl, and they waved around him like the tendrils of a sea anemone. The fat man gasped and arched his back, and Simon's fingers wrapped around his throat and pulled him off the bed.

The fat man started to scream, so Simon slid two fingers over his head and clamped his mouth shut. Simon's body hummed with energy, with power, and his muscles felt like steel, and he raised the fat man completely over his head, knelt on the floor, and dropped the man straight down onto his knee.

The killer's spine crunched apart, and Simon set him on the floor and straddled his chest. The fat man stared up at him through eyes glazing with pain and shock and fear, and Simon curled his fingers around the man's head and neck and arms and drained him dry.

Up through his fingers the blood came, the sensation so far beyond orgasmic he couldn't imagine words for it. It built with every drop he took, thrummed inside him, tuned each nerve into a high-tension wire and jangled pleasure down it. His vision darkened, returned, darkened again.

All over his body, from every pore in his skin, the blood emerged. Like a thick, dark red sheen of sweat, the flow accelerated, poured out of him in millions of tiny rivers, collected in pools on the floor around him.

Soft warm tongues licked and caressed inside his shoulders, in the small of his back, in his groin.

Tiny, thrilling touches like eyelashes flickering under his skin traveled the length of him, stroked the bones and ligaments of his feet, massaged the insides of his ribs.

He threw his head back and his mouth gaped wide and his eyes rolled all the way back in his skull, and he crowed the sensation, crowed the rush and the rapture as the fat man's body withered and dwindled and collapsed on itself, crowed the pleasure, crowed the joy.

When all the blood was gone, Simon rolled off the corpse onto his back on the floor, dripping and sticky and more sated than he'd ever felt in his life. He closed his eyes, breathed in the rich, coppery smell...

And wanted that feeling again.

Needed it.

* * *

The town was not as stunned as it could have been by the brutal mass murder because the full details of it were never released to the public. In a way, it was all very neat: victims and killer all right there, all waiting on the police.

In another way, it was grist for screaming nightmares.

The police chief at first thought it would be an isolated incident, a meteor strike of horror in an otherwise peaceful town.

But a few weeks later other bodies started turning up.

* * *

The rain slowed and trickled out of the sky in a gray, depressing haze as Janey parked the Civic in the LaCroix's private lot. She shut off the engine, and neither she nor Tim moved from their seats.

Janey stared straight ahead, while Tim gazed out the window. He didn't focus on anything. The only thing to see was a blank brick wall that ran along one side of the lot. A faint electric flash lit the rear- and side-view mirrors, and several seconds later they heard muted thunder.

"So the guy in the park," Tim said, finally, into the silence. "Simon. He was like you."

"He'd have to be. The things I saw him do..."

"And you've been looking for him."

Janey nodded.

"If you find him, what then? What're you going to do?"

"I'm not sure. It'll depend on him, I guess. But I don't think he's going to be very friendly. I mean, he didn't seem all *that* malicious when I caught up to him, just scared, mainly, but we both saw what he did to that girl."

"Yeah."

Janey shifted around in the seat to face him, unbuckled her safety belt to do it, and tucked her right leg underneath herself. "Tim. Do you believe humans are basically good? Or basically evil?"

"Jesus, Janey, that's a tired question. I'm sorry, but that's, like, college student stuff."

"Well? What do you believe?"

He sighed. "I guess...I think the human race is good. Basically. Yeah, I do, I think people will be nice if you give them the chance."

She stayed quiet for a long time. Finally looked down and shook her head sadly. "I disagree with you." She said it with regret, as if she had just lost something, or the possibility of something. "I wish I could agree, but I can't. Humans are selfish, and greedy, and...and it takes so much effort to teach ourselves to be anything but animals. I think, I believe, that's what makes us human—the ability to rise above our impulses. But so few of us do..."

Nonplused, Tim said, "That's pretty bleak."

"Have you read any history? Have you paid attention to what the human race does to itself, every day?"

Tim shook his head in denial. "Lots of bad stuff happens every day, sure... Wait. This relates to you directly, doesn't it? You think this is some kind of justification for what you do? You're rationalizing your actions?"

She bristled, but her voice stayed level. "I'm not rationalizing anything. What I'm saying is that I can have a direct effect on the amount of shit out there."

Tim gestured in the air for several seconds as he gathered his thoughts.

"I've said this before. To you, I think—but it's still true. *The only thing you can control is yourself.* It's not up to you to try to change the world…at least, not like this."

Janey looked out through the windshield and drummed her fingers on her thigh, silent, scowling.

Tim realized in a flash how exhausted he was. He'd spent the night almost without sleep, and run an emotional gamut for several hours straight. His eyelids grew heavy even as his heart thudded.

"Okay, look. I've missed a whole day of work, I'm sure the maintenance guy is about to report me missing, and I absolutely cannot handle any more surprises from you. Not for a while. I've got to go." He opened the door and was about to step out into the rain when Janey took his upper arm in one hand.

"Wait a minute. Close the door."

He did, but wouldn't look her in the eye.

"Can I trust—" She stopped and started over. "You know about me. Can we keep this between ourselves?"

He darted a glance at her. "If I told anyone..."

"If you told anyone." She paused. "It would be really inconvenient. But it wouldn't stop me. I just wouldn't have this apartment anymore."

He sighed. "Nobody's going to hear about this from me." He gently pulled her hand off his arm. "But we're going to have to talk about this some more. A lot more. Soon."

She nodded. "Fair enough. Thanks. Oh—let me give you your coat back."

Tim smiled faintly. "Nah, you keep it. I've got another one. And I wasn't lying. It does look better on you than on me."

* * *

Neither of them noticed Simon in the brown Ford, watching them. The skinny towel-head got out and ran inside the building. A few minutes later, wearing a badass knee-length gray raincoat, Janey Sinclair unfolded her long, delicious body from the car and followed after him. No sign of the gray body armor.

Simon had excellent vision, and saw Janey's tag number clearly through the rain. He jotted it down in a three-by-five spiral notebook, started the Ford and headed back out to Brenda's house.

On his way, he pulled out a cell phone and dialed eleven digits. The phone rang four times before it picked up.

"Hello?"

Not as confident as she used to be, Simon thought. *Some of that zing missing.* He said, "Hi, Mom."

In Louisiana, Anna Grove said, *"Simon?"*

"Yeah. How's it goin'?"

"Where are you? You didn't even say goodbye, I didn't know what happened! Are you all right?"

He sighed, stretched a little before he answered her. "Well... yeah, I'd say I'm all right. There's been a lot going on. I can't really tell you about much of it, but believe me, it's been an experience. Yeah, I'm fine."

"Where are you?"

"It still is an experience, if you want to get technical about it. Stuff's still happening."

"Simon?"

"Y'know, Mom, how I used to be? All timid and shit? Well, it's really not like that anymore."

"You need...need to..." Her voice shook, choked. He heard the tears in it. "Simon, you need to come home. You know you need to come home."

Simon grinned and tapped his knuckles on the wheel in time to the song on the radio. "Is Jessica there? Can I talk to her?"

"Simon..."

"I think Jess would like the new me, my new direction. I think we have some old times to catch up on, if I remember correctly. Do a few things should've been done before."

His mother cried softly into the phone for a few moments. Simon tried to figure out how he felt about that, and settled on annoyed.

Haltingly she said, "Please come home. Simon...I love you. I want to help you. Whatever's happened, whatever it is you've done, I want to help you."

He waved her words away impatiently. "Hey, listen, I just wanted to call and say, you don't need to worry about me, all right? Wasn't looking for melodrama. For the first time in my life I'm on top of things, and I wanted you to know that. Okay? Next time I'm in town I'll try and stop by."

He heard her say, "Simon!" one more time before he ended the call. He rolled his eyes and shook his head. *Okay, so that was a bad idea.*

Simon concentrated on his driving as the rain grew heavier.

CHAPTER SEVENTEEN

Janey went up to her apartment the traditional way: through the lobby, up the elevator, down the hall, through the door. Rain dripped down the back of her neck, and she scowled as she pulled off her clothes and got into the shower.

She tried to let her mind wander. It worked after a fashion. The water beat across the bruises on her chest and side and made her catch her breath, but soon she began to grow numb under the near-scalding spray. She mentally ticked off everything that had happened in the last few days—finding Simon in the park, the chase, the fruitless search, the discovery of the little girl, Tim's discovery of *her,* the visit to Adam at the home. She couldn't remember when so many things had happened to her so fast.

Janey dried off carefully and dabbed gingerly at the bruises, which had turned a sicker shade of yellow around the edges. She dressed in a loose T-shirt and running shorts and padded into the kitchen on bare feet. Her stomach growled. When had she last eaten?

Her mind was still on automatic as she prepared a breakfast-type meal of scrambled eggs, meatless bacon, and toast with honey. Tim knew who she was now. Knew *what* she was…at least, as much as she did herself. At this moment, in her apartment cooking breakfast, she could pretend that everything would continue as it had before—though she knew it couldn't.

Well...maybe it could.

She could take Tim out of the picture.

The thought came to her unwanted, dark and ugly.

With Tim gone, she could be more careful, take more precautions than before, and make sure she never repeated her mistakes. She knew fifteen different ways to kill with her hands, each of them precise and fast.

Dizzy, Janey braced herself against the counter with one hand, sick to her stomach. She washed her hands in the sink, then her face, then her hands again. "No," she said to no one. "No. No. No. *No.* What the *fuck,* Janey?"

Minutes later, after her stomach had settled down, Janey carried her loaded plate and a glass of orange juice to the couch, set them both down on the coffee table, and picked up the TV remote. She hardly ever watched TV, and really just wanted background noise. So when the opening credits of what was apparently a special televised edition of the *Good Morning Sheree* show started—Janey had never heard of *Good Morning Sheree*—she left it there, staring at the floor as she ate.

On the TV, applause from a studio audience gradually ended, and Janey glanced up just as a breathtaking redhead filled the screen. She chewed slowly and watched the redhead with narrowed eyes, her mind elsewhere. In a lower corner of the screen the word *LIVE* flashed slowly.

"Few sensations have gripped America in quite the way the topic of tonight's show has," Sheree said perfectly.

Maybe the whole thing was a bad idea. She tapped her plate absently with a piece of fake bacon. *Grown women don't do what I'm doing. When they have problems they deal with them, either alone or with someone else's help, but they deal with them. They don't do what I'm doing.*

But then, other people can't do what I'm doing.

She shook her head and closed her eyes...and snapped them open again, all her attention on the TV and Sheree Baker's voice.

"In just over one week, the mysterious character known as the Gray Widow has captured the hearts and minds of people all across the nation. She appears from out of nowhere, dishes out a brutal brand of justice, and vanishes again. More than a dozen people have come forward with stories of how the Gray Widow has helped them, claiming that she's come to their rescue as they were about to be victimized. But our guests today have a different take on what the Gray Widow is all about."

The cameras cut to focus on a couple in their late forties, seated uncomfortably in two chairs on one of the set's raised platforms. They both wore clothes appropriate for Sunday morning worship services, and both had tightly pinched faces. The man was fat, his belly spilling over the belt of his trousers, while the woman was reed-thin, approaching skeletal. Janey couldn't picture either of them smiling. A caption appeared on the screen below them: TOM & AMANDA PITTMAN. Below the names, in smaller letters: *Son was shot and hospitalized after imitating Gray Widow.*

Janey's throat turned dry as sand. She dropped her fork on the plate and forgot about it.

"Say hello to our guests, Tom and Amanda Pittman. In a widely publicized case, their son Nathan left the house a few nights ago, put on a mask, and tried to stop a robbery at a convenience store. In the process Nathan was shot, and is now in critical condition at Gavring Medical. Tom, Amanda, how are you doing?"

Janey thought her eggs would come back up, and she forced herself to drink a sip of orange juice. Her entire world had narrowed to the TV screen.

Amanda Pittman nodded bravely. "We're still here, Sheree. We're holding on."

Sheree nodded sympathetically, plastically. "And how is Nathan?"

"There's been no improvement," Tom Pittman said. His voice was gravelly and phlegm-filled. "The doctors haven't said anything about him getting better anytime soon."

"Tom, Amanda, I can only try to understand the pain you're both going through, and I extend my deepest sympathies. Now, I understand you've decided to take action based on what happened to your son?"

"We have, yes," Amanda Pittman said. "We're going to do something about that worthless, spineless vigilante that made our Nathan go out and do what he did."

"And you're talking about the so-called Gray Widow?"

"Yes we are," Tom Pittman growled. "Nathan wouldn't ever've got those stupid ideas in his head if not for that piece of trash. So we've got a lawyer, and as soon as the police catch her, we're going to make that *Gray Widow* pay for what she's done." Pittman filled the name with venom.

"So, just so there's no confusion here," Sheree said, sounding as though she barely understood it herself, "what you're going to do is file a lawsuit against the Gray Widow. Someone whose identity is unknown."

"It'll be known soon enough," Amanda Pittman chirped. She looked and sounded like an old, desiccated bird. "When the police catch that slut and pull off her mask, we'll have a lawsuit waiting for her so huge it'll make sure she never causes any more harm to any other innocent young people." The woman sounded coached.

Janey stood up from the couch, boiling inside. Captured the hearts and minds of the nation? She cursed herself for not keeping up with the news. And this kid, getting shot playing hero? How could she not have known about that?

Janey dumped her mostly uneaten meal down the garbage disposal as the Pittmans further described their hatred for her and their desire to see her brought to justice for the injury done to their son. Her hands trembling, she stood behind the couch and watched as members of the audience voiced their own opinions about her and how she should be dealt with. Some disagreed with the Pittmans, but a lot of the audience were middle-class, morally upstanding parents, and they seemed to back the couple wholeheartedly.

Janey clicked off the TV and violently hurled the remote the length of the apartment. It sailed through the door to her bedroom and punched a small triangular dent in the wall over her work table. She hurriedly dressed in dry clothes and headed downstairs.

* * *

Fields wasn't there when Simon got back. Probably off getting food or something. Simon stamped his feet on the front porch and wiped them on a bristly rubber mat before he came inside. Brenda sat on the couch, reading a Joe Lansdale novel, and looked up as he opened the door. "Well?"

Not *hi.* Not *hello.* Not *how are you.* Just *well?* Simon felt annoyed and frustrated, but when he tried to think more about that his head went sort of funny and he couldn't quite put a finger on why, so instead he decided to concentrate on what he'd been sent to do.

"Kid Creepy had it right on. I watched Sinclair get out of her car. Piece-of-shit little Honda. Got the tag right here." He handed her the notebook and went to the kitchen for a drink. She got up off the couch and followed him. "Another little tidbit for you, too. She's got herself a boyfriend, looks like."

"Oh really." Simon glanced at Brenda, saw the cogs and wheels turning. Brenda craved information, craved secrets. "Tell me about him."

He shrugged. "Just some bony sand nigger, looks like he's abou—"

Simon's whole head snapped around with the force of the backhand. He turned back toward Brenda, and she did it again, harder the second time.

"Don't you ever," she growled, "*ever* let me hear you use that word again."

Simon's face crawled with the change, back and forth. He finally settled on human and rubbed his jaw. "Touch a nerve, did I?"

* * *

Brenda glared at Simon Grove, breathing hard, while the time-distorted voices of dozens of children echoed inside her. *Nigger nigger nigger, Brenda is a nigger, nigger nigger nigger...* They'd made it into a crude song.

She wanted to kill them all. She wanted to kill Simon.

With a snarl she slapped one open hand onto Simon's forehead and pushed him backward into the kitchen wall. The scent flowed off her in a rushing chemical wave, and as she funneled it all into him his eyes glazed over and his jaw went slack.

"Forget we talked about this," she said, low and dangerous. "But do not, *ever,* in your entire *life,* use the word 'nigger' again. Got that?"

He nodded numbly.

"Good. Now I've got some information to gather. Get out of my sight."

* * *

Janey felt as if she'd been out of the country for the last several days.

Sitting in a public library in front of her shiny new laptop—she didn't have wi-fi in her apartment, not yet at least, and hadn't wanted to wait—she paged through site after site, each of them, in one form or another, featuring the masked vigilante commonly called "the Gray Widow."

She found the very first article to mention her, dated August 31. The first day she met Tim. That one didn't try to give her a name, but the appellation "Gray Widow" popped up soon enough. As near as she could tell, it had originated with a reporter named Darius Clay and gone viral from there, replacing the other names that had tentatively been put forward, such as "the Shadow Woman," "the Woman in Gray," and one that actually made her shudder: "the Woman Hood."

She'd only been truly active for, as Sheree Baker had said, a little over a week, but in that period she had made the front pages of CNN, MSNBC, and Fox News, as well as countless smaller sites. Each of them had only artists' renditions of her, except for Fox News, which featured a stylized, solid black head-and-shoulders silhouette on the cover, with a large red question mark where her nose would have been.

She found one of the renditions particularly striking. It depicted a woman in a skin-tight costume, a pair of nunchaku in one hand and a huge semi-automatic pistol in the other, and breasts at least four sizes larger than her own C-cups. The artist had taken it upon him- or herself to give her what amounted to a logo, too: a ragged, splintery cross with an evil-looking skull at its center, right in the middle of her chest.

Janey made a sound with her lips like *Pffff.*

A local news site contained a transcript of a debate which had taken place on—she couldn't believe this—the *Good Morning Sheree* show. Apparently the program normally ran very light fare, but the dialogue between two columnists, Greg Thatcher and Chirina McCallum, had served to focus the city's opinions after it showed up on Twitter and began trending. By bizarre default, the *Good Morning Sheree* forum grew into Atlanta's most common sounding board for expressing its feelings on the Gray Widow's activities.

The articles grew in frequency with each passing day. Even in just the few days she'd been common knowledge, she'd achieved the status of cultural icon, for good or bad. She was convinced of that when she found an advertisement for the upcoming *Gray Widow* web comic.

The artist who'd composed the web comic ad had obviously seen the earlier cross-and-skull drawing; the design was there, though this version of the Gray Widow also wore about sixty pounds of plate metal armor and hefted an implausibly huge gun. Janey grinned in spite of herself.

The Gray Widow buzz took a sharp turn for the serious after Nathan Pittman was shot. News of the shooting itself started out as small potatoes: lower-middle-class teenager shot during convenience store hold-up, in critical condition. Then the connection between Nathan's actions and the masked vigilante got out, and his story jumped to the front page and went out over the wire. When the *Chronicle* got pictures of Nathan's room, well on its way to being wallpapered with clippings about her, the entire nation learned the circumstances overnight.

A good two hours of Widow-related reading made Janey's head begin to spin. Eventually, after some time spent assimilating it all, three distinct things occupied her mind. The first was the image of Tom and Amanda Pittman, and the grief they felt because of what had happened to their son.

The second was guilt.

The third was an enormous sense of indignation.

Sides were taken, yes, but if what she'd read in the past couple of hours was any indication, most of the people who voiced opinions didn't care for what she was doing. Words kept cropping up such as *irresponsible* and *hurtful*. Twice she was called a negative role model. In the pieces published after Nathan Pittman was shot, the voices which had in the past been wary and suspicious bared their teeth and went after her with gusto.

"Of course she's to blame for Nathan Pittman's injury," proclaimed a noted televangelist. "What else can we expect when our children are bombarded with such images? What else can happen when an uncaring domestic terrorist stares back from every television and computer screen? The media is at fault, but even more so is the terrible individual herself. You see, this is what happens when women do not understand their place in God's plan. Whoever is behind the mask of the Gray Widow, she should be in the home, helping to raise the next generation and seeing to the needs of her hard-working husband. All this…this vigilantism? It's a perversion of God's will."

Janey had to take a break after reading that quote to let her heart rate settle back down.

In nearly every instance, those who spoke out against her were parents. The Gray Widow got Nathan Pittman shot! Catch her and lock her up before she hurts some other innocent child! Catch her and lock her up before she hurts *my* child!

At the other end of the spectrum were the twelve- to twenty-four-year-olds, particularly the teenage boys, who couldn't seem to get enough of her. One kid from Nashville, Tennessee had appointed himself president of the fast-growing Gray Widow Fan Club, which already boasted 60,000+ members.

She read about the Gray Widow Updates on BuzzFeed.com, and discovered that James Wan was talking to Paramount about a film.

Merchandise had flooded the market in record time, unimpeded by copyrights or the need to gain permission: posters, T-shirts, hats—ThinkGeek.com had a whole Gray Widow section.

Interviews taken with people stopped randomly on the street ranged from bitter hatred to mooning adoration. She hadn't quite caught on with the young teenage girls yet, but that didn't stop the females college-age and older, many of whom apparently found her both intriguing and inspiring. She saw a picture of a grinning college co-ed holding up a pair of Gray Widow boxer shorts. They looked hand-made.

The positive press still didn't outweigh the negative. She couldn't get Amanda Pittman's voice out of her head. *"Piece of trash..."*

Eventually Janey slung Tim's raincoat over one shoulder, tucked her expensive new purchase under one arm, and walked slowly to the exit, staring absently into space.

* * *

After Janey had gone through one of the six glass doors at the main entrance and started down the marble stairs, a man in a sweatshirt, jeans and Atlanta Braves cap made his way over to the reference librarian, a plump, smiling woman of about forty. "Afternoon, ma'am. Would you be the one to talk to if I had a question about the library's wi-fi network?"

The librarian's smile got broader. "I would indeed! What

would you like to know?"

Zach Feygen showed her his badge. "I'm a detective, ma'am. And I'm wondering how hard it'd be to get a look at what kind of search someone did on the public network here."

* * *

Back at the LaCroix, Janey trudged down the hallway, past the office door, to the elevator, which she rode by herself up to her floor. She didn't see anyone else as she unlocked her apartment and went inside.

Barely aware of her surroundings, Janey went straight to the empty utility closet, stepped inside, and emerged into the basement. She slept there that night, stretched out on top of a sleeping bag thrown over an inflatable mattress.

At 2:13 a.m., Janey awoke and lay motionless, staring at the ceiling. She let the night vision come to her, and moved her eyes slowly over every crack and crevice and irregularity in the poured-concrete-and-steel-beam ceiling. Eventually she rolled off the mattress and padded across the smooth, cool floor to the Vylar suit, which hung on its rack, waiting for her. She tugged the rack over next to her work bench and reached through the darkness, up to her bedroom. Scorching air flooded around her. When she pulled her hand back, she held a brush and a tube of black acrylic paint.

With a somewhat sardonic smile Janey stared at the suit and unscrewed the cap from the tube.

* * *

Earlier that night, but several hours after he left the library, Zach Feygen groaned and rolled his shoulders as Heather worked on his back. He did that partly because it felt good, and partly because he knew Heather liked to see his muscles flex. He still ragged himself from time to time for robbing the cradle—Heather was a good nine years his junior—but damned if she didn't have herself together better than anybody else he'd been out with in the last three years.

The sheets always smelled like her now. He loved it.

Feygen's eyelids were heavy, and felt as though they were lined with gravel. He was immensely tired, and knew he ought to be dropping off to sleep any second now.

Any second now. But it wouldn't happen. Not with his insides as twisted up as they were. Not with what he'd found out today.

"You're thinking about *her,* aren't you?" Heather asked, reading his mind. She worked her hands up both sides of his spine, kneaded the heavy muscles there.

"I can't get it out of my head. Her, the case, the whole thing. The way she stood there, downstairs, and talked to us. Plus..."

Heather paused. "Plus? Plus what?"

Feygen sighed and slowly rolled over, looked up at her. If anything could begin to take his mind off work, Heather certainly could.

She straddled him on the bed, wearing only a pair of filmy French-cut panties, and he reached up to run his fingers along the skin of her side, and across one tiny breast. "You're like a work of art," he said softly. She smiled and took his hand, nibbled on the fingertips.

"Most of the time that would work," she said. "But this time I'm not going to let you distract me, because I can tell, you've really got something to say. So out with it."

Feygen frowned, but he laced his thick fingers through Heather's slim, delicate ones and decided to talk.

"I think I know who she is."

Heather's eyebrows shot up. "Yeah?"

"Her father—he's dead now, died a little over eleven years ago—he was a magician, like Copperfield, or David Blaine, only not as big."

She frowned, and made him feel very old by asking, "Who's

Copperfield?"

"Oof. Doesn't matter. Never mind. But this guy, the father, played a lot at this one place, used to be a really fancy venue. And that's the place where the Gray Widow first showed up. So I looked at the original blueprints, and there's this part of it... It's got to be her. The woman I've been following, it's got to be her in the suit and the mask. I've got no proof, but I've got more than enough for a search warrant."

She slid one hand over his chest. "So...you're going to bust her?"

Instead of answering, Feygen pulled her down against him and wrapped his arms around her.

"What she's doing is illegal," Feygen said after a few moments. "I can't even count all the laws she's broken. I've got to bring her in. She's a vigilante. A criminal."

Heather took a breath as if to speak, and Feygen thought he knew what she was thinking. *If not for that vigilante, there'd be no more Zach Feygen, would there?*

"We both know what she's doing is illegal," Heather finally said, her breath hot against his neck. "But is it *wrong?*"

He pulled her more tightly to him and shut his eyes.

CHAPTER EIGHTEEN

In the control booth, Ted Swit watched Sheree, his eyes glazed. After the call from ABC they'd gone back to his place, and she'd worked him over mercilessly. He'd heard of sex hangovers before, but this was the first time he'd actually had one.

Sheree Baker's smile soared to maximum wattage as the theme music ended. Camera One stayed tight on her as she gazed out over the studio audience.

"Good morning, Atlanta!" she shouted, and the crowd bellowed right back at her. "Well, folks, I read the news today, and it looks like the Gray Widow actually took last night off!"

The audience laughed, probably would have even if the LAUGHTER sign hadn't lit. Sheree had ridden the unexpected wave of the Widow's popularity with tremendous grace, and late yesterday afternoon her agent got a call from ABC. Her smile this morning wouldn't have been any dimmer had her guest been the treasurer of a high school math club. She glowed, and the crowd picked up on it.

"That's right," she said after the laughter died down. "Not a single report of a foiled burglary, or a prevented assault—not even any gang members with broken arms."

More laughter.

"But hey, even masked vigilantes have to take vacations, don't they? So we're going to change pace here, too, and try to remember what we used to do before this became the *Good Morning Gray Widow* show."

Laughter laughter laughter.

In the control booth, the phone buzzed. He grabbed it up. "Swit, hello."

He didn't say anything else, just listened, and felt the blood drain from his face. Swit finally said, "Thanks," in a small voice, and dropped the handset back on the cradle. His eyes, which bulged hugely, never left the set.

"What was that?" the sound tech asked.

"Wuh," Swit said. He swallowed hard. "The. Um." He picked up his headset and spoke to the crew. "Guys? I, uh, don't know for sure, but—uh, something is about to happen, I think. Just...stay alert, okay?"

Sheree, still with the thousand-watt smile, said, "With us this morning is the proverbial local boy done well, recent country music sensation Chad McNabb." A young man of about twenty-three sat in one of the guest chairs, wearing a white shirt and jeans and a cowboy hat. His polished boots shined brightly as he smiled and waved at the cameras.

Sheree turned to make her way to the guest platform.

All sound from the audience died.

The Gray Widow walked out from behind the curtains that covered the back wall of the studio. With her left hand she pushed along a small podium on wheels, a set piece used when a local minister recorded his TV spots. It had a goose-neck microphone stand built into it.

No longer was the Widow's segmented armor solid gray. Now a pattern in black adorned her torso and sections of her arms and legs—eerie, symmetrical markings echoing something from an actual spider's body—and she had added six more black spots to her mask, to mimic a spider's eight eyes.

Before these decorations, the Gray Widow had been a strange, intimidating figure. Now, striding slowly out into the studio lights, she became menacing. Alien.

Terrifying.

Sheree glanced at the booth. "Is this a bit?" She giggled nervously when no one answered her.

The Widow kept walking, pushing the podium along beside her, until she stood in the middle of the set. Her eyes remained hidden behind the spots of black mesh, but wherever she looked, people felt it.

The Widow slowly swiveled her head, took in the people in the control booth, the audience, the floor crew, and lastly Sheree and Chad McNabb. McNabb, petrified, made as though to rise from his seat, but the she motioned for him to stay where he was, the smallest gesture with one gauntleted hand. McNabb sank back down obediently.

The crew only needed about two seconds to realize what they had, and immediately the Widow filled every monitor in the station. Finally she moved, stepped back behind the podium, and with her foot pushed down a lever that lowered the podium's rubber-tipped feet to the floor. With the podium secured, she leaned forward slightly and stared into the cameras.

The director took a step backward and clutched her clipboard convulsively with one hand.

Sheree Baker almost dropped her handheld when the Gray Widow turned and beckoned to her. Sheree went to her without question, and when the Widow held out her hand Sheree silently handed over her microphone. Quietly, the Gray Widow said, "Thank you." As Sheree backed away, the Widow calmly fitted the microphone onto the end of the podium's flexible neck, and clipped a small, square box onto it. A red light lit up on the box.

Straightening, the Widow pulled a 3 by 5 card out of the gauntlet on her forearm and let it drop onto the podium. She glanced down at it briefly and began to talk, in a voice that came through the speakers like frozen rainwater. Swit realized the small black box was some kind of sophisticated voice modulator.

Very slowly, the Gray Widow said, "Since I...began...I've been accused of many crimes."

A gofer named Louis skidded to a stop outside the control booth door. Swit whirled around to face him. "Well?"

"No good, man," Louis said. "Every door I tried is locked. I think they're chained." Swit cursed and turned back to watch the woman at the podium. "The cops are already pulling up outside, and a bunch of reporters, too."

On camera, the Widow continued talking. The studio audience could have been a collection of plywood props for all the movement they made.

"People have called me a racist. People have called me a terrorist. People have said that I am a negative influence on America's youth. I have a few things of my own to say about all of this."

Swit, on the verge of babbling, said, "This is going out, right? It's going out, right?"

Another technician said, "Relax. We're streaming." He chuckled. "Man, this is cool as hell."

The Gray Widow continued: "First of all, and for the record, I am no racist. I'm not black. I'm not white. As far as any of you need to be concerned, I'm not even human. The color of a person's skin makes no difference whatsoever in how I see him or her, or in what steps I take. Actions concern me, and actions only. I am motivated solely by behavior.

"Second, concerning the charge of terrorism. I think, depending on what definition you decide to use, I will accept that. What I'm doing...the reason for my existence...is the modification of behavior. I want the people of this city to *behave*. And I'll resort to terror if necessary to see that they do.

"If you—and I address every single person in this city—if you engage in criminal activity... If you sell drugs to minors. If you assault someone. If you forcibly take what does not belong to you...I have something for you, something that I promise I will give you in abundance. I will give you *pain.*"

Several members of the audience gasped.

* * *

In his apartment, his toothbrush in his mouth, Tim wandered out of the bathroom and glanced at his TV. He was going to be late getting to the office if he didn't hurry, but he thought he'd heard something strange on whatever show was playing, and he paused in his brushing to look.

The news had broken in live, and Janey filled the screen in full-blown costume. Tim yelped, and gagged on toothpaste.

* * *

In the off-white two-story house, Brenda Jorden and Ned Fields watched as the Gray Widow spoke.

"It's nothing more complicated than classical conditioning," the Gray Widow continued. "You commit a crime, I find you, and I cause you pain. No matter where you are, no matter who you are, if you are a criminal, I will gift you with intense physical agony. I will make it so that everyone, every single human being in this city, directly associates *crime* with *pain.*"

"This is unreal," Fields said. "Can you believe that bitch?"

Brenda Jorden didn't say anything. She only watched, and hoped more than ever that they could subdue the vigilante. Brenda knew her name—Sinclair, both Scott and Simon had confirmed that—but Fields didn't, and neither did Stamford. They didn't need to. Not yet.

* * *

In his hospital room, propped up on pillows and listening to the Gray Widow speak, Nathan Pittman grinned and shook his head in amazement.

The audience still sat, transfixed, as the Gray Widow went on. "Now, a good number of you have made the claim that I caused the injury of Nathan Pittman. I deeply regret what happened to Nathan Pittman, and if it were within my power I would heal his wounds. But it isn't. So I will say this: from now on, I will consider anyone else in this city who puts on a mask and tries to fight crime outside the law just as much a criminal as the most depraved murderer. I'll repeat that, so there's no confusion. If anyone in this city tries to imitate me, I will deal with that person even more harshly than I would an ordinary criminal. This is *my* job. My niche in this society. My link in the food chain. Only I will fill it. So if anyone else has the desire to become what I am, put it out of your mind. Because if I find you, I'll break you off at the knees."

A nurse stood beside Nathan with a tray of medication on a rolling cart. She gestured at the TV and said, "This is that vigilante you wanted to be like? But she's totally *slamming* you."

"Hey." Nathan waved one hand weakly. "She can *have* the job."

* * *

The Widow's voice had grown harsher and harsher, until her last seven words—*"I'll break you off at the knees"*—sounded like razor blades scraping across rock. The hairs on the back of Ted Swit's neck stood up. From the front of the building came the faint sound of police trying to break the doors down.

"The general public has also branded me a criminal. I can't argue with that. What I'm doing is illegal. However—and I say this with the utmost respect for the law enforcement community—I don't care. No one can stop me. No cell can hold me. Atlanta belongs to me, and I will see that it stays protected." She held up the 3x5 card. On the back was a symbol that mirrored the black eye spots on her mask.

"Take a good look at this. I call it 'the Eyes of the Widow.' Soon you will begin to find the Eyes of the Widow around the city. On buildings…at bus stops…carved into sidewalks and telephone poles. And when you see it, you will know that *I am nearby*. I am watching. And I *will act*."

The Widow put the card back down and tilted her head from side to side, cracking her neck. "Someone recently told me that the only thing any of us can truly control is ourselves. That may be true. It may be that my actions will change no one's minds or hearts. But I *am* in control of myself. I *will* protect this city. And I will not stop. Ever."

The Gray Widow lifted her arms out to her sides for a moment. "One last thing. As you can see, I do not carry guns. I never have. I never will. I do not believe private citizens need to hold in their hands the power to take another human being's life. To pull a trigger and end someone, instantly, with no planning, no skill, and no effort. I take a *dim view* of guns. And if I find someone out there using one in the commission of a crime, I will go hard on that person. Very, *very* hard."

She leaned forward, raking her gaze across the audience. "There is a new law in Atlanta. The Gray Widow's Law. It's easy to remember: do unto others as you would have them do unto you… *or else*. Please. Quote me on that."

The Widow plucked the card off the podium, disconnected the voice modulator, and strode back to the curtain at the rear of the studio. She turned to face the audience, gathered great folds of the curtain in both hands, and jerked violently downward, tearing it off the thin metal support rail. Multiple tiny, metallic *pings* sounded as the hooks popped loose, and the material billowed down and forward, hiding her in its folds.

It settled to the floor and flattened out, empty.

Someone in the audience screamed.

Ted Swit came out of the booth and crossed the studio before he realized what he was doing. He pulled and tugged at the curtain, which was hot to the touch and smelled faintly singed, but it was obvious even before he grabbed it that nothing hid underneath. The Gray Widow had gone, just as she'd arrived—out of and into thin air.

* * *

Simon slowly emerged from his room that evening and approached Brenda. She'd moved to a chair in the living room, but was still reading the same book. Brenda glanced up as he came in, and her lips curled as she took in the look on his face.

Brenda put the book down, uncoiled from the chair, allowing her skirt to ride high up her thighs as she rose, and moved into Simon's arms before he realized what she was doing. Her kiss felt cool and silky. Simon's hands moved down her back, then lower, but she smiled and chuckled and pulled away from him.

"No no, remember yourself."

He'd already started to react to her, a sexual ache he'd actually begun to get used to, and he frowned resignedly. "Sorry."

"I've got another favor to ask of you," she said, and took his hand. He let himself be led, and she pulled him to a small utility room off the kitchen and put her hand on the knob. "Tonight I want you to do something...*decisive* for me. But first..."

She opened the door, and Simon's eyes flickered and changed at what lay inside.

"You're still a growing boy. You can have your meal." Brenda lowered her eyelids and traced one finger along the bulging line of his crotch. "And after that, maybe you can have dessert."

She left him standing in front of the utility room door. He didn't move for several seconds, only watched.

Another teenage girl lay on the floor of the room, slumped against the wall, barely conscious. A thin silvering line ran from the corner of her mouth, and her eyes rolled back in her head. Several sheets of thick plastic covered the floor of the room and curved up at the walls.

Rail-thin, the girl wore only a ragged pair of jeans with the knees worn out of them and a dirty blue bra. Fine blond hair fell down just past her shoulders, and tracks like a miniature railroad ran up the insides of both arms. No-name junkies Brenda brought to him, junkies looking for a fix, all of them, no lives to leave behind, nothing. Wasting themselves on synthetic peace. He could always feel the drugs as they came through. Simon found himself sneering as the urge built up.

He did nothing to hold it back. His jaw unhinged and stretched, popping and sliding, his fingers lengthened and waved through the air around him.

Without taking the hard white pinpoints of his eyes off the girl's semi-unconscious body, he entered the room and quietly closed the door behind him.

* * *

Later, Simon walked out of the utility room, coated and dripping red.

Brenda had put down a plastic runner for him, and wordlessly he padded along it to the bathroom, where he stripped and got in the shower. Before he closed the bathroom door he glanced out at Brenda, where she sat at her usual place on the couch, curled up with her book. She hadn't even looked up at him.

He thought of Scott Charles. The kid hadn't left his room in a couple of days. What had Brenda said? "I think Scott's had too much, for too long. He might be broken." What did that mean? He didn't know. Not that it mattered.

Simon took his time in the shower, let the scalding water soak into him.

He didn't worry about the mess he'd left. Fields always took care of that. A small, scratchy thought popped up, and Simon took a moment to examine it: he was pretty sure that Brenda touched

Ned Fields in the same way she had just touched him, gave him the same feelings...even let him go *all the way* with her.

He paused, a bar of soap in his hand, and the water ran off the tip of his nose in a stream while he considered that. Finally he decided that that didn't matter either, and finished his shower.

Simon came back out into the living room with one towel wrapped around his waist, drying his hair with another. He wore nothing under the towel. He flopped down on the couch beside her and said, "So. You mentioned I might get dessert tonight."

Brenda put her book on the floor and stretched mightily, arching her back, so that her heavy breasts pushed against the material of her dress. Simon immediately responded, and she smiled playfully and tugged at one edge of his towel.

"You're right. I did. I'm in the mood for a little dessert myself." Tenderly she touched his face. "But I also said there's a favor I want you to do for me."

Simon trembled. "Sure. Anything."

"Anything? You'll do whatever I ask you to?"

He cupped one of her breasts, and she let him. He'd wanted her for so long... "Yeah...yeah, whatever you say. Just...just..."

"I believe you. I believe you will do whatever I ask you. But this is a very important thing, and I want to be sure I have your full attention."

"Yes, yes! Please..."

She smiled. He thought, maybe, that it was all a game for her, the way she teased him and tortured him. He didn't care. She moved over and straddled his hips, and he realized she'd removed her own underwear. He hurriedly unfastened the buttons of the dress, but she had already opened his towel and begun moving against him. His breath caught as he realized she was as ready as he was.

They moved onto the floor in a sort of crablike motion, Brenda straddling him the entire time. Once Simon lay flat on his back, she positioned herself, and his breath came in shudders as they joined.

A few minutes later they separated, and she turned over onto her hands and knees.

As Simon knelt behind her, he looked up and saw Scott Charles standing in the doorway of the dining room, watching them. Scott wore rumpled white pajamas, and his eyes were hollow and empty. He stared at them unblinkingly.

Brenda had her head down, her forehead touching the carpet, so she didn't see Scott standing there. Simon regarded Scott for a moment, his eyes narrowed in derision. He grinned, winked at the boy, and slammed into her, pumped fast and forcefully.

As Brenda began to cry out, Scott turned and drifted silently away.

* * *

Much of Scott Charles's own life he didn't understand. His memories, coherent and ordered, only started a few years ago. Before that...before that it was like looking into a sea of fog, gray and oily and bad, with *things* moving in it. Things with the faces of people he knew. Things that looked like his mother and his father.

He remembered some of what they'd told him. He remembered what they said he was. Child of evil—taken by the Devil, soul was gone, gone and eaten, had to send the body after it. Bad thing. Rotten thing.

The thing with his mother's face was named Claire.

Claire came back to him every once in a while, up out of the oily gray fog while he slept, and she'd put him back under the floor. Down under the floor, with the things he couldn't see, and he couldn't move because of the thick silver tape around his arms and legs, and one time she and the thing with his father's face left him down there for three days, and when they came back to get him a spider had built a nest over his left eye and he couldn't scream anymore. After that they wrapped him up in plastic before they put him down there.

The thing with his father's face was named Emmett.

Emmett's hair was all white, not white like snow but white like worms under rocks, white like the giant hard worm that he only showed Scott when Claire had gone away out of the house.

Mr. Vessler made all of it stop, though...he pulled Scott up out of the oily fog and made the things with his parents' faces go away, and gave him a good bed to sleep in, and food that didn't smell bad. Mr. Vessler's hair was black. He didn't look anything like Emmett.

Simon's hair was black, too, but Scott had *seen*...he'd seen the white, the white like worms, like giant worms on his hands, and... and...

Miss Jorden. Scott liked Miss Jorden a lot. She confused him sometimes, when she touched his face, and he felt like there was something he was supposed to remember, but he didn't know what it was, and she was so pretty. So pretty, and she smelled nice, and she brought him things and helped him pick out his clothes, and she didn't smile very much but, when she did, he'd do anything for her, anything to see her smile, and

touch her skin

liked her, something inside him that got all tight, and he liked her saw the giant white worms

Simon

Scott was dimly aware of some sort of reaction going on in his head, but he didn't know what it was or how to stop it. Abruptly Brenda Jorden's scent filled him, traveled through him, and his blood came alive and crawled in his veins like a billion tiny ants.

touch her skin

liked her, liked her so much Claire and Emmett and the white and

Scott felt something moving in his head, in his mind, something struggling to break through, to break loose.

Simon and

liked her

touched her skin

Simon touching her skin

Giant white worms, touching her skin, Miss Jorden and Simon there in the living room and

His stomach heaved. He shoved aside the draperies on the window nearest his bed, popped open the catches on the window and pushed it up. Night air rushed over his face and he leaned outside and vomited, as quietly as he could, into the bushes below. It smelled like Miss Jorden, very very strongly, but soon that smell faded away.

If he strained his ears he could hear them, still, through his door and down the hallway. Soft moans and grunts. Skin striking skin.

Tears welled and burst from his eyes, and Scott knelt at the window, his arms and head outside the house, fresh air on his face for the first time since Mr. Vessler pulled him out of the gray—

— and he opened his eyes and *looked*. Looked up at the stars, and out at the trees surrounding the house, and down at the grass, and he didn't want to be *afraid* anymore. He'd had enough of the fear, the fear that kept him from doing anything, anything normal, he'd had *enough*.

He felt something leaving him, the insects in his blood scraping clean from the walls of his veins and arteries and pouring out through his tears.

Not to be afraid...not to feel the fear...

Something like thunder exploded in his ears, and he didn't immediately realize that it was only in his head, not in the sky. His blood squirmed and burned inside him like electricity, and his limbs shook and convulsed.

He couldn't tell how long it went on, but it was terrible and new, and he thought it felt like...

...like being born.

Finally Scott hung on the window sill, limp and wrung out, and felt as if a huge, foul tumor had just been sliced out of his brain.

He stared out at the world around him for, in a very real sense, the first time.

"Oh Jesus," he whispered, at the grass waving in the breeze and the tall, majestic oaks and the beautiful, beautiful sky. "Oh, Jesus, it's been just like this all along. All this time."

With his world pulled out from under him, Scott would have scrambled out the window and rolled in the grass—if not for the ache that replaced his fear, the ache deep in his heart.

Simon and Miss Jorden. There in the living room. That was real. That was now.

Scott picked himself up off the floor and crept to the door of his room. He knew where Miss Jorden kept her phone.

He could still hear them. He knew he'd have time.

* * *

When it was over they both lay on the floor, breathing heavily. Simon had his head propped up against the base of the couch, and Brenda rested on his flat stomach, her left cheek pressed against the ridged muscles there. She still wore her dress, though she hadn't bothered with any of the buttons, and her right breast was exposed, the dark nipple still slightly peaked. After a few minutes she sighed and raised herself on one elbow and looked him in the eye.

"Well, if that didn't do it it's not going to get done."

Simon didn't know what that meant, but he felt sort of glazed, and it didn't matter too much. Sweat and sex and that other strange, strong scent all filled him up. He was content to lie there, savor the prickly sensation of the shag carpet against his back, and listen to her.

"I'm glad you didn't end up like Scott," she said calmly. She could have been reading the ingredients on a can of dog food for all the passion in her voice. "He didn't want to go along, and now he's just about used up. But *you*...you didn't take much convincing. And you're just fine." With the word *fine* she dragged her nails lightly across his chest and stomach, and let a husky tone enter her voice.

Even more glazed over now, Simon couldn't follow what she was saying.

It still didn't matter.

"Now. Listen carefully."

"Okay," he said, coming a little clearer. She wanted him to listen. That sounded good. Listening was good. He blinked a few times, focused on her.

"I'd like you to do something for me. You'd still like to do something for me, wouldn't you?"

"Sure."

"All right. There's someone I want you to go see. I'll tell you where to find him. He's a grumpy old man, and he's been a pain in my ass for a long time now. I want you to go to him, kill him, and kill anyone with him. Tonight."

He blinked a few more times. She looked a little weird, a little fuzzy, but he heard the words well enough. Sounded like a reasonable request.

"Yeah, sure, okay. Whatever you say."

CHAPTER NINETEEN

In his room at a Best Western in Chattanooga, Tennessee, Garrison Vessler unknotted his tie, slipped it off his neck, and slumped into one of the chairs set around the small circular table in the corner. The door itself closed slowly, and almost latched before Stillwater caught it and pushed it open. He and Wong came into the room silently. Each of them wore a dark gray suit and a dour expression, and Vessler refrained from rolling his eyes.

"You two are really the picture of it," he said, kicking off his shoes. He pulled off his socks and massaged his left foot, and thought he heard Stillwater take a breath as if to speak, but the agent didn't say anything. Vessler took hold of his ankle with both hands and shook his foot up and down, loosening up the joint, and repeated the massage and shake with the other foot. He undid the top button of his starched white shirt, propped his feet up on the tabletop and glared at the two agents.

Wong had immediately busied himself checking the room out, top to bottom. He came out of the bathroom, flicked off the light as he emerged, and nodded once. That meant "all clear." Vessler knew better than to expect Wong to say anything when he didn't have to.

The poster-boy for homegrown, apple-pie Americana, Stillwater had blonde hair, blue eyes, and the wide shoulders of a football player. And yet, aside from his slightly larger than average build, there was nothing remarkable about him at all, from his off-the-rack J.C. Penney suit to his sixty-five dollar Hush Puppies to his round, slightly underslung chin. Stillwater had learned to play up this lack of distinction whenever circumstances called for it. A practiced hunching of the shoulders, a carefully non-confrontational demeanor, and Gary Stillwater became an unknown face in the crowd. Those in charge preferred it that way.

Wong, on the other hand, could only have made himself look more conspicuous if he *tried* to blend in anywhere. An inch taller than Stillwater, Benson Wong was whip-thin, taciturn, and stuck permanently with a nickname the other operatives had given him years before. He hated it, but grudgingly accepted it, especially after they gave him a jacket with "The Asp" embroidered on the back for his birthday.

Stillwater and Wong stood several feet away from their boss for most of a minute, respectfully, their hands folded.

"All right. You can leave me alone. Get some sleep." He waved dismissively toward the door. The two men said good-night and went to their own room, the second half of a suite, joined to Vessler's by two thin doors in the wall to Vessler's left.

Vessler shut his eyes and tilted his head back. Breathed deeply, slowly.

Damn the timing. And damn Stamford and his cryptic summons back to the main office.

Two off-the-chart augments out there, doing only God knew what, and Scott had lost contact with them both. Maybe the surge did it, when he picked up the second one in the park, maybe that scrambled Scott's head around somehow, Vessler wasn't sure.

What he *was* sure of was that everything was about to come down on his head. One way or another, Stamford would make sure of it. He'd already started the humiliation, arranging for them to drive to Chattanooga, of all places, and catch a flight out of the minuscule city airport.

Vessler sighed, got up from his chair and moved slowly toward the bathroom, undressing as he went. The starched shirt fell across the dresser, and Vessler stretched. Corded, stringy muscles flexed under his skin like bundles of wire.

He gave himself a tiny smile as he finished undressing and turned on the water in the shower. He'd been practicing the tired old man routine for some time now, with apparent success. No one else in the company, except maybe the physician who gave him his bimonthly physicals, seemed to know he faked his moans and groans. Additionally, most of the new recruits simply weren't aware of how he'd gotten the nickname "Icicle." He knew someone would try him, and underestimate him, sooner or later.

Probably Stamford. Probably sooner.

* * *

In the room adjoining Vessler's, Stillwater and Wong began to settle in for the night. Stillwater had the first shift, and flipped around the channels on the hotel's TV, searching for something to help him stay awake. He watched a few seconds of MTV, another few of an infomercial hawking an exercise video called "Destroyer Buns," and finally settled on one of the premium channels, which was airing *Alice's Adult Adventures in Wonderland.*

"All right," he said happily, and propped himself up at the head of the bed with both pillows behind him.

Wong stood next to the other bed, undressing, and cast only a brief glance at the TV. He pulled a book out of his bag, turned on the reading lamp on the bedside table, threw the covers back and crawled into bed. He had trouble getting to sleep unless he read for a while first, and tonight was no exception, but his tastes normally ran to Robert Ludlum novels. Tonight he read a progressively dog-eared copy of *Men Are From Mars, Women Are From Venus.*

Wong's girlfriend of seven months, Patricia, had given it to him a week before, and told him if he didn't read it she'd leave him.

Patricia, a petite Korean-American woman, taught elementary school and used most of the precious little spare time she had to write poetry. She could cook an omelet that made Wong's eyes roll back in his head, she gave professional-quality backrubs, and she could quote, along with him, every line of dialogue from all three *Indiana Jones* movies. Neither of them acknowledged the existence of any entries in the franchise past the first three.

Wong didn't like being pressured into things in his private life, but he liked the idea of losing Patricia even less, so he took the book and promised her he'd get through it.

Fifteen minutes and eight pages later, Wong rolled halfway over toward Stillwater. "Hey, can I read you something?"

Stillwater didn't take his eyes off the screen, most of which was taken up by a curvy blonde's bare breasts. "What, from that piece of shit? I told you before, man, if I wanted to read it I'd buy a copy. On my Kindle. Like a person from this fucking century."

Wong sighed. He'd just finished a particularly compelling passage, and wanted to talk to someone about it. He would have called Patricia if he hadn't known she'd already be in bed.

As an afterthought, Stillwater said, "You ought to get your ass to sleep, anyway, you start in four hours."

Wong took a breath to speak—and froze in place, staring at the bathroom. "Hey, did you just hear something?" He set the book down on the bed next to him, reached for his gunbelt and pulled out his Browning .45.

The TV clicked off. Wong looked over his shoulder and saw Stillwater standing with his own identical Browning held ready. Stillwater's blue eyes had instantly taken on a hard, icy sheen, and Wong knew his partner was focused.

Noiselessly Wong left the bed and nodded at the bathroom. Stillwater answered his nod and approached the door, which stood slightly ajar. They couldn't see anything beyond it but darkness.

Wearing only a pair of paisley-patterned jockey shorts, Wong crept over to a position on the opposite side of the door, his tall, lanky body quivering.

They burst into the bathroom and flipped on the light, hammers cocked and ready for anything except what happened next.

Stillwater had time to observe that the medicine cabinet was gone, revealing a black hole in the wall that led into an adjoining bathroom, before white tentacles dropped from the ceiling, wrapped around his head, and twisted violently up and to the right, shattering vertebrae and severing his spinal cord. Gary Stillwater slumped dead to the floor.

Wong entered an adrenaline-fueled, hyper-alert state as Simon Grove dropped from the ceiling, where he'd been clinging, spider-like. The boy's face began to pop and distort, lengthening grotesquely, which distracted Wong just enough for Grove to fling out three of the finger-tendrils and jerk the Browning out of his hand. It clattered on the floor and slid behind the toilet. More of the tendrils snaked out, but Wong threw himself backward out of the bathroom, rolled and came to his feet. Grove immediately followed him, hissing and hunch-shouldered, and lunged.

Wong whirled, his left leg flashed out, and the heel of his foot caught Grove's temple with a thick wet crunching sound. Grove staggered and toppled over, but the finger-tendrils bunched underneath him and supported him on a bizarre coiling cushion. He trembled and got back to his feet, his skull re-shaping itself, and Wong felt a sharp spear of panic.

Grove brought one arm forward, the tendrils twitching and writhing, but Wong stepped inside the boy's reach and struck him three times, *crack crack crack*, twice to the face and once in the center of his chest.

Grove staggered again, and Wong realized he himself was bleeding.

Four of the weird spines that had replaced Grove's teeth had broken off and rammed into his forearm. He didn't feel the pain yet, and didn't have any time to, as Grove hissed and rushed in again.

This time Wong stepped inside, as before, and struck Grove solidly in the gut. As foul, rotten air whooshed out around Wong's head, he turned and slid up tight to Grove's body, yanked one attenuated arm forward and flipped the boy across the small of his back.

Grove's feet almost touched the ceiling as he sailed around

in a perfect tight arc, and Wong knew he heard bones break as the boy crashed into the floor at Wong's feet. Grove made a pained, keening sound, and Wong put him in a brutal arm lock. The weird, fish-white body thrashed and twisted, but couldn't go anywhere, and only then did Wong give himself enough breathing space to think about what it was exactly he had pinned to the floor.

He'd seen some strange augments, working with Redfell, but nothing like this. He lifted his head and looked around for his phone: there, on the table next to the TV. Too far to reach. He'd have to yell for Vessler...no problem with the thin, shoddy doors separating the two rooms.

But Grove's elbow gave way, rolled in a slick, greasy fashion like a ball-and-socket joint, and his shoulder went loose right after that. Abruptly the principle behind Wong's joint lock no longer applied, and he lost his balance as Grove kicked out from under him. Wong was fast, but not quite fast enough.

The wall slammed into him, sent skittering glints of pain along his shoulders and back, and before he could try to move Grove stiffened all the fingers of his left hand and sank them into the plaster around Wong's head, caging him. Wong wished briefly for his knives, which rested in their sheaths in his suit jacket, and thought of Patricia.

Grove wound his other hand into a slim, dagger-point horn and rammed it through Wong's heart.

* * *

Garrison Vessler had tried to fall asleep, couldn't, and sat up in bed, groping for the TV remote. He scanned through the channels quickly, paused for a moment on a naked, curvaceous blonde, and finally settled on a documentary on the Discovery Channel about the habits of scorpions.

Hotel rooms had begun to sicken him. Redfell had never been run like this before. It hadn't ever been this complicated.

Vessler realized he was hungry, and shuffled through the collection of menus he'd found in the drawer of the night table. One for an all-night pizza delivery place caught his eye.

With a small start, Vessler realized he hadn't turned his phone back on since that afternoon. Damn Stamford, and damn his own aging brain. He powered on the phone and checked his messages.

The first one made his heart stand dead still in his chest. It came from Jorden's number, but it was Scott's voice, high and breathless, and it began with, "Listen to me."

Garrison Vessler listened with total attention for just over five minutes.

By the end of the message Scott was sobbing and, still with the phone to his ear, Vessler was almost fully dressed.

He was tying the laces on his left shoe when he heard a muffled sound from next door. When something heavy slammed against a wall in Stillwater and Wong's room, Vessler jacked a round into the chamber of his .45 and glanced at the door to the outside. His skin grew slightly cooler as he weighed his options.

The decision was made for him as five bone-white tendrils punched through the thin connecting door between his room and the agents'. His eyes narrowed to slits, Vessler concentrated hard, even as the door cracked and pulled away from the frame.

As the last few scraps fell away, a fine mist, foglike, began radiating from Vessler's body, and drops of frigid water collected on his skin. His heartbeat accelerated.

"Knock knock," a young man's voice said, and Simon Grove's widely grinning face popped around the corner. Vessler fired twice at the face, which vanished as swiftly as it had appeared, and sent three more bullets through the hotel room wall where he thought Grove might be.

He took a tentative step forward, and Grove blurred into the room.

Damn he's fast, Vessler thought, and fired again, but Grove bounded around the room like a crazed monkey, and before he could pull the trigger once more the young man crashed into his chest, knocked him backward onto the floor. Three tendrils manacled his gun hand and pinned it to the carpet.

"This is easy," Grove said, and giggled. His face began to distort, and the tendrils of his free hand started to spiral together. Just before his mouth became something that could no longer produce speech, he said, "I don't know what Brenda was so worked up about."

Vessler's breath, which he'd been holding, came out in a smoky white plume at the mention of the name, and Grove paused, frowning. Vessler reached up and touched the spiral horn-blade, very lightly, with the fingertips of his free hand.

Instantly Grove's hand froze solid to halfway up the forearm.

For just a moment both men held perfectly still as the horn turned a strange blue-gray.

Grove flung himself off Vessler, clutching the frozen tendrils and howling. Vessler covered his ears as Grove's scream gained volume and the mirror above the dresser cracked. Grove barreled toward the door, slammed into it, and jerked it open with a hand that had reverted to normal. His other hand stayed fixed, the horn-blade frozen and beginning to web with fine cracks.

The muzzle blast of Vessler's gun filled the room, not quite as deafening as Grove's howl but still thunderous, and the bullet blew Grove's hand into tiny frozen fragments. Most of the pieces ricocheted off the walls and floor, but a few sliced into Grove's face, and Vessler imagined that he saw the instant when the boy's last bit of humanity disappeared. Vessler immediately jumped to his feet, slammed in a fresh clip, and fired three more shots, but Grove blurred again, and the shots passed through the open doorway and buried themselves in a Chrysler parked outside. The Chrysler's car alarm shrieked.

Vessler paused, uncertain. He couldn't see where Grove had gone...

...but before he had time to think about it, Grove exploded

up from behind one of the two double beds.

The dead-white fingers lashed out like whips. The .45 smashed out of Vessler's hand and flew clattering under the dresser, and Grove lunged for him again.

Vessler knew he wouldn't be able to get cold enough to do anything worthwhile for another half hour or so, and after that probably not for a good four or five hours, but he was far from helpless, especially against someone so thoroughly untrained as Simon Grove, augmentation notwithstanding. As Grove came forward, Vessler sidestepped and drove his right elbow into the side of Grove's neck. The distorted chin cracked into the corner of the cheap motel dresser, and spiny teeth shattered and flew from the distended mouth.

The double impact would have rendered even the toughest of men unconscious or, at the very least, no longer willing to fight. Grove rolled over, shook his head, and got to his feet again with an agitated hiss.

Vessler sprinted out the door.

His car was at the far corner of the lot, and he breathed out heavy relief as he slapped his thigh and felt the lump of the key in his pants pocket. As soon as he left the glow of lights he threw himself full length on the pavement and rolled sideways under a van.

Behind him Grove exploded outside. A young woman two rooms down opened her door and looked out, gasped, and immediately closed and locked the door again.

On his fingers and toes, with his body almost flat to the concrete, Vessler moved sideways again, this time underneath a Pathfinder. He emerged on the far side of the vehicle and glanced up. From two aisles over, where he'd disappeared between the cars, he heard a horrible squeal of rending metal, and saw a car door arc out over the lot with its hinges twisted and mangled. Glass shattered as the door landed. Grove seemed to be tearing the cars apart in his search for Vessler, scraping his way up the aisle like some sort of steam-driven machine. He still howled, though whether in rage, pain, or both Vessler couldn't tell.

Vessler got to his knees and took the key out. Grove's search was disorganized. He seemed to be thrashing blindly about rather than following any kind of pattern, which, Vessler thought, made him only slightly less dangerous.

On all fours now, Vessler crept down the length of the line of cars and prayed that Grove's hearing wasn't augmented, or that if it were, that he wouldn't be able to distinguish anything over all the noise he was making himself.

Vessler raised his head and saw the Town Car parked at the end of the line. He'd left it right next to a Ford coupe, but in the past hour the Ford owner had left. Now the Lincoln sat by itself, a gap of roughly eight feet between it and the next car. He didn't know if Grove would see him cross the gap or not.

His heart whirred in his chest as he gathered his legs under him and thumbed the key's buttons, unlocking the door and starting the engine.

Immediately the sounds of Grove's frenzied search cut off, but Vessler had already reached the car and jerked the door open.

He had one leg inside when he risked a glance over his shoulder and saw Grove barreling toward him across the parking lot, bounding over car roofs, his hands distended and reaching out.

Vessler slammed the door shut and locked it as he jammed the car into gear. He left two broad streaks of rubber on the pavement as he tore out of the parking lot. The road outside the motel was a four-lane divided highway, and Vessler accelerated all the way across, weaving through cars on both sides of the median as he powered over the narrow strip of grass.

Vessler's stomach knotted and rolled as he tramped down on the accelerator. His skin rose in millions of goose pimples as he began to let himself feel a twinge or two of tentative panic.

Simon Grove hadn't looked much like his yearbook photo.

As he sped away from the lights of the motel, a part of the

glimpse he'd gotten of Grove coming after him finally registered. He'd been reaching out with those bizarre, grotesque hands.

Hands. Plural.

The hand he'd frozen, the one Vessler saw fly apart, had been reaching out after him along with the undamaged one. Regrown from the stump in seconds.

His own hands covered over with a cold sheen of sweat unrelated to his augmentation. After about ten miles he risked pulling over. His whole body trembled as he tapped in a number he'd long ago committed to memory.

The phone rang while he stared back down the highway. Vessler didn't think he'd see Simon Grove charging down the center line toward him, waving those freak-of-nature fingers, but... better cautious and alive than confident and dead.

The line clicked, and an automated female voice said, "The number you have dialed is no longer in service."

Vessler growled and ended the call and tapped the number in again. After a click, the same automated message played, and in the middle of the word "dialed" he ended the call and dropped the phone on the passenger seat.

Vessler's eyes stopped focusing. His teeth ground together.

He grabbed up the phone and stared at it, index finger hovering over the keypad, before he acknowledged to himself that there really weren't any other numbers he could call.

"Stamford, you bastard," Vessler breathed.

He could imagine how it would look to the rest of the company. An uncatalogued augment, one he might have been able to take in before but had chosen not to, had just killed two ranking employees. Had almost killed *him*. And only hours before a full project audit.

He slumped against the wheel.

"You bastard. You and Jorden. You finally got me." He swallowed hard, tried not to be sick. How could he have slipped this far? How could he have let so much get past him?

You're getting too old, that's how. Too old and too slow.

With clenched teeth, Vessler drove back across the narrow median strip and headed for a used car lot he remembered passing a minute or so earlier.

CHAPTER TWENTY

Stover Fitz, also known as The Map Man, really hadn't expected to see Satan that night.

Stover groaned and pulled the newspapers up higher. He'd been dreaming about turkey dinners, but the dreams left him and he woke up with a sharp pain in his ankle. He reached down underneath the newspaper blanket and touched the spot, and his fingers came back bloody.

Damn rats.

His wife used to cook turkey dinners for him. Turkey dinners and pecan pies, and divinity candy, and barbecued pork chops and steak and biscuits and gravy. The food was the hardest part. Now and then he'd think about her, think about how he always called her Kiddo instead of Lori, and he'd remember her skin and her lips and how she smelled and that'd hurt for a while. But mostly it hurt the worst when he thought about the food. He could usually work on his map some, and that'd make the hurt go away, but now it was dark and he was hungry and he wished the damn rats'd let him be.

He hadn't planned it to go like this, with everything in the crapper, and don't anybody think he didn't *know* it was in the crapper, but he hadn't planned on Lori checking him into the hospital and he sure as hell hadn't planned on her walking out on him.

The hospital wouldn't keep him, of course. They had their own problems.

Had people to deal with who didn't even know where they *were*. So now he lived under a damn newspaper blanket and had rats for alarm clocks, and that was in the crapper, yeah, but he knew where he *was*. That's right.

Because he had his map.

Stover had found a spiral-bound notebook and a few broken

pencils some little while ago—he knew it was on a Thursday—and he rubbed the pencils against a brick wall until they were sharp, and he'd begun his map of all the best dumpsters in the area.

It hadn't started out as much, just a sort of connect-the-dots thing, really, but then he made a few notes along in the margins about other places nearby.

But the notes never really seemed complete, so he kept working on them and adding to them, and he drew in the locations of the other places he'd noted, and to make it a little more pleasing to the eye he drew a border around the sheet and that *really* never seemed like it got finished. Couple of days ago he sat and worked on it outside the library, on a bench, and looked at a big clock every now and then, and four hours just went right past him in no time at all. That surprised him so he didn't even mind it when the cop came and told him to move along.

Too dark right now to work on the map, but Stover rolled over—*that was a rhyme, Stover rolled over, Stover from Dover, Stover in clover, Stover Red Rover*—and touched the notebook where it rested inside his shirt. Maybe he'd take it out and see if he could make out the lines, just a little.

The first thing he thought when Satan ran into the alley was *He won't get my map.* And to keep Satan from trying for it, Stover lay perfectly still and tried not to breathe too hard.

Satan looked a lot like Stover had imagined he would. He never had bought into the horns-and-tail bit, and it turned out he was right. Satan had black spiky hair and a mouth like a cross between a shark's and a snake's, and instead of hands he had cats-o'-nine-tails all twisty and wiggly. Stover didn't know why Satan would wear Nike sneakers, but he figured the Prince of Darkness could dress however he wanted.

It looked like Satan had run quite a distance. He panted and gasped and held himself up against the wall, and turned around and put his hands on his knees and panted some more. Stover stopped breathing entirely, 'cause he thought Satan had seen him, 'cause

Satan got real still all of a sudden—and then held up one hand in front of his face like he'd never seen it before. And he changed, Satan did, so as to look like a normal human person, and Stover thought *Well, he can be right handsome when he wants to be.*

When Satan looked completely like a regular person he took hold of that hand with the other one and felt of it, and opened it and closed it and shook it around like he thought it might come off. Stover nearly peed in his pants, because Satan jumped up, still holding up the one hand, and he whooped and hollered and danced around and screamed out, "Yes! Yes yes yes! Ha ha, look at *this!* Whooooo-ha!"

He danced and danced for most of a minute, Stover reckoned, before Satan reached in his pocket and pulled out a cellular phone—which cemented Stover Fitz's opinion of cellular phones once and for all.

Satan dialed a number and talked for a bit but Stover couldn't hear any of the words. When he was finished he stuck the phone back in his pocket and strolled out of the alley.

Stover lay there for a full half hour to be sure Satan wasn't coming back.

He went out to a streetlight and pulled out his map. Before he scurried away down the street, he drew in his present location on the map, and wrote: *DONT GO HERE. SATAN.*

* * *

Hours passed by in the darkness, and the skeleton of the Hargett Theatre stood silent. The nearby highway was practically deserted, and nothing penetrated the shadows where Janey flickered and stepped out. She crouched and scanned the wreckage, as she always did.

She was about to flicker out again, down to the basement, when a tall, lean man stepped out from around a corner into the moonlight and lit a cigarette.

Janey froze, watching. The man wore a rumpled white shirt and gray slacks. The night vision lit his features clearly; he looked to be in his forties, maybe older, with a brutally seamed face and deep-set eyes. His hair slicked straight back from a widow's peak. He could have been made of granite.

Janey flickered, did a fast sweep of the theatre's grounds. An old tan Jeep Cherokee with a crumpled rear bumper sat near the main entrance. Its hood was cold. Nothing else seemed out of place.

The weathered man had just touched his Bic's flame to another cigarette when Janey stepped out of the shadows ten paces behind him and snapped open a baton.

"Hold still," Janey said.

The man froze obligingly. In a deep, unhurried voice, with perhaps a touch of Texas in it, he asked, "May I put away my lighter?"

"No. Keep it in your hand. Raise your arms, and turn around very slowly."

The man took direction well, but his eyes fixed on Janey as soon as his head had turned far enough. Janey's eyebrows rose under the mask. The man was so blatantly unafraid that she felt a touch of annoyance.

"I hoped I'd find you here," the man said. "It was a pretty long shot, but it felt right."

The man's gaze didn't waver, but Janey began to think her own voice might.

"Tell me your name and what you want." That came out cold and dangerous, to Janey's relief.

"May I put my arms down?"

"No."

"Oh, c'mon, girl, I'm old and tired. You want to frisk me? Make sure I'm not carrying?"

"No. You stay right there, and keep your arms up, and do what I tell you." The man let one corner of his mouth twitch upward slightly in what Janey thought might have been approval. It made Janey twice as cautious. She began to suspect that the man could hold up his arms all night.

"My name is Vessler," the man said. "I work for the government. And I need your help."

Janey tilted her head. "Really."

"I know what you are, girl. I know you're a lot more than a woman in a suit. You are what is called an *augment.*"

Janey's stomach tightened, and this time her words did emerge a little shaky.

"Wha —" She swallowed hard. "What do you mean?"

Vessler sighed impatiently. "It'll take a lot less time if I just show you," he said. "I'm like you. Not exactly like you, but pretty close. Here." He gestured to a small puddle a few feet to his left. "I'm going to walk over to that puddle, all right?"

Janey didn't say anything. Vessler moved to the puddle and knelt beside it, and Janey's eyes widened behind her mask as a faint fog began to roll off the man's body. Vessler reached down and touched the puddle with one forefinger, and it froze straight through with a tiny brittle sound. He wedged his fingers into the dirt to one side of it, pulled the chunk of ice out of the ground, straightened up and tossed it at Janey's feet.

The fog quickly dissipated from around him, and his shoulders slumped a bit. She motioned with the baton, and he raised his arms again.

"Go on," he said. "Take a look."

Slowly and cautiously, Janey crouched and laid one palm against the ice, and tried to let it go as stabbing pain shot through her hand. It had frozen to the Vylar glove, and she had to hit it with the baton to get it loose.

"I'm in the boat with you," Vessler said calmly. "Or you're in it with me. Either way, I need your help. I don't think I have a lot of time."

Janey tried to keep her thoughts straight. Next to Simon, this guy looked pretty normal. "I still haven't heard how this concerns me."

Vessler grew visibly irritated, but he controlled his voice. "How it concerns you involves an individual I think you've met, name of Grove." He wiggled his fingers. "Funny hands? Big teeth? Unpleasant?"

Janey drew in a sharp breath. "Simon."

"Oh, you're on a first-name basis."

"Hardly. Look…you know more about all this than I do. Obviously. So explain it. How long have there been…people like us? How did it all start?"

Vessler sighed. "If that's what's going to get you to trust me, fine. But I'm not telling you a story with my hands in the air."

Janey paused. Nodded. Vessler lowered his arms. "We don't know what causes it. What we do know is that about seven years ago, augments—that's our term for people like you and me—began appearing. The range of abilities we've documented so far goes from temperature manipulation on one end to…Simon Grove on the other. I run a private security firm called Redfell, and since I had first-hand experience with the phenomenon, I decided to start looking for others. Recruiting them if I could."

Janey tilted her head, her heartbeat speeding up. "Do you know what made us this way?"

"Only theories. Though we do have a tiny little shred of evidence."

"Tell me."

"December 12, 2010. A SETI radio telescope picked up a signal. It only lasted for about a millisecond, but near as they can tell, it flashed down to the Earth's surface from somewhere in a low orbit. A week later we picked up an augment thirty miles from where the signal landed."

Janey processed that. "Someone's using a satellite to…to do this to us?"

Vessler slowly shook his head. "It wasn't a signal anyone had ever seen before. We've been trying to analyze it ever since. No luck so far."

"So what does that mean?"

Vessler shrugged. "Some in the company think it's a, for lack of a better term, a mad scientist. Some lone genius, light-years ahead of the rest of the world, playing with this new technology. Others think it was extraterrestrial."

"Aliens?" Janey started to scoff, but Simon's spine-teeth and writhing fingers made her bite her tongue. She gestured with the baton. "All right. Move over against that wall."

"Does this mean you believe me?"

"Just move."

Vessler did it. Janey stepped up behind him and patted him down. "I'm going to take us somewhere private, and we can talk some more. This is going to feel a little weird." She put one hand on Vessler's shoulder, and they flickered out.

* * *

Exactly five seconds after Janey and Vessler disappeared, a dark, bulky figure stood up from behind a ruined brick wall and turned a high-powered flashlight beam on the spot where the two of them had stood. It revealed nothing but dirt and concrete dust...but when he walked over and laid his hand on the ground, it was as hot to the touch as an Arizona sidewalk at high noon. He swept the beam side to side, but only lit up more dirt, dust, a few sections of unbroken concrete flooring—and the two sets of footprints, big as life there in the dirt.

Reflectively, Zach Feygen said, "I'll be damned."

With a chill racing around his spine and shoulders, Feygen pulled out a photocopy. As if reading a treasure map, he turned and walked about thirty feet to his right, put away the photocopy and shined the light on a fallen slab of concrete, propped up at a slight angle by a twisted I-beam.

Feygen dropped to his belly, wriggled underneath the slab as far as he could go, and played the beam in front of him. Far back in the darkness, a metal ventilation grille was set into the floor. Feygen lay perfectly still, strained his ears and tried to filter out the occasional sounds from the highway.

Faintly, like the tiniest whisper, he thought he could make out the sound of voices.

* * *

Vessler blinked his eyes in the darkness until Janey lit a candle. She led the way to a couple of Salvation Army chairs in one corner.

"I can't offer you much in the way of hospitality, but I've got some bottled water."

Vessler said, "No thanks," and sat down. Janey perched on the back of the other one and leaned against the rough concrete wall. They stared at each other for a few seconds, and Janey almost laughed at how absurd they must have looked.

Vessler gazed out into the darkness. "This is the old parking garage, isn't it? Under the theatre? The one reserved for wealthy patrons?"

Startled, Janey thought about denying it, but finally nodded. "It got sealed off during demolition. I'm sure they planned to knock out the ceiling and fill it in, but they never got to it."

"I think I parked here once, years ago. Came to see *Othello*. Back when it was a real theatre, and didn't have all these hack shows, magicians and whatnot."

Janey bristled. "Look, you said you needed my help. With Simon...what'd you say his last name was? Grove?"

Vessler nodded. "It's not just him, though. I've got to give you some more background here, all right?"

"Go ahead."

He cleared his throat. "As I said up top, I run—until tonight, I ran a company that's been dealing with people like you. Now, by my way of thinking, that means observing people, determining whether or not their abilities could be useful, and if they are, recruiting them."

"Recruiting them how?"

"Offering them positions. Giving them jobs."

"Like your job now?"

"Well...I'm an administrator, much as I hate to say it. We mainly train and farm out operatives. Very specialized operatives. Until very recently, I was among the more powerful augments we knew about…until Simon Grove came into the picture. Until *you* showed up. Just imagine how much mileage the CIA could get out of your abilities."

"I'd rather not. A minute ago you said 'by my way of thinking.' Someone else doesn't share your opinion?"

"That's right." Vessler looked old and tired for a moment. "Three years ago I took on a business partner named Derek Stamford. I didn't realize it at first, but Stamford thinks any augment who doesn't sign up needs to disappear. Feelings in the company started polarizing a couple of years ago, and people with the wrong idea started to outnumber the rest of us. Stamford got it in his head to get rid of me and claim Redfell for himself. So he and his cohorts set me up. Grove was my responsibility, you understand, I was supposed to bring him in. Tonight Grove showed up at my hotel and killed two of my men. Tried to kill me. That was exactly what Stamford was waiting on—for me to either end up dead or be proven incompetent—and now I've been...eh...sanctioned. Cut off."

"Wait, I'm confused. Simon was already in this other faction?"

Vessler blew out a long breath. "Here's where it's good that you're an augment. You'll be able to accept this. One of our people—until tonight I believed she was *not* an augment—her name is Jorden, Brenda Jorden. She seems to be able to exert some sort of influence over people. I think it's chemical, something her body produces, and she's used someone very close to me, a boy named Scott. She's done this thing to both of them—Scott and Grove—used this control. Now Grove's still out there, and she still has Scott, and as long as she has power over them she can find us, either one of us. And send Grove after us."

"How would she find us?"

"Scott's a remote viewer. We've trained him to look for other augments. He picked up on Grove for the first time a couple of weeks ago, and the second time he tried it he found you, too. Of course, we didn't know at the time we were looking at the world-famous Gray Widow."

"Wait, wait, if she knows where we are, she can tell anybody, right? The other people in your group?"

"Right—but I don't think she will, at least not just yet. She enjoys hoarding information too much, waits to see how she can best use it. The point is, neither of us is safe as long as the situation stays the way it is."

"This is…it's a lot to take in all at once. Before I saw Simon, I didn't think there *was* anybody else like me. Then him, and now you, and you're telling me there's, what, hundreds? Thousands?"

"No. Dozens at most, at least in this country. We're not as certain about foreign matters." Vessler abruptly grew impatient. "Look, let me help you along. I got cut off tonight. I don't have any support. *You* have the means to put an end to this whole sorry mess, and you need to get off your ass and do it, *Ms. Sinclair.*"

Janey gasped. She couldn't help it.

"There's a surprise for you, huh? Didn't think anybody knew? Scott managed to clear his head enough tonight to contact me and tell me what's going on. Saved my life. He knows who you are, along with Brenda Jorden and Simon Grove. Your name, where you live."

Janey put her face in her hands. "Oh my God."

"Yeah. Now, I don't know if Jorden's told anybody else. Maybe not, she may be holding on to it, seeing if she can use it for something. But aside from making sure Grove doesn't hurt anyone else, I'd say it's in *your* best interest to do what I'm asking you to."

"If you were going to blackmail me the whole time, why all this song and dance?"

Tightly: "Because I'm not a total son of a bitch. I thought I might convince you."

Janey breathed slowly, in and out, in and out. "How do I know *you* won't tell anyone?"

Vessler shrugged. "You take out Grove, get Scott back to me safely, I figure I'll be in your debt."

"That's it? My debt?"

Vessler folded his arms across his chest. "That's all you've got."

CHAPTER TWENTY-ONE

3:36 a.m.

The dancing blue-white of a television screen was the only light visible in the house, which looked exactly as Vessler had described it: slightly run-down and isolated. One car sat in the driveway, a late-model Ford matching Vessler's description of the car Brenda Jorden had been assigned.

Janey flickered onto the screened-in back porch and crouched close to the wall. Inching forward, she peered in through the glass door that opened onto the living room. An infomercial played on a big RCA television. No one watched it.

Another flicker, and she crouched beside the sofa. The house smelled...not bad, quite, but *thick* with something. She sniffed experimentally, tried to identify the smell. Musky, a little like perfume, but not as well-defined.

Her head felt funny.

Janey blinked a couple of times and moved carefully to the hall doorway. Scott was probably in one of the bedrooms, if he was here at all; Vessler wasn't sure whether or not Jorden knew about the call Scott had made to him. If she did, Scott may be lying in a ditch somewhere with a hole in his head. Janey took a deep, slow breath and started down the hallway.

A door on the left stood slightly ajar, and Janey pushed it a few inches open, standing to one side. She'd cranked her night vision up to the top, and immediately saw a countertop and linoleum on the floor.

Bathroom.

She moved to the next door.

Even before she touched it she knew Scott was inside. She could hear slow, labored breathing. It didn't sound healthy. Janey didn't know what kind of shape the boy would be in, or whether or not he'd be able to walk. Not that that mattered, really, as far as getting him out of here.

Outside the bedroom door Janey wondered whether or not the house's peculiar odor was related to Jorden's "persuasive" personal scent. Vessler's words stayed with her: "I only know what Scott told me tonight, and he didn't have time to say much. But if she can control people like he says, for God's sake stay away from her. He said she does it mostly through touch. Maybe if you keep the suit on, and she can't get to your skin, that'll help. What's your sexual orientation?"

That took Janey off-guard. "Wh-huh? Why?"

"Jorden's damned attractive, and I don't know if she'd use that along with the control thing or not, but be aware of it."

"I like men," Janey said, feeling lame.

"All right, well, just get in, get Scott, and get out. Once we have him we can use him to locate Jorden and Grove."

That bothered Janey. *We can use him...* Cold phrasing for someone Vessler claimed to care about so much. Or maybe that was the only way Vessler knew how to talk.

Janey eased open the door to Scott's room.

Scott Charles lay on the narrow twin bed. Vessler had warned Janey about Scott's appearance, but even considering the lack of both pigment and exercise, Scott Charles still looked like hell. Janey glanced around the room and checked the closet before she went to Scott's side.

"Scott," she whispered, next to the boy's ear. "Scott, wake up. Vessler sent me here to get you."

The breathing faltered, and Scott opened his eyes and turned his head. On impulse Janey ducked down, out of sight. She couldn't take her mask off just then, and she didn't want to scare the boy to death.

"Who's there?" Scott murmured weakly. "I can't see you."

"It's okay. I'm here to help."

Scott muttered something incoherent and shifted on the bed. He seemed *atrophied,* everything about him, not just his musculature. Weak moonlight fed through the slatted blinds and silvered his face.

Slowly, his tendons creaking like an old man's, Scott rose up and fixed his eyes on Janey. The mask didn't alarm him in the slightest. "*You.* You got here." Scott's words mixed fear and reverence. "I've been reading about you."

"Yeah?" Developmentally, Scott Charles didn't look a day past eleven. A tiny old man inside a sick boy's body. He wore only frayed pajama bottoms, and ribs poked out from his pitifully thin torso.

"We've got to get out of here, *right now,*" Scott said. "I don't know where they are, but they're here somewhere. You can get us away, can't you?"

"Yes," Janey said reassuringly. "Can you stand up?"

"Lie back down, Scott," a gorgeous female voice said behind Janey, just as a floor joist squealed. Janey whirled around to face Brenda Jorden, standing in the doorway, a goddess in the faint moonlight—and a hand like a brick crashed into the side of Janey's head. She staggered sideways.

Ned Fields didn't give Janey any time to recover. The small man jumped on her, and the impact was like getting hit by a car. The two of them crashed to the floor, multi-colored spots flashing in Janey's eyes. She scrambled for the two extra items clipped to her belt as she remembered Vessler's description.

"Fields is dense," the older man had said. "And I don't mean mentally. He's not but about five-five, but last time I checked, the man weighed nearly four hundred pounds. He's got muscles like concrete, and skin like iron. I don't think you could lift a gun big enough to do him any serious damage, and forget trying to get a needle into him."

"Great," Janey said. "So what, then?"

"So we have to get a little imaginative." Vessler picked an item off Janey's pegboard and held it up in the candlelight. "With a little modification, this will do just fine. I don't suppose you have another?"

On the floor of Scott's room, Ned Fields balled up a fist like the head of a sledgehammer and drew it back. Janey knew that fist would break whatever bone it hit, so she didn't give it the chance. She pulled the customized stun-gun off her belt, rammed it into Fields' crotch and turned on the current.

Brenda Jorden and Scott Charles both watched open-mouthed.

Fields yelped like a shot dog and exploded backwards, and with a wrench in her stomach Janey watched as one of Fields' flailing hands clipped Scott across the chin with a sickening crack. The boy crumpled on the bed. But Fields' eyes didn't close and he didn't lose consciousness, and Janey knew he'd be back at her in a matter of seconds. So she took the other stun-gun off her belt, the one that she'd fitted with a cord and male adapter, found a wall socket next to Scott's computer desk, and plugged it in.

When Fields surged back up off the floor and lunged at Janey, Janey slapped Fields' head down face-first into the carpet, stuck the stun-gun in the back of his neck and let him have it.

What few lights burned in the house flickered madly, the scent of overcooked pork filled the bedroom, and Fields' screams faded and stopped.

Janey kept the current on him for three more seconds before she turned it off and felt for a pulse. She found one, a little spotty but definitely there, and Fields' arms and legs kept twitching, so Janey didn't worry that she'd killed the man. Fields made no further attempt to get up, and Janey edged away from him and stood.

She swallowed hard. Her head abruptly felt very weird, and the smell she'd noticed earlier got thicker.

Scott Charles lay on the bed, unconscious and bleeding from his mouth, his breathing ragged.

Janey snapped open a baton and turned to face Brenda Jorden, who said, "I don't think you want to hit me." It was like a purr. "I think you'd rather just talk to me."

Jorden flicked on the overhead light. In the incandescent glow she looked twice as beautiful as she had in the near-darkness. She wore a clinging, soft blue blouse and flowing black skirt, and any words Janey might have used to describe the woman left her head. The hand holding the baton began to shake. The scent grew stronger, filled up her head, and oh, God, it smelled *good,* better the more she got of it.

At her feet, Fields stopped twitching, but Janey could hear him breathing.

Brenda smiled, and Janey began to feel a sort of detachment from reality—as if she hadn't just almost killed someone, almost been killed herself, as if she weren't here to rescue a sick child—and she was ashamed to feel herself responding to this woman physically. Janey noticed Brenda wasn't wearing a bra beneath her thin silk blouse, and her nipples were very visibly erect. The heavy curves of Brenda's breasts pressed at the material.

"Of course, I don't *really* want to talk," Jorden said, and took a step forward. She sensuously trailed a hand from her cheek down the front of her blouse. Buttons fell open in its wake. The hand slid farther down, outlined the curve of her waist and the generous flair of her hips. Janey noticed a sprinkling of caramel-colored freckles on the smooth skin between Brenda's breasts, and felt a sudden and irrational need to taste them. Her head filled to overflowing with Brenda's scent.

No, no, dammit, what the hell am I doing?

"I know you'd much rather put off talking till later, and... maybe...get a little more...comfortable?" Brenda's voice grew low and sultry, and her lips seemed to sparkle dark red, like sweet cherry syrup. She gracefully nudged her blouse aside, fully exposing her left breast, and Janey's breath stopped completely. It started high, near her collar bone, and swept down into an achingly perfect teardrop, the milk-white skin contrasting splendidly with the tightened dark brown nipple.

A wave of heat began in Janey's stomach and rushed down

through her groin. An involuntary moan escaped Janey's lips, and Brenda smiled. Janey could smell, feel, taste her scent, and her eyes shook with tiny tremors as she whipped them over Brenda's body, from eyes to lips to breasts and back.

Stop it, stop it, stop it!

Brenda smiled again and slipped the blouse completely off. Janey's entire body trembled, and she almost dropped the baton when Brenda spoke again.

"Come on," she sighed. "Come with me. Let me take care of you." Brenda's hand slid forward, took the baton, and dropped it on the floor. That was all right. Janey didn't need it anymore. "I know you'd like to be with me...face to face...let your skin touch mine."

God, she was right. She was so *right.* All the pain and loneliness since Adam got shot, all the tension with Tim, all the stress Janey had jammed down deep inside herself, all of it she'd condensed into a tiny shard that constantly stabbed through her, soured her emotions, tainted every breath she took. As Brenda Jorden's thrilling scent filled her body, Janey knew Brenda could make all of it go away, that a night in her arms would be better than a thousand pain-killers, that Brenda could pour herself over Janey's wounds and heal them in a soothing, tingling rush.

Brenda's fingers ran up Janey's arm and across her shoulder, leaving a trail like sweet fire behind them. Janey felt Brenda's essence enter her skin, wash over the jagged rents and tears inside of her, fill her up and smooth her over.

Brenda's fingertips brushed Janey's neck, toyed with the edge of the mask, searched for a grip...

...but couldn't find one. The mask zipped to the suit, the pull-tab concealed at the back of the neck. Brenda's caresses turned insistent as she tried to find an opening in the fabric.

Why is she pulling at my neck?

"You need to take your mask off, Jane," Brenda breathed into her ear.

Jane. *Jane?* She *hated* that name. The only person who'd ever called her Jane was her father, and then only when she'd gotten in trouble.

What the hell is she doing?

Janey took a step backward and brushed Brenda's hand away from her face. The scent still coated her nostrils, filled her lungs, and it smelled so good—but Janey shook her head, tried just to breathe through her mouth. "My name is not Jane." She took another step away, and her heel bumped Fields' shoulder, and Fields let out a low, agonized groan.

Janey's head cleared. As it did, Brenda's perfect features contorted with rage.

Brenda abandoned her words, her other hand came up, and Janey noted somewhat dully that it held an enormous, serrated butcher knife. Brenda raised it in both hands, took a step forward and rammed it down into the center of Janey's chest.

The impact hurt, since it struck several of her bruises, but the Vylar turned the blade aside easily.

With a grunt, Janey planted one gloved hand between Brenda's perfect breasts and shoved as hard as she could, which wasn't all that hard at the moment. Still, Brenda stumbled backward through the doorway into the hall, tried to catch herself on the doorframe, missed, and fell hard on one elbow. The knife spun out of her hand.

Janey stepped over Ned Fields and flicked off the overhead light. In the darkness, she pulled Scott Charles off the bed and flickered away.

* * *

Alone in the bedroom with Fields, Brenda Jorden panted in the sudden heat and pulled her blouse back around her. Janey Sinclair and Scott were both gone.

For the first time in years, Brenda was afraid.

* * *

Vessler waited for them at the Jeep, which he'd parked in a dark alley behind a drug store. Janey and Scott flickered out of the shadows, and as Vessler came forward he immediately saw that Scott was hurt. His face tightened.

Janey carried Scott to the Jeep, the sight and sound and smell of Brenda Jorden still buzzing in her head like a band saw. Her physical reaction had diminished, for which she was grateful. She had to try twice to make her tongue work before she could say anything.

"Fields hit him accidentally. I think his jaw might be broken."

Vessler took Scott from her and placed him gently and carefully on the back seat. Not the way someone handles a possession, either; Janey could tell in an instant that Vessler loved the boy dearly. The mask hid her surprise.

Scott breathed, but only shallowly, with ice-cold and clammy skin.

"What should we do with him?" Janey asked. "Get him to a hospital?"

Vessler paused with the back door open. "No. Stamford would find out. I can set his jaw, if it needs it. We need to get him somewhere private. And safe." He looked pointedly at Janey.

Janey's eyes narrowed behind the black mesh. "I can't take him back to the basement. If I had to leave, you couldn't get in or out."

Vessler didn't like that. "Hhmmm...fine. Another motel, then."

Janey shook her head, not in disagreement, but in an attempt to dislodge the last lingering effects of Jorden's scent.

Vessler said, "All right. Follow me. I'm sure you don't want to be seen with me in a car, with or without the mask."

Janey nodded. "Go ahead. I'll be right behind you."

Driving away, Vessler tried to look in the rearview mirror for the exact moment when Janey flickered out, but only saw shadows.

* * *

Tim couldn't decide whether to be insanely frightened or insanely envious—and he couldn't tell if either feeling was genuine, considering his recent lack of sleep. The last time his sleep patterns had been so thoroughly mucked up was spring semester finals week of his senior year at college. His eyes had popped open at 3:30 this morning, and he couldn't get them to stay closed; now it was just past four, and he was wired tight.

What happens when fantasies come true? What happens when you know someone actually *can* fly? He pushed the button and waited for the elevator.

Tim wasn't a kid anymore, and this wasn't a fantasy. He'd seen Janey do it. Had her repeat it, in fact, and he couldn't deny it. After all the initial hysteria, after the painful process of warping a new convolution into his brain so he could accept it, he'd come to a single, possibly irrational conclusion.

Janey's teleportation was without question the coolest thing he'd ever seen.

In the hours since he'd last spoken to her, Tim had gone through a mental list of hundreds of practical applications for her talent. She could do virtually *anything*. Because sooner or later, no matter what, the lights went out *everywhere.*

They couldn't keep her in a cell. Lights out, and zap, she's gone.

She could take anything she wanted, from anywhere. Just wait till the store closes, zap, she's in, zap, she's out, and nobody knows any better.

She could save a real bundle on air fares. Wait till the sun goes down, and zap zap zap right across the country.

And dammit—why couldn't he do it too?

Why her, and not him? Why couldn't he have been *chosen,* if that was the right word? Seven years ago...that would have put him smack in the middle of his eighteenth year, and God in Heaven, could he have used something like this.

The elevator pinged and opened. Tim got in the car and pushed the button for Janey's floor.

He found thinking about Janey's talent easier than thinking about his feelings for her—or about the emotional bear trap she was caught in with Adam.

Not that he really *needed* to think about his feelings. He knew how stupid it was, to feel this way about a woman who obviously had serious problems relating to...well, to anyone, and was *married,* for crying out loud. Well, sort of married. But again, that was a bottomless well of guilt he didn't feel like dipping into just then.

Janey was also the most talented, gorgeous, fascinating woman he'd ever met. And there it was, there he went, head and heels and everything, and he knew if he didn't talk to her soon his brain would spin right out of his skull.

The elevator door slid open, and he stepped out into Janey's hallway. It was deserted. Tim went to her door, rapped sharply five times and stepped back to wait. After a minute had passed, he knocked again and said, "Janey? Hey, Janey, are you home?"

The door opened.

A young man dressed in black, wearing the dark gray raincoat Tim had given Janey, stood there in the doorway.

The mugger from the park. *Simon.*

He grinned and said, "Hi there."

Tim jerked back, tried to run, but something like a cold white whip lashed across his wrist and his hand went numb. The same whip-thing curled around his throat, cinched tight, and jerked him off his feet.

Simon kicked the door closed as he dragged Tim into Janey's apartment.

Tim crashed to the floor hard on one shoulder, and the impact sent splinters of pain through his arm and neck. He rolled onto his side as the whip-thing uncoiled from his throat, only to find his cheek pressed against the side of Simon's boot. He glanced up in time to see Simon's jaw begin to contort before Simon drew the boot back and drove it into Tim's face. Agony speared through him as his nose crunched inward, and immediate tears blinded him.

"You're not who I was looking for," Simon croaked out. His voice was grotesque, razor-edged. Even through the pain it sliced along Tim's nerves. "But you'll do just fine."

The whip-thing encircled one arm, then the other, and Simon hauled him to his feet. Tim blinked rapidly and tried not to cry out or choke on the blood filling his nose and mouth. His vision at last cleared enough for him to get a good look at the man holding him, and he took it all in in a flash: the needle teeth, the white-on-black eyes, the finger-tendrils extending from grossly lengthened forearms.

"Oh shit, oh shit, oh shit," Tim whispered, and tried to look away from Simon, but couldn't. Simon's mouth writhed and shrank back into something closer to normal.

"You'd be better off saying prayers." Still through needle teeth, the words couldn't have been produced by anything like a human throat.

With a grunt, Tim drove his knee upward into Simon's groin as hard as he could, and felt his kneecap bash through the softer tissues and connect solidly with Simon's pelvic bone.

As though Simon's hands were loaded with explosives, Tim flew across the room away from him. He crashed into the wall next to the coat closet, hard enough to leave a head-and-shoulders indentation in the wall, and his vision dimmed—but he refused to lose consciousness, and struggled to his feet. Blood poured down his face and onto his shirt.

Simon lay curled on his side on the floor, his hands shoved between his legs. The finger tendrils had distended crazily, spinning out to twig-like strands more than a yard long. He started chewing on the carpet.

Not for a second did Tim believe one knee to the groin would put Simon out of action for good. With what felt like quarts of adrenaline pumping through him, he didn't stop to think at all about the insane distortions Simon's body was going through. Tim saw him only as a threat—a threat specifically to himself and to Janey. If he ran, Simon would only chase him down. He needed to stop Simon, not just escape from him.

Tim took a step toward the kitchen, looked around for a likely weapon, saw a block of knives and started toward it.

He never got there. The impossibly thin tendrils of Simon's left hand wrapped around his ankle like steel wire, and as Simon pushed himself upright, he pulled Tim's feet out from under him and dragged him across the floor. Simon still breathed heavily, but he no longer seemed to be in pain.

"I wouldn't have hurt you," he said into Tim's face. His breath smelled like raw hamburger. "Well, okay. That's not true." Two tendrils snaked over Tim's eyes and lips. "But now you've—"

He would have finished the word, but Tim caught one of the tendrils between his teeth and bit cleanly through it.

Simon's blood, thick and nearly black, sprayed out of the tendril as though from a high-pressure hose. Tim had time to spit a mouthful of blood and the severed bit of finger back in Simon's face before the tendrils from the other hand wrapped completely around his head. The short length of still-twitching finger stuck to Simon's cheek like a leech.

Simon heaved Tim off the floor using only the grip on his head, and Tim both felt and heard his neck pop.

"You *bastard!*" Simon screamed, and slammed Tim's head against a wall.

"You fucking bastard!" He did it again, with greater force. Tim went somewhere past pain.

Somehow, in the flailing, Tim's hand found something hard and heavy, possibly a bookend. His fingers closed around it, and the muscles in his arm tensed to swing it, but Simon rammed his head into the wall again, and whatever it was fell out of his grip. Crazily the apartment tilted away, and Tim tumbled slowly into a dark, wet place.

CHAPTER TWENTY-TWO

Simon Grove let the towel-head thud to the floor and dropped to his knees next to him. He peeled his severed finger off his face and waited for a new one to grow. It didn't—and for a few frantic minutes Simon tried to reattach the severed bit, holding it to the stump in hopes that it would magically reattach itself. But the stump and the severed finger weren't quite the same size anymore, so he tried to get the stump to stretch out further, and it did stretch, but he couldn't stop it from getting too thin, and he howled in frustration.

For a few moments he sat on the floor next to the sand-monkey and stared at the finger, which had finally stopped twitching.

Slowly he brought it to his mouth, placed it on his tongue, and swallowed it.

That made the pain a little better, he thought.

Simon turned his attention to Tim Kapoor: reached out and encircled his throat again. He felt the tingle, just a little bit, but at Brenda's suggestion he'd fed earlier in the evening, taking a delicious blonde hooker. The hooker was a big girl, at least five-ten, taller than Simon, with bee-stung lips and breasts larger than her head. He hadn't felt anything that intense or prolonged in months.

"You need to be focused tonight," Brenda had told him. "You shouldn't take the chance on getting distracted."

She was right, of course. If he hadn't fed so much, hadn't gotten such a hard, lasting rush, he never would've kept it together with the old man and the two morons in the motel. Going for Janey Sinclair tonight was an improvisation, too, and he might otherwise have gotten a little freaked out over the sudden change in plans, but he could still feel the hooker's blood rush in the small of his back, and he was cool.

Like a cucumber.

No problem.

He hadn't planned on encountering Janey Sinclair's skinny boy-toy tonight, but he knew he could use the guy. Somehow. He'd think of something. He could just call Brenda and ask.

Kapoor's fading pulse fluttered beneath his fingers, but reluctantly he took his hand away.

* * *

Vessler stopped at a Howard Johnson's. Janey flickered in by the Jeep's rear bumper as Vessler got out, and watched over Scott as the older man went in to get a room.

Vessler came back from the office a few minutes later, drove the Jeep around to the back of the motel, and carried Scott inside. Once he lay the boy down on one of the room's two double beds, he turned off the lights and pulled the door open.

A second later, from the back of the room, Janey said, "All right." Vessler let the door swing closed and turned the lights back on. Janey stood in the bathroom doorway.

"His jaw's not broken," Vessler said, examining Scott's face. "Thank God. That would have been hard."

Vessler stood and turned back to Janey. "Look, I'm going to go and get him something to drink, maybe some orange juice. If he wakes up before I get back, talk to him, all right?" Janey nodded, and Vessler moved to the door. "And take off that mask, will you? You're giving me the creeps."

He didn't wait for Janey to do it. The door closed behind him with a slight hydraulic hiss.

Dazed by everything that had happened in the last several hours, Janey went to Scott's side and sat down on the edge of the bed. Scott made a tiny noise, but didn't wake up. Reluctantly, Janey took hold of the concealed zipper pull at the back of her neck and unfastened the mask from the suit. She pulled it off slowly. That felt weirder still, given the circumstances, but the air was cool and soothing on her skin.

Vessler returned a few moments later. He stopped just inside the door, as it swung closed, and regarded Janey's face with open curiosity. "You're younger than I expected."

Janey couldn't think of a good comeback. "Oh yeah?"

Vessler didn't respond. He had a paper bag in one hand. He pulled a can of orange juice out of it, went to Scott's side and gently touched his face.

"Scott? Scott, can you hear me? Can you wake up?"

The boy's eyelids twitched and finally opened. The whites of his eyes had turned partly red with ruptured vessels. Weakly, he said, "Sir. I don't feel very good."

Vessler nodded. "Here. Drink this. It'll help." He propped Scott up with pillows and held the orange juice to his lips. Scott shakily raised one hand and took the can, drank from it. Drank more. He glanced over at Janey, and down at Janey's suit.

"You're younger than I thought," Scott said, and Janey laughed. Scott continued, "Thank you. I don't think she was planning to keep me alive for very long."

"It's not over yet," Vessler said sadly. "I need you to tell me where they are. Both of them."

Scott grimaced, and for a moment Janey thought he'd start crying, but as soon as it had come the grimace faded. Janey was once again impressed by how *old* Scott Charles seemed to be on the inside.

"All right. I can do it...but, would it be okay if I didn't get up? If I could just describe what I see from here?"

"Sure, of course," Vessler said soothingly. The more time Vessler spent around Scott, Janey thought, the more human he seemed to become. It was a welcome shift. Garrison Vessler could probably write the definitive text on rigid and intimidating. "You just tell us where they are."

Scott nodded and closed his eyes. Seconds later they opened

again, focused on nothing. "I…can see…Simon." Janey started to ask him something, but Vessler put out a hand, shushing her. Scott went on. "He's walking into a…a building."

Vessler spoke gently. "Can you tell what building it is? Can you see numbers, or a name?"

Scott's brow furrowed. "I…don't…I don't know how to pronounce it." He stumbled over the unfamiliar letters in his mind. "Lah…lah-kroiks?"

Janey felt as if she'd been kicked in the stomach. *The LaCroix.* She threw herself into the darkness of the bathroom, and a blast of sweltering air washed out over Vessler and Scott as Janey vanished.

* * *

Vessler turned and went back to Scott on the bed. "You're doing fine, Scott," he said. Scott's eyes focused and he smiled feebly. Vessler knew how much it must have been taking out of the boy, in such a weakened state. But he had to ask. He had to know.

"I just need you to do one more. You have to tell me where Miss Jorden is." Scott nodded again and closed his eyes. He seemed so eager to please. A few moments later he exhaled sharply, and started talking.

* * *

Drenched in sweat and terrified, Janey flickered out of a shadow across the street from the LaCroix and stared up at the window of her apartment. It was lit, but she couldn't tell from street level whether or not anyone was inside. She'd already checked Tim's apartment as well as the office. Both were empty.

The thought of Simon Grove with Tim made her physically ill. She tried chanting the alphabet backward to herself. It didn't help.

Another flicker and she stood on the ledge outside her living room window, and if anyone saw her, to hell with them. She didn't care.

The living room was empty, but every light burned and the coat closet stood open. Carefully Janey opened the window and stepped through it, her boots noiseless on the carpet.

One of her neighbors had a stereo going a few doors down the hall, just loud enough so that all Janey could hear was an incessant drumbeat. Aside from that, the apartment remained still and silent.

Just then there was a rustle and a *slide-click* that Janey recognized, and she rushed for her bedroom and went into a low roll, knocking the door wide with her shoulder. She tumbled across the floor and came up on one knee next to the bathroom door, a baton ready, staring at a blank, open window. A small, circular section of her shower curtain melted as she flickered out.

On the ledge outside the window, which faced away from the street, Janey looked around wildly, her night vision transforming the world about her into crisp, clear images in glowing yellow and green. It only took her seconds to notice the small holes punched into the mortar between the bricks of the building's wall. They led upward.

The glass of her window rippled and cracked as she vanished.

The roof of the LaCroix looked like a lot of other roofs in the city, covered with a thin layer of gravel and spotted with air-intake housings. The view to the west was blocked by a nearby building, a recently completed twenty-story apartment tower. Janey stared across the thirty-foot gap between the LaCroix and the other building, and was about to flicker out again, when she thought she saw something at the building's edge. Movement? She walked quickly to the edge of the LaCroix's roof, still staring.

There. She saw it again.

"Simon?" Janey strove to keep her voice from shaking. It carried well across the space between the buildings, reaching forty feet to the other roof.

There, right at the edge, Simon Grove rose up and stood in

plain view.

That bastard stole my coat!

He looked human—except for his right hand, which he slowly raised into view. Janey gasped. Simon's extended fingers wrapped around Tim's head as if he were holding an oversized highball, keeping Tim upright. Tim wasn't moving. Bruises and lacerations and blood marred his face.

"*Tim!*" Janey screamed. "Tim, can you hear me? *Can you hear me?*"

"I've got some instructions for you," Simon called out, his voice smooth and unhurried. "You're going to do just what I say, or I'll drop this asshole over the side. First things first: come out of that suit."

Neither Simon nor Janey moved.

"Hey! I said *come out of that suit!*"

Silently Simon lengthened his right forearm, looped two finger tendrils under Tim's arms, and stepped forward. Tim's legs swung free of the roof, suspended two hundred feet above the street below.

Janey eyed the building's wall. A wide concrete ledge circled the building directly below them, and if Simon dropped Tim, he'd probably land on it.

Probably.

But that was still a drop of at least ten feet, and Janey could tell he wouldn't be able to make even an attempt at landing properly. Ten feet was plenty of room to break your neck.

"He's still breathing, if you're wondering," Simon said. "But just barely. We had an argument."

"You don't have to involve him in this," Janey shouted. "Just put him down slowly."

"*Involve* him? What's wrong with you?" Simon's eyes began to glow white. "Lost your memory? Lost your *mind?* Do you think he got here on his own? I can't just turn him loose. *Please.*"

"Let him go and I won't hurt you." The words came out

clichéd and ineffectual, and Janey gritted her teeth.

"No, no, no, let's not go through all this movie good-guy bad-guy bullshit here, *Janey.* I've got your guy, and I won't feel bad at all about dropping him, so *take off that fucking body armor!*"

* * *

Even as Simon screamed the last few words, he saw Sinclair drop down out of sight behind the low wall surrounding the rooftop. A moment passed, and he was just about to call out something like, "Where'd you go?" when a steely arm clamped around his throat. It would take very little pressure to crush Simon's throat or even snap his neck, and he knew it.

Simon kept still.

Tim hung as if suspended from a crane.

"Simon, listen to me." Sinclair's voice in his ear. "None of this is necessary. The woman you were with. Brenda Jorden. She's like us. She's an augment."

Simon didn't answer, didn't move. A gust of wind blew, and Tim's feet swayed back and forth.

"She controls people. She's controlling *you.* You don't have to do any of this. If you'll let me...I can get you to someone who can help you."

"Take your hands off me."

"She's been playing you, Simon. Made you a puppet. Come on, I know you don't want that."

Simon slowly turned his head completely around, 180 degrees, until he stared the Sinclair bitch in the face. He grinned a little when she tried not to flinch away. "Understand this, you cunt," Simon said slowly. "Brenda hasn't done a damn thing to me except show me that I don't have to let bitches like you push me around anymore. And I will drop this stupid ni-...ni-..." He trembled slightly. "I will drop this son of a bitch unless you get away from me."

Simon swiveled his head back around to the front.

"Please," Sinclair murmured. "This is pointless. I never did anything to hurt you. The only reason you're here, the only reason you're doing this now, is because she *told* you to do it. This is what *she* wants, it's not what *you* want. We don't...we don't have to do this. This is unnecessary, this whole thing."

"That's nice, coming from the chick who's got me in a choke-hold. And don't you even try to tell me what I want. This is not just a threat. I will drop him. Now back off me."

"Simon...I don't want to hurt you, I've never wanted to hurt you. All I've ever wanted to do was talk to you. But I'll tell you this, and you better believe it. If you drop him, I will end you."

Simon felt power humming through Janey Sinclair's arm like a high-voltage line where it clamped around his neck, and through the mask Sinclair's breath touched his face, so hot he thought his skin might blister.

For just the tiniest of instants, Simon felt numbing, paralyzing, *familiar* fear.

But Brenda's words, Brenda's message came back to him, and her reassuring fragrance filled him up again, and the anger rose in his blood. *He* had no reason to feel fear. *He* was a prince, destined to become a king. Fear was for the weak. And Simon Grove was *strong*.

In the space of one second he said, "Fuck you," and wrenched forward, and yanked his fingers away from Tim Kapoor's body.

Kapoor fell like a brick.

Something like a wrecking ball smashed into Simon's face, and the night sky turned blood red and faded out.

* * *

Janey's world slowed to a crawl as Simon let go of Tim. The space between Tim's body and Simon's finger-tendrils as he released him struck out at Janey like a physical blow, only a few millimeters, scarcely significant, but the distance shrieked Tim's death.

Simon stood in the way, and as Janey shoved him Simon swung around, his face already distorted into a gigantic leer. With a snarl Janey hammered a baton into Simon's face, crushing his nose and knocking a spray of broken spines down his throat. Simon staggered and crumpled.

That action took less than a second. Janey leaned over the roof's edge in time to see Tim thud onto the concrete ledge below, as she'd prayed he would if Simon dropped him.

Janey screamed as Tim slid bonelessly over the edge and fell.

* * *

Brenda Jorden tried not to let her hands shake on the steering wheel of Ned Fields' car.

Derek Stamford's words still played in her head.

"This was your idea from the start. I'm sorry it's blown up in your face, but there's really nothing I can do."

Nothing I can do. Smug, condescending bastard. Probably twirling his cane while he talked.

She kept just under the speed limit. No use in attracting unwanted attention. She doubted Stamford would send Redfell after her directly now, since there wasn't really any need to. Without their direct support, he'd look for her to crash and burn on her own.

She'd be disappointed to have to crush his expectations. Underneath the passenger seat rested a mid-size gray overnight bag. Inside sat 125,000 dollars in tens and twenties, along with two alternate ID's, complete with passports. Brenda Jorden was a survivor. How many times had she proven that? How many times had life thrown its absolute worst shit in her face? She couldn't remember. Fields wasn't in quite as good a position—with no hope of moving him, she'd left him there on the floor of Scott's room. At least he was breathing.

But Fields was *so* not her problem.

A couple of months, maybe a year. She'd be back in Derek Stamford's life.

Long enough to end it.

Pine trees flashed by her on both sides of the road. On the horizon to the east was a glow of pink.

She'd just begun a mental list of prioritized actions for when she reached safety when a battered tan Jeep Cherokee rammed into her from behind. She fishtailed in the road and the Cherokee hit her again, harder this time. Her right rear tire caught the curb at a bad angle and she lost control of the car entirely. It flipped, rolled down a steep embankment, and jammed nose-first into a dry drainage canal.

She stayed just conscious enough to hear a car door slam somewhere above her. Her own door opened, and a deep, slightly Texan voice said, "Hello, Brenda."

She couldn't quite see Garrison Vessler through the gas and dust from the deflated airbag, but she plainly felt the sudden, intense cold near her face, and screamed as the ice took her.

* * *

Without hesitation Janey vaulted over the wall and dove after Tim.

One hundred eighty feet.

She saw him there below her, and beyond him the pavement rushed up like an enormous gray fist. A detached part of her knew what he'd look like if he hit. Not like in the movies, where the jumper lies on the pavement as if asleep, maybe with a tiny, harmless pool of blood around his head.

One hundred thirty feet.

Not like that at all. If Tim hit the ground from this height he'd be unrecognizable. Every bone in his body pulverized, every bit of flesh torn and ruptured.

Ninety feet.

Tears streamed from Janey's eyes as the rushing air found its way through the fabric of her mask. She had to reach him. *Had* to.

Fifty feet.

She stretched, reached out as she fell. Tried to angle her body to slip through the air faster.

Oh God. The momentum. *"So what happens if you take a running start?"*

She hadn't even thought about it. What would happen to their fall if she took them out of shadows at ground level? Would their velocity transfer, smash them to bloody bits even if she did catch him? How could she compensate for it? How could she channel it?

Twenty feet.

She'd have to redirect the energy somehow, send the force of their fall away, take it and shove it away from them. ...How?

There, right below her, Tim was *right there.*

She had no idea how.

Ten feet.

Janey's hand closed around Tim's left ankle six feet off the ground.

A broad column of flame erupted from their point of departure. It scoured and scorched the pavement, and sent sheets of fire skittering sixty feet up the sides of both the LaCroix and the building where Simon had stood before they flickered out. A sudden, sharp peal of thunder crashed. Fierce winds roared away from the spot where Janey and Tim disappeared.

All the windows in the walls facing the flame column exploded savagely inward as something very like a bolt of lightning smashed out of the air and into the ground where they would have crashed. It coruscated blood red and brilliant gold, and in the microseconds of its duration it dissipated the fire and gouged a pit twelve feet deep through the concrete and into the earth.

Bits of glass, some molten, rained down around the crater.

The pavement at its rim burned long after the power discharge faded away.

CHAPTER TWENTY-THREE

Chief Resident Carla Gates walked swiftly along a corridor in Gavring Medical's emergency center, staring at a patient's charts.

She worked with a few doctors who could weave words like *tumor* and *inoperable* into a kind of poetry that, if it did not soothe, at least served to numb the terror. Gave the patients a sense of control in the face of their own mortality.

She'd never been a poet. She could try, had tried in the past; she would try again in a few minutes, when she spoke to a fifty-three-year-old man named Bernard Stein, but she didn't think Mr. Stein would take any comfort from her. Spoken in layman's terms, Bernard Stein's right lung was little more than a huge cancerous mass, and the cancer had metastasized. He had weeks left, maybe even days. Only the facts, she could give him, like a journalistic report. No soothing...no real ease. She hated that facet of herself.

A dozen yards ahead of her, on her right, was the door to a certain janitorial supply closet, and for several days now she'd watched it suspiciously whenever she passed it. The image of the two black eyes staring out at her was a lasting one. Even though the shopkeeper, Rico Ruiz, swore the vigilante had saved his life, the Gray Widow still made Gates' skin crawl. Hero or not.

She'd thought a few times about propping the door open permanently, maybe leaving the light on inside. Tonight, for some reason she couldn't put a finger on, that seemed like an excellent decision, and she wondered why she hadn't made it before.

Gates stopped directly opposite the door and started to glance around for a chair to prop it with when something slammed into it from the inside.

Carla Gates dropped her charts and gasped.

Another impact and the door burst open, torn halfway off its hinges. The Gray Widow came out of the darkness with a young man cradled in her arms. At a glance Gates could tell the man had been beaten severely. The Widow's head turned, and black eyes tracked across the ER. Activity ground to a halt with her arrival, and everyone from attendings to clerks stared at her openly.

The black eyes settled on Carla Gates. The Widow came toward her.

Gates thought the woman must have been at least seven feet tall.

"This man needs help, *right now,*" she said, and Gates recognized panic in her voice. An empty gurney stood nearby, and the Widow lowered the man gently onto it. "His name is Tim Kapoor, he's twenty-five, he's suffered blunt head trauma, and..."

The vigilante's composure slipped further, and Gates realized she was crying.

"...And there might be...broken bones, maybe his collarbone..." She turned to Gates again and took a step toward her. "You can help him, right now, right? No waiting, no bullshit about insurance, right?"

Two security guards rounded the corner at the far end of the hall, and the black eyes lifted to them. Gates stammered a little before she got the right words out. "Yes, yes, of course." She glanced over her shoulder at the guards. They both had guns drawn. "But we can do that best if we don't have any other conflicts here."

The Gray Widow nodded. Before she turned to go, in a voice thick with pain, she said, "Make him better. Help him. Please." She spun and bolted through an exit.

Gates barked orders, and two nurses moved to wheel the injured young man into a trauma room as the two guards rushed past.

* * *

Starting at the roof of the apartment building next to the LaCroix and moving in concentric circles outward, a searing wind blew through Atlanta. At its head was a woman in gray with acid tears in her eyes.

Janey had never used the flickering the way she did now. She never fully entered it, but skimmed along its edge, shadow to shadow, neither in one place nor the other. With grinding teeth and tear-blurred vision Janey *became* shadow, and tore through the city with a speed close to flight.

She searched. As she searched, from time to time she repeated words to herself, and the pain grew worse with each repetition.

Not again. Not again. Not like Adam.

Twice she came upon people in the commission of crimes, and both times she acted swiftly and harshly before flickering away.

The first was a young man with a bandanna pulled down over his eyebrows, using a sheath knife to threaten a middle-aged woman behind a rundown clapboard house. It looked as if she'd come outside to empty her garbage. The woman might have heard a sigh, might have seen the hint of movement, before the man with the knife wrenched away from her and did a twisted, frenzied dance as Janey's baton worked him over. The man collapsed to the grass-covered dirt like a marionette with its strings cut, both legs and one arm folded the wrong way. The grass around him scorched and died as Janey vanished. The woman, screaming now, ran back inside her house and slammed and locked the door.

The second was a blonde, tanned, muscular frat boy trying to force himself on a teenage girl in his car, which was parked out of sight in a drainage canal below a freeway overpass. The girl, who couldn't have been more than sixteen, screamed and thrashed as he pawed at her breasts and tried to jam one hand between her legs.

The girl had managed to get her door open and put one foot on the ground when the frat boy balled up his fist and punched her in the jaw. She screamed louder and tried to kick him—and stopped dead still when she looked over his shoulder and saw a looming gray shape outside the car.

The driver's side door jerked open and the frat boy vanished through it. A number of sharp, violent impacts rang out as the girl clambered out of the car. She looked over the roof in time to see the gray shape deliver four devastating kicks to the frat boy's crotch. The boy thudded to the ground, landing partly in and partly out of the car, his eyelashes and eyebrows singed off.

The girl stared into the darkness for a few seconds, straightened her clothes, fished her phone out of her purse, and dialed 911. The frat boy groaned loudly and threw up his dinner.

For over forty minutes Janey's search continued, and storm clouds had begun to gather overhead when she saw a glimmer of something white disappear through a metal door at the side of a low brick building. With a tiny rush of recognition, Janey realized she was at the television studio where she'd made her unannounced guest appearance on the *Good Morning Sheree* show.

Somewhat familiar with the building's layout, she flickered into the lobby and pressed against one wall, deep in the shadows.

From the lobby, the building split into two hallways which ran its length, one on the north side and one on the south. Between the corridors, studios took up most of the building's floor space, while small offices lined the outer edges. The door she'd seen something disappear through was halfway down the southern hall, between two offices, and let out onto the parking lot. Janey flickered into the shadows and emerged on the other side of the locked glass doors separating the lobby from the hallways.

She identified the steady background hum as air conditioning, which ran even though the temperature outside couldn't have been more than sixty. The building's interior felt like a freezer, still and morgue-silent. Janey soundlessly edged her way to the corner of the southern hallway, started to peer around it, and paused.

Reaching into a shadow, Janey carefully pulled a small dentist's mirror to her from the basement. Moving slowly so as not to create any sudden flashes that might register on Simon Grove's peripheral vision, she extended the mirror past the corner's edge and got a full view of the corridor.

A studio door gracefully clicked shut.

Something flashed in the opening just before the lock engaged; something that might have been the hem of a long gray coat. Janey was surprised to find a trace of indignation piled on top of everything else. *Can't believe the bastard went through my closet.*

In a series of flickers, Janey moved down the hallway until she stood outside the door. She opened another small portal to the basement and replaced the mirror, and put her hand cautiously on the doorknob.

She knew it was some kind of trap. It had to be. Simon was playing with her, leading her on. But he was here, now, and Janey couldn't let him escape, trap or not.

She turned the knob. All she needed was the tiniest of openings, just a glimpse into the studio, and she could flicker inside, reach a point of safety.

The knob worked smoothly, and the latch slowly disengaged. Janey pulled, gently, gently, and the door left the frame, millimeter by millimeter. She only needed one crack, just a hair wide, and her night vision would take care of the rest. She could take the room.

Another millimeter. And another—

— and the door exploded outward. The knob tore out of her hand, and Simon crouched there with a needle-toothed grin that nearly split his head in half. A long, forked tongue flicked out at Janey, and Simon's finger-tendrils rushed forward, snaked around her like demonic worms. The tendrils entangled both her arms immediately. Simon swiveled at his hips and hauled Janey completely off her feet.

Simon let out an ungodly hiss next to Janey's ear as he heaved. Her arms still trapped, Janey tried to twist away, but Simon's strength was immense. He whipped Janey over his head as if she were a rag doll and hammered her into the concrete floor.

Janey felt her left leg snap halfway between her foot and knee. All the air slammed out of her lungs as she screamed, and she jerked and pulled at her mask and got it off her face less than a second before she vomited, her stomach spasming painfully. She kept control of her bladder, but only just.

Silence. The tendrils had withdrawn at some point.

It took her a few seconds to realize Simon had moved away. Gasping at the pain, Janey tried to orient herself. She lay in the middle of the concrete floor of Studio 2, according to the sign above the exit. No lamps burned, and her night vision still worked, though brilliant red flashes filled the edges of it. The pain in her leg overwhelmed her. She vomited again, and wondered if what she felt swiftly approaching was shock. She tried to concentrate, tried to flicker away—

—and the room flooded with blinding white light. The flickering shut off with a painful shearing sensation, and her night vision fled in ragged neon tatters. Janey shielded her eyes and squinted. A dozen spotlights on portable stands ringed the roughly circular area where she lay.

Simon Grove stepped into her field of vision, hands and face normal, wearing an expression of smug contempt. "Bet you weren't expecting this." He sounded very young.

Janey tried to steady her breathing as she lay on the cold concrete. The flickering, the teleportation, had never been cut off like that before, and she felt as if the outer layer of her brain had been roughly peeled away. She tried to get her good leg under her, but the room wouldn't stop spinning, and she collapsed again.

Simon said, "I'm not stupid. It only took so many times watching you jump in one shadow and out another." He cracked his knuckles and slowly walked forward. Janey searched around her for the baton but couldn't see it. When she looked back up, Simon stood over her, and his grin began to widen again. "By the way, I really like this coat."

"Simon," Janey said, and tried to lock her gauntlets' steel knuckles into place, but before she could get the first one set Simon kicked her viciously in the ribs.

Everything went black for a moment. Janey drew a stabbing breath. "Simon, listen to me."

"Screw that. You have been a *severe* pain in the ass, honey."

He circled Janey, and kicked her in the ribs again. "Brenda didn't want you hurt, y'know. Not at first, anyway. She just wanted to use you. Take possession of you before Vessler and his goons got to you. She thought you were too powerful and dangerous not to be on her side."

Needle teeth began to grow out of Simon's gums.

"But I don't think you're so powerful, and I sure as hell don't think you're so dangerous. What I *do* think...is you *really* piss me off." He straddled her chest and reached down with his right hand, the fingers extended and writhing. The intense light rendered a network of fine blue veins visible in each one.

The tendrils encircled Janey's head, flicked her mask the rest of the way off, and Janey knew she was about to die. One tendril mashed her eyes closed, and she saw...

Her father, blasted and dead in the kitchen chair.

Adam in his hospital bed, head swathed in white and tubes snaking out of his nose and mouth.

Tim, torn and broken, bleeding in her arms.

"This is going to hurt," Simon breathed in her ear, and began draining her.

Janey felt the blood leave her body through the skin of her face and neck and scalp, and tried to scream, but Simon's tendrils held her mouth shut. Janey squirmed and thrashed, but the movements grew weaker with each heartbeat. Every rhythmic pump channeled her blood into Simon Grove's body. Every contraction brought the end closer.

I never had a chance at this. Connections felt as if they were shorting out and dying in her brain. *I couldn't have planned for it. I couldn't prepare.* She thought fleetingly of what her father would look like when she met him again.

The tendril over Janey's eyes slipped a fraction of an inch, and Janey's right eye opened. Simon had his head thrown back, and at that moment the blood emerged from the pores of his skin and rained down on Janey in a hot, sticky shower. The coat hung loosely on Simon, soon to be soaked through and ruined, a slick gray death shroud.

Janey's eye widened, and one of the vessels in it burst as Simon drank deeply.

There, in the folds of the coat just beneath Simon's armpit, lay a deep, inviting pool of darkness.

And Janey's right arm remained free.

Janey reached into the darkness through a rapidly dimming burgundy haze.

* * *

Simon Grove realized something had gone wrong when an intense burst of heat blossomed against his left side. He would have slapped at it, but to do that he would've had to let go of Janey Sinclair, and he didn't want to, so he simply looked down...

. . .as a blinding pain speared through him so intense it made his vision flare red. . .

...and saw the hilt of a Japanese katana protruding from the left side of his ribcage.

* * *

The dead-white tendrils whipped loose of Janey as Simon pitched over backward and scuttled away from her in a hitching, crab-like motion. Janey took a deep breath and tried to open her left eye, but it was gummed shut by Simon's blood—*her* blood—and she had to pull it open with her fingers.

Simon screamed. It hurt Janey's ears, and might have gotten even louder, but the sound cut off with a strangling gurgle. Janey figured the katana she had brought from the basement—her father's katana, whose blade had solidified inside Simon's torso—had at least skewered one of his lungs. She wasn't sure about the angle. Maybe it had touched the heart, or the spine, too.

Janey fought her way up to her one good knee, crying out from the pain in her shattered leg. Black waves rolled across her vision. She didn't think it would have hurt any worse if her leg had been ripped completely off.

Simon flopped on the floor, spastically wrenching at the katana. He tore off the gray coat. Janey saw the blade tenting the back of his shirt, and as she watched, the tip pierced the fabric, revealing the blood-coated steel. Simon screamed again. "What have you done to me what have you done to me you bitch I'll kill you I'll kill you *I'll kill you!*"

Simon's finger-tendrils wrapped around the katana's hilt. With an inhuman bellow that blew out one of the Klieg lights, he began pulling the sword out of himself.

Janey locked the second set of steel knuckles into place and threw herself on top of him.

The impact and weight of her body shoved the katana's blade sideways inside him, and he screamed again and drummed his hands and feet on the floor, and Janey smashed a steel-reinforced, gauntleted fist into his face. The impact stunned him, but only for a second, and the tendrils sprang up, writhing and waving all around her. One brushed across her face, and suddenly they locked around her throat.

The pain in her leg shrieked at her, but what felt like an oil tanker's worth of adrenaline flooded her bloodstream, and before Simon could choke her or snap her neck she pulled herself up to a full mount.

He seemed to realize what was coming, and through the haze of pain in his eyes she saw what might have been fear, and he said, "Don't—"

Janey rained punches down on Simon Grove. Every bit of fight training she'd ever had, every bit of augmented strength in her bones and muscles, every bit of savage, brutal advantage the steel knuckles gave her, she poured into this display of ferocity. Simon's tendrils never had the chance to tighten around her neck. Janey landed blow after blow, breaking off spine-like teeth and lodging them into the flesh of Simon's mouth. Blow after blow, until she felt the bones of his jaw break and grind against each other. Blow after blow after blow, until his eye sockets gave way and his nose collapsed and his face became unrecognizable as anything but a wet, red, pulp-filled crater in the front of his skull.

When the tendrils went limp and Simon's arms smacked down, lifeless, on the concrete floor, Janey pitched over to one side and rolled away from him. She lay there and gasped, and panted, and fought off a wave of rolling darkness that threatened to overtake her. With a monumental effort of will she turned her head to look at Simon's corpse.

As Janey watched, Simon's skin began to take on a lizard-like, scaly texture, and small, hooked barbs emerged all over it, but Simon remained motionless, and blood spread out from him in a puddle across the floor.

Janey held still, stared and bit her lip as the pain in her leg redoubled. She took the time to crawl over to one of the spotlights, which she turned off, allowing her to open another portal to the basement.

Behind her, Simon twitched. Janey heard the sound and turned to look.

The pool of blood halted its advance, shimmered and pulsed, and began oozing its way back across the floor. Simon's fingers writhed out, found the blood, and thirstily reabsorbed it.

Janey's insides went sort of loose, and tears started from her eyes.

Convulsively Simon began flailing his way across the floor toward Janey, pulling with his extended fingers. Janey watched, horrified.

She thought Simon tried to speak, but the younger man's

ruined mouth yawed grotesquely and couldn't form words. His eyes, though…Simon's eyes emerged from the carnage of his broken sockets. They had turned solid white, and light poured out of them, and they left faint trails in the air when he moved. As Simon drew closer, Janey saw that the finger-tendrils had hardened to points, each one with a razor-sharp, back-swept blade at the end. Blood burst from Simon again, not just from the wounds but from his skin itself, and he seemed to be covered in wet red lacquer as he squirmed closer and closer.

Janey didn't dare put any weight on her left leg, but she used the crutch she had pulled from the basement and struggled to her feet.

Simon Grove's body had lost most of the features that define human beings. The blood on his skin moved, rippled and danced like tiny red flames. A sickening thought clamped down on Janey's mind: *Is this what Simon truly is? And if that's true for him—if he's really not human—is it true for me, too?*

It didn't need to end like this. There was so much to say, so many questions to ask. So many experiences to share. All the information and knowledge they could have accumulated together, gone, all gone, shoved into the trash. Pointlessly.

Simon hitched forward another few inches.

Janey thought of Tim.

When he reached her and reared upright, Janey braced herself with the crutch and wrenched the katana out of Simon's body. He screamed again, his blue-green forked tongue flailing around his neck and shoulders, and Janey swung the katana with every bit of strength she had left.

Simon's head hit the floor and rolled a few feet. His body spasmed, crumpled backward and landed on the concrete with a wet, spongy smack.

Janey watched the corpse, expecting all the scales and tendrils and barbs to shrink or withdraw, like in the movies, the way they always did on monsters when they died, so that Simon Grove could be found in the morning and identified. So his perverse truth could be kept a secret.

That didn't happen. The body on the floor in front of her, especially now that it was dead, didn't seem even remotely human, didn't seem ever to have *been* human. The eyes in the severed head darkened, the alien light dying, until the eyeballs looked blank, like burned-out light bulbs.

All the blood, both on Simon's skin and the floor around him, abruptly congealed and turned a rank brown.

Janey tried to think of something to say, like a eulogy of some kind, but couldn't.

Biting her lip to keep from crying out, she maneuvered herself over behind an unused, slightly battered writing desk that had once served as a prop in a children's program called "KidzNews." She figured it would provide shadow enough. She knew she'd have to come back very soon to dispose of Simon's body, but she also knew that if she didn't get medical attention even sooner, she stood a good chance of succumbing to shock. She'd vomited twice more, and the room had a good spin on it now that showed no signs of slowing down.

She had just pulled her good leg under the desk when the studio door burst open. Janey froze and stared out through the space between the desktop and the modesty panel.

Six men in white hazmat suits rushed into the room, two of them carrying a stretcher. Two of them hoisted Simon's ruined body onto the stretcher and carried it out the door. The remaining four produced cleaning materials and began mopping up both the brown, crusted blood and the small pools of Janey's vomit.

A seventh man, not wearing one of the hazmat suits, stayed back near the door, leaning against a wall and watching. He carried a cane with a silver head.

One of the men cleaning the floor noticed the smeared blood trail leading to the desk. He jerked his head up and stared straight at Janey, who needed no further prodding and flickered away.

EPILOGUE

8:30 p.m.

Two days later.

A tiny article had appeared in the *Chronicle,* providing sparse information about an unidentified woman found dead on the shore of Lake Lanier. The article only made the paper at all because of an unusual feature of the corpse. "Worst case of frostbite I've ever seen," were the words of the medical examiner. "Like she'd been locked in a freezer."

Lying in bed in a shabby motel room, very close to the middle of nowhere, Scott Charles set the paper down beside him—no using the Web, not yet, too easily traced—and used the remote to click on the TV. An old *Wheel of Fortune* had just started. Maybe that would keep his mind off how hungry he was.

Vessler was out at the moment, gone to get Chinese food. Scott had never had Peking chicken before, but he'd agreed to try it on the strength of Vessler's recommendation. His stomach growled.

They won't find us, Vessler had said. *I've got plenty of tricks up my sleeve yet.* Scott couldn't really wrap his mind around everything Vessler had promised. He'd used the term "normal life" a lot. Scott wasn't entirely sure what Vessler meant by that, but he was certainly willing to find out.

A heavy truck roared past the motel. It made Scott shiver, and for a second he thought about jumping down and crawling under the bed. But only for a second. The sound wasn't really that bad. Not really.

A key turned in the lock, and Garrison Vessler walked in, holding a small cardboard box filled with white cartons and Styrofoam cups.

"Hi...Dad," Scott said. *Dad.* The word tasted strange and good.

"Hello, son," Vessler replied. "Do you like duck sauce?"

"I don't know." Scott smiled. "But I guess I can try it."

* * *

Detective Zach Feygen leaned back in his chair and eyed the thick stack of paper on the corner of his desk. On the first sheet was scrawled a name in Feygen's writing: *Jane Sinclair.* Below that a horizontal line, and below that, again in Feygen's writing, the words *Gray Widow.*

For forty-five minutes Feygen stared at the papers. In that stack he had what any jury would consider proof of the Gray Widow's identity, where she lived, what she did for a living...for that matter, who her parents had been and how much she made in a year. As a *painter.* Feygen laughed a little, but his shoulders slumped.

He remembered the night in the Hargett Theatre when Janey Sinclair prevented Maurice Tell from making hamburger out of him. He remembered the Latino clerk in the hospital, and how he said the Gray Widow saved his life. But foremost he remembered Laura Jean Troland, shackled there in her parents' cellar like an unwanted dog, with big blue eyes that sparkled up at him over the thick rusty chain.

Janey Sinclair was making a mockery of the American criminal justice system almost nightly. She was taking everything Feygen had been taught to believe, everything he'd sworn to uphold, and tossing it in the toilet. She was thumbing her nose at the Atlanta PD.

With what he had there in that stack of papers, Zach Feygen could put the Gray Widow behind bars for the next two hundred years.

Heather's voice came to him. *I know what she's doing is illegal. But is it wrong?* Then Sinclair's, from that ballsy TV appearance: *No one can stop me. No cell can hold me.*

Feygen knew a lot of cops who'd taken that as a challenge, but he figured Sinclair was probably just telling the truth.

And none of this even *touched* what he'd heard Garrison Vessler say, in the ruins of the theatre. All of that about augments and signals and freaking *aliens.*

"Jesus Christ," he said to the empty air. "I need to have my head examined."

Feygen picked up the papers, opened the bottom drawer of his desk, set them far in the back, and covered them with two ancient telephone books and a box of crackers. He locked the drawer, picked up his jacket and left the office.

* * *

Dressed in a baggy sweatsuit, wearing a thick cast on her leg and walking on a pair of crutches, Janey flickered into Tim's room at Gavring Medical. His step-mother, Kay, back from Cincinnati, had left only a short time before, most likely to get some much-needed sleep.

Tim lay still on the bed. They'd put a body cast on him, his left arm hung in traction, and bandages covered most of his head. An IV sprouted from his right arm. Janey could tell his thick, wavy hair had been shaved. His eyes were closed.

The room was mostly dark. A small light burned in the bathroom near his bed, just enough to drive away Janey's night vision, so she couldn't see him as well as she would have liked. Squinting, wincing from the pain in her leg, Janey moved carefully to his side. He lay so still.

Janey felt the tears accumulate, and didn't try to stop them as they ran down her welt-covered face. Tim's lips had taken on a gray cast, his cheeks were sunken, and both his eyes were severely blackened. Bandages covered his nose. Janey balanced herself on one crutch, reached out and let her fingertips brush his face, barely enough pressure to feel. He gave a small sigh and turned his head.

Janey's leg ached, and twinged hard enough to make her grunt.

She hadn't been able to ask a doctor about Tim's condition, but he was placed in a normal room, not in ICU. That was something, at least. It must at least mean his condition was stable.

Footsteps padded down the hallway outside, probably a nurse, and Janey watched the door, ready to vanish in a second if it began to open. The footsteps faded.

"Tim," she said softly. "Can you hear me? It's Janey."

Tim stirred, slightly, and after a few seconds his eyes opened just a fraction of an inch. His lips parted, and he tried to moisten them. Janey saw a plastic cup with a giraffe-neck straw beside the bed and poured some water into it, held it to his lips. He drank a little.

When he released the straw his eyes opened wider, and Janey saw panic as they darted around the room.

"He's gone," Janey said. She took his hand. "He's gone. He's dead. I killed him."

His eyes closed again, and his face relaxed. He whispered, "I thought you would."

A tremor moved through Tim's body, and Janey watched as he used the big toe on one foot to scratch the instep of the other. *Oh thank God. He's not paralyzed. Thank God. Thank God.*

"Tim...I'm so sorry. All this is my fault, and I never meant...I never meant for you to get hurt...I'm so sorry..." One of her tears splashed on the sheet next to him. "I wanted...I wanted to protect you...I'm *so* sorry... "

Tim squeezed her hand, a tiny, trembling pressure. "We'll talk..." He swallowed carefully. "...We'll talk about this. Later."

His hand eased in hers, and she said, "I love you," but he had already fallen back to sleep.

Janey stayed there by his bed, watched him sleep, listened to his steady, shallow breathing, until a nurse came to check on him. As the door opened Janey flickered away into the dark.

* * *

High in the sky, past the border of the atmosphere, the Sender plummeted in freefall. He had maintained the low orbit around Earth for many years, and the parts of his cognitive apparatus that still functioned made sure the orbit continued. Every so often, carbon-fiber muscles relaxed, jetting gases out in the precise ways needed to keep him falling, ever falling, just past the curve of the planet below.

The Sender's body had no true parallel among Earth's fauna. His asymmetrical physiology, a combination of organic tissue and super-dense metal, most closely resembled that of a whale. A series of parabolic protrusions along his axis rendered him functionally invisible. No Earthly instrument could detect him. Light bent around his body to prevent him from being seen with the naked eye, and he modified his orbital path as needed to stay away from any manned space flights.

A communications array near the Sender's cognitive apparatus sprang to life, and as the Sender glared down at the surface far below, words came to him across the vastness of interstellar space.

You have missed your last two message points. Report.

The Sender fell, ever forward, ever down. He made no response. The array flared again.

You have missed your last two message points. Report. We require details of the experiment.

The Sender remained silent.

A third of his cognitive apparatus had gone dark, thanks to the ragged hole punched through it by a fist-sized meteor destined for Earth. His orbital programming hadn't accounted for that random factor, and hadn't been able to evade it. Now the Sender could still see the tiny organisms squirming across the planet's surface, could still monitor them and select suitable specimens to receive the mutagenic signal, could still fire the signal and record the results.

But he could no longer follow the protocol. The meteor had struck him, scrambling the signal, shortly before he targeted the specimen designated "Simon Grove." Instead of modifying the subject's DNA to conform to one of the military archetypes he was supposed to create—as he had done, so effectively, with the specimen designated Janey Sinclair, who had become a near-perfect Scout—he had, in effect, scrambled Simon Grove's body on a molecular level, transforming him into an abomination wholly unsuitable for the experiment.

Exactly as he had done for eight other subjects since then, with varying results.

The Sender had no idea he had done any of this, thanks to the devastating trauma his cognitive apparatus had sustained. Neither could he communicate. The array lit up one last time.

Your status must be verified. A unit has been dispatched. Expect arrival in one hundred eighty local days.

The Sender did not acknowledge the message. He plummeted, watching and falling, ever falling, ever falling.

To be continued in

GRAY WIDOW'S WEB

About the Author

Dan Jolley started writing professionally at age nineteen. Beginning in comic books, he has since branched out into original novels, licensed-property novels, children's books, and video games. His twenty-five-year career includes the YA sci-fi/espionage trilogy *Alex Unlimited*; the award-winning comic book mini-series *Obergeist;* the Eisner Award-nominated comic book mini-series *JSA: The Unholy Three*; and the Transformers video games War for Cybertron and Fall of Cybertron. Dan was co-writer of the world-wide-bestselling zombie/parkour game *Dying Light*, and lead writer of the Oculus Rift game *Chronos*. Dan lives somewhere in the northwest Georgia foothills with his wife Tracy and a handful of largely inert cats. *Gray Widow's Walk* is his first original adult novel.

Learn more about Dan by visiting his website, www.danjolley.com, and follow him on Twitter @_DanJolley

From Bram Stoker-Award-winning Michael Knost

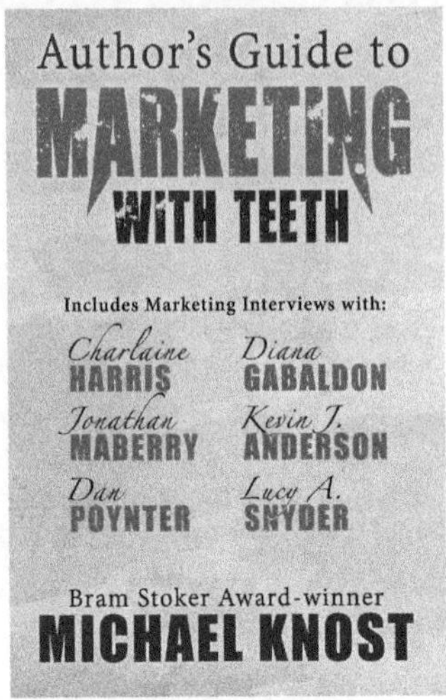

Softcover ISBN: 978-1-941706-27-5
eBook ISBN: 978-1-941706-29-9

Author's Guide to Marketing with Teeth is a collection of essays and interviews on marketing and advertising for authors and books. Michael Knost has spent more than a quarter of a century in marketing, working in the radio, television, and newspaper industries, as well as serving as marketing director and chief marketing officer for several large companies, including those in the automotive industry.

Mr. Knost has taken the lessons he's learned from his extensive experience and captured the best tips and advice for authors (or anyone in the publishing industry) who hopes to increase sales and/or name brand recognition. Each chapter covers a different subject with tips on theory and execution.

And let's not forget the interviews. Michael is also including several with successful authors to learn about their personal marketing strategies—from when they began their careers to now. You'll hear from superstars such as Charlaine Harris, Diana Gabaldon, Jonathan Maberry, Kevin J. Anderson, Lucy A. Snyder, and Dan Poynter.

From Bram Stoker Award-winning Michael Knost!

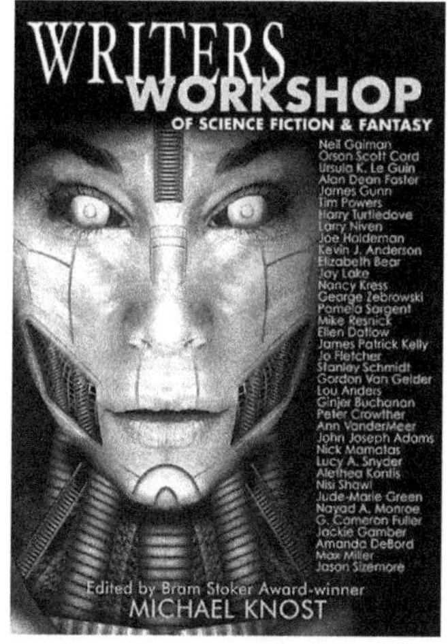

Softcover ISBN:
978-1-937929-61-9
eBook ISBN:
978-1-937929-62-6

Writers Workshop of Science Fiction and Fantasy is a collection of essays and interviews by and with many of the movers-and-shakers in the industry. Each contributor covers the specific element of craft he or she excels in. Expect to find varying perspectives and viewpoints, which is why you many find differing opinions on any particular subject.

This is, after all, a collection of advice from professional storytellers. And no two writers have made it to the stage via the same journey-each has made his or her own path to success. And that's one of the strengths of this book. The reader is afforded the luxury of discovering various approaches and then is allowed to choose what works best for him or her.

Featuring essays and interviews with:
Neil Gaiman, Orson Scott Card, Ursula K. Le Guin,Alan Dean Foster,James Gunn, Tim Powers, Harry Turtledove, Larry Niven, Joe Haldeman, Kevin J. Anderson, Elizabeth Bear, Jay Lake, Nancy Kress, George Zebrowski, Pamela Sargent, Mike Resnick, Ellen Datlow, James Patrick Kelly, Jo Fletcher, Stanley Schmidt, Gordon Van Gelder, Lou Anders, Peter Crowther, Ann VanderMeer, Joh Joseph Adams, Nick Mamatas, Lucy A. Snyder, Alethea Kontis, Nisi Shawl, Jude-Marie Green, Nayad A. Monroe, G. Cameron Fuller, Jackie Gamber, Amanda DeBord, Max Miller, Jason Sizemore.

CPSIA information can be obtained
at www.ICGtesting.com
Printed in the USA
BVHW04s1419290518
517644BV00001B/22/P